FIRE CURSED TRILOGY

By

J.E. Taylor

J.E. TAYLOR
SUPERNATURAL SUSPENSE
& DARK FANTASY AUTHOR

FIRE CURSED TRILOGY

Lucifer's daughter rises.

Faith Kennedy's mother hid the awful truth from her daughter for sixteen years. Until she lay on her deathbed. Only then did she reveal who sired her daughter, and the revelation terrifies Faith.

The devil may have sired her, but he only wants her beating heart ripped out of her chest. After all, that's where her angel grace fueling her fire power is stored, and that will give him what he needs to bring about humanity's fall.

And Lucifer will take down anyone who gets in his way.

When Faith is given an ancient knife that can kill the devil, she faces the toughest challenge of her young life. She must hunt Lucifer and put him down. Otherwise, the world will burn.

But if she succeeds, she may wipe herself, and everyone she loves, out of existence.

Fire Cursed
Chapter 1

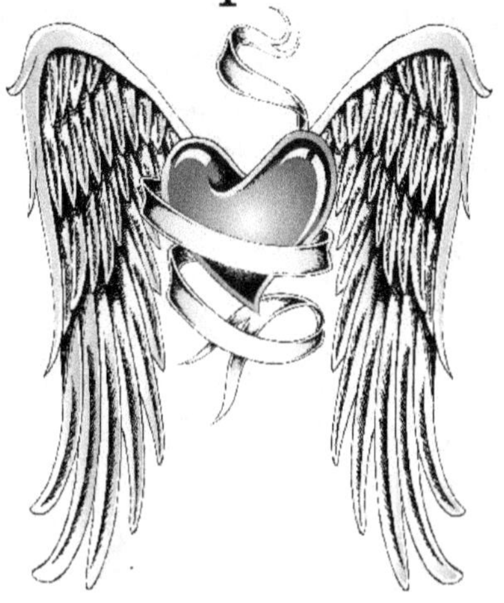

THE ONLY THING WORSE than holding my dying mother's hand was her whispered confession just before she took her last breath.

I stared at her, dumbstruck with horror.

She'd chosen this moment to tell me her darkest secret? Her breath wheezed, and she nodded, her gaze lucid enough to make me tremble. As if losing her wasn't devastating enough.

My knees gave out, and I tumbled into the chair next to the hospital bed. After all these years, she'd finally told me who my father was, and it was enough to strike fear in my soul.

Lucifer.

The Lucifer.

Not some arbitrary fool she'd met in a bar with the same name.

My father was the devil himself. The fallen. The archangel, Lucifer.

Nurses surged into the room and peeled me away from my mother. I hadn't even heard the monitor flatline. Annie, one of the junior staff members, led me out to a seat in the hall.

I stared at the floor tile pattern as the chaos gave way to silence and a lingering stench of antiseptic and Death.

THE FUNERAL HOME WAS just as quiet as the hospital had been. My mother didn't have many friends. I guess when you live off the grid for so many years, that's what happens, but it still struck me as odd and sad at the same time.

I glanced at the photos I had propped on the receiving table. Hollie Kennedy had been a stunning woman before cancer ruined her beauty and her mind. The paper on the counter next to the picture ruffled as the door opened, reminding me of the whopping hospital bill that I was responsible for. I didn't think I'd ever be out of debt due to my mother's death.

I glanced up at the door, and the woman from the state stood waiting to take me to a group home in Bangor. There was no one else, and because I was only sixteen, the state would not let me go back home. My mother had left no will, no provisions, and apparently owned nothing, not even the cottage where she'd raised me, tutored me, and taught me control.

There was a reason my mother lived off the grid.

So, I lingered. The thought of mixing with society left me cold to the bone.

"FAITH, IT IS TIME to go," Mrs. White, the mortuary assistant, said.

She gently took my elbow in her hand to help me to my feet. I pulled out of her grip and crossed to the table, taking the backpack that had the sum of my belongings packed inside. I grabbed the frame and maneuvered it into the front pocket, and hesitated with the zipper between my fingers.

I stared at the hospital bill, gritting my teeth. Crumpling it, I stuffed it into the mesh holder meant for a water bottle and then hauled the pack over my shoulder.

I turned to Mrs. White. "What will happen to my mother's ashes?"

"You can pick up her ashes tomorrow, or you we can mail them to wherever you are staying," she said.

Mrs. White had let me pick out a simple urn for my mother's ashes, even though I had planned to dump them in the ocean. That was what my mother had asked me to do, but I couldn't bring myself to transport her remains in a cardboard box. My mother had made me promise her I would find my way to the Atlantic Ocean. She wanted her ashes scattered in the sea, so she could travel anywhere she wanted in the afterlife.

It was a silly thought, but one I was compelled to honor.

Mrs. White squeezed my hand, and I tried to smile, but I wasn't sure I pulled it off. My heart thundered in my ears as I turned to the state child services woman who stood in the doorway and tapped her foot impatiently.

My legs stiffened as I crossed to her. She took hold of my arm in a grip that I didn't like, but I didn't fight her as she led me to a car parked at the edge of the parking lot.

I got in the passenger seat of the sedan and dumped my backpack on the floor between my feet. She closed the car door behind me. The woman slid into the driver's seat and clipped her seat belt before she turned to me.

"I'm Sue, by the way." There was no warmth in her gaze. It was as cold as a snake. "I'm sorry for your loss."

I just nodded and looked out the window. The populated city of Bangor still was a shock to my system. We had been in Williamsburg for so long, and the town center only consisted of a veterinarian, a doctor's office, a gas station, and a country store. So, the transition from there to the hospital, to the funeral home, and now to the wayward home for girls, was too much stimulation for my brain to handle.

My fingertips sparked, and I curled my hands into fists to staunch the burn.

Sue parked on the curb next to a building with a sign on top that said Home for Wayward Girls. It reminded me of the old wing of the hospital. She stepped out of the car and came to the passenger door, then opened it for me.

Even though I lacked a lot of the social graces normal people had, everything about her mannerisms was weird. She took my arm again in that iron grip that was tight enough to stir my instincts into a frenzy.

A chill skittered through me.

By the time we stepped inside, the heat had bled from my skin in waves that warmed the air around me. If I didn't get control of my nervous energy...

Sue stopped inside the great open hall.

A handsome couple stood from the bench near a door marked Office.

The woman had kind eyes and blonde hair that reminded me of my mother's. She was pretty, but not stunning. Her gaze jumped between Sue and me, and a tick twitched the side of her mouth.

The man had his gaze locked on me. He was handsome in a way that made my knees weak, even though he was probably more than twice my age.

Sue's gaze hardened even more, which I didn't think was possible until I saw the knot in her jaw. "We are closed for the evening," Sue said, her voice clipped with authority. Her grip on my arm tightened as she led me toward the door opposite the office.

"I am related to Faith."

He knew my name. I stopped, and the air in my lungs sucked out as if a boulder had landed on my chest.

The man glanced at Sue's grip on my arm.

She tugged me, but I stayed in place, just staring at him.

His eyes narrowed. "I suggest you let her go," he said, his voice lowering into a dangerous tone.

"Her mother's records stated there was no next of kin," Sue snapped, still gripping my arm and trying to get me to move towards the interior door.

It made me wonder what was on the other side of this grand atrium, and I found myself decidedly not wanting to find out.

The air shifted, caressing my skin with a discomfort so severe that I nearly yanked out of Sue's grip and bolted for the outside door. I was willing to take my chances in the harsh world instead of this questionable institution.

"I'm not related to her mother," he said.

I blinked. If he wasn't related to my mother…

I shook at the sudden thought that swelled in my mind. This was Lucifer. This man was my father.

His gaze turned to mine and softened. "I'm not your father," he said as if he had read my thoughts, or somehow felt the fear broadcasting from every cell.

"There is paperwork that needs to be filled out," Sue said, and her grip tightened painfully.

I winced.

The man stalked towards us. "I am her uncle, and I am taking her home. Right. Now. Please see that you file the paperwork accordingly." The words sounded more like a growling command than a request.

Sue's hand dropped from my arm as if she had no choice. As if an invisible force made her release me. Her face scrunched, and she glared at the man.

The moment Sue released me, the blonde woman stepped to my side and hooked her arm through mine. She turned me towards the outer doors and hurried us away from the bristling state worker.

"I'm Bridget Ryan," she whispered as we left the atrium and started down the stairs. "That's my husband, Tom. I'm sure you have a million and one questions going through that brain of yours. Once we get settled in the truck, we will answer every one of them."

Unease burned in my belly, and my nerves started firing in overdrive, creating a prickly heat itching every inch of my skin. I didn't know if staying in that institutional building was safer than going with these strangers.

I almost pulled out of her grip, but a hand landed on my shoulder, shocking me. It felt like an electrical surge, and I jerked away from the connection with my heart lodged in my throat.

His touch had almost ignited my fingertips.

Tom Ryan stared down at me with an apologetic smile. "We need to go." He traded a glance with Bridget.

She looked at the building, and I sensed fear.

"What are you?" I blurted as my mind started truly working again for the first time since my mother had imparted my heritage. Tom said he was my uncle. Which meant he was Lucifer's brother. Which meant he was an archangel. I shivered despite the warm spring air.

"I'm not an archangel. But we need to move because whatever *that* was inside was not alone."

Bridget bolted down the stairs and climbed into the front seat of the truck.

"What do you mean?"

"That thing was not a state worker," he said. "It was a soul eater, and once they figure out you are gone, they'll come after us." He glanced up the steps, and a nervous energy singed the air.

"Why should I trust you?"

"You need to make that choice, but I'm kind of partial to my soul." He started down the stairs and stopped like he knew I was debating about running. "There are worse things than the foster care system, and I think you sensed that even before that woman dragged you into the building."

"It could have been because you were in there," I said.

"Tom, there's movement up there," Bridget said. Her voice sounded as on edge as I felt.

He nodded. "We need to go. I will not force you, but I'm not going to stay and fight, either. So, the choice is yours." He turned, trotted down the steps, and climbed in the back seat of the truck.

Bridget started the truck and the engine idled.

I glanced at the Home for Wayward Girls sign, and unease wrapped around me, squeezing my abdomen. There were very few times in my life that I'd felt that kind of unease, and my mother moved us the moment I'd mentioned it.

The front door opened, and what stepped out made my eyes widen and my heart stall in my chest. It was wearing the outfit Sue had on, but its face didn't have any eyes or nose. Just a gaping mouth with rows of teeth.

I turned and ran toward the truck. Screw the illusion of choice. I didn't want to stay behind and find out just what a soul eater did. I skidded around the front of the truck and hopped into the passenger seat. I didn't even have the door closed all the way when Bridget gunned the gas.

I just prayed I wasn't making the biggest mistake of my life.

SILENCE FILLED THE CAR. I didn't know which question to ask first, and neither Bridget nor Tom seemed to be inclined to break the silence. When I turned towards the back, Tom met my gaze and handed me a pair of leather gloves.

I stared at the soft fabric and then back at him.

"While I can probably survive a fire, Bridget can't."

I recoiled and fisted my hands around the gloves. He knew my secret. My gaze jumped to Bridget. She glanced at me and then back at the road, and all I could sense was her discomfort.

"How..."

"Fate." Tom said nothing more.

Fear laced my mouth, making it taste like rusted metal. "Gloves won't help," I finally said.

"Those will. They've been warded. I know you have some sense of control, but some things we need to talk about may trigger... a reaction." He glanced out the window and waited.

Bridget's knuckles whitened like her grip on the steering wheel was the only thing keeping her together.

If I were going to have a reaction, it would have been on the front steps of the home, but I slipped on the gloves, anyway. The burn in my hands cooled like when my mother used to plunge me into a cool bath before I could set the cottage on fire. It calmed my nerves, and I glanced at the man in the back seat like he had just given me the best gift in the world. That euphoria faded as he began to speak.

"Fate came to us the day your mother passed away and told us—"

"Wait. Fate's a real person?" I asked, unable to contain myself.

Tom smiled, and it reached his eyes, creating crinkles at the edges and dimples in his cheek. He certainly was nice to look at when he smiled.

"Your mother really kept you off the supernatural grid," he said with a laugh. "Yes. Fate is an actual being. So is Death. Just like Lucifer was an archangel... and I am not. I'm just a man, but if you want to get technical, I'm Lucifer's great grandson, by so many generations removed that I'm not sure what the number is. My brother could tell you the exact number of generations between us."

My hands fisted. "Was. You said Lucifer was an archangel." The rest of his explanation had faded out after those words.

"Your father is dead."

"Lucifer is dead?"

He nodded.

"How do you know that?" I crossed my arms, skeptical. No one could kill the devil, could they?

"Because I was there. I saw it with my own eyes."

"I didn't think you could kill the devil." I narrowed my gaze, unsure of what kind of dung he was shoveling in my direction.

"Angel fire is pretty damn good at wiping out any supernatural creature in its path, even an archangel." He shifted and stretched out his legs. "I guess your mother begged Death to send someone to help you. To protect you. So Fate made a house call, and that's why we were there today when you arrived."

"Is my mother..." I pressed my lips together, unable to ask where she had ended up.

If he heard my thought, he ignored me.

"You were pretty much dumped in my lap because I'm a descendant of your father, and *I* harbor his grace." His gaze turned to almost a glare, and he closed his eyes, taking a few breaths to calm whatever beast had crawled into his tone.

Calm seemed to cloak him once more, but the chill had already settled into my center. When his eyes opened, they nearly glowed.

"I wasn't happy. The idea of being responsible for *his* child... But the moment I saw you, I realized you were just another piece of his collateral damage." He studied his hands. "I don't think your father knew about you. Otherwise..." He didn't finish and when he glanced up at me, I shuddered at the intensity of his gaze. "And I think he'd be pissed to know you were in my care."

The smile that formed on his mouth sent a tremor through me, and I began to doubt this had been the right choice.

His smile faded. "I'm sorry if I have made you uncomfortable," he mumbled. "It's just your father..."

"Was the devil." I focused out the window in front of me.

"No. It isn't because he was the devil. It's because every memory I have involving him opens some deep wounds."

The sorrow in his tone pulled my gaze back to him. It reflected intensely in his blue eyes.

I sighed. "I never knew my father."

"That's a good thing. I think if you had, you would be dead. Blood meant nothing to that bastard."

"And what does it mean to you?" I asked, curious at the sudden thickness in the air.

"Everything," he said. "Family means everything to me."

Fire Cursed
Chapter 2

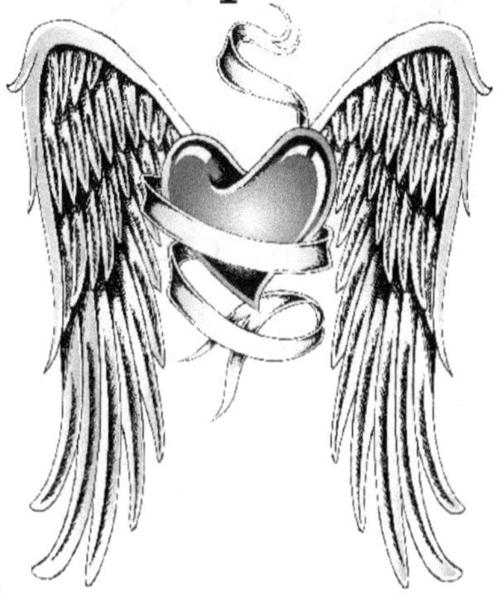

I COULDN'T SHAKE THE uncomfortable feeling that I had made a mistake.

There was far more venom in Tom's tone than I thought he meant to reveal. But I didn't get the same level of discomfort when I looked at Bridget. She reminded me of my mom. Soft on the outside, but I was sure a warrior lurked on the inside.

"So, where did you find these?" I held up my gloved hands after we pulled off the exit for York and Ogunquit.

"The gloves I found at the trading post, and a friend of ours put a warding spell on them." Bridget glanced at me.

"And what did you think was going to freak me out so badly that I might lose control?" I crossed my arms.

"I didn't realize you knew who your father was. And I'm sure if I was told Lucifer was my father, I would have freaked the fuck out," Tom said from the back seat.

"Tom," Bridget scolded and glared in the rearview mirror.

I laughed. "It did, but not in the fire-starting sense. It numbed me. But with whatever affliction I have, the *why me* question finally made sense."

"It's not an affliction. It's the angel blood in you. Being a direct descendant of an archangel has some side benefits."

"Benefits? You call spontaneously setting things on fire when you lose your temper a benefit?" Anger bloomed, lacing my voice and tingling my skin despite the warded gloves.

He shrugged. "Pyrokinesis, telekinesis, clairvoyance, telepathy, precognition, astral projection—it's all related. Psychic abilities are part of the package."

My brain couldn't wrap around what he was saying, and too many crazy questions fired off in my head, but my worst fear blurted from my lips. "How do you know I won't turn out just like my father?"

"Because your aura is pure light, much like my brother's."

Surprise raked its claws across my skin. "You see auras?"

He smiled. "Yes. But I wasn't born with that gift. I kind of inherited it. I was born with the ability to see ghosts, which seems like more of a sideshow trick compared to what you were born with, or what my brother was born with."

Bridget turned into a beautiful Victorian home across from a bluff overlooking the ocean. She parked in the space closest to the house. But it wasn't the home that caused me to raise my eyebrows—it was the sign over the front door.

Ryan-Okeefe Paranormal Investigation Agency.

Tom stepped out of the car as shock filtered through me. I glanced at Bridget and pointed at the sign.

"It's where we live. And it's what we do." She gave me a strained smile.

Light spilled from the front door, pulling my attention away from her. My brain stalled at the figure standing on the porch. The backlighting from the house looked like white wings, and his face was so familiar that I gasped.

I rummaged in my backpack, focused on confirming what I saw. I pulled out a CD and stared at the cover. The same person who stood a few feet away was branded on the front of the CD package.

Bridget touched my arm, and I jumped in the seat.

"CJ Ryan is Tom's brother," she said.

It hadn't just been a cold bath that calmed my spontaneous combustion tendencies. It was CJ Ryan's magical voice. I blinked and shifted my gaze between the CD cover and the man on the steps.

My car door opened, and I stared up at Tom Ryan. My hands shook. Hell, my entire body shook.

Tom crouched down next to me. "This all has to seem so strange to you. I know you're trying to come to terms with a lot right now. I don't even think you've had the chance to mourn your mom's death."

I stared into his bright blue eyes and nodded.

"It takes time. I lost both my parents when I was nine, and it messed me up, so I know where you're coming from. Just remember, being Lucifer's daughter does not define you. You have a choice of what direction you take in life. A choice on whether or not you let the darkness in. If you're looking for a role model to emulate beyond your mother, CJ is a great choice."

"What about you?" I asked in a small voice. Whether or not I wanted to admit it, I felt some weird connection to him, especially when his gaze was so open and sincere.

"I'm not the best person to model yourself after. I've made some truly shitty choices in my life, but I'm trying to do right by people now that I've got myself together." Tom's gaze scanned around me and then met my eyes again. "The best advice I can give you is to let yourself grieve. If you keep it bottled up, it will eat away at your inherent goodness. And if you're worried about setting a fire, the gloves should help."

My chin trembled. "What if they don't?"

"Then I guess we'll have the fire department on speed dial." He glanced over his shoulder and then back at me as Bridget got out of the car and went into the house. "Are you feeling up to meeting my family?"

Family. That word cut through the wall I had erected, and I looked down at my covered hands.

My vision blurred, and the back of my throat burned.

"I can sneak you in the back if you need time," he said.

I nodded. I couldn't imagine walking into a roomful of strangers right now. When he stood and offered me his hand, I took it, letting him help me out of the car and take my bag. He led me toward the side of the house, away from the famous man on the front steps and the commotion I could hear coming from the doorway.

The kitchen was dark and so was the stairwell. The dimly lit hallway at the top of the stairs had three doors. Tom opened the one on the right. The room had a large bed and a dresser.

"There's a bathroom over there." He pointed to the corner. "The room across the way is my daughter's. She's a few years younger than you are. You can meet her when you're ready."

"Thank you." I swiped at my eyes. The bedroom was as big as the cottage we had stayed in for the last few years, and the homes before were not much bigger.

He closed the door behind him, and I grabbed the backpack he'd put on the end of the bed. I did not expect a room fit for a princess. This was too much to take in. It was more than I had ever had.

I climbed into the center of the bed and clutched my backpack in my arms. Tears came in a deluge. I covered my face with the soft fabric of the gloves. Losing my mother finally caught

up with me, shredding my insides to a pulp with
every shaking sob.

Fire Cursed
Chapter 3

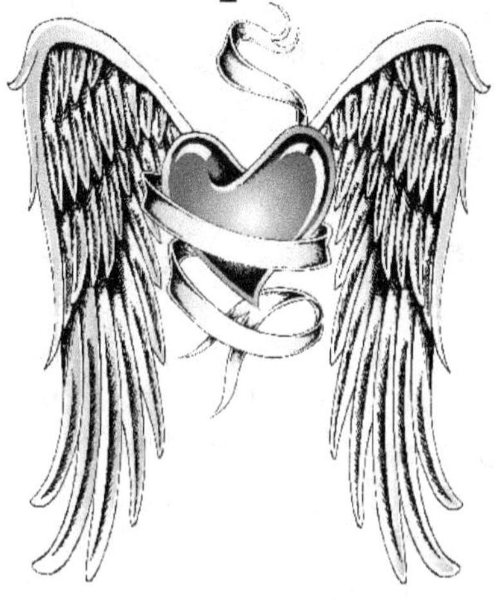

A LIGHT KNOCK ON the door pulled me from sleep. Light spilled through the curtains, and I gripped my bag in my arms in an unfamiliar room. My hands were covered in leather.

"Breakfast, then school," a deep voice said through the door.

I stared at the wood as everything from last night flooded back.

When his words registered, fear ballooned in my belly. My mother had kept me at home. She'd never subjected me to an institution, and I wasn't keen on the idea. I stayed in place and hugged my backpack.

The door opened. Tom stood in the hall and crossed his arms. "My house, my rules."

"Don't be such a dick, Dad," a girl's voice called from the other room.

His face bloomed red. "Pancakes are waiting." He walked off.

A pretty blonde a few years younger than me poked her head into the room. "I'm April." She crossed to stand a few feet from me. Her head tilted as she studied me. "I love your hair." She stepped closer, reaching for my fire-colored locks.

I pulled away, but she didn't seem deterred.

She leaned against the side of the bed and smiled. "Do you like pancakes?"

"Yes," I said. They were one of the few treats my mother used to let us indulge in when she had something to trade for the mix at the local country store.

April leaned close. "My dad makes the best pancakes, but don't tell him I said that."

"Why not?"

"Because it will just go to his head." She rolled her eyes and took my gloved hand, then pulled me along with her, out of my room, down the stairwell, and into the kitchen, where plates were already set out on the table. She released my hand and took a seat, nodding to the chair next to her.

I thought the bedroom was big, but the kitchen was the equivalent of a palace. My gaze jumped from the row of cabinets to the long counter with all sorts of appliances. The table shined with polish, and the colorful placemats reminded me of a bouquet of spring flowers. My mouth watered at the scent of buttermilk pancakes.

Tom turned from the stove. He set an overflowing plate of fluffy stacks down in the middle of the table. I still stood by the door, clutching my backpack.

Tom glanced at me. "Eat. Then we can talk about school." He glanced at his watch and then at his daughter. "You have ten minutes until the bus comes."

April rolled her eyes and dug into the pile of pancakes. She pointed to the seat again before drowning the poor pastries in syrup.

I gave in to the growling in my stomach and took a seat. The backpack stayed on my lap, but that didn't deter me from taking my share of the flapjacks.

April handed me the syrup and smiled. She was certainly a cheery one. Tom sat down at the head of the table.

"Where's Bridget?" I asked.

"She's not a morning person." Tom took what was left on the plate in the center of the table.

My first bite was heaven. The pancakes were fluffy and sweet enough that they didn't need syrup, but the sugary liquid just increased the experience. I closed my eyes and let the food settle on my taste buds before I swallowed. I must have made a noise, because when I opened my eyes, both Tom and April were staring at me. April's expression warned me not to say it, and Tom's was a smug smile of satisfaction, like he knew these were the best-tasting pancake I had ever eaten.

I licked my lips and devoured the rest of the food.

April dumped her plate in the sink. "Maybe when we get home, Mom can take us shopping?"

Tom nodded and sipped his coffee.

April stepped out the door and ran down the driveway just as the squeak of brakes and the rush of exhaust sounded.

"I have the paperwork for high school," Tom said, pulling my attention to him.

The quaking in my soul began again, and I slowly peeled off my gloves and dropped them on the table before I pressed my palms onto the wood. The hiss of burning fibers filled the room.

"Do you really think a public school is such a great idea?" I lifted my hands and curled them into tight balls.

Tom stared at my handprints burned into the wood.

"That's what being nervous does to me." I couldn't help the snap in my voice. The idea of being in a place surrounded by strangers left me shaking.

His gaze narrowed. "Did I say I was sending you to public school?" He leaned back and folded his arms. "That's as much of a disaster as putting me in a room full of angry angels."

"Oh." I didn't quite understand his metaphor, so I folded my hands in my lap. I stared at the marred wood. "I just assumed."

"You assumed wrong. The papers are for home schooling."

I glanced up at him as hope flared.

His lips pressed together. "I am not homeschooling you. My brother is. He is a damned good teacher, and if you can keep up with his kids, then you'll be Harvard material. If not, we can talk about alternatives."

My heart clanged in my chest. "CJ Ryan is going to homeschool me?" The mere thought of it was enough to make me woozy.

His eyebrows rose. "Are you... fangirling?" His voice carried a measure of disgust.

Heat filled every pore as I stared down at the designs on my nearly clean plate. I knew what fangirling was. My mother had accused me of it, too, but she was more of a CJ Ryan fan than I could ever be. I raised my shoulders in a meek shrug.

My mother would die if she knew.

I closed my eyes at my last thought, and my heart constricted with pain that nearly folded me over. I hated cancer and what it had taken from me.

"My mother died at the hands of a serial killer who was practicing surgery on me. He put her severed head at the foot of the table I was chained to. So even though cancer is a hideous disease, there are far worse ways to die."

My eyelids flew open wide, and I stared at Tom. His words scraped my skin like a blade and turned the pancakes in my stomach sour. I recoiled in the chair. "Why would you tell me that?"

His lips formed a smile that did not reach his eyes. "It shocked you out of that pity party you were throwing, didn't it?"

I didn't get this man. He was so different from any of the handful of people I had met. "I thought you said I should let myself grieve," I mumbled and traced my handprint on the wood.

His smile faded, and his gaze dropped to the table in front of him. "I did say that. I'm sorry." Remorse filled his voice, and I could almost see him mentally kicking himself.

"Was that even true?" I hugged my backpack to my chest.

"Unfortunately, yes." He stood and cleared the plates. "My life has been pretty much a shit show since I was four."

The way he freely swore around me made me uncomfortable. That was the one thing my mother couldn't stand, and she rarely ever let an expletive pass between her lips. I'd heard more curses since I stepped into that godforsaken hospital than I had all my life.

He cast a quick glance in my direction. "I can't seem to wrap my head around being so sheltered. And I'm sorry that my language makes you uncomfortable. I'll try to watch what I say."

"You read minds?"

He nodded without turning my way and continued to clean the dishes. I cleared the rest of the table and stacked the dirty plates on top of the pile he was working to clear.

"In the interest of not assuming anything, do you know what your education equivalent is?" He glanced at me, turned off the water, and wiped his hands on a dish towel.

When he folded his arms across his chest, I noticed just how thick his biceps were. The strength in those arms unsettled me. I could feel it surrounding him, and it made my skin buzz. I still wasn't sure this was the right place for me to be, but I was willing to play along. Especially if it meant meeting CJ Ryan in person.

"I've been taking online college courses."

"Did you get your high school diploma?"

I bit my lower lip and shook my head. "My mother got sick before she could file the final papers."

"Well, CJ will probably insist on an assessment. Then we will need to let the superintendent know where you fall on the grid."

I crossed my arms, annoyed at the prospect of having to repeat classes based on a stranger's opinion, even if it was CJ Ryan.

He glanced at me again, scanning me like he was seeing me for the first time this morning. "Did you want to shower and change before we go?"

I glanced down at my clothes. The same clothes I had on yesterday, and the day before. I had nothing else to wear with me. I shifted and shook my head.

His gaze clouded over, and he pointed at my backpack. "I just assumed you had clothes stuffed in there." He sighed and inspected me, cocking his head. "You're a little too tall to fit in April's clothes, but Bridget may have something you could wear if you want something clean."

I didn't know what to say. Wearing a stranger's clothes didn't feel right, but a shower sounded more heavenly than I wanted to admit. I hadn't cleaned up since the day my mother died.

"There are towels in your bathroom. I'll get Bridget up to help pick out something for you to wear." He scooted me back up the stairs and disappeared into the main bedroom at the end of the hall.

I brought my backpack into the bathroom, set it next to the sink, and turned on the shower. I engaged the lock on the door and then ran my hands over the thick towels on the bar. They were plush and large. Eons better than anything that had touched my skin before.

The shower was blissful. I stood under the water for much longer than necessary, lathering my skin with the pomegranate body wash. The combination of scents between the body wash and shampoo lulled me into a state of calm I hadn't experienced in years. The water pressure was so much better than that of the cabin, and it was steamy, unlike the lukewarm showers I was used to.

The knock on the bathroom door jerked me out of my stupor, and I turned off the water. With one of the plush towels wrapped around me, I crossed to the door and cracked it.

Bridget stood near the door with clean undergarments in her hand. "These should fit. I also laid out a couple outfits on the bed from my younger days for you to choose from. When you get back, we can go shopping, okay?" She smiled and handed me the underwear and sports bra and then left the room.

Awkward heat filled my cheeks. I closed the bathroom door and leaned on it, staring at the soft fabric in my hand. Every encounter with both Tom and Bridget had been weird, just like my encounters with the doctors and nurses at the hospital.

While my mother taught me social graces in the confines of our home, I wasn't comfortable interacting with people.

My sum total of conversations had been maybe two sentences at the general store and learning about what type of cancer was killing my mother at the hospital. Even the negotiation for the urn was difficult.

I realized just how used to silence and squalor I was.

This environment was as strange as if I had been launched to Mars. Perhaps I should have taken my chances with the soul eaters.

You can't think that way, my inner voice scolded. I knew it was right, but I couldn't help but feel like an outsider in these people's home.

My eyes widened. *The urn. I need to call the funeral parlor.*

With that single thought, my temporary paralysis broke, and I slipped on the borrowed undergarments. They were smooth and silky and fit better than my old pair of cotton briefs. When I stepped out of the bathroom and into the bedroom, I stared at the outfits spread out on my bed. There were three of them, and all three were prettier than anything I had ever worn.

I picked up the soft jean skirt and pulled it on. The waist was perfect, but the length seemed a little short at the top of my knees. The white shirt was comfortable with one shoulder covered and the other bare. I pulled on the long black cardigan and took a seat on the bed to put on a pair of socks. I slipped into my sneakers and returned to the bathroom to see what I looked like.

I stared in the mirror. I looked... normal. A smile formed, and I hand combed the knots out of my hair before I picked up my backpack and headed down to the kitchen.

Both Tom and Bridget glanced up from their phones, and Bridget smiled.

"You look fantastic," she said.

Tom stood and handed me the gloves I had left on the table. "Just in case you go all fangirl and set CJ's house on fire." He cracked a smile.

A blush heated my cheeks as I put them on.

Bridget rolled her eyes at Tom. "I'll see you in a few hours," she said to me. "Be nice," she said to her husband.

"I'm always nice," he muttered under his breath and held the door open for me.

"Before we go, can I give the funeral home this address?"

"We already took care of that for you," Tom said. "They said your mother's ashes would arrive tomorrow."

My mouth popped open.

"Mind reader, remember?" Tom tapped his temple.

I blinked and looked at Bridget.

"It is annoying," she whispered, as if Tom wasn't within hearing distance.

I was ambiguous about Tom, but I definitely liked Bridget.

He huffed and stepped out the door.

"Thank you for the clothes." I followed Tom out. He was waiting in the truck, and I took the passenger seat. "Are you always this moody?"

"I'm not moody." He started the car.

I snorted a laugh. He was as moody as I had been when I first got my period. That had been harrowing. I spent more time doused in cold water than all the prior years I had graced this earth, and it was all because of puberty.

He glared at me, and his jaw tightened.

I guessed he didn't like being compared to a hormonal teenager. I smirked and glanced out the window at the rolling Atlantic.

He pulled down a hill and parked in a spot overlooking a sandy beach and the ocean. "Okay. I am moody. And I'm just as ambiguous about you as you are about me. I can't help but think this is a disaster in the making, but that could just be my slant on life these days."

His fingers drummed the steering wheel. He exhaled loud enough to make me shift in the seat, and he wouldn't look at me. The air thickened in the car as he glanced out at the water beyond me. When his gazed moved to mine, it was conflicted.

"I'm not sure how to get past this." He dropped his gaze.

A lump formed in my throat. I had no idea what he was fighting to get past, but then one name flared in my head. Lucifer. I was Lucifer's daughter.

"What did he do to you?" My voice was barely a whisper, but even though I'd asked, I really didn't want to know. Not when his eyes held such pain.

Without words, he reached out and pressed his fingertips to my forehead.

The car disappeared, and a slide show of horrific images flashed before me. But it wasn't just images—it was the depth of emotion accompanying each one. Fear, heartbreak, despair. They pummeled my insides as much as the visions. And every one of them had my father's touch.

Tom Ryan had lost his wife, his child, his best friend, his adopted parents, and his dog to the wrath of Lucifer.

The images would haunt me for the rest of my days. What that bastard did to the man sitting next to me would have driven me mad.

When Tom pulled his hand away, I gasped for air and threw the car door open, then fell to my knees on the asphalt. The most horrific thing about the mini-mind movie that Tom had subjected me to was the fact that I recognized some expressions my father wore. I recognized them because I had seen those same expressions in my own mirror.

Heat encompassed me, and I counted my breaths, getting a hold of the wild beast in the center of my being. Perhaps Tom *had* gone mad. After all, he collected the daughter of his greatest nemesis when asked to do so.

Who does that?

Could I have done that given the same set of circumstances?

I knew with a cold certainty that I would have wanted retribution for all the ills that had been rained on me.

Tom sat in the car and stared out at the water, waiting for me to get myself together. His face was stoic, but I could feel the boiling conflict beneath.

I finally got control over my emotions and my stomach and climbed back into the car. "And you still came to get me after all that?" I asked with a voice I barely recognized.

"I went to kill you," he said softly, unable to meet my gaze. His cheeks flared red, and I couldn't tell if it was from anger or embarrassment.

I shivered, studying his profile. A new thought rose from the ashes in my mind. "Was that what Fate told you to do?"

He shook his head. "No. Fate did not order your death. If she had, we wouldn't be sitting here right now." He shifted the car back into drive and glanced over at me. "Your instincts were right to be on edge, but as I said last night, it only took me one glance at your aura to realize you were just another piece of his collateral damage. An innocent. But that still doesn't..." He pressed his lips together.

"My existence haunts you," I said with a heavy sigh.

He nodded. "Whether I want it to or not."

"So, you're still ambivalent about killing me?"

He shook his head. "No. I'm not on the fence about that. I can't kill an innocent. It's just the way I'm made."

I blinked and narrowed my gaze at him as the litany of visions played back in my mind. "Yet you killed your best friend."

"I did." He nodded, not trying to sugarcoat his actions. "But Damian was far from innocent. He was the one who originally stole your father's grace. He was a former vampire who had been born centuries before Christ."

Wait. Vampires exist?

Tom continued as if he hadn't heard my thought. "Damian was my bargaining chip to get my daughter back."

A chill skittered down my spine. He had been so ready to trade his friend's life for his daughter, but something deep inside him couldn't go through with it. He had killed his friend, but instead of giving Damian's heart to Lucifer, he had eaten it himself, absorbing Lucifer's grace.

My brain turned that scene over in my head. Disgust clenched my stomach, creating a dark spot in my soul. I shook the cold out of my head, focusing on the heat tingling my fingertips. Danger pulsed in every nerve, and I shifted in the car seat.

"Does Bridget know?"

"Know what?" he asked, as if he wasn't privy to my thoughts.

"That your intent was to kill me?"

"She would have never let me." He took a right turn.

It wasn't an actual answer, and from the set of his jaw, I guessed pushing him for more information would just aggravate him further. When we pulled up to a gate, the house beyond captured all my attention. I thought Tom's house was big, but CJ Ryan's home was stately. It was what I would imagine lined the Hollywood hills.

Tom snorted as he punched the code into the gate. "This isn't a mansion. There are far bigger, more elaborate houses over on the lighthouse bluff."

Before we were parked, the front door opened. CJ's glare landed squarely on his brother.

Tom got out and crossed his arms, staring his brother down.

"You haven't done it yet?" CJ said as I climbed out of the car.

Fear ballooned in my throat as I returned to the conversation a few minutes ago. My gaze darted to the gate for an escape, but the gate had already closed. My backpack dropped to the ground, and I struggled with my gloves, Hell-bent on protecting myself.

Tom turned towards me. "Calm your ass down. This isn't about me killing you," he snapped.

I paused and glanced at him over the roof of the car. My gaze moved to CJ's, and his brow creased. When he glanced at me, his eyes widened and then went back to his brother. CJ stomped down the steps.

"Fate told you to give her his grace," CJ said, approaching his brother.

My stomach clenched, and I backed away from the car, putting my hands out in front of me. There was no way I would even consider eating a human heart.

CJ's gaze jumped to mine. "That's not the only way to transfer grace." He turned hard eyes at Tom. "I can't believe you shared all that with her. Way to make her feel a part of the family, bro."

The contempt in his voice almost made me smile. But my mind was too preoccupied with the ability to transfer grace. My head spun, and the scene before me altered.

CJ AND TOM STOOD on the front lawn. Tom had his hand clamped on the back of CJ's neck, and his other hand was centered over his own heart. Light ballooned around and through his fingers, coming from his chest in pulses that matched a heartbeat. When the last of the light exited his chest, Tom turned his hand and slammed the glowing ball into CJ's chest.

The result was epic.

It was as if Heaven's gates had opened and shined their light on the man. Golden wings fluttered inside the majestic radiance.

I GASPED, BLINKED, AND the scene disappeared. CJ and Tom just stared at me with their jaws hanging open.

I shouldered my backpack, unnerved by the weird vision and more so by the open-mouthed stares. I just wanted my diploma and to get on with my life. I rounded the front of the car and headed towards the open door.

I turned my gaze from the two men by the car to the front door, and my feet faltered. At the front door, a younger, more handsome version of CJ Ryan stood with the same open-mouthed awe. When his gaze moved from the yard to me, my heart clanged in my chest, and the rest of the world disappeared.

Heat filled me, and it wasn't the same as my scorching fire. This was at the cellular level, drawing me closer, yet I remained in place, afraid to move. Afraid this wasn't real.

He took a tentative step toward me, his gaze locked with mine.

The world around us darkened until we both stood a few feet apart, just staring at one another while surrounded by a black void.

I peeled my glove off and stepped closer. He raised his hand. I mirrored his move, pressing my palm to his. Wind whipped my damp hair around. It was as if the two of us stood in the center of a tornado.

His gaze widened. His fingers curled around my hand, clutching it tight. I mimicked him.

Everything about the moment felt right. It felt like I had found the piece of my soul that had been missing since the day I was born.

My body jerked away from him. I blinked and then stared up at an angry tiger. My brain couldn't reconcile the peaceful feeling that had overtaken me and this sudden rush of fear. My skin prickled, and I went to raise my hand intending to burn the snarling animal.

An invisible force held my hand on the ground at the same moment as someone body slammed the tiger and rolled away with the cat in his clutches. I had a second where our eyes met, and it wasn't the boy that spoke to my soul. This one was different. Older. More rugged. Still handsome, but not in the captivating way that CJ's spitting image was.

"Cut the shit, Grace," the man snarled in the tiger's ear while he stared at me.

CJ dropped the enchanted glove onto my stomach, and the hold on my hand released. He brushed his fingers through his hair and surveyed the pandemonium. Even he looked perplexed as to what had just happened.

"Alex, go inside," CJ said to his look-a-like.

Alex met my gaze for a second before he glanced at the hissing tiger and then turned and retreated into the house.

My hand still tingled where Alex had touched it. I slid the glove on and climbed to my feet slowly, still trying to make heads or tails of what was happening.

"That... that thing shouldn't be here," a female voice spat.

I turned toward the voice, and the handsome man who had hurled himself at the tiger stood next to a dark-haired woman who pointed at me with an equal amount of venom as the tiger had tackled me with.

Tom stepped in front of me, blocking my view. "She isn't what you think."

The girl huffed and glared at him. "You are defending her? *You?*"

Tom's hands dropped to his sides, and he glanced at the ground. After a few beats of my heart, he nodded. "Yes. I'm defending her."

She launched at him. Mid-air, she transformed into the beast that had attacked me.

My heart lurched in my chest. I blinked incessantly, but each pass of my lashes confirmed what I was seeing.

The tiger crashed into an invisible barrier separating her from Tom. It slid down almost like the coyote in those cartoons my mother let me watch.

"Please go home." CJ's command broke the tension.

The tiger transformed back to the wildly angry woman. She let out a scream of frustration and marched away, leaving me with Tom, CJ, and the one who had tackled her.

"Thanks, Gabe," Tom said.

Gabe nodded, and his gaze met mine. There was no trace of warmth in his piercing stare, but there also wasn't the malice present in the woman's. "Grace just went ballistic." He wiped his face and then crossed to where I stood. His sharp glare landed on me. "The second you stepped out of the car, she went crazy." His voice carried accusation as if I had any control over how that woman acted. "My sister can be... volatile, but it is usually with good reason." He glanced at Tom and CJ. "And Lucifer's daughter is enough of a reason for us all to be a little on edge."

I blinked and crossed my arms. Anger burned below the surface. When his gaze came back to me, I did my best not to fidget. As much as being Lucifer's daughter unnerved me, this stranger had no right to throw accusations. He didn't know me. He didn't know how I was raised, and he certainly didn't have the right to sneer at me the way he was.

The more his judgmental stare lingered, the more my skin burned. I kept eye contact and my mouth closed. I inhaled, quenching the beast roaring inside me.

"Nice to meet you, too," I finally said when I was sure my voice would be steady.

He blinked, nodded, and turned on his heel, marching across the lawn in the same direction the woman had gone.

Relief made my muscles rubbery. I turned to Tom. "Thank you."

"For what?"

"For standing up for me. I know how hard that must have been."

His cheeks turned pink, and he traded a glance with CJ. "CJ, meet Faith Kennedy. Faith, my brother CJ." He waved his hand between us.

His formal introduction was as awkward as everything else that had happened this morning, and I couldn't help but wonder what else lay in wait to pounce on me today.

Fire Cursed
Chapter 4

CJ LED ME IN through the kitchen to the family room. "Have a seat. I need to have a word with my brother before he leaves." He waved towards the soft couches.

I could hear their harsh whispers from the other room, and I wished Alex was with me to calm the brewing storm building inside. He seemed to make me forget about all my ailments. When we'd gripped hands, it was as if everything that had come before didn't matter. Only the connection between us mattered.

I glanced out the back door and jumped to my feet. The glass I had been holding fell and shattered on the table. The scene outside rattled me more than anything that had happened recently.

I bolted to the slider and laid my splayed hands on the glass. Darkness painted the landscape, which was a far cry from the bright sunny morning out front moments before.

Each pant of my breath fogged the glass, but it didn't mar my view of the apocalyptic scene.

TOM AND HIS DOG stood at the far end of the backyard. Tom's eyes were wide, and his hands slowly curled into tight fists. Fear and anger radiated from him. His entire form shook, even from this distance, and I had a pretty accurate guess at what could make Tom react that way.

What waltzed into view stalled my mind. A mirror image of Tom, but something was off with his gait. The man's stride was predatory, and his mannerisms sent a tingle of recognition through me. This was my father playing some sick game.

A wave of creatures followed, flowing into the backyard from both directions. Hulking red-eyed men with dagger-like nails poured in, along with sleek hounds the size of Great Danes. Their eyes were as red as the demons', and their teeth reminded me of razors. Long canine razors.

CJ and another man stepped onto the battlegrounds. Their gazes jumped from Tom at the back of the yard to his doppelgänger on the left.

"Tom is back there!" I cried and pointed to his image at the far side of the yard, but no one heard me.

My heart leaped into my throat as the demons attacked.

They didn't flow towards Tom's doppelgänger. Instead, they separated and attacked CJ and

Tom. The man next to CJ went after Tom's mirror image.

Blood splattered against the glass separating me from the battle. Arrows and gunshots pierced the air. One knocked CJ off the bluff, leaving Tom to fend for himself against the band of demons.

Each punch pulled a flinch from me, and I could almost feel the pain where the demons' fists hit Tom's flesh. My breathing came in fast pants as I watched the massacre.

I turned away because I couldn't watch Tom get pummeled.

My gaze landed on his doppelgänger, and for a moment I glimpsed underneath the façade he wore. I saw Lucifer in all his beautiful glory. My heart stopped in my chest and I gasped. Understanding of why my mother could ever entertain having a relationship with the devil wove into my psyche. He was too breathtaking to look away from, never mind deny. She couldn't have said no to his shining, angelic beauty.

The moment passed when he ripped the man's head off and tossed it toward Tom.

Despair wrenched my gut, and I nearly doubled over from it. How could a mere mortal stand up to that sort of power?

"Your turn," Lucifer growled, and he pointed at Tom.

Two demons grabbed Tom's arms. Tom spun, wrenching his wrist away from one demon, and landed a throat punch to the other. He snapped the demon's neck and dropped the limp body before two others stepped in. He parried and twirled out of the way of many of their attacks, but his luck ran out when he backed right into Lucifer's reach.

My father punched Tom, lifting him right off the ground. Tom collapsed on his knees but rolled away before Lucifer could do the same thing he had done to the other man.

The two remaining demons circled him. Tom executed the type of spin kick I once saw in an old kung fu movie I had found on my computer. The demon's head snapped with the force, but when Tom landed, he stumbled. The grimace on his face broadcasted the pain.

He shuffled a couple of steps to get his balance, but it wasn't enough. A demon drove his boot into Tom's supporting leg with such force, I actually heard the snap through the glass.

Tom fell, clutched his knee, and bellowed to the Heavens. The agony in his scream curdled the contents of my stomach. Before the demon could connect another kick, Tom swept the demon's leg out from under him. Luck favored Tom this time because the demon hit his head on a rock post and didn't move.

Somehow, Tom climbed to his feet.

I was awed by his tenacity and will to survive. He stumbled toward the house with eyes that radiated fear.

"Where do you think you're going?" Lucifer growled. He grabbed a fistful of Tom's hair and yanked him backwards into his grasp. Lucifer's hand wrapped around Tom's throat.

All I could see was the despair in Tom's eyes. It was enough to crush my heart. Tears blurred my vision, and I wiped at them.

"I promised you pain," Lucifer hissed.

A steel blade reflected in the light, and I cried out a warning that wouldn't breach the void.

Lucifer gutted Tom. Blood spilled out of Tom's abdomen along with his entrails. He frantically tried to put himself back together while Lucifer smiled with satisfaction.

"This is only the beginning. I have a very special place for you in Hell, and my staff has instructions to make your suffering more horrific than anything ever seen before." Lucifer's hand formed a claw. "Now give me my fucking grace."

Lucifer's fingernails pierced Tom's chest.

Tom's cry of pain and fear weakened my knees. I slowly slid to the floor. In that moment, hatred bloomed in the center of my soul. Hatred so pure I couldn't run from it if I'd tried.

I hated my father.

I hated what he stood for.

And I hated what he did for his insane pursuit of power.

An arrow pierced Lucifer's throat, making me jump. Hope flared inside me, and I climbed to my feet as Lucifer released Tom.

Lucifer turned towards the door where I stood, and his gaze met mine. It wasn't an illusion. It wasn't a manifestation of whatever was happening to me. Lucifer was actually looking at me as if I had been there in the flesh. His eyes widened with recognition, and his mouth popped open.

A second arrow pierced his chest, breaking whatever had been taking place between us. I dropped to the ground, gasping for breath.

He waved his hand, and a breeze brushed my cheek. His face formed a hateful glare as he yanked the arrows from both his neck and chest like they were annoying gnats instead of deadly projectiles.

He stepped toward Tom, but the appearance of CJ from the right side of the yard pulled both Lucifer's attention and mine. CJ had the same stunning golden wings that I had seen in the front yard. White light radiated from him as if Heaven had opened up and supplied him with God's wrath.

Righteous fury pulsed over the clearing, and CJ moved like he was made of heavenly intent. When he decapitated Lucifer with his own hands, flames of pure white rolled over the entire yard, licking as high as the doorframe.

I shivered on the floor, staring out at the carnage. The rise and fall of Tom's chest slowed. I bit my lower lip, and hot tears rolled down my cheeks.

A HAND LANDED ON my shoulder, and the darkness surrounding me faded with a blink. I glanced out the window, expecting to see blood and gore still painting the yard, but only green grass and a clean rock wall met my gaze.

I turned toward the owner of the hand, and Alex's concerned eyes stared at me. His lips tilted in an awkward smile.

"Thank you," I whispered and covered his hand with mine.

He squeezed, and I wondered if I would have gotten stuck in that horrifying scene if he hadn't pulled me back.

Angels, demons, vampires, soul eaters, shape shifters, psychics. Outside of what was written in the bible, I had not been taught about these things. Not in the practical sense. Nothing my mother had taught me had been grounded in this type of reality. I shivered again, and this time my whole body trembled.

Alex helped me to my feet, keeping his arm around my waist to steady my sway. My breath shook, and I glanced across the room to where CJ and Tom stood staring at me with the same wide-eyed expression that I imagined still graced my face.

"You shouldn't have survived," I whispered, staring at Tom. I forced myself into control despite the tingling across my skin. Shock kept my heart galloping. "What is happening to me?"

"I have no idea." Tom glanced out the door. Apprehension settled into his features. "It's almost as if you are creating echoes of my past." His haunted gaze found mine.

"You saw it, too?"

All three of them nodded. I gulped down the fear now threatening to burst from my fingertips despite the gloves. If it had just been me, I could chalk it up to the stress of losing my mother, but since I'd pulled them into whatever that was, it scared the daylights out of me.

And what scared me the most popped out of my mouth.

"Lucifer saw me," I said. "He looked right at me." I pressed my lips together.

"You were standing where Bridget had been standing when she shot him with the arrow," Tom said. "He wasn't looking at you. He was looking at Bridget."

"If he was looking at Bridget, she never would have gotten that second shot off that hit his chest," I said. I was as certain as I was of Alex's arm supporting me at this very moment. There was no arguing my point. Not with how fast he'd swatted her away once he reclaimed himself from my vision.

Tom and CJ's heads tilted like puppies who were trying to figure out a foreign word. Tom's gaze narrowed as he looked at the door. A crease appeared between his eyes, and he blinked rapidly. Then all the lines in his face smoothed. His gaze returned to mine, and it filled with wonder.

"Faith, you have an entirely different kind of astral projection than we do."

CJ's head snapped in Tom's direction, and he gasped. "Time travel?"

Fire Cursed
Chapter 5

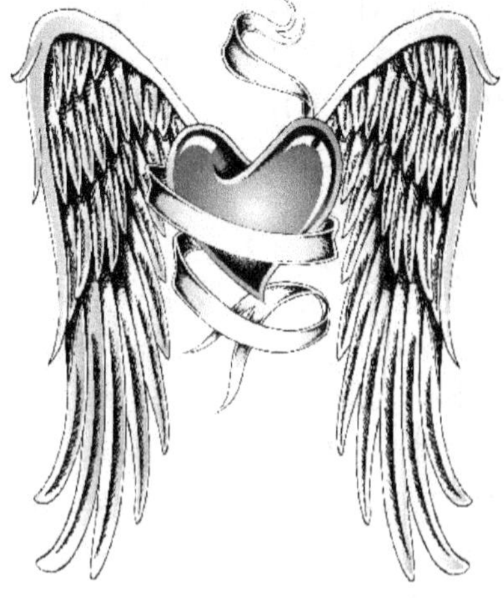

"WHAT TRIGGERS IT?" CJ asked.

I shrugged. We had been sitting at the kitchen table for at least an hour trying to figure out my newest manifestation.

"If I actually time traveled, wouldn't you have been able to hear my warnings?" I asked. While I was certain my father had seen me that night, I was not certain of anything else.

Tom leaned back in the chair and ran his hands through his hair. It seemed to be his go-to move whenever he was exasperated, and he had done it enough times so his hair wasn't neat any longer.

"Maybe it's more of an echo, like Tom alluded to, but I don't understand how just an echo of the past could allow Lucifer to see you," CJ said. He chewed on his bottom lip and stared out the kitchen window as if the bright sunny sky had the answer.

"Have you ever done anything like that before?" Tom asked.

I shook my head. "Out on the front lawn was the first time anything like this has ever happened, and CJ triggered that one when he said there was another way to transfer grace."

"That was wild," Alex said, pulling my attention to the basement door. "I hadn't seen it when Uncle Tom gave my dad Michael's grace, so it was truly awesome to get a glimpse." He gave me the kind of smile that made my heart flutter and my stomach flip. "Are we going to do any schoolwork today?" he asked, but his gaze still lingered on me.

"How are Amber and Arianna doing with the math problems I gave them this morning?" CJ asked.

Alex's gaze flicked to me and then back to his father. "They finished a while ago and have been playing video games ever since. They didn't hear anything that happened up here." He nodded to the back door. "So at least your range of pulling people into the echo is limited."

CJ stood from the table. "I'll be right back." He looked at me. "When I get back up here, we can talk about your schooling. I don't think we need to solve this right now." He waved towards the table. "And you can go home if you want," he said to Tom.

CJ crossed to the stairwell and started down. "You have schoolwork too, Alex."

Alex rolled his eyes and smiled before he disappeared down the stairs with his father.

Tom leaned back in the chair. "Do you want me to stay?"

I met his gaze and glanced towards the back door. Something had happened during that vision. Whatever ambiguity I'd had about the man across the table had gone away. Even with some of his missteps, I knew his heart was in the right place.

Instead of answering his question, I asked, "How did you not die?"

"A miracle and a little angel grace," he said. "My sister-in-law is a healer, and CJ gave me Raphael's grace. Considering I'm his descendant as well, it helped."

"You are from two angel bloodlines?"

"Yup. My brother is from three." He pointed towards the basement stairs.

"I thought you were twins?" I had read in one of the entertainment rags that my mother bought from the store that CJ Ryan had a twin brother, but that didn't jive with what Tom was saying.

"We are. Fraternal twins sired by different fathers. My mother had both Raphael and Lucifer's blood in her, and CJ's father had Uriel and Lucifer's bloodlines. So CJ was actually the first natural trilogy ever born. You met the only other set of trilogies to ever be born outside this house." He nodded towards the front door.

"Tiger woman?" I hooked my thumb over my shoulder.

"Yes. They are my best friend's kids." For a moment, his eyes darkened and then he looked down at the table.

"The one you killed?"

He nodded. "Damian was Gabriel's son. He would have been your cousin."

I laughed. I couldn't help it. "You mean those two are my second cousins?"

Tom grinned and shrugged. "I guess that would be accurate. So, do you want me to stay?" he asked, leaning back in the chair.

"Do you want to stay?" I countered.

"I don't have any cases right now. My schedule cleared as if..." His expression darkened. "Damn it. Fate?" he yelled at the ceiling.

The air next to the table shimmered and a girl who couldn't have been much older than me appeared. I imagined Fate as some glamorous model with long, flowing hair and an elegant dress. This was not what I envisioned. The hair fit, but that was where my mind's eye and reality diverted.

She glanced at me and then turned her stark gaze at Tom. "Did you give her your grace?" she demanded.

"No. Did you divert all my cases?"

"Yes. Kylee and Michael have gladly agreed to resolve anything outstanding, so you can focus on Faith."

"Bridget isn't going to like that," he said.

"Bridget agreed. She thought you needed a break."

Tom's jaw tightened. "It's my responsibility," he hissed.

Fate shrugged. "You still have to follow through on the rest of the deal," she said, then turned to me, dismissing the man who looked like he was twice her age. She stuck her hand out. "Hi, Faith." She smiled. "I'm Julia."

"But..." My mind misfired. I thought her name was Fate.

"Fate is more of a role. It isn't my name. Just like Death. His name is Nick. Although you really don't want him showing up out of the blue. While he is a sweetheart, he tends to be a buzzkill, if you know what I mean."

Tom snorted and looked away when Fate glanced at him.

"Anyway, I'm glad Tom took my advice and collected you from that home. I was never a fan of state-run homes, especially ones that harbored soul eaters." She shivered.

"Thank you."

"You're welcome. Even if it had been a true state-run facility, child services are not equipped to help you the way Tom and his family can." She gave me a pat on my shoulder and then swirled into a smoke tornado that dissipated a moment later.

"So... Fate..." I waved at the air, feeling more like Alice after she fell into the rabbit hole.

"Yeah. She's a pistol." He smiled, and there was a fondness in his eyes. "I used to babysit her before her family moved to Florida."

"Fate's from Florida?" It all just seemed so ludicrous. I almost wished I was back at the cottage in the woods buffered from any of this. My mother certainly hadn't prepared me for the real world.

"I don't want to mislead you. This is not the real world. This is beyond the real world into something that only a few see. Calling on deities like Fate and Death, meeting archangels, battling Lucifer, hunting the supernatural—all of this is *not* normal. People in the real world know nothing of these things. They only know their version of reality. Of normal." He glanced at the stairwell and then back at me. "You've never been normal. We've never been normal, either, and that is probably why Fate intervened on your behalf."

"Family is everything to you," I said, echoing his words from last night.

"Yes. And family doesn't always mean blood. The couple who took us in after our parents died taught us that. We were lucky, and I never quite understood the responsibility that was put on my adoptive father until now."

CJ walked into the room, interrupting the barrage of questions Tom's last statement had brought to the forefront of my mind.

CJ glanced at his watch. "Valerie should be home soon," he said. "And we have done nothing in relation to your schooling." He pointed at me and raised an eyebrow.

"I'm taking college courses online." I straightened my back. "I'm already past high school."

CJ pursed his lips as he studied me. "Tomorrow I will give you the opportunity to test out. If you pass, I'll make sure they issue you a diploma, and we can start your college curriculum."

"I'm already enrolled in online classes," I repeated, as if he hadn't heard me the first time.

"Then bring your work tomorrow, and you can use the time after the test."

I narrowed my eyes at him. He was a bit cocky.

CJ leaned on the dinner table. "I'm a member of Mensa. I earned the right to be cocky."

I stood, and my hands itched inside the gloves. "I'm not some ignorant little girl off the street," I snapped. Something got my hackles all in a bunch.

Tom's arms were crossed, and an amused smile played on his lips, like he was enjoying my challenge to his brother.

CJ waved his finger at me. "We can discuss this tomorrow."

"You're leaving?" Alex said from the doorway, cutting through the tension. He actually looked disappointed.

My heart jumped in my chest, and I found I wasn't quite ready to go. "I would like to see what Alex is working on," I said, stalling. I didn't want to fall back into awkward conversations with Tom and Bridget until April came home, and the way the boy was looking at me compelled me towards him.

"Come on. I'll show you," Alex said, and his smile brightened my world.

Fire Cursed
Chapter 6

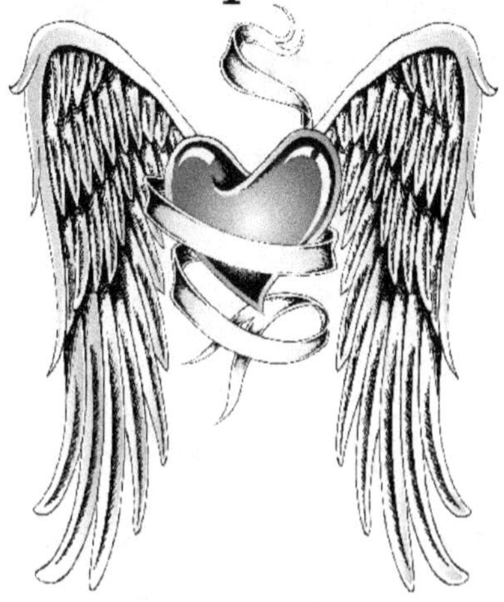

THE BASEMENT WAS MORE awesome than the rest of the house. Two girls sat at a table, both focusing on whatever CJ put in front of them.

Alex cleared his throat. They glanced up and identical eyes widened. Their smiles radiated, and they dropped their pencils and ran to where I stood.

"I'm Amber," the one on the right said.

"I'm Arianna," the one on the left said.

"I'm Faith," I replied, smiling at them. I would never remember which was which.

The affection in Alex's eyes as he gazed at his sisters was clear, and it remained when he glanced at me.

"How old are you?" Arianna asked.

"I just turned sixteen," I said.

"You're younger than me?" Alex asked, surprise arching his brows.

I looked directly into his bright blue eyes. His eyelashes were dark, and they framed his eyes perfectly. "How old are you?"

"I turned sixteen last fall," he said, hooking his thumb over his shoulder like his birthday was an object behind him instead of a date in the past.

"We're basically the same age," I said, almost forgetting there were others in the room.

"Go study." Alex pointed at the papers the girls had left. His commanding tone reminded me of his father.

The girls obeyed without a bat of an eyelid.

Alex took my hand and led me into the far room where four computers sat. He stopped in the middle of the room and turned to me. His gaze was almost as intense as his father's, and he stepped close, searching my eyes for something. He glanced toward the outer room and then reached out and cupped my cheek. His thumb ran over my lower lip.

"What are you doing?" I whispered, enamored enough that I held my breath.

He licked his lips and shrugged. "I'm not sure."

I didn't stop him when he leaned close and pressed his lips to mine. They were soft and tender, and his hand threaded into my hair, pulling me closer. That swirl of air that encompassed us outdoors returned. I opened my mouth to say we should stop, but his tongue slid in between my teeth and slowly tangled with mine. The slow tongue dance created a spiral of heat inside me that burned brighter with every swipe.

He pressed me against him, and I wrapped my arms around his neck. The kiss deepened, sucking the air out of my lungs. It left me lightheaded and wanting this to never end.

My first kiss was as heavenly as I'd dreamed it would be.

He pulled away slowly and searched my eyes. His breath was just as ragged as mine. His slow smile nearly dropped me to my knees.

"What are you doing?" CJ's harsh voice rang out.

We both jumped away from each other, spinning towards CJ.

My throat throbbed with every beat of my heart.

Alex glanced at me, and his cheeks bloomed red. "I was kissing her." His voice rose in almost a comical lilt. His shrug wasn't any less humorous.

I touched my lips still awed by the feel of the kiss. Deep down, I knew I should be ashamed for letting someone I just met kiss me. But I couldn't conjure up an apology, not when I still felt Alex's breath mingled with mine.

Disapproval rolled off CJ in waves, and I glanced beyond him at Tom. Tom's brow was creased, but he didn't look upset the way his brother did. He actually looked quite amused.

"I should go," I whispered.

Alex sighed, exasperated. "I haven't shown you what I am working on." He waved to the computer behind him.

"Tomorrow." CJ gave no leeway in his tone.

"Fine," Alex said, but he wasn't fine. His voice was filled with the same raging disappointment riding my blood.

I scooted by CJ, and Tom escorted me out of the house. I crossed to the passenger side of the car and reached for the door handle. Weight slammed into me, and the tiger's hateful eyes reflected in the window just before my head banged into the glass. I saw stars. Sharp pain pierced the back of my neck. It took me a moment to realize the tiger was biting me. Panic filled me, but then as soon as it came, the weight disappeared. Hot paths rolled from the holes the tiger's teeth had made. I glanced up, dazed.

Tom stepped around the front of the car. His eyes held fury, and black wings unfurled behind him in a majestic, angelic display. A shiver cascaded up my back and pulsed in the cuts left by the tiger's teeth.

Tom looked frighteningly like my father when he was angry.

I made a mental note to never get him that mad.

"Cut the shit, Grace," he growled to the tiger crouching on the ground behind me. He opened my car door.

I slid into the safety of the passenger seat, and he closed the door.

The cat transformed into the woman. "You were supposed to kill her. You promised me!" she screamed.

"I told you if she was evil, I would end her. She is *not* evil."

Grace's face turned crimson. "But Alex... Alex is mine," she hissed.

Tom pressed his lips together and shook his head. "He isn't anyone's property. You know that. What the Hell is wrong with you?" He crossed to his side and slid into the driver's seat.

She lay on the grass, her face streaked with tears and her glare as murderous as Lucifer's had been.

I felt sorry for her.

Just when I didn't think it could get any worse, Tom opened his mouth again.

"Grace thinks Alex was meant for her. Alex is a very special child. He has the blood of four archangels. Michael, Lucifer, Raphael, and Uriel. And if he and Grace were to get together, their offspring would be something the world has never seen."

I shivered. They would produce a child who had bloodlines of all the archangels. What the Hell would that do to a child?

Tom chuckled. "I've wondered that for years. Especially being the brother of someone who could end it all with a snap of his fingers," he said as he pulled out onto the main road. He didn't speak again until we were closer to the house. "What were you thinking?" he asked, but it wasn't accusatory.

I knew exactly what he was referring to. "I wasn't thinking anything. Alex kissed me." I glanced at my gloved hands. "It was nice."

"Nice?" He laughed. "I almost felt the earth move from the intensity between you two." Humor tinged his voice. "Nice isn't quite the right word, is it?"

His grin lifted my heart. I shook my head. "It was kind of magical."

"I know I should be scolding you the way I'm certain CJ is blasting Alex, but I can't help it. I've only seen that look from one person in my entire life."

"What look?"

"The way Alex looks at you. It is the exact replica of the way my father used to look at my mother. That look could set the upholstery on fire." He sighed. "There isn't a damn thing any of us can do now that the train has already left the station."

I didn't get what he was trying to say.

"That look is the stuff legends are made of."

"I still don't understand."

"You and Alex." He chuckled and shook his head. "Just be smart." He glanced over at me, raising an eyebrow.

I might have lived a sheltered life, but my mother had already given me "the talk," and I didn't need it from Tom too. Heat filled my cheeks. "You aren't going to warn me to stay away from your nephew?"

"Nope."

"Why not?"

He chewed on his lower lip and pulled into the driveway. "First, it would be futile. Second, the same thing that happened to you during that echo happened to me. You chose a side, and I'm no longer ambiguous." He met my gaze and threw the truck into park.

"So, just like that, you accept me?" I didn't buy it. Not when this morning he confessed to wanting to kill me the night before.

He smiled. "And just like that, you accept us?"

I turned and stared at the house. "Only if we can get a dog." I slid my gaze to his.

His smile faded. "No." He pulled the keys from the ignition and got out of the truck.

Moody Man was back. He stopped and glanced up at the sky before he turned to stare at me through the windshield.

I climbed out of the cab.

"I don't want another dog." His expression was unreadable. "Sometimes you just shouldn't tamper with perfection." He turned away. "Come on. Let's patch up your neck."

I had forgotten about the tiger bite, and my hand went to the back of my neck. I winced and followed Tom into the kitchen. He grabbed a few sheets of paper towels and dampened them under the tap.

I pulled my hair up and out of the way.

"Damn it," Tom muttered under his breath and pressed the paper towel to one side. "Bri!" he called towards the front of the house.

He grabbed another bunch of towels and did the same on the other side of my neck. Bridget stepped into the kitchen.

"What happened?" she asked as she hurried over to the sink where Tom had me leaned over.

"Grace happened. Can you call Valerie? Tell her to swing by, even if she's already left the hospital. Tell her it's kind of urgent." Tom's voice was calm, but his words made my head spin. He pulled a chair over. "Sit down," he breathed.

Bridget stepped out of the room.

I took a seat, and he pressed both towels to my neck. The pressure was hard enough to be uncomfortable.

I tugged at the gloves. "If the cuts are that bad, I could cauterize them."

Tom eased up enough for me to glance up at him. He bit his lower lip and lifted one of the paper towels. All I saw of the makeshift rag was red.

"Won't that burn?" he asked.

"Yeah, but it will stop the bleeding."

"Can you focus your power like that?"

I'd had to do something similar to a cut on my foot when we were at the cottage. The pain made me lose control. Thankfully, my mother had a bucket ready and doused the fire. My foot hurt like crazy for a while, but the aloe my mother slathered on it helped.

He checked the cuts again. "You aren't going to bleed to death in the next half hour, so I'd rather have Valerie take care of this than risk a house fire."

"Okay," I said, and he resumed the harder pressure.

"I can work with you on control if you'd like. I could always use the practice," he said.

I nodded. The side door opened, and a familiar pair of high-top sneakers and frayed jeans came into view. My backpack dropped on the floor next to the sneakers. Electricity filled the air, and I knew who it was before he spoke.

"She forgot her backpack," Alex said. He crossed to my side.

"Grace bit her," Tom said. "We're just waiting for your mom to stop by."

Alex's hands clenched for a second, and then he dropped to his knee so I could see his face. Concern and anger danced in his eyes. "I'm sorry."

"You didn't bite me. What are you apologizing for?"

He smiled and everything inside me warmed.

"She bit you because she thinks she has some claim over me. She thinks we are destined to be together." He rolled his eyes. "She's been like this all my life, and it drives me crazy. I've never thought of her as anything but an annoying older sister, and lately, she's just been creeping me out." He glanced up at Tom and shrugged. "I think I need to set her straight."

"Set who straight?" a female voice said from the door.

Alex stood. "Grace. She needs to chill."

The pressure on the back of my neck loosened.

"Grace bit Faith. Think you can fix her?" Tom asked.

I glanced up through the strands of hair that had fallen. Valerie Ryan still wore her hospital scrubs, and even in the unflattering blue fabric, she was beautiful. Her eyes were even kinder than Bridget's. I had seen her a few times on television with CJ. She was just as pretty in person in her scrubs as she was in her evening wear.

She crossed and shooed Tom away. He stepped back, holding the bloody rags.

"I'm sorry, sweetie. This is going to hurt a little." She kissed the top of my head.

Nothing happened. I glanced up at her and raised an eyebrow. Her brow knit.

"Fix it, Mom," Alex said.

"I... I thought I just did." She traded glances with Tom, and her eyes widened in horror.

Tom turned and grabbed a knife, then sliced his palm. He held it out to Valerie, his eyes just as wide as hers. She placed a kiss on his skin, and light danced over the cut. He winced as it closed, leaving not even a hint of a scar.

They stared at his palm, and then all eyes landed on me.

Bridget stepped into the room as Valerie tried again. The results were not any different. Hot trails still flowed down my back.

"Okay. Looks like this is the old-fashioned way," Valerie said. "Get me your first-aid kit." She twirled my hair, took my hand, and put it on top of the messy bun on my head.

Bridget came back with a small first-aid kit like the one my mother had under the sink at the cottage. She rummaged inside, then a cool pad swiped my cuts. The sting started almost immediately. I clenched my eyes shut, and a hissing wince escaped.

She worked fast. She finished with the last bandage and then turned to the sink to wash her hands.

"You're going to want to rinse her hair in the sink and use a washcloth to get the blood off. No showers for a couple of days. I assume she will be at the house tomorrow?" Valerie asked Tom.

"Yes. CJ's testing her to see if he can apply for her diploma."

Valerie crouched in front of me. "I may have to stitch one of those cuts tomorrow when you get to the house. Until then, make sure Bri or Tom check the bandage and change all four of them tonight before bed and again in the morning. Does that sound good?"

"Yes. Thank you, Mrs. Ryan," I said.

Her eyes sparkled with her smile and a blush bloomed on her cheeks. "You're welcome, and please, call me Valerie." She glanced at Alex. "You rode your bike over here?"

He nodded. "She forgot her backpack." He pointed to it on the floor by the door.

"Did you want to hitch a ride home with me?" She stood.

Alex shook his head, and his hands curled into fists. "If I go home now, I'll end up kicking Grace's ass."

Valerie crossed her arms and narrowed her gaze.

"I'm angry and I would prefer to cool down before I head home." He shifted and shoved his hands in his pockets, keeping eye contact with his mother.

The set of his jaw almost made me swoon, and when his gaze turned to me, the flutters in my chest brought Tom's words he'd said in the truck home. This was the stuff legends were made of.

Valerie glanced at Tom, and her brow creased.

"He can hang out here for a few if he wants."

"I can drive him home later. We're supposed to go clothes shopping when April gets home," Bridget said, stepping closer.

Valerie pointed at Alex. "Be good."

"Aren't I always?"

She smiled. "It was nice to meet you, Faith, despite the circumstances." She traded a look with Tom, and I swore there was some silent communication between them. She turned and walked out the door.

I glanced at Alex, and that calm warmth spread through me despite the deep throbbing in my neck. I tore my gaze away from him and looked at Bridget. "How bad is my hair?"

She crossed and took my hand. "Let's go get you cleaned up, and then you can visit with Alex in the family room."

The avoidance of a direct answer was clear. I was a mess.

"I'll be back," I said to Alex.

"I'll be right here," he said, and I believed him.

Fire Cursed
Chapter 7

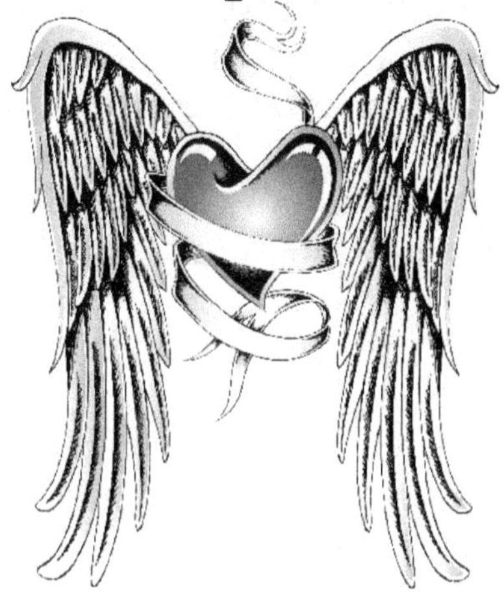

BRIDGET LED ME INTO the bathroom and folded a towel, then put it on the edge of the sink. She helped me with my sweater and stepped back with a wince on her face. "I think we need to take the shirt off before I help you clean up."

I wasn't comfortable undressing in front of a stranger, but one glance in the mirror told me to shelf my modesty. "I'm sorry about the shirt." The blood stains covered the shoulder and seeped downwards. I didn't want to see what my back looked like. I could already feel the tacky quality of my hair and I cringed.

Bridget helped me with the shirt, clipped my hair up, and gently cleaned the blood off my skin. The white basin streaked pink each time she rinsed the cloth.

"Now the hair." She patted the dry towel.

The gentle strokes of her fingers through my hair relaxed me.

The water shut off and I started to stand, but Bridget put her hand on my shoulder.

"Not yet." She grabbed the towel on the rack, wrapped my hair in it, and squeezed out as much of the water as possible. Then she wrapped it around my shoulders. "Now."

I stood, and she picked up the brush and gently combed the knots out while I stared at our reflection in the mirror.

"I've only seen Valerie's healing power fail once." She sighed and continued to work the knots out of my hair. Her gaze finally lifted to mine, troubled.

I was afraid of the answer, so I didn't ask the question.

She smiled. "Let's get you dressed."

She led me into the bedroom, picked up the flowing black shirt, and helped me into it. She retrieved the bloody towels, shirt, and sweater from the bathroom and headed down the hall to a small laundry closet, then dumped the soiled clothes inside the washing machine.

She turned to me. "I think those gloves need washing, too." She put her hand out.

I gulped the sudden swell in my throat. "Are you sure?"

"You don't just spontaneously combust, do you?"

I shook my head.

"Then I think you will be okay for a couple of hours."

I peeled the gloves off, and she dropped them in with the rest of the laundry and started the washer before she escorted me downstairs to the front of the house.

The family room encompassed the entire left side of the house. The front atrium had a desk in the center and what looked like an office on the other side. I turned back to the family room, and I didn't know where to look. The most inviting-looking couches graced the middle section as I entered. To my right sat a bar with bar stools and a large television over the top, and near the front was a billiards table.

Tom and Alex were studying the colorful balls, and Tom glanced over at us.

Alex turned and smiled. "Hey. Want to play?" He waved to the table.

"I've never played before." My skin itched with a sudden bloom of nerves, and I curled my hands, so I didn't start sparking.

Alex leaned his stick against the table and came to me, took my hand, and led me to where he had been standing. The contact of our skin settled calm over me like his father's music used to.

"Can you sing, too?" I blurted.

Alex grinned at me. "What do you want me to sing?"

"I think I'll leave you two to finish this game." Tom hung his stick on the holder in the wall and left, shuffling Bridget with him.

His exit was as subtle as an anvil falling from a cliff in a cartoon.

Alex leaned close. "Are we going to do this or what?" he sang and winked. His voice was much like his father's, lyrical, and almost a spiritual experience.

And I knew the song.

Blood rushed to my cheeks, and I shifted as he finished the chorus.

His gaze flicked to the door and then back to mine. He closed the distance and planted another kiss. Heat filled the space between us, and it wasn't coming from me. Alex moved me backwards until I was pressed against the wall. Our tongues intertwined, and his hands gripped my waist.

"That's not the kind of game you should be playing in my house."

My heart leaped into my throat. Alex pulled away from my lips and glanced at Tom, but he didn't jump away like he had in his basement.

"It's not a game," Alex said.

"You are sixteen."

Alex laughed. "From what I understand, you weren't exactly a saint at my age."

Tom's stare made me push Alex away.

"Come on. Teach me how to play this." I didn't want to cause tension, and as much as I enjoyed kissing Alex, there was something deeper at work between us. Something ignitable. Maybe even legendary.

Tom smirked and headed back into the office across the hall.

"I'd rather kiss you," Alex mumbled and grabbed a stick off the wall. He turned toward the table while handing me the stick. "Are you any good at geometry?"

"Math in all forms is easy for me."

Alex rolled the white ball to the end of the table and collected the rest in a wooden triangle on the opposite side, setting them. He picked up a yellow ball. "Solids." He replaced the ball at the head of the triangle and picked up a white ball with a blue stripe. "Stripes." He put the striped ball back and set the balls before he removed the wood.

I smiled. When he was in teaching mode, he was so cute and focused. That fluttery sensation filled me again.

He picked up his stick and came to the side where the white ball was. "We'll start with a simple game of eight ball." He held up the white ball. "This is the cue ball. It's the one you hit your stick with to get whatever balls are yours into the pockets."

"So, which ones are mine?" I looked at the tightly clustered balls.

"We don't know yet. We won't know until after I break." He placed the ball a little left of center on the side he stood on. "There are a few ways to hold the cue stick. I curl my index finger loosely around it, but Uncle Tom just rests it on the V of his thumb and uses his index finger as a guide." He showed both holds. "Use whatever you are most comfortable with."

He leaned over the table, lining his cue stick with the ball. "When I break, if one solid or one stripe goes in the pocket, then that's my color. If one of each goes in, then I get the choice." Then he looked at me and delivered the smile that turned the warmth in my soul to liquid heat. "You ready for an ass kicking?"

That was a challenge if I ever heard one. I shifted my stance. "Let's see what you can do." I clutched my stick, focusing on the table and all the possible geometric patterns and probabilities.

The *crack* of the cue ball against the rack made me jump, and the balls rolled in all different directions. Nothing fell in.

I glanced at him.

"The table is open. You can pick any color you want."

After studying the table, I lined my stick up with a solid ball.

"Faith?" he asked.

I looked up at him.

"You need to hit the white ball with your cue stick."

"But you just said I could pick any color." I straightened and scanned the table again, blinking. "Oh. I get it. It's not simple geometry. It's more complex with two balls in the equation."

Alex smiled. "Precisely. And the white ball is always the lead. The one you are using to get the angle just right."

"Gotcha." I positioned myself behind the white ball and lined up the cue stick.

"One more thing."

I lifted my gaze.

"If you sink the eight ball before the rest of the balls have been pocketed, you lose."

I stared at my shot and adjusted away from the black ball still near the center of where the neat rack had been.

Geometric patterns overlaid the table, and I chose the solids because those seemed to have the most unobstructed sites. I pulled the stick back like he had and slammed the tip into the white ball. It hit the yellow ball with such force that the cue ball shot up off the table, sailed towards the picture window, and smashed right through the glass.

I gasped and covered my mouth.

Alex burst into laughter.

Tom and Bridget skidded to a stop in the entry.

Alex walked over and plucked the stick out of my hand. "Maybe pool isn't your thing," he said, still laughing.

"I guess not." Tom cracked a smile, too. "Go get the ball, Alex." He pointed to the front door and then took a deep breath and closed his eyes. A crease appeared between his eyebrows, and his lips pressed together.

The scraping of glass pulled my gaze away, and I stared as the window pieced back together and fused as if nothing had happened. My gaze snapped to Tom.

"You could catch flies with that," Alex said when he stepped back in the room and put the cue ball back on the table. He crossed to me, and his smile faded.

Out of everything that had happened in the last twenty-four hours, the repairing of a glass window finally pushed me over the edge.

I walked over and fell onto the couch, clutching my hands into tight fists. Tremors started in my hands and then encompassed my whole body. Alex sat next to me and stroked my back. My breath wheezed.

Bridget took a seat on the coffee table in front of me. "I know."

I looked up at her.

"To them, it's normal. To us, it's the stuff nightmares are made of."

"I'm sorry, it's just... I guess..." I couldn't articulate all that was flying through my mind. "I have too many questions, and the only thing that seems real is Alex." I looked at him, and he took my fisted hand in his. "Everything else..." I shrugged. "It's all just too much." My gaze landed on Tom and clouded over in a wave of tears. I swiped at my face and met Bridget's gaze. "Before last night, I was the only monster out there." I opened my right palm, and a small flame danced in the center.

Alex stared at the flame, and so did I. I expected it to flare, but it remained in control. I closed my fist, and the flame snuffed out. I opened my palm again. The flame had indeed gone out.

I huffed a small laugh and glanced at the hand that Alex held. A certainty bloomed in my stomach, and I stared at him as I peeled my hand out of his grip. With my gaze locked on his, I opened my right hand again, letting the flame rise.

His gaze jumped away from mine, and his eyes widened. I didn't need to look. I felt the heat.

Bridget moved back.

I closed my fist, and the fire still licked at my skin. When I took his hand, it was the equivalent of submerging my hands in icy water.

I looked at Tom. He didn't look surprised at all. He retreated to the office across the hall. I glanced back at Bridget, still shaken by things, but not as bad as when I'd first sat down. I took a deep breath.

"What monsters are real?" I asked. If I knew what was out there, I might be more prepared for surprises, like putting broken things back together.

Bridget bit her lip. "Well, you saw a soul eater last night. And ghosts are real. Tom has had run-ins with vampires. Sirens are real. You've apparently met a shapeshifter..." She sighed.

"No werewolves?" I asked, thinking of all the books I'd read over the years.

"Not that we have run into, but I'm sure Kylee can fill you in on the things she's seen whenever she and Michael return."

"Michael?" I pointed to the ceiling because having archangels mingling on earth didn't seem that far-fetched anymore.

"No. Grace's brother. He took off last summer with Kylee, who is a supernatural bounty hunter," Alex said.

"Fate's real. Death is real. Demons are real. What about witches?" My brain swirled already.

"We actually have a friend who is a witch. Her husband is another with angel blood in them, and they live here in York, too."

"What is this, some supernatural mecca?" I asked.

Bridget laughed. "No, not really. But this *is* the only town that has anyone left of angel descent, but that's only because of CJ and Tom's efforts before the bottom dropped out."

"How many of us are there?"

"Thirteen, including you," Alex answered.

"How many were there before?"

Bridget looked down at her hands. "Thousands worldwide."

Her answer sent a shockwave through me. I had seen enough in the visions Tom had fed me to understand what happened. "My father killed them all?" My voice cracked.

She met my gaze and nodded.

I shivered. "So basically, all the things that terrified me in childhood nightmares are real." I swallowed with a tight throat. And that list didn't cover any of Alex's family's powers. "Including Lucifer."

"He's dead," Alex said.

An uncomfortable itch started at the base of my spine. "Don't the dead either go to Heaven or Hell?" I glanced at Alex. "Even angels?"

"What's your point?" Tom said from the hall.

"If he still exists..."

"Every portal on this earth was closed." Tom crossed his arms. "That is something I am certain of because *I* closed them. All of them. Including the only one to Heaven that existed." He studied me. "Lucifer is dead."

I chewed on my bottom lip. "Isn't dead relative where archangels are concerned? Or do they truly cease to exist in any manner, anywhere?" I knew I was digging, but something deep inside me told me to pursue this line of questions.

Tom's arms dropped to his sides, and he licked his lips. He glanced out the window he had just fixed. "I suppose he still exists in Hell the way Michael and Gabriel exist in Heaven."

"So. Not dead." I unclasped my hand from Alex's and wrapped my arms around me, holding my elbows to stop the quake from forming inside.

"He can't get here. Just like the archangels in Heaven can't. And even if he did, I doubt he'd be anything more than human this time." His hand pressed to his chest almost like a reflex.

I bit my lip. The squeal of brakes and the exhale of exhaust outside closed the conversation. I wiped my face and shook off the dread clinging to every cell so April wouldn't walk into a roomful of tension.

She bounded inside, and her grin widened at the sight of her cousin. Alex smiled back and gave her a big, warm hug.

"Are you coming shopping with us?" April asked him. The hopeful lilt in her voice broadcasted her wishes.

He turned and glanced at me. "Did you want me to come?"

I glanced at my ungloved hands and shrugged. I wasn't so sure about going out in public without the warded leather, and having Alex along would probably make it safer for everyone. "Only if you want to."

"Come with us!" April said, giving him wide puppy eyes that brought a smile to my face.

"Fine." He rolled his eyes and grinned at me.

"I can take your bike home for you," Tom said to Alex.

"Thanks, Uncle Tom."

Bridget disappeared and came back with her pocketbook. "Do you need anything?" she asked Tom.

"No. I'm good, but I'd imagine Faith and Alex are hungry. We never had lunch at CJ's."

My stomach growled, and it wasn't the only one making noise at the mention of food.

Alex shrugged. "I could eat a burger or two."

"Sounds like a plan." Bridget gave Tom a kiss before corralling the three of us out to the car.

In the back seat, I clutched Alex's hand as another uncomfortable, people-filled adventure awaited.

Fire Cursed
Chapter 8

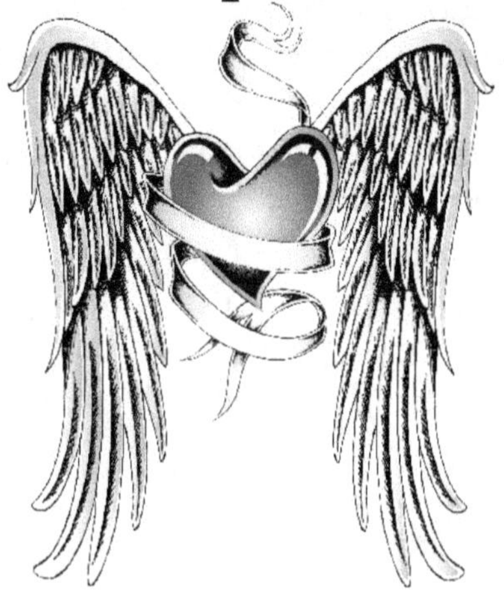

GOING SHOPPING WITH BRIDGET, April, and Alex ended up being much more fun than I'd expected. Bridget took us to a diner in Portsmouth before we headed over to the mall. There were so many choices on the menu that made my mouth water that I couldn't decide.

"I don't know what to get." I glanced up at Bridget and April.

Alex took the menu from me and smiled at the waitress. "We will both have the barbeque cheeseburger, fries, and a chocolate milkshake." He waved his finger between us.

"How would you like that cooked?" she asked.

"Medium rare," we both said at the same time.

Bridget and April ordered, and the waitress stepped away.

"I hope that didn't bother you," Alex said.

I shook my head. "I'm not sure I could have decided with all the choices. So, thank you."

He squeezed my hand under the table. "You looked like you were getting a little stressed."

April studied the two of us. "You like each other." Her eyes sparked with glee and she beamed. Then it faded almost into a warning. "Grace isn't going to like that."

"F..." Alex started and clamped his lips together at the glare Bridget sent. "Forget Grace," he said. "She doesn't have claim to my heart."

Bridget's dimples appeared, and she tried to suppress her smile. "Shouldn't you be more worried about school than your heart?"

Alex shrugged and leaned back in the seat. "I'm not worried about school. I'm not sure I'll have a choice, anyway. It seems my mom has her heart set on me going to Harvard like she did."

"For?" I asked.

"She wants me to be a doctor." He met my gaze. "What about you?"

"I don't know what I want to do. I thought about being a veterinarian, because I love animals. But animals aren't fireproof." I shrugged. "I'll probably do something with computers, so I don't have to be around people."

"Why wouldn't you pursue what you love?" Bridget asked.

I glanced at Bridget and raised my hands before folding them back in my lap.

"You totally should go for it," April said, but she didn't understand, and I wasn't about to enlighten her about my curse.

"We'll see." I smiled.

The waitress came and set our drinks down.

The chocolate shake was delicious, and when the food came, I took my first bite and had to agree. This was the best choice on the menu.

I swallowed the bite. "Thank you."

"It's my favorite." Alex took a sip of his milkshake.

I cataloged that to memory and wondered if Bridget would teach me to make it if I asked her.

The rest of the lunch flew by, and before I knew it, we were standing in front of racks of clothing. My gaze didn't know where to go. We only had the country store, and they had very little variety. Even the online shops didn't overwhelm me the way standing in front of so many choices did.

April was like a winter flurry, running from rack to rack and grabbing whatever struck her fancy.

Bridget took my hand and crossed from the junior department, where April was gathering a monster pile to the women's section.

"Just start with something simple, like jeans." She brought me to a rack of pants. "And then look through the shirts for something you like. And please, do not worry about how much things cost. Money is not an issue at all," Bridget added and squeezed my hand. "Now, I need to go rein April in." She smiled and took off.

Alex stood next to me, his hands deep in his pockets, looking as uncomfortable as I felt.

"Are you okay?" I asked.

The moment his gaze landed on mine, he smiled. "Not exactly the most exciting afternoon."

"I'm sorry," I muttered and stared at the clothes.

"What size are you?" he asked.

"Six."

"Did you want help finding stuff?"

I shrugged, but inside my head, I screamed yes. I didn't know where to start, even though Bridget had given me a road map.

As if he could read my mind, he took my hand and led me to the other side of the rack. He shuffled through the jeans and handed me three different pairs. I draped them over my arm.

He led me to the shirts and picked out a pretty green sweater and an equally pretty blue one. He also grabbed a black button-up shirt as well. We walked by a mannequin dressed in black leather, and he stopped, raising an eyebrow.

"You would look awesome in that," he said.

He rummaged on the shelf, found the top and pants, and put it over the growing collection in my arms. He even grabbed the open-toed, lace-up boots that matched the outfit.

He added a couple of dresses to the pile and then led me to the dressing rooms, where Bridget stood outside the entrance. She raised an eyebrow at the pile in my arms and then glanced at Alex.

"Try them on," Alex prompted when I stopped at the doorway.

April came bounding out in a colorful outfit consisting of a bright pink skirt and a turquoise shirt. She beamed at me and grabbed my arm, pulling me into her dressing room. It was big enough for the two of us and she took the clothes from my arms and deposited them on the bench.

She pointed to a hook on the wall. "That's the keeper hook, and the one on the door is the pass one."

I glanced between the two and when April put the current outfit on the empty hook on the wall; I smiled. The one on the door already held three outfits.

I slipped my sneakers off and put them right next to hers.

"Try on that leather outfit first," she said, spying the last outfit that Alex had picked out for me. She pulled on a red dress that drained her of color.

I must have had a less than pleasant look on my face because she turned towards the mirror and scrunched her nose.

"Yuk." She peeled it off, and it went on the hook on the door. She didn't seem to have a problem changing in front of me. "Go ahead." She nodded at the pile of clothes as she grabbed another dress off her try-on stack.

I took off my skirt and stuck it behind the massive pile. The leather pants slid on easily and hugged my form comfortably. I pushed the pile back and put the boots on, then tightened the laces. When I took off my shirt, April's eyes widened.

"What happened?" she asked with a gasp.

"The tiger bit me." I tucked the shirt where I'd put the skirt.

"Grace bit you? Why?"

"She doesn't like me," I said, and then pulled the leather and silk shirt over my head. It felt so decadent and I turned, looking at the mirror.

April's eyes widened. "You have to show Mom and Alex." She grabbed my hand, and I nearly tripped on the boots' heels as she dragged me out the changing room door.

Alex's eyes widened, and his pupils grew. His cheeks flared pink just before he licked his lips. "Wow." He slowly looked down to my feet and up again.

The scrutiny of his stare made me shift.

"Hot," he whispered.

"Um, no," Bridget said.

"Why not?" April argued. "She looks fantastic."

"She does, but it looks too... risqué." She crossed her arms.

"Okay," I turned back towards the dressing room. Bridget was right. It was too sexy, but the fabric felt as good as having Alex look at me the way he just had.

"Then I'll get it for her," Alex said.

I took a quick look behind me at him, and he squared off with Bridget, adopting the same crossed arms and stare as she had.

"You can't deny she looks great in that."

"I agree, but I can't see your uncle agreeing to let her wear that out of the house, can you?"

"I see your point," he said just as April closed the door behind us.

I took the outfit off and went to hang it on the no pile.

"That belongs over here." April put her hands out.

"But..."

"It would be a crime not to buy that for you."

I relinquished the outfit and tried on one of the dresses. April changed back into her clothes and grabbed all the yes outfits, including the leather one. She headed out to where her mother and Alex waited and dumped everything into the cart.

"Now that's more like it," Bridget said, smiling at me in the royal blue dress.

April went back into the dressing room with me and helped by holding items and saying yes or no.

When I peeled the last shirt off, I winced and handed it to her before I reached for the clothes I had come with. All the effort left me a little light-headed.

"Um, Faith?"

"Yeah," I said, pulling my skirt on with my back to her.

"You're bleeding through one of your bandages."

I sat down on the bench, my brain swirling, and heated panic raced across my skin and pooled in my palms. I clenched my fists. "Go get Alex," I barked.

She balked. "This is a women's dressing room."

"Get Alex," I yelled.

April backed out of the room with her arms full. Before the door could close all the way, both Alex and Bridget stepped into the room.

"What's wrong?" Bridget asked, and I turned so she could see what April had seen.

"Sweet Jesus," Bridget whispered. "We need to get you to the hospital."

That was the last place I wanted to go. I reached out and grabbed Alex's hand, grounding myself before my nerves ignited. "I don't want to go to the hospital."

"You are bleeding. A lot."

"I need help to cauterize it." I glanced up at Bridget, and then to Alex. "I need you to help me so I don't set this entire building on fire."

"Okay," Alex agreed and squeezed my hand.

"Your mother said that if it got worse..." Bridget said.

"I know what my mom said, but she's already pale and we'd still have a twenty-minute ride if we left now. I can help her. You go with April and check out. We'll be out just as soon as we are done."

"If anything happens to you..."

"I've got this," Alex said.

"You're sixteen."

"Why is everyone throwing my age in my face today?" he asked, exasperated. "We will be fine. Now go, before Faith passes out." He pointed at the door.

The conflict was clearly written in the creases around Bridget's eyes.

"We don't have time for this," Alex whispered. "Please, just trust me."

Bridget took a deep breath and nodded. "I'll wait just outside the changing rooms."

Alex closed the door and locked it before he sat down behind me. He moved my hair to the side and placed his hand on the back of my neck.

His soft touch sent tingles all over my skin, and I became aware that I was only in my skirt and bra. Both heat and chills ran through me.

"What do you need me to do?"

"Take the bandage off," I said, and winced when he did.

He dropped the saturated bandage on the ground and sucked in air. "Now what?"

His voice shook, and I glanced back at him. "Keep my hair away from the flame and guide my finger to the cut." I pulled my hand from his and raised my index finger, willing the flame to ignite. Heat flared, and a blue flame rose from my fingertip like a blowtorch.

Alex grimaced, but didn't hesitate. He wrapped his hand around mine and pulled it toward the cut on my neck.

I clenched my teeth, waiting for the pain. The sizzle of burning flesh filled the air a split second before agony clenched every muscle.

He brought my hand away. "Done," he whispered.

The pain was too much.

"Control," Alex commanded sharply, but I couldn't. His hand left my neck, and he wrapped it around my finger, squeezing.

His reaction slapped me into full control, and the fire fizzled out. But I wasn't fast enough to pull it back. Alex pulled his hand away, wincing.

"Why did you do that?" I whispered and took his hand in mine. Angry red blisters formed on his palm.

He closed his eyes and took a deep breath before glancing at my back. "Your back looks as painful as my hand." He met my gaze. "Come on, before the smoke alarms go off."

I pulled the shirt over my head gingerly and slipped my shoes on.

Alex grinned at me.

"What?"

"This is not how I imagined being alone with a half-dressed girl."

I snorted laughter. "Let's go."

We walked out of the dressing room.

"We're going to need some aloe." Alex showed Bridget his hand.

Her gaze narrowed, as did her lips. "Alex…"

"I'll be fine. It's a burn. It will heal. Besides, her neck is just as bad." He wrapped his good hand in mine.

He headed towards the checkout counter, and the rest of us followed. The back of my neck stung like hornets had found a new playground. I just wanted to get home, slather my sore with aloe, and sleep for six weeks.

Bridget stopped in the underwear department and grabbed a handful of things, then tossed them into the cart before she paid for everything and herded us to the car.

She didn't even notice the black leather going into the bag. I had a feeling that would prompt a discussion when we got home, but right now, all I wanted was something to soothe the fiery burn on my neck.

Bridget made one stop to grab antibiotic ointment and bandages and then headed over to drop Alex off. Tom's truck was in the driveway. Instead of dropping off Alex and leaving, Bridget turned off the car. She grabbed the bag from the drugstore and headed inside.

I hesitated with my hand on the door. At least I was on the side closest to the front door. Alex glanced at me before he closed his door. He crossed around the car and helped me out. April seemed to understand my hesitation as well, like we had been sisters all our lives instead of just for twenty-four hours. They flanked me to the door like body guards.

The silent communication we had was odd, but it gave me a sense of peace like I'd never felt before. I took a moment to silently thank Fate for bringing me here.

Fire Cursed
Chapter 9

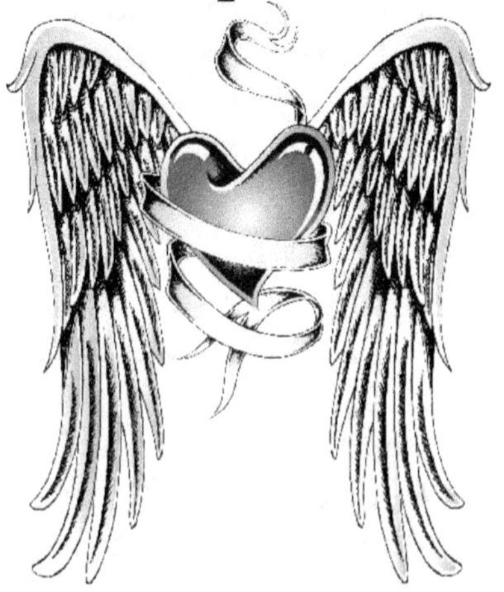

BRIDGET STOOD JUST INSIDE the doorway to the kitchen. Her gaze locked on the family room. We stepped in behind her and stared at the scene.

Tom lay on the kitchen table with his shirt unbuttoned and his chest and face bathed in sweat. Valerie held his wrist and was staring at her watch. CJ stood on the opposite side of the table.

"You have to stop," Valerie said.

"What are you doing?" Bridget asked.

Tom sat up and banged his head on the chandelier over the table. He exchanged a glace with CJ as he rubbed the spot that took the brunt of the collision. "Trying to extract Lucifer's grace." He mopped his face.

"I gather from your faces it didn't work?"

They all shook their heads.

I didn't quite understand the tension filling the room and glanced at Alex.

He let go of my hand and approached his mother with his injured hand outstretched. "Think you can take a second and fix this for me?"

"What happened?" Valerie said with a sharp tone that made me shrink back a step, especially when her accusatory stare landed on me.

"She needed to cauterize one of the bite wounds."

"And she burned you?" CJ asked, his lashes batting wildly as if he couldn't quite reconcile his son's calm demeanor with the severity of the burn on his hand.

"I didn't mean to." All eyes turned to me, and I shifted in place. "I just..." I dropped my gaze to the floor, letting my hair block my view.

"She lost control, and I reacted," Alex explained, but no one seemed to grasp the magnitude of what could have happened if Alex hadn't been there.

"She has blood in her hair?" Tom's voice cut through the tension.

I glanced up in time to see him slide off the table. He nearly dropped to his knees but steadied himself with a hand on the wood. Bridget moved like lightning and was at his side in a blink. He lowered into a kitchen chair looking sickly, almost the same pallor as my mother had near the end. My chest tightened with concern.

"She was bleeding pretty badly," Alex said, pulling my attention away from Tom.

Alex hissed when his mother pressed a kiss to his palm. Light danced over his skin like a hundred fireflies had taken flight. Sweat broke out on his forehead and his jaw tightened. He blew air out of his puckered lips slowly as his blisters flattened and then melted away. The redness in the center of his palm lessened but did not completely fade. He flexed his hand and glanced up at me. He didn't quite manage a smile, but it was there in his eyes.

Valerie turned to me. "Let me look at you." She waved me over.

I crossed as I gathered my hair into a twist and piled it on top of my head so Valerie could look at my wounds.

After a quick look, she pulled out a chair for me. "We're going to get you cleaned up a bit. Get me a clean, wet washcloth, please," she said to Alex.

"I have antibiotic ointment." Bridget handed her the bag she'd brought in.

"Go get my medical bag upstairs. And grab a couple hair clips while you're up there," she said to CJ. "I think it might be a good idea to address these tonight, so there isn't any chance you have to do that again," she said, leaning so I could see her. "What were you doing?"

"Trying on clothes," I replied.

"You probably should have held off on that," Valerie said.

"I didn't even think..." Bridget started, and then closed her eyes. "I guess I've gotten used to having you around." Her cheeks turned red. "I'm sorry," she said to me.

"It's not your fault." I glanced at Bridget and then across the table at Tom. "Are you okay?"

He nodded and tried to smile, but he didn't look okay. Dark circles rounded his eyes, and his cheeks now had some blotchy red marks, like a fever had set in.

"Maybe you should go lie down on the couch," Bridget said to him. She helped him to his feet and guided him to the couch, where he sat down hard. "I'll get you some juice."

CJ came down with Valerie's medical bag, hair clips, and clean towels draped over his arm. He spared a glance at his brother and his brow knit, but he continued to us at the table and handed a handful of hair clips to his wife. He set the bag on the table and waited until she clipped my hair before he handed her the towels. "What do you need me to do?"

"Wipe down the table. Tom sweat all over it, and it can't be sanitary."

CJ crossed to a plastic container of disinfectant wipes and started wiping the table down in front of where I sat.

Alex returned with a handful of wet washcloths. "Where do you want these?"

"On the table where your father just cleaned off."

"Did you find anything you liked?" Valerie asked, as she tucked a towel around the collar of my shirt.

"She did," April said. Her gaze was planted on the back of my neck, and her usually high color had faded.

Valerie wiped the skin around my burn with a wet washcloth.

Pain flared, and I inhaled sharply, my back arching away from the source. I clenched my hands into fists.

"It probably would be a good idea to have a couple pots of cold water nearby," I said, my voice higher-pitched than normal.

The cloth stopped moving.

"I'll get it." Alex left my side. He grabbed two saucepans, filled them with water, and set them on the table in front of me.

His mother resumed cleaning my burn. Alex sat in the chair and threaded his hand into mine. I locked gazes with him and the softest smile on his lips made the sharp drills of pain fade. He was my elixir.

"Soulmates."

The word pulled us out of whatever trance we had fallen into, and I looked at April. Everyone was looking at April.

"Well, they are." She waved at us.

I glanced back at Alex, wondering if April had put a name to the completeness I felt when I was near him.

The pull at the back of my neck sent another tremor through me, and I winced, squeezing Alex's hand harder.

The back slider opened, and the cause of my pain stepped into the room with an older woman leading her. The stern set of the older woman's lips, along with her hand on the back of Grace's neck like she was forcing Grace to step foot in the house, almost made me smile, but I was in too much discomfort to manage it.

"Grace has something to say," she said.

Grace glared at me and pressed her lips together. She crossed her arms like a petulant child.

"She isn't welcome here." Alex stood, holding my hand in full view.

"Alex," both CJ and Valerie said. The scold in that single word was clear.

"I'm sorry I bit you," Grace said, but she didn't sound like she was sorry. It sounded exactly like what it was. A forced apology.

I gave a nod. "Apology accepted."

"The Hell it is," Alex snapped. "You attacked her twice for no reason."

"She's Lucifer's daughter. That's reason enough."

"And I suppose being a vampire's daughter is any better," Alex said.

"Alex, she apologized." I squeezed his hand.

The sharp look he gave me shut me up.

"You almost bled out at the store, and you want me to accept that half-assed apology?" He shook his head. "Nope. Not happening." He glared at Grace. "You need to let go of whatever fantasy you've concocted about me. It will never happen, Grace."

Her lips thinned, and her hatred pulsed in the air in time with the throb of each of her puncture marks on the back of my neck.

"They belong together. They are soulmates. Can't you feel it?" April waved at us, interrupting the growing tension, sending it into ignite mode.

Grace snarled, and the woman's arm tensed. "Let me go, Mom."

My free hand tingled with heat, sensing the danger as much as the thrum of my heart. I clenched it into a fist.

"Please just go," Valerie said. "You attacked her on *my* property, without provocation."

"But..." Grace started, but her mother nodded, dragging her out of the house.

The peel of another bandage coming off pulled my attention, and I closed my eyes.

"You don't get to tell someone that they aren't welcome in our house," Valerie said.

Alex sat down and stared at the table. "She won't stop."

Tom huffed from the couch. "She will if she knows what's good for her." He sat up with a half-empty glass of juice in his hand. His gaze flitted around me and then landed on mine as if confirming something only he could see. "You need to talk to Naomi," he said to Valerie. "Grace's aura is threaded with more darkness than light."

The hands working on my injury stalled. Silence fell on the room.

"Grace has already chosen her path," April said in a voice I did not recognize. "Death surrounds her now."

Fire Cursed
Chapter 10

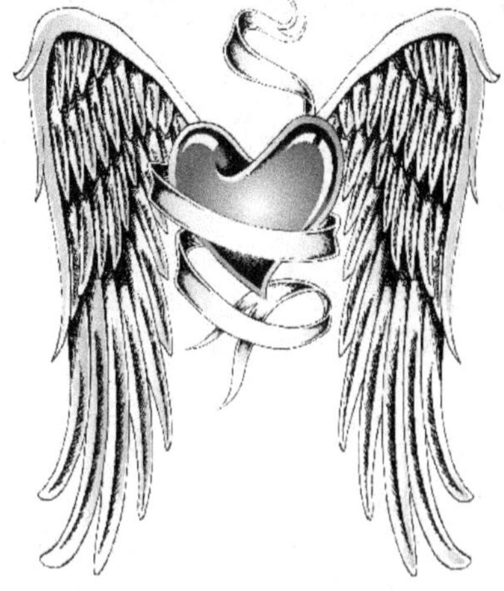

APRIL'S REVELATION HAD LEFT a chill in the air. No one spoke as Valerie finished her patch job and gave Bridget the rundown of bandage changes I would need. By the time she finished, Tom had gotten his color back.

"Same drill as earlier," Valerie said, as we stepped out the door. "Don't get those bandages wet for another day or so. Sponge baths and wash her hair in the sink."

"Thank you." Bridget led me to her car, April at my side.

Tom walked with us and made sure I got in the car without incident before he crossed to his truck.

"I'm sorry," I said from the back seat once we were all belted in.

Bridget looked in the rearview mirror. "You have nothing to be sorry about."

April turned to me, her gaze pleading. "Promise me you'll watch your back whenever you are here."

I nodded.

"You can't let your guard down when you are outside. Okay?"

"Okay."

My agreement with her didn't seem to wipe out the underlying urgency in her eyes, even after we drove out of the gate. I shifted in the seat and looked out the window.

"How do you feel?" Bridget asked.

"Like someone took a thousand needles and stabbed them into the back of my neck," I said, keeping my hands clasped so I didn't try to rub the prickle away.

"I'll clean you up, and then you can rest," Bridget said.

All I wanted to do was sleep a dreamless, dead-like slumber that would renew the energy I'd lost today. Not even Alex could bring the spark back right now. Only a decent night's rest would do that.

In a repeat of what we'd done earlier in the day, Bridget washed the blood off my back and washed my hair in the sink. Then she rummaged through the pile of clothes April had left on top of the dresser. She came back in the bathroom with a nightgown, helped me into it, and then fixed my damp hair in a single braid.

We didn't speak. Just went through the motions.

As soon as she tucked me under the covers, she sat on the edge of the bed. "I've been thinking about how to say what I want without you taking it the wrong way."

My stomach tightened.

"Tom didn't want any more children after his daughter died." She glanced at her hands. "When he left, he did not know I was pregnant."

I shifted, uncomfortable with her unloading their past on me.

"Anyway, he's been back long enough to regret his decision." She met my gaze. "He made certain he would never have any more."

Understanding trickled into my brain. "Oh."

She licked her lips and sighed. "So, what I'm trying to say in my round-a-bout and terrible way is that I'm glad you're here."

"Even after today?" I asked before I had the sense to keep my mouth shut.

Her light laugh filled my room and swelled my heart. "Yes. Even after today. A few bumps, bruises, and a little blood are all part of parenthood. Now get some rest. I'll come check on you in a little while."

"Thank you."

She closed the door when she left. I stared at the ceiling. I had only been in York for less than twenty-four hours. That single thought boggled my mind, and I wondered if this was all a dream. If everything, including Alex, was just a figment of my imagination.

It would make total sense. The perfect guy. The near perfect family who unilaterally accepted me. The existence of things that I never imagined were real. It was all too bizarre.

Maybe I would wake up in the morning in our cabin to Mom making some oatmeal on the old stove and we'd have a really good laugh at my dreams.

I closed my eyes, letting the exhaustion pummeling every muscle have its way.

I SAT UP IN a dark room, disoriented. The only light filtered from the moon coming through the thin curtains. Voices interrupted the silence of the night. I rubbed my eyes, swung my legs over the side of the bed, and crossed to the door.

I cracked the door ajar and looked out into an unfamiliar hallway. It took a few moments for my memory to clear. I was at the Ryans' house, and everything that had happened was real.

I closed my eyes and leaned my head on the door, but the voices below moved me forward. I turned towards the stairwell and silently padded downstairs. The voices were coming from the partially open door of the office.

I crept closer, my mind racing with the possibilities of what could make Bridget and Tom raise their voices at each other.

"You have to!" a voice that wasn't Bridget's insisted.

"I have no fucking clue how to," Tom's voice snapped. "Believe me, we tried."

"Do you not understand what is at stake?"

"I tried, and then I had CJ try. It almost killed me," Tom said.

"What?" Bridget asked, her voice agitated.

I could almost see his head spin towards her, and his wide-eyed expression that screamed he had just screwed up.

"There is a breech. We have no idea where on earth it is, but alarms are going off all over Purgatory, which means..."

That voice sounded an awful lot like Fate's.

"A portal to Hell is opening," Tom said. He sounded completely deflated.

"Yes. Anything leading to Heaven wouldn't set off alarms. And we have dominion over Purgatory, so any hole there would be found like that." Fate snapped her fingers loud enough for me to recognize the sound.

"What changed? What set off the first alarm?" Bridget asked.

"I don't know. Things were fine, and then this morning, the alarms started going off."

"Before or after we spoke?" Tom asked.

"Before."

Silence fell on the room, and I closed my eyes. This morning was the first time I'd ever done that weird time travel thing. It couldn't be a coincidence. I sagged against the wall.

"How long have you been listening?" Tom asked, and my eyes flew open. He stood in the doorway.

"Long enough," I said. "I'm responsible for it?"

Tom opened his mouth and then closed it. "I don't know."

"Yes, you do. The timing is too odd to be a coincidence." I took a deep breath. "You shouldn't have brought me here."

Fate stepped out of the office, followed by Bridget.

"If they hadn't gone to get you, you would be operating without a soul." Fate crossed her arms. "That path would have killed far too many people before their time. Which would have been much more disastrous. Lucifer does not need permission to claim a soulless body."

The rush of my blood flowing through my veins nearly drowned out Fate's words. I trembled with a shiver gone rogue and wrapped my arms around myself to keep from triggering my fire nature. My mind raced as fast as my heart.

I locked my gaze with Fate. "Are my fire abilities tied to my soul?"

She slowly shook her head.

"Holy Mary, Mother of God." My knees gave out, and I slid down the wall. "So as long as my soul is intact..."

"He can't claim your body, and by default, your powers, without your permission. However, without his grace, you cannot shut the rift between worlds."

"Tom has his grace. Can't he close it?"

"He doesn't wield fire," Fate said.

"Yes, he does. He has angel fire," Bridget said.

"Angel fire may be enough to send Lucifer back to Hell, but it cannot repair the tear. Only *his* daughter filled with *his* grace can repair that." Fate's eyes closed. "If he gets through again, there is only one thing on earth that can truly kill Lucifer. It isn't angel fire. It isn't tearing his head from his body. It's a rare knife he had given to Lilith. It was forged with Heaven's light and can obliterate anything, even Death. And when I say obliterate, it's far more permanent than killing. It's removing something from existence. No Heaven. No Hell. No Purgatory.

Just gone. And more importantly, there is no way back.”

I trembled in place on the floor.

“Kylee doesn’t have it in her arsenal?” Tom asked.

“I don’t believe so. It’s been missing since before Lilith was turned.” She pulled a piece of paper from her notebook and handed it to Tom.

He looked and crossed back into his office. I stood and followed Bridget and Fate into the office. Tom stood with his back to us, dropped the paper on the desk, and ran his hand through his hair.

I glanced at Bridget. A tear tracked down her cheek.

When Tom turned, deep-seated pain reflected in his gaze as it met Bridget’s. He shrugged and tried to smile, but it looked haunted.

“We’ll figure this out.” Bridget wiped at the tears on her face.

“There’s only one way to get his grace,” Tom said.

It took a moment and then my eyes grew wide. “No.” I backed out of the room and ran upstairs, then slammed the door to my bedroom. I leaned against it.

The memory of Tom eating his best friend’s heart turned my stomach.

I could never take his life like that.

Not even if it meant hell on earth.

Fire Cursed
Chapter 11

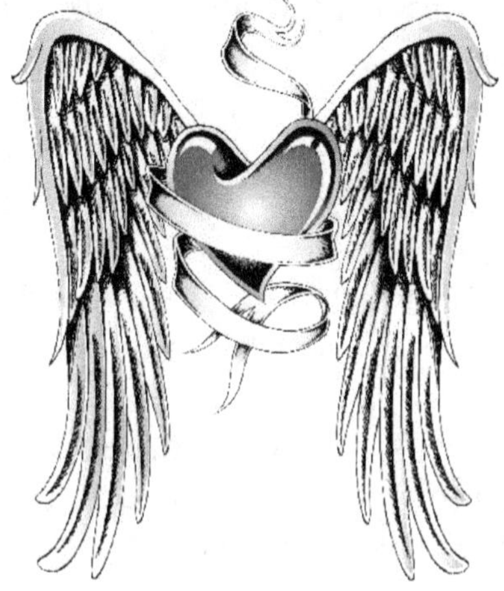

A KNOCK ON THE door interrupted my frantic swarm of thoughts.

"Let me in," Tom said.

"No." I continued to press my back against the door.

"I promise you won't have to eat my heart today."

"Not ever! Promise me you'll never make me."

"I can't promise you that."

His voice was soft enough to calm some of the storm brewing inside me. The man was talking about his own life as if it wasn't worth bargaining for. I opened the door and stared up into his bright blue eyes.

"I won't kill you." I crossed my arms.

"I'm a dead man walking if Lucifer gets loose, and everyone I care about will be a target. Including you."

I pressed my lips together to stop my chin from quivering.

"When the time comes, you will have to. Otherwise, your father will take it from me. And honestly, if I'm going to die, I'd rather it be by your hand than his."

My vision blurred, and heat filled my hands. I balled them and stepped back. I shook my head. "I can't."

"We are stressing over something that might be years away. Let's not do that. It's not something we need to worry about right this second."

I scoffed. Any thought of digesting a heart was not welcomed, whether it be tomorrow or ten years from now.

"You have other things to worry about, like getting your high school degree, and learning how to control your fire."

"I already know how to control it."

"No. You know how to suppress it most of the time. But you don't know how to wield it."

He was right. I knew how to put it under wraps when I was stressed, and it had a habit of getting away from me when I used it under duress.

"I also have to deal with the tiger," I whispered, trying to focus away from the dull panic throbbing in my muscles.

"Yeah, well, Grace is something of a wild card. But Alex should be able to keep her in line. If not, CJ will."

The mere mention of Alex's name soothed the beast inside me. "I'd like to get to know him better," I said, and my hand went to my lips.

"You mean kiss him more?" Tom crossed his arms.

Heat filled my cheeks.

"On second thought, don't answer that. It's time for you to get some rest." He nodded toward the bed. "You have that test with CJ tomorrow."

I laughed. Sleep would bring nightmares, which would likely bring fire with it in my current condition.

Tom's eyes darkened, and his gaze dropped to my hands. "Where are your gloves?"

I pointed towards where the laundry closet was at the end of the hall near the stairwell.

He crossed and opened the folding doors. He came back to the doorway and sighed at the melted leather bundles in his hands. "I don't think these should have gone into the dryer."

I snorted a laugh.

He crumpled them in his fist and turned, marching away.

I closed the door and climbed into the bed, staring at the window, my thoughts swirling like a wild storm in my head. I kept my fists clenched tight, but I didn't know if that would be enough. Not with the images that kept pushing to the forefront of my mind despite my efforts to push them away.

A few minutes later, the door opened, and my light switched on. "I always have a backup plan." Tom handed me a second pair of leather gloves.

These were softer than the other pair and fingerless. I slid them on, and they dampened the heat in my hands the same way the other gloves had. These were much more fashionable and would go beautifully with the black leather outfit that we had bought. I liked them much better than the last pair.

He pointed at my hands. "Don't let Bridget throw those in the washing machine, okay?"

"Okay." I flexed my fingers. These felt like a second skin. "I really like them. Thank you."

"I would have given you this pair to begin with, but we decided to play it safe and see if it worked before switching up. If you need another pair, I have one more in my desk drawer downstairs. Now, get some more sleep. You need it." He turned the light off and left me to my own thoughts.

I tried to focus on Alex, but the visions of the past kept congregating, clouding my focus and keeping sleep out of reach.

When the clock reached two, I climbed out of bed and grabbed the bathrobe on the back of the bathroom door. I wandered down to the family room and stretched out on the couch with the television remote in my hand.

I studied the tool and pressed the power button. The television blared to life, and I quickly pressed the volume to the lowest setting before mute. I surfed the channels, going one by one, unable to choose what to watch.

"I need to be more decisive," I whispered to the dark. "Too many choices, and I freeze." I sighed and rubbed my eyes. "Just choose something," I scolded myself, while doing another round of switching channels.

A scene with a little girl throwing fire from her hands caught my attention, and I put the remote down. I watched with curiosity, hugging my knees as it became tense.

"*Firestarter*? Really?"

I jumped at his voice.

Tom stretched out on the other couch and crossed his arms. "I couldn't sleep, either."

I gave him a cursory glance and then focused back on the movie. Hot tears tracked down my cheeks as the credits rolled across the screen. I sniffled and wiped my face. The girl in the movie had lost everything. A deep pain filled my chest. If she couldn't save those she loved, how could I?

"It's a movie, Faith."

"But..." I waved at the television.

He glanced over at me. "I'm going to ask CJ to try to extract the grace again."

Tears still tracked down my cheeks. "You said you almost died today when he tried."

"I may have been embellishing that a little." His lips formed a goofy grin. "Not only am I moody, but sometimes I embellish for effect."

I wiped my face. "Bullshit," I said. The word felt foreign on my tongue and I cringed inside, but it was the only one that would slap the truth out of him.

His eyebrows rose, his mouth popped open, and he sat up, facing me. "Faith."

I put my hand out. "Save your placations for someone else."

"You are worse than Bri." He ran both hands through his hair and stared at the ground.

"I've been sheltered all my life. I don't need you to sugarcoat things for me. I will come to terms with everything that's been dumped on me since you picked me up from the state home." I took a breath when his gaze met mine. "I have to, because otherwise, everyone I care about will be at risk, too."

He huffed and smiled. "You are much more prepared to take on the world at sixteen than I was when I was thirty."

"I just want—"

"Don't say a normal life," he interrupted. "Normal is boring and underrated." He grabbed the remote and started flipping through channels.

"Normal might actually be nice," I said, feeling a little more argumentative after watching that movie.

He sighed. "Being powerless and clueless..." He chewed on his bottom lip. "I've been powerless, and believe me, you never want to be in those shoes. But clueless might be nice. To never know what really lurks out there... Yeah, I could get on board with that." He smiled over at me.

"I was clueless all my life. If my mother hadn't died, I'm sure I would have been clueless for quite a long time." I raised my hands to stare at my palms. "And I would have thought I was the only real freak out there." I curled my fingers and dropped my hands to my lap. "So, thanks for making me not feel so alone."

He belted out laughter. "We are a bunch of unnatural freaks," he said. "Except for Bri. She's normal, as you categorize it."

I raised an eyebrow. "Alex and his sisters?"

"Nope. Angel descendants. Same with Austin, the witch's husband. No powers, but he is angel blood, too, so that does not qualify as normal, like Bri."

I stared at his profile. "April?"

"She has visions sometimes. Grace, beyond her tiger transformation, seems in tune with angel radio." He pointed to the ceiling. "Michael and Gabriel don't show any signs of supernatural powers, though."

"I think Alex has powers," I said. "He has the power to calm the fire, just like these gloves."

Tom chuckled. "Are you sure he isn't just turning it into another kind of fire?"

I stared at the television trying not to allow a blush to heat my face. I failed miserably. Alex's touch brought on some powerful and highly inappropriate emotions.

"Be careful with him." Tom's smile faded, and a serious light shone in his eyes.

I nodded. I had no intention of hurting Alex.

"I'm not worried about Alex. I'm worried about you."

"Why?"

He inhaled deep and glanced at the ceiling. "I have no idea if he's experienced or not. But at his age, I was... wild. CJ had had a steady girlfriend ever since we were nine. He never looked at anyone else until after she dumped him. And then he met Valerie and married her. But me... I started sleeping around when I was thirteen. I was kind of a whore in that respect." He glanced at me. "In other words, I don't know if Alex takes after his father or not."

I traced my bottom lip with my finger. I couldn't imagine him kissing anyone else, and the thought spurned an uncomfortable flare across my skin. I shifted on the couch and yawned.

"Please stop talking about Alex," I said. I didn't want to broach that subject with Tom. He'd already planted the seeds of doubt.

"Don't doubt that he is into you," Tom said. "That isn't what I'm saying. I'm..."

"I know what you're saying. I just don't want you to keep talking about Alex. At. All."

"I'm making you uncomfortable?" He had the audacity to grin.

"Very," I admitted.

His smile faded. "I don't know if I'll be around to torture April like this."

Now I wished he had just kept on razzing me.

Fire Cursed
Chapter 12

HANDS SHOOK ME.

I blinked my eyes open to Bridget standing over me. The television still played some movie. Tom snored on the other couch.

"CJ called wondering where you were." She rubbed her eye. "Go get dressed and I'll take you over."

I rolled off the couch, stiff from sleeping at an odd angle. I headed for my bathroom and the toothbrush first. My braid still held, and outside of a line on the side of my face from the piping on the throw pillow, I didn't look bad. I used a washcloth to clean up and crossed to the bureau where my new clothing had been stashed.

I chose my jeans and the green shirt that Alex had picked out for me. There was a pair of green underwear that matched the shirt and white socks, and a bra that was similar to the one Bridget had let me borrow.

I dressed, used deodorant, and slipped on my beat-up sneakers. By the time I got downstairs, Bridget was waiting in the kitchen. My backpack was on the stool by the door.

"What about Tom?"

"Letting him sleep." She yawned and headed outside with her keys in her hand.

I hooked my arm around my backpack and headed outside. My stomach fluttered with both excitement at seeing Alex and dread that I might have another run-in with Grace. I adjusted in my seat and hoped like hell my day would be better than yesterday.

I made it into the Ryan's house without incident. CJ led me downstairs, past Alex and the girls, into the computer room. A monitor was on waiting for me, along with a pencil, a sheet of paper, and a simple calculator.

The test.

"I'll take your backpack." CJ put his hand out. "Did you need to go to the bathroom or get a drink before you start?"

"No, thank you." I crossed to the desk, took a seat at the computer, and started the exam.

The questions were simple, and I made my way through the five-hundred-question test. When the submit button came up, I rubbed my tired eyes and pressed it. I leaned back in the chair and waited while the program calculated my grade.

My stomach growled, and I licked my lips.

CJ walked into the room and put a sandwich down on the edge of the desk, along with a glass of milk. His phone beeped, and he glanced at it.

The screen dissolved into a grade. I stared at the ninety-eight percent blinking on the monitor and sighed. It wasn't a perfect grade, like I'd expected.

"What did I get wrong?" I turned to CJ.

He scrolled through his phone. "A couple grammar questions, one of the macro-economics questions, a history question, a sociology question, two calculus questions, a science question, and a couple psychology questions. Until the last hour, your answers were all correct. Every question you got wrong was within the last hour, so I think hunger and mental exhaustion played a role. Overall, you did excellent. I'll bring your results to the school board and let them know I am recommending your certification of graduation with high honors."

I picked up the sandwich and leaned back in the chair. "Thank you." I took a bite. I just wanted to feed my growling stomach and take a nap.

"When you're done, why don't you head out back? Alex and the girls are playing soccer, and the fresh air should help. I shouldn't be long." He leaned over and pressed the print button on the screen. A printer whirred to life at the back of the room.

Instead of waiting, I picked up the plate and the milk and headed upstairs. I stood at the counter and watched Alex with his sisters in the yard. When I finished the sandwich and drained the milk, I put the dishes in the dishwasher and headed outside.

The day was warm, and it got warmer when Alex glanced up at me and smiled.

"Where's my dad?" He handed one of the twins the ball and came over to me.

"He went to drop off my test at the school board and request my diploma."

"That's impressive."

I shrugged.

He took my hands and inspected the gloves. "I like."

My cheeks flushed, and I pulled my hands away.

"Can we go watch our show?" one of the girls asked.

"Sure," Alex said.

After both girls disappeared into the house, I turned to Alex. "I'm never going to figure out which is which."

"That was Amber. If you look at her eyes closely, you can see a ring of green around the blue. Arianna doesn't have that green ring, but *she* has gold flecks in the blue of her irises. That's the only way I can tell them apart." He stepped closer, and an impish light filled his eyes. "My parents are gone." He wrapped his arm around my waist.

The moment our bodies connected, overwhelming desire squeezed every cell. I looked into his deep blue eyes framed by long dark lashes, noticing the silver flecks mingling with aqua flecks in his irises.

Tom's warning whispered in my ear, so I pushed out of Alex's grasp, unnerved by the lack of logical thought when I was that close to him.

"Am I the first girl you ever kissed?"

"Does it matter?" He closed the distance.

Did it? A very large part of me didn't think so, but that nagging voice that sounded an awful lot like Tom wouldn't let it go. I glanced at the ground.

"Am I the first boy you've ever kissed?" he asked, trying to catch my eye.

I met his gaze and nodded.

He cupped my cheek. "You are not my first, but I have the distinct belief you will be the last girl I ever kiss. And kiss. And kiss." He leaned in and demonstrated. His soft lips caressed mine with a heat that burned brighter than the fire inside me.

A sting on my neck yanked me away from him. My gaze fell to a small plume of feathers that stuck in Alex's neck. He blinked and stumbled. I tried to catch him, but the world went dark.

Fire Cursed
Chapter 13

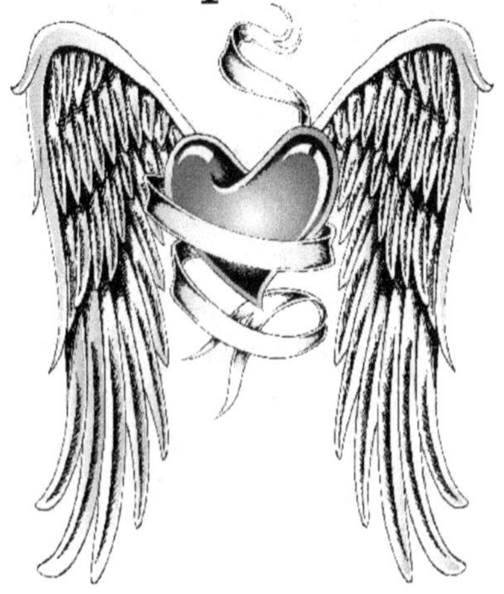

MY HEAD POUNDED, AND I blinked my eyes open. The unfamiliar room sent shockwaves through me. The last thing I remembered was kissing Alex and then seeing that fuzzy feather stuck in his neck.

I shifted on the hard chair and blinked at my bound arms. The sleeves of my shirt were rolled up to my elbows. My gaze landed on the skin of my hands, and my heart leaped into my throat. My gloves were gone.

"Alex?" Hot pulses of panic ran through me.

"Faith?"

His voice was as perplexed as mine.

I twisted my hands and pulled, trying to move my arms so the edge of my palms touched the rope. The progression was slow and painful, to the point sweat rolled into my eyes. I blinked the sting away, concentrating as my internal alarms got louder with every second that ticked by.

"Where are we?" I asked.

"I'm not sure. The last thing I remember was being in my backyard."

The door opened. Grace waltzed in, wearing my gloves like they were prized diamonds. The beings following behind her made my heart plummet. Three soul eaters followed her into the room.

"I promised you a feast." She waved toward us. "Make her death as painful as possible. I expect he will not be touched this time."

"What the fuck, Grace?" Alex said from behind me.

"You can't have a soul mate without a soul." She smiled and closed the door behind her, leaving us with these things.

My right hand was just about where I needed it. My heart pounded in my chest as I focused on the rope. If I didn't break my bonds now, we would be in trouble. I let the fire flare. The sight of flames leaping from my hand halted the soul eaters' steps.

I yanked at the burning rope, and my hand freed. Before I turned the flame to the soul eaters, I fried the rope on my other hand. I was on my feet and standing between them and Alex before they could come to their senses.

"Back off," I growled. "Or you won't see tomorrow."

Yellow flame licked my splayed fingers. I held tight to the weapon inside me, afraid that if I let go, I wouldn't be able to stop the fire from consuming everything in the room, including Alex.

I reached with my other hand, finding the rope binding Alex, and let my flames devour the string.

He winced. "I need help with the other one," he said.

I stepped in front of him, never taking my eyes off the creatures, letting Alex guide my hand to the rope.

Alex stood and took my hand in his. The flames sputtered.

The soul eaters charged.

I ripped my hand from Alex's grip and pointed both palms at the charging monsters. I screamed, and fire sprayed with a jolt. It consumed everything in its path. The monsters, the walls, the ceiling. The door. Half the room was engulfed. I closed my palms, shaking, and turned to Alex and stared at the solid wall behind us.

Panic as hot as the flames behind me lit through my veins. I had blocked our only exit.

"Are we underground?" I asked, praying we weren't. I didn't know if I could keep Alex from being burned if we were.

"No. I think we are in Naomi's panic room."

"Get down." I closed my eyes. I clenched my fists and let the panic feed my power. When every inch of my skin burned, I opened my eyes and pointed my palms toward the back wall.

The explosion blew outward, turning the wall to dust. The cool ocean air rushed in.

I grabbed Alex's arm, yanking him towards the opening. "Run!"

We hit the cool air outside just as the room behind us flashed over.

I kept running with one focus—the ocean. I needed water, or otherwise, the fire burning inside me would engulf everything around us. Alex kept pace with me and didn't hesitate when I jumped off the cliff. He jumped with me, our hands clasped tight.

The frigid Atlantic swallowed us, chilling the fire out of me. By the time we surfaced, sirens pierced the air. Alex pulled me towards our right and around an outcrop of rock. Beyond sat a small dock, and we climbed onto it, out of breath and shivering.

He clasped my hand and dragged me towards a rock ledge. When we skirted around a boulder, a small space between the rocks opened. We slid inside out of sight. He leaned against the wall and let go of my hand to wipe his face. His gaze locked with mine in the semidarkness.

"She tried to..." He closed his mouth. Anger flared in his eyes, and then his gaze fell to my hands. He took them in his and brought them to his lips. The next moment, he pulled me to him, wrapping his arms around my numb body.

We shivered against the wall as the sirens outside got louder and louder. My adrenaline faded, and my knees wobbled. Alex held me steady.

"You saved me," he whispered in my ear.

I let out a high-pitched laugh. "But I nearly burned you alive."

He pulled away and cupped my cheeks, searching my eyes, and then smashed his lips against mine. The kiss was as desperate as I felt.

"Come on," he said, breaking the kiss. He took my hand, leading me farther into the dark cavern.

We stopped when all the light faded. Four tones rang softly, and then a door swung open in front of us.

Alex led me into a dark room. A moment later, the lights came on, and Alex punched numbers on a keypad next to the door.

"Our panic room has multiple ways out."

I raised my eyebrows. The room looked like just another play room with soft chairs, a table and a small kitchenette, instead of the one we had been in that was barren except for the chairs we'd been tied to.

I still couldn't grasp the need for a panic room at all.

Alex crossed to another keypad and punched the sequence again. The wall moved, opening to the basement of his house. He put his hand out, and I crossed to him and clasped mine in his. Dripping, we crossed the threshold into his basement. The door slid closed behind us.

We were halfway across when the basement door flew open. Feet pounded down the stairs, and we both froze in place.

"Alex!" CJ's voice rang out just before he flew around the corner.

Behind him, Grace appeared, and her panicked features hardened. "She set my house on fire."

My gaze dropped to the ground as shame heated my cheeks.

"You sicced three soul eaters at us." Alex glared at her.

"Bullshit!" Grace said. "She's got you brainwashed."

My head jerked up, and I squeezed Alex's hand as the source deep inside me let loose. The room altered around us, except this time Grace and CJ were in the room with us, staring at Alex and me tied to chairs in the barren panic room.

The vision ended with me blasting the monsters back to Hell.

"You were saying," I said softly.

CJ spun and glared at Grace. "You put *MY* son in danger," he growled. "My son!" His bellow shook the foundation beneath us.

Grace's eyes widened, and she turned and bolted up the stairs. I would have run, too, but not because of the sight of the golden wings forming in the air behind CJ. The fury filling his face was enough for me to shake all over again.

He turned to us, focusing solely on his son. "You didn't call?" The venom in his voice was enough to make me shrink behind Alex.

"Honestly, I didn't think to call. I was still trying to come to terms with what Grace was doing." He combed his hair with his hand. "Besides, Faith took care of it."

"By almost killing you?" His gaze moved from Alex to me.

"I couldn't control it," I whispered.

"Well then, we're going to have to work on that before you fuck up and get someone killed."

"Yes, sir." I dropped my gaze to the floor.

He marched upstairs, and we followed like wet puppies.

"Your diploma is on the table." CJ pointed to the paper at the opposite end of the table that

Amber and Arianna sat eating a snack. "And Tom is on the way to pick you up." His forehead broke out in sweat, and the vein at his temple throbbed.

"What are you doing?" Alex asked.

"Making sure the fire doesn't spread beyond their property."

The front door opened, and footsteps fast approached the family room.

"What the fuck happened?" Tom asked as he stepped into the room.

CJ sent a glare at him, and I could almost make out the admonishment.

"Sorry," Tom mumbled, and an awkward smile appeared.

"Grace tried to kill Faith and leave me soulless." Alex summed it up with a matter-of-fact tone, as if we hadn't just had a near-Death experience.

Tom blinked and then the confusion marring his features turned to raw anger that sizzled on the air. "She struck a deal with the soul eaters?" His gaze jumped to his brother.

"Yup," CJ said. "But the newest addition to our fun little family blasted them and nearly everyone else in their house to hell."

My skin grew cold. "Who else was in the house?" My voice shook.

The look CJ gave me settled my nerves a little. His gaze didn't hold accusation or regret, so I knew I hadn't killed.

"Gabe had just stepped in the front door when you blew out the back of their house. He's okay."

"Naomi?" Tom asked.

"Working at the school," CJ answered.

Tom took a deep breath. "And Grace?"

CJ's jaw tightened and that anger I had seen downstairs shuffled to the surface. "She's fine," he said through clenched teeth. "But if she pulls anything like that again..." His eyes were like ice.

I shivered and rubbed my arms. My teeth chattered as the chill reached down to my bone marrow. Alex put his arm around me and pulled me closer.

Tom's gaze traveled over the two of us. A crease appeared between his eyes. He stared at Alex, blinking rapidly, like his mind couldn't wrap around something. "Um, Alex? Are you feeling okay?"

"Fine. Why?"

CJ's full attention was now on his son. "Because your aura is almost gone," he growled and stormed out of the room.

"What does that mean?" Alex asked, turning to Tom.

I studied him as well. He seemed like the same boy who made my heart flutter. His touch still calmed me and set me on fire at the same time, but there was no anxiety in his question like what was burning through me.

Tom turned and walked outside where CJ had headed. We followed.

The house next door imploded like a giant foot had slammed down on the structure, smothering the fire. The air rippled with heat and smoke and underlying aggression coming from CJ.

Grace stood beyond the iron gate, her glare pronounced even at that distance. Danger prickled my skin as we approached. A car skidded to a stop outside the neighboring house, and Grace's mother jumped out. Her gaze was locked on the demolished house.

"You need to leave this town and never come back," CJ said to Grace over the sounds of the fire engines and rescue personnel.

"She started the fire." Grace pointed at me.

"You stole my son's soul." CJ's growl was feral.

Alex wasn't fazed in the least by CJ's accusation, but I stopped moving, dumbstruck. How could she let one of those things touch him if she professed to love him? It made no sense to me at all.

"Not all of it," Grace said, confirming my worst fears. "But enough of it that this crazy soulmate thing would be taken care of." She put her gloved hands on her hips. "And if that witch hadn't started the fire..."

The first hint of anger reached Alex's face, and he let go of my hand and closed the distance to stand next to his father. "No matter what you do, there will never be an *us*. You had every intention of letting those things kill Faith. You had every intention of taking an innocent life. That makes you a monster. Tell me, Grace, what do your angels say about your actions? What does Heaven think of you now?"

Grace's face turned bright red. "The angels haven't spoken to me in years. The last time they spoke, it was for me to tell Tom all was forgiven," she said. "Heaven has forsaken me, and so have you." A tear escaped from the corner of her eye.

"I will never forgive you. Soul or no soul, I know what you did today was wrong. And so help me God, if you *EVER* attempt to harm Faith again, I will kill you with my bare hands."

The venom coming from Alex was even scarier than the anger radiating from CJ. His growling voice sounded more like his father's than his own. And I swallowed hard, believing his threat.

Grace stumbled back, right into her mother, whose attention was now on us.

"What happened to my house?" she asked.

Grace turned to her mother and opened her mouth.

"Zip it," CJ said. The surrounding air rippled with the force to silence her.

Naomi's eyes narrowed at CJ. "Let her speak," she ordered.

"Your daughter is evil," Alex said. "She knocked us out and tied us up in the panic room. When we came to, she let soul eaters into the room and told them to kill Faith."

Naomi's mouth popped open. Her gaze darted to her daughter.

"She is no longer welcomed anywhere near this property," CJ said.

Naomi's shock transitioned to disgust. "And the fire?"

"That was me, ma'am." I studied the ground in front of me. "I didn't mean to burn the house down. I just wanted to save Alex from getting hurt."

"She disintegrated the soul eaters. But I guess the damage had already been done before we woke up." Alex glared at Grace. "She left just enough of my soul intact for me to grasp her duplicity. And had she not stolen Faith's gloves, Faith would have died in there, and then *I* would have killed Grace myself." He moved his glare to Naomi. "So just be glad that your daughter is alive. And take her as far away from me as possible, so she stays that way."

"We forgave him," Grace started, pointing at Tom.

"That is not the same," Naomi spat, silencing Grace with a voice as cold as ice. "And it certainly is not an excuse for your behavior lately." She turned to CJ. "Let Valerie know that I'll text her when I get settled."

CJ nodded.

"Get in the car." Naomi pointed at the car, and Grace climbed into the back seat. Naomi crossed to where the fire trucks were and stepped behind the barricade. A few minutes later, she came out with Gabriel by her side, and they climbed into the car and took off without another word.

I turned to Alex. His fearless gaze met mine. The deep compassion I had seen in his eyes every time I looked at him the last couple of days was gone, but the spark of interest remained.

Could someone without a soul still feel love?

"Don't look so devastated." He stepped closer and palmed my cheek. "I'm still me."

I closed my eyes and leaned into his touch, balling my fists so my nerves wouldn't get the best of me. His hand was warm, but it didn't stop the shakes gripping me. My clothes still dripped, and the cool air filtering through the wet fabric of my shirt didn't help.

"Come on, let's get inside so you two can get into something dry." CJ headed towards the open front door where Amber and Arianna stood with wide-eyed gazes.

Alex left me in the kitchen with Tom and CJ, and as soon as his door closed upstairs, Tom and CJ both sagged against the kitchen counter.

"What am I going to tell Valerie?" CJ asked softly.

"He didn't seem all that different," Tom said, but I could tell there was some underlying angst. He glanced at me. "Right?"

"I don't know," I said.

Tom glanced at the stairs. "He still looks at you the way our father looked at our mother, so that is still there."

CJ's eyebrows shot up. "What?"

Tom rolled his eyes. "Come on, you can't see it?"

Alex came down the stairs with his wet clothes in one hand and a pair of sweatpants and a sweatshirt in the other. His gaze landed on me, and he crossed the distance as if we were the only people in the house.

"I thought you might like something dry, too. The bathroom's back there." He nodded towards the hallway and handed me the dry clothes.

I caught CJ's open-mouthed expression before I turned and headed to change. I stripped out of the wet clothes and piled them neatly on the toilet lid. I debated on keeping my underwear and bra on, but they were uncomfortably wet. So, I peeled them off and added them to the pile.

Alex's sweats were big around the waist, but with the drawstring pulled tight, they settled on my hips enough to be comfortable. The large sweatshirt fell in a baggy bunch to mid-thigh. I rolled up the sleeves and opened the door.

Alex stood straight and put his hands out. "Your clothes."

I handed him the pile. He stared at my undergarments and then raised his gaze to mine. His lips formed a smile that I'd never seen on him, and my cheeks heated in response.

"I'm going to go put these in the laundry," he said in a husky voice that sent chills through me. "And then maybe we will sneak down to the panic room."

"I don't think so." Tom stepped around the corner and raised an eyebrow at his nephew.

Irritation flashed in Alex's eyes, and he turned and headed towards the laundry room.

Tom led me into the kitchen and picked up the diploma. "Congratulations."

I crossed my arms. "I told you."

"Yes, but he's the one that makes the recommendations to the school." He pointed at CJ. "If I tried, they would laugh me out the door."

"Where are the girls?"

"Doing more work downstairs," CJ said. His gaze was glued on the ocean outside.

"I'm fine, Dad. Don't stress about it," Alex said.

CJ turned. "Maybe you two should head out."

"But her clothes..." Alex said.

"We can bring them by later, after your mother gets home."

"I'll go get my stuff." I headed downstairs. My bag sat outside the computer room and I shouldered it. "See you two tomorrow," I said to the girls who were busy at the computers.

"Bye," they said in unison.

I wished I were their age again and blissfully clueless. I turned and bumped right into Alex.

He licked his lips and pulled me to the corner near the entrance of the panic room. His mouth found mine. The kiss started slow, but escalated quickly. I put my hand on his chest, and the strong beat of his heart echoed in my palm. It matched mine in strength and speed.

He pulled away from my lips, and that decadent smile appeared. Raw hunger reflected in his eyes, and when he leaned in for another kiss, I locked my elbow, holding him off.

"I have to go."

He stepped back and raked his hair with his hand. "I'll see you later." He waved me toward the stairs.

I stopped halfway across the basement and turned back towards him. "Eighteen."

He blinked and tilted his head to the side.

"Save that look and everything that goes with it until we are eighteen." I grinned.

He laughed and cocked an eyebrow. The silent challenge in his gaze flushed my entire form. I nearly ran up the stairs, and by the time I sat down in Tom's car, I was convinced that only the primal part of Alex's soul was left.

Fire Cursed
Chapter 14

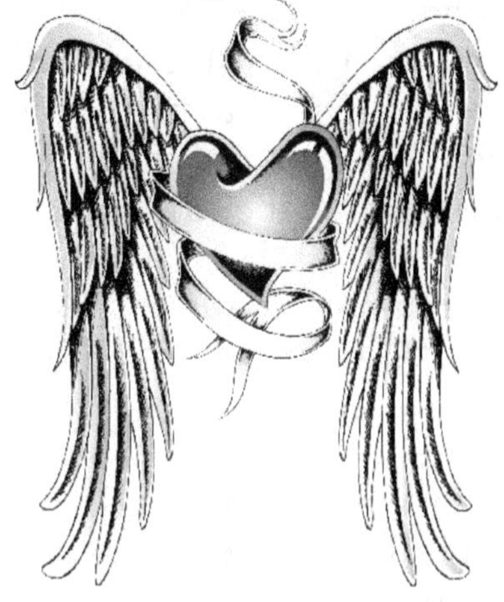

"ARE YOU ALL RIGHT?" Tom said after we pulled out of the driveway and away from the commotion.

"I don't know." I stared out the window at the water.

"Your mother's ashes arrived just before I left to come get you."

I nodded. A knot developed in my throat, and my chest constricted. I fisted my hands against the wave of emotions threatening to break down my defenses and wrapped my arms around my midsection.

The reality of everything that had happened today hit like a demolition ball. In all my life, the only danger I had been aware of was from my fire curse. That and possibly freezing to death when we ran out of firewood in the winter. Now, someone wanted me dead. It wasn't figuratively speaking, either.

Tom's hand landed on my shoulder, and he squeezed gently.

Fury welled to the surface, incinerating all other emotions and leaving only wild and unchecked wrath. "You brought me into this," I roared in the small space and tried to shake his hand away.

He kept his hand in place. "Yes. I did." His voice was soft. "And I would do it again, despite the fallout."

I was tempted to knock it away, but I was terrified to move my hands. All I needed right now was to set the upholstery on fire. "Damn you," I whispered.

Tears prickled the corners of my eyes. I blinked them back as despair threatened to engulf me. The same sense of being overwhelmed that I'd had yesterday crushed down on me, and my lungs constricted until I could only get a wheeze of air through.

"Breathe." He pulled into the empty driveway and put the truck in park. "I've said it before. This is all normal to me, but it took some getting used to for Bri. She understands stepping into this blind, so if you need to talk..." He pulled his hand away from my shoulder.

The absence of contact caused my breath to hitch. "I killed those things," I finally squeaked out, saying the thing that had haunted me the most about today. The ease with which I had taken life, even the life of a monster, startled me.

He turned off the truck. "Yes. You did."

"I almost killed Alex in the process." I met his gaze.

"But you didn't. You got him out of there without harm. Although, I wish you had been awake when they were siphoning Alex's soul."

I closed my eyes and leaned my head against the headrest, willing the tears not to come, but it was a futile command. "Alex lost a lot of himself today," I whispered. "That wouldn't have happened if you hadn't taken me in."

Tom drummed his fingers on the steering wheel. He didn't agree or argue with my statement. Instead, he opened his door and stepped out of the cab.

"Go get changed, and then we can go do what you promised with your mother's ashes." His door closed, signaling the end of the conversation.

My fingers ached from holding them so tightly balled, so I slowly opened my hands and wiped the tears from my cheeks. I didn't know if I would ever consider any of this normal. I inhaled slowly and then exhaled before I opened the door and climbed out of his truck.

Inside the house, Tom crossed from the desk in his office and handed me the last pair of gloves.

"Don't lose those, and don't let Bri wash them." He walked into the family room.

I made my way upstairs and stared at the choices of clothing. My gaze kept being pulled to the black leather. It was the only black outfit I had, and while one of the dresses probably would be better suited, I decided I needed to be badass instead.

I dressed quickly and undid my hair, then ran a brush through the damp locks. The last thing I did was pull on the gloves. The boots had a higher heel than I was used to, so I walked carefully down the stairs and into the entry.

Tom stepped into the entry and his eyebrows rose, but he didn't say a thing. He handed me the box that held the simple urn inside and headed back outside.

Bridget wasn't in the office. April wasn't home, either, and a quick glance at the clock confirmed she should have been. I went out to the truck and Bridget's car wasn't there. I hadn't noticed the absence of the car when we'd arrived.

I needed to be much more vigilant.

I climbed into the passenger seat.

"Where to?"

"I have no idea."

Tom nodded and drove down a few winding roads, over a bridge, and then parked in the marina parking lot and turned off the truck. He opened the console between us and pulled out a pair of keys.

"Where are we going?"

He nodded towards the boats. "*Raven's Gift* is mine." He pointed at one of the bigger boats on the dock. "I'm going to take you to the perfect place to honor your mother."

I followed him to the boat and waited while he unsnapped the cover. Once the boat was ready, I handed him the box and helped him untie the ropes from the moorings. With the last of the ropes untied, we stepped aboard, and I settled into the passenger seat.

Tom started the boat and pulled out of the slip. I watched the shoreline, fascinated at the different view as we cruised out of the marina and into the open ocean.

He headed towards the far bluff with a lighthouse. When we passed another outcrop, he pointed. "That's CJ's house."

The home looked different from the water, but I recognized Alex. He stared out at the sea from behind the rock wall. Even at this distance, I could see his stiff stance. I glanced at Tom.

"He's processing everything right now. Much like you did on the ride home."

"Is he upset?"

Tom sighed and focused on where we were headed. "I'm not picking up emotion, just thoughts." A troubled expression crossed over his face, but he didn't expand on what he'd said.

My gaze dropped to the box in my hands and my current task. I would worry about Alex later. Right now was time for goodbyes.

Tom slowed the boat as he approached the lighthouse on the bluff. "I would have brought you there, but they don't really like ashes thrown from the park, although people still do. This is Nubble Lighthouse, and I'm sure being from Maine, you've seen pictures of it before."

"It's beautiful."

"It is." He turned off the throttle and put the boat in neutral about fifty yards from the outcrop of rock that held the notable lighthouse. He dropped anchor and turned the engine off. "The wind is blowing offshore, so just be mindful of where you toss the ashes. I'm sure you don't want a face full of your mother."

A smile surfaced at the image his words painted in my head. Guilt followed. I shouldn't be smiling at such a solemn time.

"Why not?" Tom asked, surveying the seascape. "I'm sure your mom had a sense of humor. She wouldn't be upset with you for smiling."

"Please stop listening to my thoughts." I sent a sideways glare at him.

He sat down in the pilot seat and waved for me to get on with it.

I stood, pulled the urn out of the box, and gasped. This wasn't what I had picked out. It was one of the top-of-the-line urns. "I think there's been a mistake."

"No. No mistake," Tom said.

I turned the sapphire urn and stared at the gold etching inscribing my mother's name, birth date, and death date on the side. I pressed my hand over my mouth. Tears burned my eyes, and I sat down on the back bench, overwhelmed yet again.

"You did this?" I asked.

"Yes. I thought you'd appreciate something that was as beautiful as your mother and not some cheap knockoff."

I traced the letters and pressed my lips together against the sudden quiver. "But it was so expensive."

"But it was the one you wished you could afford."

I wiped the tear from the corner of my eye. He was right. This was the only one I really wanted, but with the hospital bill and my mother's savings depleted, I had to choose the most economical choice instead. Besides, I was just going to dump the ashes, anyway.

"Thank you."

"You're welcome." He turned back to the controls, busying himself with the boat and giving me the space I needed.

The boat had swung around so the back now faced the open sea, away from the lighthouse. I stood at the stern and held the urn against my chest.

"I promise I'll live up to your expectations," I whispered. "I'll make you proud. I miss you." I unscrewed the top and slowly poured the ashes out into the ocean. "Go explore the world, Mom." I sniffled. "I love you."

I screwed the top back on and just held it tight while the ashes disappeared beneath the water. When it all was gone, I turned back towards Tom and gave him a silent nod before I took the seat next to him.

He handed me some tissues, retracted the anchor, and started the boat.

"Can we stay out here a little longer?" I didn't want to go back and be reminded of my failures. I just wanted this sense of peace to last a little longer.

"Sure. I can go up the shore for a bit."

"That would be nice."

Tom trolled slowly along, narrating what we passed, but I wasn't listening. I was just enjoying the calm seas and the stunning coastline, letting my mind rest.

I glanced at his profile. "What is it like to absorb angel grace?"

He slowed the boat down and chewed on his lip. "It's hard to describe," he said. "My only conscious experience was eating Damian's heart, which was beyond gross, but I knew if I didn't..." He looked away and wiped his mouth. "If I didn't, Lucifer would."

He stared out at the ocean long enough for me to believe he would not finish.

"I don't know what I expected. I had seen Damian do the same thing years before, and it bathed him in light, kind of like you saw in the vision of me giving CJ the grace." He sighed and glanced at me. "It wasn't difficult to do that, either, because Michael and Gabriel's grace didn't bond with my cells. It seems Lucifer's did. And I'd venture to guess Raphael's as well because I do have both lines in me. But that doesn't explain the fact CJ can gift grace at will." He let out a sarcastic laugh. "Maybe I am some kind of freak. I don't know, but when Lucifer's grace bonded with me, it felt like I was being shredded from the inside out. Raphael's was different. It exploded from the very core of me, and I woke with his insignia on my chest. None of the others were ever marked in the same way." His hand went to his chest and rubbed his shirt over the spot where I had seen the mark. "The fact I can't pull either grace out..." He pressed his lips together and shook his head. "I don't know if it will be the same for you. CJ said he felt like the light of Heaven had filled him. I never asked Damian or Valerie what they felt."

He let the silence fill the space between us as he slowly passed by CJ's home.

"So only four people ever experienced angel grace?"

"All the descendants of archangels have angel grace within us. That's why your father was feeding on the blood of descendants. It gave him a boost that he didn't have without his grace."

I waited for him to answer the question.

He glanced at me. "Yes, only four of us have ever consumed an archangel's grace."

I nodded. It made sense, although only two had truly consumed grace.

Tom rolled his eyes at my thought, but he didn't point out the semantics, thankfully. We pulled into the slip and secured the moorings, and I waited on the dock while he snapped the cover in place.

"Why *Raven's Gift*?" I asked, pointing at the name.

"Raven was my first wife." He shoved his hands in his pockets. "She was very special. I inherited her gift of reading auras when her tongue was transplanted into my mouth. I wanted to honor her, and this boat was the best I could think of."

I swallowed hard. It was an incredibly sweet gesture, just like the urn in my hands. "April is very lucky to have you as a father," I said, and then his actual words hit. "Tongue transplant?"

Tom laughed. "I thought that one just breezed right over your head. Yes. My wife worked it out with Valerie. If anything should happen to her first, then I was to get her tongue. The same psycho who killed my mother took mine when I was eight."

"The one who put her head on the table you were tied to?" My throat tightened around the words and I trembled in place.

"Yes." Tom stopped before we climbed the ramp. "You need to promise me something," he said, his gaze as sharp and intense as I'd seen so far.

"What?" Dread filled every pore.

"When you get his grace, you won't allow it to taint you."

I shook my head. "I've already told you, I am not eating your heart. Ever. Unequivocally, no."

He chuckled. "Humor me."

"Fine, if I ever get my father's grace, I promise I will not let it taint me, even though that will never happen." Ever. Nothing could ever make me rip a heart out of anyone's chest. No way. Not ever.

Somehow, I thought I heard the Fates laughing at me.

Fire Cursed
Chapter 15

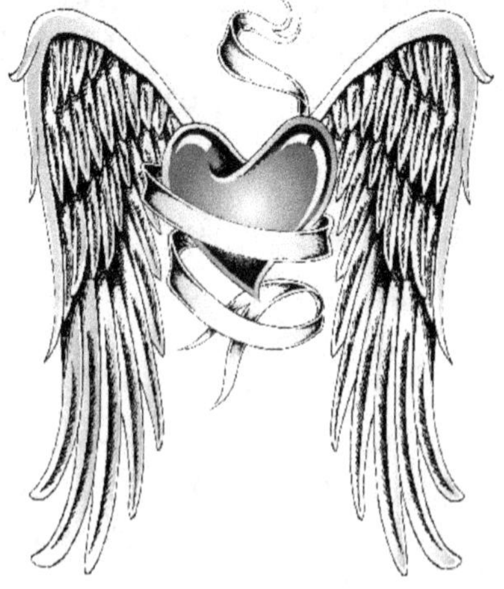

I WALKED IN THE front door holding the urn, and Bridget choked on a sip of coffee. Her eyes nearly bulged out of her head.

"I thought I said no to that one," she said through her coughing while waving her finger at me.

"I put it in the cart," April said. "She looks awesome in it."

"You didn't go over to CJ's in that, did you?"

"No. It was the only black outfit I own." I held the urn so she could see it, and her gaze softened.

"I'm sorry I wasn't here for that. April had a field trip this afternoon," she said. "If Tom had waited until we got back, I could have lent you a dress." She pressed her lips together and glared at Tom. "How was your day otherwise?" she asked me.

I didn't know how to articulate the day we'd had. Thankfully, Tom crossed to her.

"We need to talk." He shuffled Bridget into the office, leaving April and me staring after them.

I turned toward April, and her normally bright sunshine of a smile was absent. The seriousness of her expression made me shift my stance. I didn't know what to do, so I set my mother's urn down on the table near the door.

April stared at the office doors and cocked her head. Then her gaze turned to mine and her eyes widened. "You went outside, and you weren't watching your back."

I had no idea how she knew, but I couldn't deny it. Especially after her warning. A warning that hadn't even entered my mind after taking that grueling test. "Yes. And your cousin paid the price."

Her eyes darkened in a way I never would have fathomed. The office door burst open a moment later, and both Tom and Bridget stared at their daughter. April's eyes turned nearly black.

"Remember when I told you York would burn?" she asked, staring at her father.

He nodded slowly, all the color in his face drained.

"The entire world will burn if he isn't stopped." April's eyes rolled in her head, and she fell in a dead faint.

Her progression to the floor stopped before she connected with the hard wood, and her body lifted, drifting to the couch. Tom and Bridget were by her side in a flash, and I just stood still in the foyer next to my mother's urn.

I wasn't sure how long I stood in limbo, but my nerves pulsed and my chest tightened the way it always did before a panic attack started. I wasn't sure what was happening to me. Black edged my vision, and I tried to blink it away. When the edges turned red like someone had poured fresh blood over me, I shivered.

The door opened behind me, and I turned, welcoming the break of whatever had gripped me. Alex's bright blue eyes met mine. His gaze slowly dropped down the length of me, and the salacious grin that formed made me even more nervous than I already was.

CJ followed him inside and slapped the back of Alex's head. "Clean up your thoughts, boy."

I escaped Alex's scrutiny, sliding into the family room where April was just coming to.

"Something has happened," CJ said as he stepped into the doorway.

Tom looked up at his brother. "I felt it, too." He glanced beyond CJ. "Where's Valerie and the girls?"

"She needed to change and call Austin and Paige before she came. They all should be here momentarily."

"Felt what?" I asked when my brain caught up to the conversation.

"The darkness," April whispered. She blinked her eyes and sat up.

Alex crossed the room and stepped behind me. He wrapped his arms around my waist and kissed my neck. "You didn't feel it?"

His breath tickled my neck, and despite how being wrapped in his arms felt like coming home, I didn't appreciate the display in front of his father and Tom and Bridget.

"What are you doing?" I whispered and looked at him sideways.

"Saying Hello." He acted as if invading my personal space was the most natural thing in the world.

CJ cleared his throat. "Boundaries?"

"Pft." Alex didn't let go. "She doesn't mind."

I glanced back at him.

"You don't, right?" His forehead creased.

"It makes me a little uncomfortable, especially in front of your parents."

"Oh." He let go and stepped to my side, threading his fingers through mine. "Better?"

I squeezed his hand and nodded. I would have to remember that he had no real sense of improper behavior anymore, or if he did, he didn't heed whatever mental warning came with having a soul.

The squeak of the front door silenced the room. When a dark-haired woman and a taller, sandy-haired man walked into the living room, the woman's gaze jumped to mine. Her tense features relaxed into a smile.

"You're Faith, right?" She crossed to me and put out her hand. "I'm Paige."

I released Alex's hand and shook hers.

She didn't release mine right away, instead she inspected the glove. "I hope these helped. I wasn't sure if the dampening spell would be enough."

"They work fine," I said.

"Well, if you need more, let me know."

"She will need more." Tom stood. "Bri washed a pair and Grace stole the other one, so that's it."

The front door opened and closed once more, this time followed by the fast patter of feet. I knew even before the twins slid into the room who they were. With all the people in the room, it felt more crowded than the mortuary had.

The squeak of the door sounded once more, and Tom spun towards the hall. His features became guarded, and I tensed in response. I didn't know what to expect, but a petite blonde stepped into view with a baby strapped to her chest. The room hushed. I understood a moment later when the spitting image of Gabriel walked in behind her.

It was so quiet you could hear the ice machine dropping cubes in the kitchen.

"Well, I haven't had this kind of reception in years," the woman said.

Tom pressed his lips together and shot a glare at CJ. "Kylee, Michael, Page, Austin, this is Faith." He waved at me. "Everyone else has already met her."

They nodded in my direction.

"Have you been home?" Tom asked Michael.

"No, why?" Michael said.

Tom ran his hand down his face and glanced at me, but before he could tell Michael there was no home to go to anymore, CJ spoke up.

"I figured I would get everyone together and go through this once," he said. "Please sit." He waved toward the couches.

I remained in place and leaned against the pool table. Alex stayed by my side and clasped my hand in his as everyone else settled on the couches.

"Are we going to wait for the rest of my family?" Michael asked.

"No, we aren't," CJ said.

Michael jumped to his feet, and his eyes shifted between CJ and the door like he was going to bolt at any moment.

CJ put his hands out. "They are okay. Just sit." He waited until Michael lowered back onto the couch. "There was a... situation."

"Does it have to do with the devil's daughter?" Michael snapped and waved at me.

CJ glanced at Valerie and then at Alex. "She was involved. Yes. But only because Grace went off the reservation. She hasn't been right for a while, and bringing Faith here just seemed to push her off balance in the worst of ways. Because of Grace's actions, your mother's house burned to the ground."

He blinked and then turned a glare in my direction. I shifted under his dark stare.

"Grace was a total fucking cunt," Alex said, and everyone's gaze jumped to him. "She's gone dark."

I jerked away from him, shocked by his vulgar language. I wasn't the only one. Everyone in the room sported the same open-mouthed look of surprise.

CJ's face reddened. "Language," he snarled with his jaw tight.

Valerie blinked a few times, and then she looked at her husband. "What's wrong with Alex?" she said with a voice that shook.

"Grace made a deal with a soul eater," CJ said.

"Why?" Valerie asked.

"Because she said you can't have a soulmate when you don't have a soul," Alex said with such venom, I shrank away from him. "She was dead wrong." He raised our clasped hands.

"He doesn't..." Valerie began, and then she covered her mouth.

"Grace let those things take most of my soul today. And then she tried to kill Faith, but Faith defended both of us, and got us the Hell out of Naomi's panic room before we died." Alex's grip on my hand tightened with each word.

Michael crossed his arms. "Is she controlling you?" He nodded towards me.

"No. She isn't." Alex squeezed again, but loosened his grip when I winced. I could feel the buildup of anger through the connection between us. "Your sister made it so I can only feel two distinct emotions. The rest are gone. One minute I was me, and the next..." He snapped his fingers. "Can you guess what she left me with?"

"Anger," Tom said.

"And desire," CJ added.

"And I only feel when I'm around Faith. When I'm away from her, I'm in an empty wasteland. So, when you see your sister, tell her I said thanks. Thanks for stealing my compassion. My humanity. And if I ever see her again, I will kill her."

I tried to pull my hand away, but he clamped down harder.

"You can also tell her, whatever she did had zero effect on what my heart wants. So, she failed." Alex glanced at me and slowly loosened his grip.

His blue irises sparked with both emotions, and they traveled into his fingertips, transferring into me like some mystical connection between us. I needed him to dampen my fire abilities, and he needed me to feel human emotions.

God help us both.

"And Fate can't retrieve his soul?" Kylee asked. As if on cue, the image of Fate appeared from a swirl of smoke near Kylee.

"It's not that simple," Fate said.

"Doesn't the soul eater pass through Purgatory?" Kylee pushed.

"They were already escorted to their destination." Fate glanced at the ground before sending her sharp stare at CJ and Tom. "If you had told me right away, I possibly could have intervened, but now…"

"But there is a way?" Valerie interjected, her eyes begging for the answer she wanted.

"No. Not without releasing every monster imaginable from Hell, and I can't do that."

"There has to be a way." Valerie bit her lip and glanced at Alex.

"I'm afraid what was taken is gone." Fate gave Valerie's hand a squeeze.

"I'm still me," Alex said, irritation flushing his voice and his cheeks. "Albeit with zero filter, but it's still me in here, so stop looking at me like I'm already dead."

Valerie recoiled, blinked like salt had gotten into her eyes. "I'm... I'm sorry."

"Give her a break. She just found out her son's soul was severely depleted," I muttered in Alex's ear.

He nodded and gave me a sideways look that nearly scalded my insides.

"Do you have Heaven's blade?" Fate asked Kylee.

Kylee's head jerked back. "That exists?"

"Yes, and she is going to need it," Fate said, pointing at me. "If Tom can't give her Lucifer's grace..." Her lips pinched together. "Then that knife is the only thing that can stop Armageddon."

The color in Tom and Bridget's faces drained, and April's chin quivered. A shiver started at the base of my neck and cascaded down to my toes. I didn't realize I was shaking until Alex pulled me into his arms.

He still had the seeds of compassion inside him, or otherwise, he would have just let me fall to pieces. I knew what was coming, even though I didn't want to hear the words. I started out of the room with Alex on my heels, but I wasn't fast enough.

"The breach is weakening." Fate's words followed me into the hall.

I let go of Alex's hand and ran. I couldn't get up the stairs fast enough, and I then threw myself face first on my bed. People were going to die, all because of my weird time travel.

The mattress depressed next to me, and I looked over my shoulder. I already knew who it was because of the calm that seemed to blanket me, but it didn't stop the tingle over my skin when our eyes met.

Alex smiled, and his hand drifted from my calf up my leg.

I rolled to my side and batted his hand away. "Stop."

His smile faded. "You can't stand to be near me anymore."

I closed my eyes and fell onto my back, covering my face. "Not true. You just have to be patient with me." I moved my hands down so I could see his face. Just staring in his eyes flushed my skin. "I still feel the electricity."

The crease of concern between his eyes smoothed, but his expression remained serious. "I'm not okay. I know I should be afraid, but I'm not. The only instinct I have is to protect you."

I sat up and took his hands. "That's sweet, but in case you didn't notice, I can protect myself."

He barked a laugh. "No, you can't. You don't have mastery over your fire. You need to have that before I will believe you can take care of yourself. Until then, I'm at your side. And I need you to keep me grounded. You. Not my parents." His hand drifted to my thigh. "Grounded and in line." His fingers walked higher, and he looked at me and licked his lips.

I grabbed his wrist when he reached mid thigh.

"Aren't you the least bit curious?"

"No. I'm not ready for all the repercussions that come with it." My heart galloped in my chest. "Besides, we have only known each other for what, two days?"

His smile softened. "But you are my soulmate."

I brought his fingers to my lips. "But I'd like to be friends, too, before we go down that road."

He blinked and sighed. "The old me would have been cool with that, no matter how disappointing those words are." He tucked a strand of hair behind my ear. "What if, when you get to know me, you don't like this version of me?"

I looked at the floor. I didn't have an answer for him.

He tilted my chin back up and planted a soft kiss. "When I kiss you, I can feel my soul flare. I feel whatever emotion I had for you before Grace tried to take it away," he whispered against my lips. Then he continued the kiss, and when I opened my mouth to protest, the swipe of his tongue silenced me.

My soul screamed for him. The connection was as solid and complete as the fire locked within me. My need for him terrified me, and I pulled away. I proceeded to stand up, and he stood up alongside me.

He pushed me against the wall and crushed my lips with his. His fingers dug into my waist, and an animalistic growl came from him.

The feel of his weight against me ignited my desire. We fit with one another. Ying and yang, despite the loss of most of his soul. We still molded to each other in all the right ways, and all the right places. When his hands slid under my shirt and slid up my sides, I pressed my palms on his chest, and pushed gently enough to break the kiss.

He didn't seem deterred. He stared into my eyes as if we were the only beings on the planet.

"Alex."

"My first name is actually Ty. I'd like *you* to call me by my first name."

Something about the name triggered a heat so all-consuming that I nearly lost all sense.

His hands slid higher, and my brain kicked back into control.

"Stop... Ty," I whispered and moved my arms over his in an attempt to stop his progression.

He actually shivered when I whispered his name. The slow grin that surfaced along with the spark in his eyes weakened my knees, and I wasn't sure I could really say no to him. Not with that consuming look in his eyes.

"But I don't want to." He leaned in for another kiss.

"You better before I launch you across the room," Tom snarled from the doorway.

I jerked at his voice. Alex never looked away from me, although his hands stopped their upward movement, and he paused just before his lips met mine. His thumbs caressed the skin right below the fabric of my bra, sending a web of goose flesh over my arms.

"Ty Alexander Ryan, step away from Faith." CJ stepped into sight behind Tom. His voice was less menacing and sterner than Tom's.

The heat inside me turned to icy mortification, and I pushed at Alex's arms.

Alex turned to his uncle and his father, pulled his hands out from under my shirt, and stepped away with his hands up. He looked squarely at Tom. "You really shouldn't be the one to give dating advice. From what I've heard, you were quite the stud in high school." He cocked his head, challenging Tom.

"Enough, Alex," CJ said, but his admonishment didn't stop Tom's face from going beet red.

"It's a real good thing that you are my nephew, because that would have earned you a black eye if you were anyone else." Tom stepped into the room, crowding Alex.

Alex stood his ground. There wasn't a hint of fear or regret in his frank stare, but I held enough of both for the two of us.

"Alex," I whispered, and he raised an eyebrow. "Fine. Ty. Stop this."

"You can't use that name," CJ said, glaring at his son.

Alex laughed. "You're the one who gave me *that* name. It's clearly printed on my birth certificate, so I have every right to be called by my first name if I choose."

CJ's lips pressed together, and he and Tom exchanged a glance. "You've always been Alex to us."

"Well, I want her to call me by my first name." He pointed at me.

"Why?" CJ asked.

Alex crossed his arms. "Because hearing it actually makes me feel something. And I like that feeling."

"What it makes you feel is not appropriate for a sixteen-year-old boy."

Alex laughed. "So, you are going to stand here and tell me you didn't experience the same things at my age?"

"No. But I didn't act on it at sixteen," CJ said. He glanced at me and then back at his son.

Tom kept his mouth shut and looked out the window. "Why don't you two come back downstairs and help us all figure out the next step." He met my gaze. "That isn't a request, either."

That was the last place I wanted to be with everyone staring at me with an accusing eye.

"They don't blame you," Tom said to me. "Michael is just coming to terms with the fact his sister has chosen a path he doesn't agree with, and it's easier to place the blame on someone he just met than on his sister."

"Can I change before I come down?"

"Do you need help?" Alex asked.

"No," all three of us answered at the same time.

"Fine." Alex walked out of the room.

CJ followed, and Tom shut my door.

The sudden quiet of my room pressed down on my chest. I didn't want to go back downstairs, but Tom hadn't given me much of a choice. I unlaced my boots and tossed them into the closet. I chose another pair of jeans and a blue tank top. I stopped to inspect myself in the mirror to make sure I looked more like a teenager than some leather-clad badass.

I ran a brush through my hair, combing out the knots from the boat ride, and when I was satisfied, I padded downstairs in bare feet. I stopped in the doorway between the kitchen and the atrium. Naomi and Gabriel were just inside the front door.

"Please, I don't know where she's gone, and the things she said before she disappeared..." Naomi shook her head.

Even I could tell she was desperate.

Tom stood next to Alex, blocking them from entering farther. Alex's stance was one I would have recognized anywhere. The tightness in his shoulders and the back of his thighs moved my feet towards them.

"You aren't here to help us," Alex said in a deadpan voice.

"Ty," I said as I approached, knowing the use of that name would call his attention from anything.

He turned, meeting my gaze with one filled with heat and anger.

"They have a right to be included. They have a right to know what we do." I couldn't believe those words were tumbling from my lips, and from the look on Alex's face, he couldn't believe it either.

Michael stood in the entry to the living room, and he cocked his head at me.

Tom stepped aside, but Alex held his ground.

"Grace did this to me," Alex growled. "She took my soul, and you stood by her. You are not on our side."

I took Alex's hand in mine. "What's done is done. You can't take it out on her family. If it had been your sister that did it, wouldn't you stand by her?"

"No, because it was evil. I don't stand by evil. Ever," he said.

I bit my lip and squeezed his hand hard.

Alex stood down.

Naomi looked at Tom and then over at me. "Thank you," she said, and I could tell it was heartfelt. She turned to Alex. "You are family, too," she said to him. "Despite what you think, what Grace did hurt me just as much as it hurt your parents."

Alex remained unfazed. He continued to stare at her, but at least the fury was no longer present in either his features or his eyes.

Tom dragged a few chairs from the office into the living room, and I sat in one. Alex stood behind me with his hands on my shoulders. Tom took the seat next to me, and Michael took the one next to him, leaving space on the couch for Naomi and Gabriel.

Fate had a map spread out on the coffee table and circled a large section of eastern United States and Canada. The farthest western corner encompassed Toronto. The farthest east included St. Johns, and the farthest south was North Carolina.

"This is as far as we have been able to narrow it down," she said.

"York seems to be the epicenter," CJ said.

"Yes." She straightened and dropped the pen on the table. "We are trying to narrow it down further, but that will take time."

"How much time?" Tom asked and traded a glance with Bridget.

"I don't know. A week. A month. A year." Fate shrugged. "But the more time that goes by, the more chance of a catastrophic breach."

"And the world burns."

April's statement drew every eye in the room, and we collectively shivered. Even Alex's hands tightened on my shoulders.

"How many of us die?" Tom asked, his gaze locked on Fate's.

Fate looked at the map. "There are so many different scenarios... Besides, no one lives forever."

"Let me ask in a different way. How many of us are destined to die because of the breach?"

Fate stared at Tom without speaking. Then the swirl of smoke started, and she disappeared a blink later.

"What does that mean?" Bridget asked, looking around the room.

Cold settled on the air and everyone stared at the floor trying to decipher whatever Fate was attempting to convey.

Tom's chair scraped the floor, and he crossed to the window. Both Valerie and CJ joined him, flanking him on either side. The three psychics stood together in silent solidarity. No one else in the room had the power to read minds, and when CJ and Valerie each put their hand on Tom's shoulder, I knew what Fate had communicated.

Fear laced my mouth, leaving a tin aftertaste that made me want to spit. I moved Alex's hands away from my shoulders and stood.

I turned to Kylee. "Can you find that knife?"

She blinked at me and shrugged.

Despair wrapped around my midsection, and I stepped out of the room. Nothing anyone could say could wipe out the guilt creeping into my bones.

Instead of heading upstairs, I crossed to the front door and walked out. I needed fresh air. I needed the calmness of the ocean. The walk to the harbor beach Tom had taken me to wasn't long, and when I got there, I settled on a rock near the lapping water.

Alex took a seat next to me.

"I wanted to be alone." I didn't turn to him.

"I told you I'm your shadow from now on until this shit blows over."

"Can you please not swear around me?" I glanced at him and then back at the water.

"I'll try, but it seems my filter and good sense are pretty much broke, so..."

I smiled. I couldn't help it, and I accepted his offered hand. "I'm sorry," I whispered.

He squeezed my hand, and we sat in silence. The waves provided the only conversation with their soft whispers and clattering pull of the stones. It settled over us like a warm blanket. But I knew this quiet solace was only temporary.

A storm was coming, and there would be blood and death and despair riding on the wind.

Fire Cursed
Chapter 16

ALEX AND I HAD stayed down at the shore long enough for the tide to noticeably change before we headed back. The conversation had all but died down, and people were dispersing, so our timing couldn't have been better.

We said our goodbyes and collapsed on the couch for some mindless television. April and the girls curled on the opposite seats, and no one spoke. Tom, CJ, Bridget, and Valerie went across the hall to the office to continue whatever planning they were doing.

It wasn't until the doorbell rang that the adults came out.

"Dinner," Tom announced, and the group of us headed into the kitchen.

I took the seat at the dinner table that had my palm prints scalded into the wood. The center of the table carried at least a dozen containers of Chinese food. Alex sat on one side of me and April on the other. CJ and Valerie flanked the girls. Tom and Bridget took the heads of the table.

CJ and April put their hands out. I glanced around the table as everyone clasped hands. I joined the circle.

Tom bowed his head. "Thank you, Lord, for the gifts you've given us. Please give us the strength to get through the hurdles you see fit to place in our path and guide us with your light. Let us not wander into temptation, and help us keep our minds on doing no harm, no matter what may come. Blessed be."

"Blessed be," everyone at the table repeated.

It was the strangest saying of grace I had ever been privileged to share in. My mother usually just recited the Lord's Prayer or something equally of Christian nature. But this was from the heart and not something done out of habit. It made all my mother's dinner prayers seem superficial.

Alex squeezed my hand, and then everyone's hands unclasped and grabbed at the containers in the center of the table like a feeding frenzy. Alex helped me, adding a little of everything to both our plates before the clatter of silverware and chopsticks filled the room.

The dinner conversation remained light even with the heavy weight hanging over us. Bridget and April talked about the field trip. The girls talked about their current favorite books. Laughter mingled with daily quips, and my throat tightened.

This was what it was like to be part of a family.

Tom's haunted gaze traveled over each member at the table as if he were trying to memorize this moment. It gave me goose bumps when his eyes met mine, and the smile he concocted did nothing to settle the jumbled nerves riding my spine.

Nothing of the darker events were discussed, and I was thankful.

"What were you doing out in the boat?" CJ asked.

Tom nodded towards me.

"Saying goodbye to my mother," I said, and like the snap of bone, the light mood ended. I looked at Bridget. "I never thanked you and Tom for the beautiful urn."

"I'm glad you liked it." She glanced around the table at the nearly empty plates. "Anyone in the mood for ice cream?"

All the children raised their hands. So did Valerie and CJ. Alex hadn't raised his hand, and neither did I.

"You don't want ice cream?" CJ asked both of us.

I wasn't in the mood for dessert. All I wanted to do was get some sleep. Today had worn me out. "Not really. You all can go. I think I just need some time alone."

"I can stay here with her if you want," Alex said.

"We will drop you off at home." There was no bend in CJ's tone, and for once since this afternoon, Alex didn't talk back.

We cleared the table in no time and cleaned everything up. The group loitered by the door, getting their shoes on and getting ready for an ice-cream run.

"You sure you don't want to go?" Bridget asked.

"Yes. And I'm sure I don't need you to stay," I said to Tom when he went to open his mouth.

He gave me a nod and closed the door. All the locks in the house engaged as if by remote, and I waved from the side window. I debated on whether to settle in the living room or go upstairs. I was tired but restless and opted for the couch instead of my room. I wasn't more than ten minutes into the program I found when a knock at the front door interrupted me.

I scooted to the window and peeked out the glass. Alex stood on the stoop, looking at the driveway. I hesitated, but the lost look on his face clinched my decision. I crossed and opened the door.

He stepped inside. Once the lock was engaged, I turned away from him and headed into the family room again with my nerves in overdrive.

I plopped down in the same spot I had been in with my back to the side arm of the couch and my knees bent in front of me, putting a physical barrier between him and any possible advance. "How much trouble are you going to be in for this?"

"A shit ton." He sat next to me on the couch. He faced me and crawled between my legs, forcing one leg off the couch and the other into the soft backing.

"Alex!" I gasped when his hands clasped my waist and moved me into a fully reclined position.

He kneeled over me and ever so slowly lowered himself on top of me. His mouth covered my protests. My arms wrapped around his neck, and the kiss deepened. He broke the kiss first and ran his tongue down the line of my neck. A delicious shiver took hold.

He grinned down at me and shifted, leaning his elbow on the inside of the couch. His lips tickled as he kissed the exposed skin at the curve of the tank top, and his hand caressed my breast through the shirt.

His strokes were gentle, but his gaze held no hint of hesitation.

"You've done this before," I said with certainty.

He chuckled and shook his head. "I've had my fair share of kisses before, but that's where it ended." His thumb circled slowly, almost painfully. "You need to block them from your thoughts," he said while still manipulating my breast, clouding my instincts.

"H-how?" I managed to say, but even that came out shaky.

He tugged on the edge of my tank top, until most of my bra cup was visible, and then lowered his mouth to my skin. Nibbling as he moved down the edge of the fabric. "Think of multiple things at once," he whispered against my skin. "Anything non-linear blocks them."

He sucked on the exposed flesh of my breast. His hand slid down the side of my shirt and over my hip to the inside of my thigh.

I ran my hand into his thick hair as heat wound through me, pooling wherever his hand was. He slid his fingers closer to my core, moving his mouth higher up my flesh to my jaw. The moment his hand found its mark, his lips crushed mine.

The rawness of the kiss, coupled with the increasing pressure of his hand between my legs, turned on a heat I wasn't prepared for.

I pushed away from the kiss to gasp air, to try to gain my senses, but the problem was I was in sensory overload. His gentle stroke blasted logic from my brain.

"Ty…"

"Yes?" His bright blue eyes gazed down at me, and I swear that warm look he had before he'd lost his soul was there, alongside the wild need.

"You need to stop."

His stroke slowed, and his smile faded. Fleeting doubt crossed his features, and in a blink, it was gone.

I pulled his hand away. "Please," I whispered. Desperation gripped me, and I almost put his hand back where it had been. My body cursed me for stopping the bliss he was creating. As ready as I was for him, I was not ready for this.

His fingers traced my lips, and then he balled his hand into a fist and closed his eyes. His jaw tightened like stopping caused him physical pain. But he nodded and pushed himself up.

He waved me aside, took the spot against the back of the couch, and pulled me between his legs so I leaned on his chest. He wrapped his arms around me and kissed my shoulder. "Sorry," he whispered.

I nodded and just let him hold me while we watched the movie.

"Love is a strange emotion," he said after a while.

I glanced back at him, but his gaze was glued on the television.

"What do you mean?"

He chewed on his lower lip. "It can leave you hollow when it's not reciprocated."

"You think my rejection was because I don't care about you in that way?"

"Well, isn't it?"

"No." I laughed. "I stopped you because I'm not ready for a sexual relationship. Not because I didn't like it," I said. "On the contrary." I turned back towards the television. "It's all I can think about now."

His hands shifted, one up and one down, and he playfully stroked me.

I squeezed my thighs together and squirmed under his touch. He nibbled the side of my neck and then released me, settling back into the comfortable embrace, but the grin remained on his face.

"I think I can drum up some patience." He laughed and kissed the back of my head.

"Do you think this dependency we have is unhealthy?" I blurted.

He didn't say anything.

I waited, and when he didn't answer, I glanced over my shoulder at him.

"That never occurred to me, but I see your point. The course of my life changed drastically the moment our palms touched in my front yard." He sighed and squeezed tighter. "I would walk away from everything for you. My family. My fortune. Everything. This morning that scared the living sh—daylights out of me. But now, it just is, and there is no fear attached to it.”

“I would never ask you to choose between me and your family.” I settled back in his arms just as car lights crossed the front window. I went to move, but his grip tightened.

“Chill. We’re just watching a movie.”

“Alex?” CJ’s voice barreled from the stairwell.

Footsteps came closer to the family room entrance, and we both looked over our shoulder. CJ’s face held the same fury as he had this morning, but instead of being directed at Grace, it was now directed at his son.

My head tickled, then a raw force blinded me, and I winced.

“Get out of her head, Dad,” Alex snapped.

My vision cleared. I rubbed my temples.

“I underestimated you,” CJ said, his voice calming a fraction.

“Me or Faith?” Alex asked, his gaze never moving from the television. “I told you I would not leave her here all alone. There are too many things out there, and if Grace was twisted enough to strip me of my soul, what else is she capable of? No way I’m leaving Faith open to another attack, and being alone in the house was an open invitation. I thought I made that crystal clear.”

“And I thought I made it clear you were not to leave the house.”

Another pair of lights crossed over the window.

"It's time to go home."

"I'm not leaving. I'll sleep on the couch and come over with her in the morning."

"Don't I get a say in this?" I pulled out of his grip and swung my legs off the edge of the couch.

Alex did the same. "I don't have a good feeling, Dad. Something right in the center of my chest is telling me to stay put, and it is not because I want to sleep with her."

CJ scoffed.

"Stop with the judgmental shit. I'm not without rational thought. And I know that this foreboding isn't quite in line with being soulless. Have a little faith in me."

"Your judgement is skewed."

Feet shuffled into the house.

"My filter is fucked. I'll admit that, but my judgement isn't. Neither is that sixth sense of mine. I have one, you know." Alex glanced back at his father. "As insignificant as it seems compared to what you live with, my intuition has never been wrong. My internal sirens were blaring. They calmed a little when I got here, but something is watching this house."

Tom walked into the room and stood next to CJ.

"Something is watching, and whatever it is, it can breach Tom's protection sigils."

CJ and Tom traded a glance.

"You should go with your father," Tom said. "I can protect the house."

"I would rather not have you in harm's way," I said. "If anything else happens to you..."

"I'll be fine."

Of course he would say that. I stood. "I'm going to bed. You all can hash this out without me." I headed upstairs, yawning.

April stepped out of her room just as I reached mine. "Good night, Faith." She gave me a quick hug before disappearing.

I didn't even get a good night out before her door closed.

The nightly routine was fast, and with my teeth freshened and my nightgown on, I climbed into bed. My thoughts swirled, but it wasn't Alex that kept coming to the forefront. Instead, it was that moment just before Fate disappeared that kept invading the nice thoughts of Alex's hands.

I stared at the ceiling with sleep just out of reach. A car door closed, and the engine started. The rumble faded away, and I wondered if Alex was downstairs or not. My question was answered a moment later when my door opened.

Alex came in and sat on the edge of my bed while Tom waited at the door.

"Good night," Alex said.

"Good night."

Tom cleared his throat, and Alex obeyed whatever silent command that throat clearing meant. He left, and Tom closed the door.

I rolled on my side. Knowing he was in the house did nothing to quell the growing nerves plucking at my skin like a league of bed bugs. I fidgeted under the sheets, rolling from side to side, pushing away the doom overshadowing my life.

Fire Cursed
Chapter 17

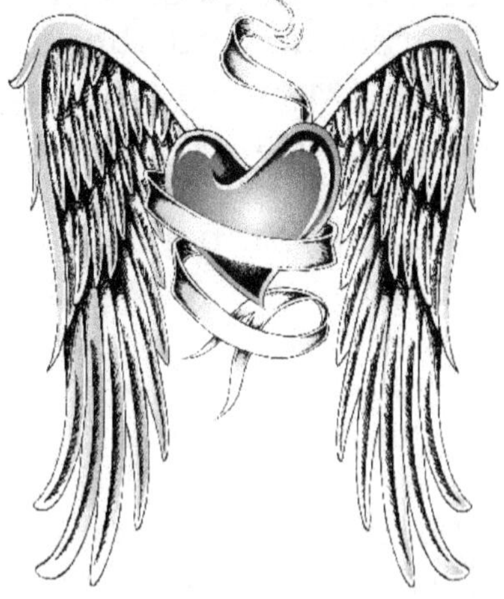

MY NIGHT REMAINED RESTLESS, and I fell asleep in the wee hours from sheer exhaustion. Between what happened with Alex on the couch and the rest of the day, my brain just wouldn't be quiet. What sleep I had was broken with flashes of bloody scenes and whispers from beyond.

The mattress under me moved, and my eyes fluttered open.

"Move over," Alex whispered.

I did, and after the covers adjusted, an arm slid under my neck and Alex pulled me against him.

"Get some sleep."

His order followed me down into a dark, dreamless sleep.

"WHAT THE HELL?" TOM'S voice snapped.

I shot up into a sitting position, blinking and disoriented. I turned toward the door, and Alex rolled onto his back next to me and covered his closed eyes with his arm. My hands shook, and I couldn't stop blinking. I thought Alex crawling in bed with me had been part of my dreams. I glanced up at Tom with my mouth still hanging open.

"What are you doing in her room?" Tom asked in that I'm-going-to-throttle-you voice of his.

"She was having nightmares." He lifted his arm and folded the covers back. "I'm still dressed, so don't have a coronary." He threw the blanket over his jean-clad legs and returned his arm to cover his eyes.

"What are you doing?"

The repetition of the question was getting to me as well.

Alex moved his arm enough to view Tom with one eye. "Trying to get a little sleep."

"Not in here, you aren't." He crossed his arms. "You don't want me to drag your ass out of that bed, do you?"

Alex glanced at Tom. "I'm just going to sleep, Uncle Tom," he said, and irritation crept into his voice.

"Not. In. Here." Tom's words hissed through clenched teeth, and his arms flexed under the tight T-shirt.

"Maybe you should listen to your uncle," I said. My shock had finally receded enough for me to speak.

Alex turned a single blue eye in my direction, the other still covered by his arm. "Do you want me to leave?"

"She doesn't have a choice," Tom said.

I shrugged. "You really need to go." I didn't want another altercation. It wasn't the greatest way to start the day, and I prayed Alex would see that. "Thank you for coming in when you did. You helped keep the nightmares away, but it's time to go."

Tom's arms fell to his sides, and he rolled his eyes. "Come on, lover boy, let's go figure out breakfast for everyone." His hostility changed to exasperation. He turned and disappeared, leaving the door open.

Alex put his arm over his eyes again, so I pushed him with my leg. He sighed and lowered his arm. "You want me to go?"

"I don't want any more fighting. If this is how you all are normally..." I bit my lip and shook my head.

"This isn't how we are normally." He swung his legs over the edge of the bed. "It's usually fun to be around my family." He ran his hands through his hair and stretched. "And Uncle Tom is usually the first to crack an inappropriate joke or take us out fishing or something like that. He's been more of an adult the past few days than I've ever seen him."

"What about your dad? What is he normally like?"

"He is exactly as you've seen him. Intense and damn strict. But he's kind to a fault, and we all know he loves us no matter what. Even when we disappoint him." He shook his head and stood up. "I should go before he comes back up and attempts to beat my ass."

Alex didn't look back as he shuffled out of the room and down the stairs. I rolled out of bed and into the bathroom. As much as I would have liked a shower, I was still on the no-shower list with my stitches. Instead, I did my best with the sponge, washed my face, and brushed my teeth before finding something suitable for the day.

When I got down to the kitchen, both Tom and Alex were at the stove. Tom was manning the bacon, and Alex was scrambling eggs. April grabbed two slices of toast from the toaster and slathered butter on them before putting them on the already respectable stack in the center.

Tom glanced over his shoulder. "Do you mind pouring the orange juice?"

"Sure," I said.

Alex winked at me, and my face heated despite the icy blast from the refrigerator.

It was stocked full, so I had to move the milk to reach for the orange juice. I poured four glasses and set the container on the corner of the table in case people wanted more. No sooner had I taken a seat than everyone else sat. Alex set the pan of scrambled eggs on the hot pad, and Tom placed the bacon next to it.

"Dig in," Tom said.

Before I knew it, my piled-high plate was clean, as were Alex's, Tom's and April's.

April grabbed her schoolbag and ran out the door just as the sound of the bus reached our ears.

I gathered a few of the plates and piled them into the sink. I took off my gloves and set them aside. Without prompting, I started cleaning the morning dishes. Alex stepped beside me and helped me load the dishwasher. He dried the pans, and before long, the kitchen was back in order.

Tom sat at the table with his cup of coffee, watching us.

"What?" I finally asked when it felt like his gaze was burning a hole in my back.

He smiled. "You two are cute together."

Good lord, that was not what I expected to hear. Alex rolled his eyes with his back to his uncle, and I nearly broke out in a smile.

"Do you have your driver's license yet?" Tom asked.

I turned off the water and wiped my hands before I slid the gloves back on. "No."

"Did your mother teach you to drive?"

"Of course. Who do you think got her to the hospital?" I leaned on the counter.

Dimples appeared in his cheeks. "So you drove illegally."

I squinted at him. "What's your point?"

"We should probably get you a driver's license. But in order to do that, you need a permit. The genius beside you already has his license."

I bit my lip. "That requires paperwork."

"And?"

"And unless you have my birth certificate—"

"Not a problem," Tom interrupted.

I crossed my arms and sent the most skeptical look I could drum up.

"How do you think CJ got your diploma?"

"You have my birth certificate?" My voice cracked in a high lilt.

"Yes. And we have legal guardianship papers." Tom took a sip of his coffee. Smile lines around his eyes showed his amusement. "We can make miracles happen." He winked as he put his cup in the sink and then pulled out his keys. "You can drive us to CJ's house."

My mother had taught me to drive out of necessity, and our little compact car wasn't in the same league as Tom's truck.

"I don't know..." I said.

"I can drive us." Alex reached for the keys.

Tom snatched them away. "Did I ask you if you wanted to drive?"

"Well... no," Alex muttered and shoved his hands in his pockets.

Tom turned back to me and put the keys in my gloved hand. "You are driving. You don't need to worry about the truck. It's just a truck, so if you back into anything, it's no big deal."

I closed my hand around the keys and nodded, although my stomach had dropped to the floor at the thought. I picked up my backpack, and we all headed out to the truck.

I put the keys in the ignition with a shaky hand and adjusted the seat until I was comfortable.

"Buckle up." I turned the key. The truck roared to life.

"Turn around in the driveway so you don't have to back out onto the main road," Tom said.

My K-turn ended up being more like a crazy W. It took me three times to get the truck turned around, despite the extra parking spaces.

Neither Tom nor Alex made any comments and when I finally got situated, I took a right instead of a left. Tom ended up guiding me through the town center and onto the back road in order to circle around to CJ's house.

Tom's hand gripped the handle with white knuckles, but his voice was calm and instructive despite the Death grip.

As we rolled toward the security gate, it opened without us stopping and punching in the number. I pulled up the driveway and put the truck in park.

"Set the parking brake," Tom said. "It's the pedal to the far left. Push it until it can't go anymore."

I pushed it down, pulled out the keys, and handed them to him.

"I need to take a trip to Brooksfield today." Tom glanced over his shoulder. "If your father says it's okay, did you two want to take a day trip?"

"Sure," Alex said. "Do you mind if I clean up first?"

"Not at all. It'll give me a chance to talk your dad into it."

Alex headed inside before us.

"I really should check in with my online class. The last thing I sent out was that my mother had passed away, and I can't afford—"

"Don't worry about the money," Tom interrupted.

"That's easy for you to say," I mumbled under my breath. He didn't have a whopping hospital bill hanging over his head and nothing in the bank.

"The hospital bills have all been settled."

I stopped short and stared at him. "What?"

"Faith, when we signed the guardianship papers, that made us responsible for you. That includes making sure you have a roof over your head, meals on the table, and an education." He shuffled his foot on the ground. "And I didn't think a sixteen-year-old should have to have that kind of burden over her head."

"But that was a lot of money." I blinked up at him, still trying to wrap my head around it.

He patted me on the head. "We can afford it." He walked into the house with me still gawking at him.

A chill settled over my neck, and I hurried inside. With the door closed, the uneasy feeling faded. I crossed into the kitchen. CJ leaned against the counter, waiting for the coffee machine to finish.

"Do you mind if I go use the computer to check the college courses I'm enrolled in?" I hooked my thumb towards the basement.

"Sure," he said.

I traded a glance with Tom and headed downstairs. The basement was dark, and it took me a minute to find the light switches in both the main area and the computer room. I turned on the same computer I had taken the test on and navigated to my college blackboard.

My shoulders sagged. Every class was marked as incomplete. I closed my eyes and laid my forehead on my crossed arms as disappointment stabbed through me.

"Damn it," I whispered and sat back up. With a deep breath, I closed out of the screen.

I stared at the browser, thinking about mine and Tom's conversation this morning. Out of curiosity, I typed in the question, *What is Tom Ryan's net worth?* I received a few hits, but nothing on the screen resembled the man upstairs, so I typed in: *What is CJ Ryan's net worth?* His information came up immediately. And with it came the fact that he and his brother were the richest people in Maine at a combined estimated net worth in the billions.

I couldn't comprehend that much money. I closed the browser and just stared at the computer. My reflection showed my shock, and I closed my mouth.

Alex stepped into the room a moment later along with the clean smell of Irish Spring soap. I turned in the seat and stared at him. My brain was still overwhelmed by what I had read, and Alex just made it harder to believe. He was so down to earth. Not pretentious at all.

That hungry look was in his eyes again, and he pulled me out of the seat. Before I could speak, he kissed me, tightening his grip around me. His hands slid down until they cupped my bottom. He squeezed and broke the kiss, grinning at me.

"Looks like we are going to be able to go with Tom," he said. "And I'm driving."

I moved his hands back to my waist, holding them in place. The last thing I wanted was for his father to catch us again.

"I haven't been to Brooksfield in years," he said. "Not since my grandparents were alive." He leaned in for another kiss, this time moving me towards the darkest corner of the computer room.

"What are you doing?" I asked.

"Finding some privacy." He pushed me against the wall. His hands roamed up my sides as he kissed my neck gently. "How are the stitches feeling today?" He licked a line at the edge of my shirt, following it to the V between my breasts and coming up the other side.

My skin tingled. "Huh?" I stared at the mischievous glow in his eyes.

"Your back. How does it feel today?" Both of his hands cupped my breasts, and his thumbs gently circled.

My brain stalled, and he raised an eyebrow, expecting me to answer. "Um, okay."

"Stitches aren't pulling at all?" he asked and kissed the underside of my jaw. When his hand moved between my legs, rubbing softly, he created enough friction to ignite a fire deep inside my soul.

"No. The stitches are fine." My voice turned husky. I had an idea of what he was doing—this conversation to throw off my thoughts—but from the way his eyes sparkled as he gazed at me, I knew I was in trouble. Eighteen was so far away.

Alex closed his eyes and drew a deep breath. And then he stepped away, putting his hands out to the side. When his eyes opened, the strength of the longing in his gaze made my knees wobble. He took another step away.

"If I don't stop, I'm not going to stop," he whispered.

I remained against the wall. Every cell vibrated with the heat he'd created in me. I wasn't sure I would be able to move or speak, never mind carry on a coherent conversation.

He put his hand out. "Come on. Let's go somewhere where I won't get us in trouble."

I took his hand.

He looked down at the connection. "You're trembling."

I laughed. "Your fault."

Concern made a brief appearance and then dissolved into a killer smile. "Oh man, if that does this to you, imagine what will happen when we finally do the deed?"

And then he'd opened his mouth and ruined the moment. "The *deed*?"

"You know what I mean."

I did, but I wasn't going to let him off the hook so easily, not when he had been so smooth moments before.

"Come on." He nearly dragged me out of the room, only stopping to shoulder my backpack and carrying it upstairs for me.

"How are your classes looking?" Tom asked.

"Every last one of them was marked incomplete." Even my voice carried my disappointment, and Alex squeezed my hand.

Tom stood from the table, fished out his keys from his pocket, and handed them to me. "You're driving."

"I thought you said I could drive," Alex said.

"Maybe on the way home if you're good," Tom said.

"Bring him home after. He's staying here tonight," CJ said with his arms crossed.

If I didn't know better, I would say both Tom and CJ knew what had happened downstairs.

Tom met my gaze and pressed his lips against a smirk. *Darn it. He knows.* My cheeks warmed, and I turned, heading out the door to avoid comments.

I climbed into the driver's seat, and Alex got in behind me. Tom lingered at the door talking with CJ.

"Why eighteen?" Alex asked.

I looked in the rearview mirror at him. "Because we will be legal adults and can deal with any ramifications."

"What if neither of us live to see eighteen?" He leaned his chin on the edge of the seat, meeting my gaze in the mirror.

I absolutely refused to dignify his question with an answer. "Maybe it's a good thing that you are staying home tonight."

He sat back in the seat and glanced out the window. "I want to have that experience." His eyes drifted back to mine. "With you. My first. My last." He shrugged and looked away.

"Not after only three days, Ty," I whispered just as Tom crossed in front of the truck.

Air whistled between his teeth, and a slow smile appeared on his lips. Whatever he would have said had we been alone died on his lips the moment Tom opened the door. But his gaze positively sizzled.

Tom glanced at the two of us as he got in the passenger seat. He buckled in, and his hand went around the handgrip on the door. "Take a right out of the driveway."

My K-turn was more controlled this time, and I pulled out and followed Tom's directions. The highway we took was sparsely populated, but it still made me nervous.

Alex leaned forward and put his hand on my shoulder, calming my nerves. It was as if he knew I was anxious by this drive. I quickly glanced in the rearview mirror, right into his baby blues.

By the time we took the turn onto the dirt driveway, Tom's grip on the car door had loosened a fraction, and I thought I had a handle on driving. I rolled up to the garage and then put the truck in park and engaged the parking brake before I turned the vehicle off. I handed Tom the keys and slumped in the seat.

At least on this ride, I wasn't worried about my hands igniting the steering wheel like I had been when I drove my mother to the hospital, but even so, the stress of driving drained me. The bites on my neck throbbed to the beat of my heart, and my hands felt as if I would never be able to straighten my fingers.

The ride was only an hour and a half.

I wondered how people who drove long distances felt at the end of the day.

"Pretty much the same." Tom opened his door.

"Huh?"

"Driving long distances." He smiled and got out of the car.

Alex followed and opened my door for me. He held his hand out and helped me from the vehicle.

"I am going to Paradise Cove," he said over the car.

"There's nothing left. I toasted the entire area, but you're free to check it out." Tom surveyed the landscaping and then headed for the house.

The log cabin was charming in a way that I couldn't put words to. It had both modern and rustic charm with large windows that offered ample light and highlighted the arched ceilings.

Alex guided me around the side of the cabin, and a beautiful lake with mountains surrounding us took my breath away. I turned away from the lake view and stared into the large picture window that covered the entire wall facing the lake. The cabin was beautiful. Exposed beams lined the ceiling between clean panels of drywall. An enormous stone fireplace graced the wall opposite the door. It gave me a sense of peace.

Alex tugged on my hand, and I turned and followed him across the lawn. The little gazebo looked like it needed work, and so did the dock. When he stepped onto an overgrown path, I glanced over my shoulder at the cottage. Tom stood in the window watching us. He waved his hand right before I lost sight of him.

I turned just in time to slam into Alex's shoulder. He had stopped at the entrance of an area that looked as if someone had charbroiled it yesterday. It reminded me of what his backyard had looked like after his father decimated Lucifer.

We stepped onto the blackened moss. It crunched under our feet. When we were halfway across the glade, Alex turned back to the noise behind us. Tom stood just beyond where the charcoal started.

I crossed to the water. Even it looked blackened. I took my glove off, shoved it into my back pocket, and crouched down. I wanted to feel the moss to see if it was actually as crunchy as it sounded under our feet.

The moment my hand connected with the ground, the blackened cove gave way to a different moment in time, like a sudden pan of a camera.

TOM STEPPED ONTO THE lush green moss, so different from the blackened blight my hand had originally touched.

"Holy fuck," Tom said, and his eyes widened at the rabid beast contained in the salt circle.

"Yeah, Lucifer is more of an asshole than I gave him credit for." CJ crossed to his brother. "He turned Dad into that."

The thing growled, its gaze bouncing between the two of them as saliva dripped from its sharp teeth.

CJ sighed. "I was going to step in the ring, but I have a feeling he's too far gone and would try to kill me."

Tom nodded in agreement, his eyes still glued to the massively scarred Hellhound.

"But there is one person he wouldn't attack," CJ said, and Tom's gaze ripped from the beast and met CJ's.

"Mom," they both said at the same time.

Mist rose off the frozen water, and the shift in air pulled my attention to the cove. A beautiful woman, one I had seen in pictures at both CJ's and Tom's houses, stood a few paces away from the wild dog. Their mother had come down from

Heaven with just a word. I had a moment to wonder if my mother could breach the divide before the woman's gaze locked on the beast.

The Hellhound's snarling subsided. His snout rose in the air and he sniffed, and then a pitiful whine escaped. He stretched on the ground, crawling forward until his paws stopped at the salt barrier. He laid his head on his paws.

The woman's eyes welled with tears. "Jesus, Ty," she whispered.

That name. I glanced at Alex, but he was so consumed with the vision that he wasn't looking at me.

The woman kneeled on the other side of the salt barrier, and the dog's head lifted parallel to hers. He whined again.

Her hands moved, breaching the barrier, and cupped his massive jaws.

Tom's best friend laid a salt ring around the woman, and then she wiped away the barrier keeping the hound from her. He crawled forward and laid his muzzle in her lap.

CJ's chin dropped to his chest, and if ever a man looked devastated, it was him right now. Tom reached out to his brother, and his hand gripped CJ's shoulder with such brotherly affection that a lump formed in my throat.

Wonder filled Tom's eyes. "Look," he whispered.

The woman's tears fell on the dog, and light filled each prism, wiping out the blackened form, replacing it with human skin, until it was actually a battered and beaten man lying on the ground with his head in the woman's lap. Tattered clothing covered his body, and he lifted his head, pushing himself to his hands and knees to stare at her.

His hand rose to her cheek, but his eyes held doubt so strong, I wasn't sure he believed she was real. But underneath the doubt, it was a look of complete and utter love.

A look so familiar to me I shivered. That was exactly the way Alex looked at me. Tom was right. It was eerily similar.

"Baby, I'm here," she whispered.

His forehead dropped to her knees, and he crawled closer, wrapping his arms around her waist. His form shook.

"If this is another game, just kill me," he whispered, his voice hoarse and filled with agony.

"It's not, Dad," CJ said, and the man's body stiffened like he expected more horrors.

The glare he sent CJ scared the Hell out of me.

"Dad?" Tom stepped closer, blocking his father's glare.

Their dad blinked, his eyes refocusing on Tom as he crouched lower just outside the salt ring. His gaze moved between Tom and the woman. Confusion clouded his eyes and wrinkled his forehead enough that I wondered what exactly my father did to this poor man beyond turning him into a Hellhound.

When his gaze landed on CJ, his jaw clenched, and the pain in his eyes was deeper than even the pain I had seen in Tom's memories.

CJ took a step closer, and his father flinched and his grip on the woman tightened. CJ reacted like he had been punched in the stomach. His gaze became frantic, and he stepped over the salt line, putting himself into the same circle as his delusional father.

His father shot to his feet and his hand flashed out, grabbing CJ's throat as his fury seemed to override every sense he had. CJ's father's face screamed murder.

Tom stepped into the circle at the same time as his mother, and they both tried to break the grip his father had around CJ's throat.

"I wasn't going to leave you there for...ever," CJ squeaked.

Alex's hand clamped down on mine, and we traded a quick glance.

CJ was crying as his father attempted to squeeze the life out of him. He didn't defend himself. Not even with his father snarling foul curses and promises that he would pay dearly for everything he had done to Jessica. His father didn't seem to realize CJ was his son. That was as messed up as it gets.

"Ty!" their mother yelled, pulling the man's gaze to hers. "Let go of our son!"

The order she issued didn't appear to compute at first, and his incessant blinking announced his confusion. His grip loosened but remained clasped on CJ's throat.

"Dad," CJ whispered.

His gaze dropped to CJ's chest and the ruined jacket before popping back to his face. After a moment, he looked around at where he was, and he dropped his hand and pressed against CJ's chest like he was testing the boundaries of his sanity.

He glanced at their mother again. "Is..." He stopped and licked his lips with another scan of his surroundings. "Is this real?"

"Yes. Our boy decided a rescue mission was in order." She glanced at CJ. "Despite the waves it caused upstairs."

He stepped back and stared at the ground. Each time he began to speak, he seemed to rethink his statements and closed his mouth. Finally, he said, "Paradise Cove?" and looked up at CJ.

CJ gave a weak laugh and nodded.

He was slow to respond, but his gaze traveled upward and all around at each one of them before landing on Damian. "I... I think I remember..." When his gaze landed back on CJ, he bit his lip and covered his mouth. "He really fucked with me," he whispered, and tears shined in his eyes.

"Yeah. Just like he screwed with Valerie," CJ said.

His gaze moved from CJ to Tom and then to their mother, and in the next instance, he squeezed all of them together in a tight hug.

"He told me I died in the complex. That everything else was my mind's last-ditch fantasy to deal with Jessie's death. He made me watch her die before the chains tore me to pieces. It never stopped... and it never changed."

His body shook, and his sobs layered over them like a blanket of rain. They held him just as tightly as he gripped them. When his shakes subsided, they all slowly let go of the family hug.

I WAS STILL CROUCHED with my hand on the moss. When I stood, light spiraled from the place that I'd touched, transforming the burned and blackened moss into the lush green that had been in the vision.

Tom's eyes widened and shot to me.

I gripped Alex's hand hard while the little light tornado swirled, acting almost like Tom's mother's tears had, renewing, erasing the damage Tom said he had caused. Flowers lining the water bloomed bright right in front of our eyes.

"Holy shit," Tom whispered.

Alex stared at the lush cove. "This is more of what I remembered."

The light spun into the sky and exploded into an umbrella of fireworks before it faded away.

"Did you just..." Tom stared out at the water, and tears filled his eyes.

I turned, and a redhead drifted across the water, holding a little girl's hand.

"Aye. She did." The woman wrapped her arms around Tom. When their embrace broke, she asked, "I understand you remarried?"

Tom nodded and crouched down to be eye to eye with the little girl. "Hannah," he whispered and touched her face before glancing at me. "Thank you."

I shrugged. "For what?"

"For opening the portal to Heaven," he said.

My skin broke out in gooseflesh. I hadn't done anything consciously. If I hadn't crouched down to touch the moss, I didn't think any of this would have happened.

Tom smiled.

The woman glanced at Alex. "Is this our nephew?" she asked, her eyes sparkling with wonder. "Why if he isn't the spitting image of CJ."

"Hi, Aunt Raven," Alex said.

Her smile faded as she glanced at our clasped hands. "So, you're the one who has all worlds up in arms."

I raised an eyebrow.

"Don't worry your pretty little head about what is happening in the great beyond," she said. "And trust your heart." She turned to Tom. "We need to get back, and so do you." She stepped close and kissed his cheek. "Come on, Hannah, it's time to go play in the garden." She gave us a wink and poof, she was gone.

I understood why Tom had chosen her as his first wife. She glowed with kindness and heart, and she was a ginger just like me.

I looked out at the water and wished for my mother. The surface of the cove shimmered, and I blinked. Tom stepped beside me as the woman I once knew before cancer had turned her into a husk stepped onto the moss in front of me.

"Hollie, I presume?" Tom asked, extending his hand.

My mother looked at his offering and stepped in, giving him a hug instead. "Thank you," she said. "For everything you have done and everything that you will do for my daughter."

"You're welcome," he said.

She pulled me into a hug next. Her arms were warm and inviting, but I couldn't help but think this was a dream. That I had somehow short-circuited when I touched the moss. It was only the tightening of Alex's hand that kept me grounded.

"You are in very good hands," she whispered in my ear, and then stepped back and inspected me.

"Did you know I could do this?" I waved my hand in the air.

She shook her head.

"Did you know about the things that are out there?" I asked.

"No. I didn't. I only knew angels existed because of Lucifer," she said.

"Why him?" I blurted. I needed to know. What I saw in the time glimpses was a being so hateful and heinous that I couldn't imagine what the Hell my mother was thinking, even with the glimpse of his natural form.

"I found him crawling in the woods. I thought he wouldn't last the night, so I brought him to my small hunting cabin. I didn't know who he was, just that he was hurt beyond humanly possible." She stepped away and stared at the ground. "It was a few weeks before he was strong enough to show me his gratitude, and I was unprepared." Her cheeks heated. "It was only after that he told me who he was. I made some excuse about needing something at the store and I ran. I don't know if he ever tried to find me. He certainly never knew about you. But he knows about you now.”

I held on to Alex’s hand while my mother rambled about Lucifer. Hearing what happened didn’t help. I knew I had been a surprise, but the circumstances just compounded my discomfort. This really wasn’t what I wanted to talk about, but I had been the one to ask the question.

“Come on, Alex. Let’s let them have a few minutes alone,” Tom said.

My mother glanced at Alex and gave him a smile. “Just remember who you were, and that will guide you.”

He nodded and let go of my hand. It was jarring not having him ground me, especially in such a sacred place. I watched until he and Tom were out of sight. When I looked back at my mother, she was looking at the path, and worry lines formed around her lips.

“Watch out for him.” She met my gaze. “And if Lucifer is ever freed, do not let Alex near him. Otherwise...” She closed her eyes.

“Otherwise what?” My heart clattered in my chest at the thought of Alex being in danger.

“He doesn’t have enough of his soul.”

Her gaze pierced mine, and Fate’s words from the other night came back. The thought of Lucifer taking over Alex’s form repulsed me, and my ungloved hand tingled with nervous energy. I pulled out the glove and slid it on before I did any damage to the cove.

“That boy could be the Death of you,” she said.

I said nothing because I already knew he was fast becoming my greatest weakness. Soul or no soul, we were inexplicitly connected, and I only felt whole when I was around him. When he wasn't near, I was much more on edge.

My mother studied my face. "You've already fallen for him?"

I met her gaze. "He calms the fire even better than these." I lifted my gloved hands.

She crossed her arms. "He may calm your fire-starter abilities, but he ignites something else in you, doesn't he?"

I shifted and shoved my hands into my pockets. My gaze jumped everywhere except at her, and she cleared her throat. I nodded.

My mother closed her eyes. "Just be careful." She looked at the path.

"I met CJ Ryan," I said, trying to move the conversation away from Alex. "He's just as nice in person as he was on television."

My mom smiled. "I gathered. His son looks just like him."

"He sings just as well, too," I whispered, and heat filled my cheeks.

She glanced up and sighed. "I need to go." She gave me a tight hug. "I love you, sweetie." She gave me a peck on the cheek before her image faded.

Tears blurred my eyes, and I stood in place, feeling the grief of losing her all over again. A hand landed on my shoulder, and I turned, looking up at Tom's kind eyes.

"It's never easy to leave here, but we need to go." He glanced at the rejuvenated glen. "But at least now you know you can come back here and see your mother any time you'd like."

"Really?"

"Yes. Both CJ and I own this property, and now that this is open again, I'm sure we will stop in periodically and not just to make sure the house hasn't been broken into." He led me back to the truck.

Alex leaned on the driver's side door, twirling the keys on his finger.

Tom pulled his phone out of his pocket and stared at the text. The tendons in his neck tightened, as well as the muscles in his shoulders. "I'm driving." He tucked his phone away. He held his hand out.

"What happened?" I asked.

Tom shook his head and nodded towards the truck. I climbed into the back seat.

"I can get us there fast," Alex said.

"No," Tom said.

I closed the back door because I was too tired to deal with the mounting tension.

Alex handed Tom the keys and opened the back door, shooing me to the other side. Tom didn't argue with the seating arrangements.

"Buckle up," Tom said after Alex closed the back door. He started the truck and spun the car around before I could clasp the seatbelt. "And no funny stuff back there," he added with a glare in the mirror aimed directly at Alex.

"No, sir," Alex said, but I could tell from his tone I would probably have to worry about where his hands were.

I stared out the window, processing what had just happened. "So, not only do I have this fire thing and this time jump curse, I open portals."

Tom glanced in the rearview mirror. "It seems that way." He continued to navigate the roads at a much higher speed than the posted limit. The urgency in his driving didn't make it into his voice, but it certainly reflected in the tightness of his shoulders and jaw.

Alex took my hand. There was no playfulness in his eyes, like he sensed the tension in the car and reacted accordingly. I wanted to fall into his arms and just stay there, safe and whole, but I had a feeling whatever was waiting for us back home would shake the very foundation we stood on.

Fire Cursed
Chapter 18

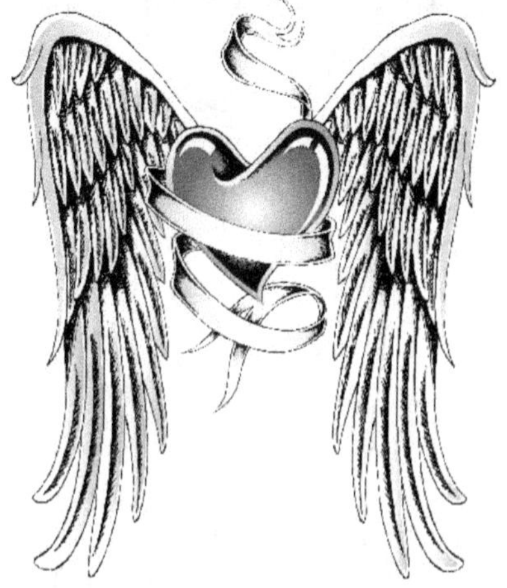

THE DRIVEWAY WAS NEARLY full at Tom and Bridget's home. We pulled in behind Bridget's car in the only space available.

Tom turned the truck off and sat still in the front seat. I didn't move either. He nodded like he was giving himself a silent pep talk and then stepped out of the vehicle. He never turned around to prompt us to follow.

Alex didn't move either. We both watched Tom enter the front door.

Dread pierced through me, and I did not want to leave the comfort of this cab. Alex unhooked both our seatbelts and pulled me into his arms. The tightness which he held me along with the hammer of his heart compounded my already frayed nerves.

When he loosened his grip, his lips found mine. The intense kiss stirred that heat that my mother had spoken about, and I couldn't help but think this might be the last time I had this luxury. I didn't break the kiss when he pushed me down onto the seat and moved on top of me. His full weight stretched out over me as he held my head and kissed me into oblivion.

He finally pulled away and laid his forehead on my shoulder. "Whatever happens, promise you will come back to me."

I kissed his cheekbone, and he turned his head to look at me. A hint of fear danced in his eyes.

"Why do you think I'm leaving?" I asked.

He huffed a laugh and glanced up at the car window and then back at me. "Tom left us alone in his truck. He didn't even look back. And he already told me I couldn't go whenever the shit hit the fan. Everyone is here. So, I think the shit has hit the fan."

I wanted to say so what? I wanted to say I had no idea what he was talking about. I wanted to believe that all our lives weren't on the cusp of changing. But I knew better. Something deep inside was on warning mode, like a silent alarm calling for the cavalry.

I palmed his cheek. "I'll always come back to you. If not, there's always Paradise Cove." I smiled, trying to feign bravery.

He shot backwards into the door at the far side of the cab. "Don't even joke about that." His hands actually shook as he put them up in front of him.

"Alex..." I started.

"No." He shook his head.

"Ty," I said, and this time, his façade crumbled.

"If something happens to you, this will be the last time I feel anything. I don't want to live life as an empty shell. I want to feel this warmth in the pit of my stomach. This fondness I feel for you." His chin trembled. "Please promise me."

I moved towards him and planted a kiss. It was the first time I'd actually made the first move. He sighed and pulled me to him in a grip so tight he actually constricted my breathing.

"Ease up," I whispered against his lips, and he did.

The truck suddenly rocked, and we both sat up straight. The glass behind us shattered. Alex rolled, and we fell off the seat. I hit the floor with a thud, and all of Alex's weight landed on me. His wide-eyed stare met mine before he turned his head and glared at the hiss coming from the window.

My hands were stuck between us, and the sight of the tiger trying to work its way into the cab with murder in its eyes did little to calm my frantic heartbeat.

Alex pushed up on his knees and threw a punch that landed square on the tiger's nose. "Back off," he yelled.

That only seemed to make the tiger more feral and determined.

A wave of power hit the truck, rocking it more than the mad tiger. The feline went flying. Alex moved fast, opening the door closest to the house before grabbing my hand. He yanked me from the floor, and I had just enough time to grab my backpack before we were sprinting to the front door.

CJ and Tom stood outside. Both of their hands splayed out in front of them. The truck door closed on one of their silent commands, and then they shuffled us inside the house. Tom closed and locked the door and then leaned his back against it, staring at the two of us.

"The shit has indeed hit the fan," he said, looking at Alex, and then his gaze turned to me. "You might want to change into something else. Something you don't mind getting a little blood on."

I recoiled.

"Just in case." He smiled.

The smile was all wrong, but I nodded and headed for the kitchen. I didn't want to glance in the family room where everyone was gathered. The hushed whispers were enough. I reached my room and closed the door before heading to the bathroom.

I peeled off the gloves and splashed cold water on my face. I stripped my new shirt and jeans and neatly folded them, leaving them on the counter in the hopes that it was an omen that would bring me back to this house. I pulled on the black gloves and glanced at my hair, debating. If I were going to be using my fire, I didn't need fly-away hairs burning to a crisp.

I braided my hair into a single strand and secured it in a hair tie I found in the top drawer. At least the black bra and underwear wouldn't show blood, but I had no idea what else I owned that would be appropriate for a battle.

I crossed to the dresser and pulled it open, rummaging through everything we had bought. Not one of them would hide blood. Nothing in these drawers was battle worthy.

A throat cleared, and I jumped. Alex leaned against my door, staring at me. He reached for the hem of his shirt and peeled it off as he closed the distance. I stared at his well-formed chest and tight abs. He was lean and hard, and when he reached for me, I stepped into his arms.

Having his skin against mine pulled a soft moan from my lips. Lips that he covered with his mouth a moment later. Our tongues mingled, and his hands wandered as if there was no rush. He dropped to his knees in front of me and ran his hands down my sides. I stopped him when his fingers hooked my underwear.

"No," I whispered, even though right at this moment, I was so tempted to let him continue his exploration. The way his eyes begged almost cracked my resolve, but I continued to shake my head slowly.

He put his cheek against my stomach and wrapped his arms around my waist. I played with a strand of his soft hair, memorizing the feel of it in my fingers. He turned into me and kissed his way up, like he was doing the same. When we were eye to eye, he pressed his lips to mine gently.

"Wear the leather," he said. "You look every bit of the badass that you need to be."

He pulled away and swiped his shirt off the floor. He didn't look back when he walked out of the room.

I turned and stared at the outfit on the chair. It was black leather like my gloves. Although I thought twice about the boots. They weren't made for a fast getaway. I made quick work of putting on the clothing and sat to lace up my boots. Badass. When I stood, I almost believed it until I tripped on the way to the door.

I caught myself before I fell, but it was a reminder that I was only sixteen and I certainly wasn't Lara Croft.

Still, when I walked out of the kitchen, the murmurs quieted.

Alex's serious expression morphed into that sparkling smile that boosted my confidence. It was totally out of place with the solemn mood blanketing the house.

"I told you she was ready." He sent a glare at his father.

I stared at CJ. "Protect him." I nodded toward Alex, unsure why it was imperative that I get a confirmation that the strongest supernatural being alive protect his son. It was a given, but I still needed to hear him say he would.

"With my life," he said.

I bit my lip and blinked back the sudden sheen of tears blurring my vision.

"Grace…" someone beyond the wall of people started to say. I thought it was either Michael or Gabriel, but Alex interrupted them before they could finish.

"Has gone crazy." Alex held my gaze.

"She needs to know," Tom said, and Alex glared at him.

"What do I need to know?" I walked right to Alex.

He took my hands. "Grace said Lucifer has my soul and is looking to bargain. If she brings me to him, he will give her my soul."

I narrowed my gaze.

"She was attacking like she wanted to kill both of us."

"Apparently, it doesn't matter if I'm alive." He shrugged.

A dark veil crossed over my eyes, and I squeezed his hands, trying to resist it taking hold of the rest of my being. My jaw tightened at the dangerous game my father had started. One I would end with pure fire.

Alex pulled me into a tight hug. "You should have let me make love to you like I wanted to upstairs," he whispered.

My gut twisted with his perfect use of words, and I swallowed the bitter lump of regret. But I didn't want my first time to be saying goodbye. And that's what it would have been. A goodbye. This way, I had the incentive to come back in one piece, and I knew deep down I would desperately need something to cling to.

"I disagree," I whispered in his ear. "It gives us both the motivation to make it through whatever is coming."

"Sure does," he said louder than I thought he meant to.

I pushed away, but he tightened his hold. "I promise I'll come back to you, Ty," I whispered, and he squeezed tighter before his arms unwrapped from around me.

I turned to Tom. His complexion was ashen, but he at least attempted to smile.

"We know where the breach is." He turned his phone. On screen was a Google Maps satellite view of a very familiar cottage.

"My house..." I stepped back as if someone had hit me with a physical blow. It was where my mother and I had last been before I rushed her to the hospital. That was the beginning of the end, and it was only a month ago, right after I turned sixteen.

"Yes. And we need to go there and fix the breach. Now," Tom said.

I met his gaze, and a shiver captured me. I slowly shook my head as my eyes widened. Fixing the breach meant the unimaginable.

He huffed, and a crooked smile formed. "Everybody's gotta go sometime," he said with a shrug.

I turned and ran right out of the kitchen door, peeling my gloves off in case Grace was crazy enough to attack me. A part of me welcomed turning her into a barbequed tiger. That part also wanted to set the world on fire and just let it consume me. Then I wouldn't have to see the end of those I had grown close to.

Tears blurred my vision, and I kept running until I was knee deep in the ocean at the same beach I had run to before. The cold bit through the leather, and my toes numbed within seconds. When I turned, the person walking through the sand towards me surprised the Hell out of me.

Bridget wrapped her arms around her elbows, pressing her lips against the tremble. In her hand were my gloves. She waited for me to come out of the water with a steady stream of tears sliding down her face.

I almost turned and swam until I couldn't anymore. Let the sea take me so I wouldn't have to experience the icy hand of death yet again.

I walked out of the water and stopped in front of her. "I'm going to close it without Lucifer's grace," I said, jutting my chin out.

"I'm sure you will." Despite her words, her tears continued. "But in the event..." She hugged herself tighter and met my gaze. "Bring him back to me."

My hands shook, and I nodded. I would do my best to bring him back alive, and if I couldn't do that, I would bring back what was left of him so she could say a proper goodbye.

She handed me my gloves, and we headed back up the hill. Tom stood halfway up the road. His arms were crossed, and the tension left him rigid. He didn't smile as we approached.

"How's April handling all this?" I asked before we reached Tom.

She didn't answer me, and I didn't blame her. If I were April, I would blame me for wreaking havoc on their lives.

When we reached Tom, Bridget hung back a step and took his hand. They walked behind me, and I felt as if I were being escorted to the gallows. Even the group standing outside the front door was enough to turn the chill in my bones into an outright winter storm.

CJ's hands were clamped on Alex's shoulders, and just from Alex's expression, it wasn't just his father's hands holding him in place. CJ's magic kept him locked away from me. In front of Alex stood April.

I had a full view of what was on April's mind. Her hands were folded over her heart. Tears stained her face, and yet when her eyes met mine, she somehow managed a smile.

My heart broke. Bridget opened the passenger side door of the truck for me. She gave me a quick hug and made sure I was buckled in before she looked at Tom.

"I love you," she said.

He nodded. "Ditto," he said in a gruff voice that I didn't recognize.

I wasn't sure he could have gotten the words out even if he'd tried. He pulled out of the driveway and drove away without a glance in the mirror. His jaw was tight, and he reached over, flipping the radio on and scrolled through the stations until classic rock came on blaring Blue Oyster Cult.

Every song after had connotations regarding the devil or death, and Tom shivered. He reached for the dial and I grabbed his hand as "Sympathy for the Devil" transitioned into the very identifiable opening notes of a Kansas song.

It was suitable in our current situation, and it seemed to turn the tides of the choice of songs. The closer we got to the cottage, the more the music changed. It was as if the gods knew we needed something to change the course of our thoughts.

Once the tide changed, we sang every song. Loud. Off-key. With passion.

When we turned onto the dirt road that led through the woods to the cottage, Led Zeppelin came on in kick-ass fashion. Just the bass beat itself was enough to kick my heart into overdrive. It felt like a setup to battle, and as we rounded the last bend, I knew that was exactly what it was.

There, to the right of the cottage, was a tear in the fabric of the universe. It crackled and popped like a thousand tiny campfires. I could make out fingers lining the edges like the creatures inside were trying to tear it open. Every inch of the breach was covered.

Why here? What could connect Hell to this place?

I glanced at the cottage as my mind raced. Was there something inside that I could destroy and, therefore, cut off the connection?

"I don't think it works that way," Tom said. His voice carried defeat.

"What if my mother had something of his?" I asked.

"Like what?" Tom asked, mesmerized by the sizzling air in front of us.

"I don't know, but nothing is getting through yet. The place isn't much bigger than my bedroom at your place, so help me look to see if there is any reason why..."

"You created the breach. Not Lucifer," Tom said, his voice turning hard as he glanced at me.

"Can we at least get a few things before we attempt this?" I wanted to grab a couple of things if they were still here and suck down a bottle of Gatorade before I wiped myself out completely.

"We can't take too long. They are starting to make some headway." He nodded toward the light breaking the air.

"Okay. Come with?"

He let out a laugh. "You aren't going anywhere alone." He put the keys in the cup holder, and we climbed out together.

The inside was in the same state of disarray as when we'd left, except now there was no light. Tom pulled out his phone, shining it around the small space. I couldn't quite make out his expression until I reached one of our hurricane lamps and turned it on. The place bathed in light.

Tom looked truly perplexed as he glanced around the place. The one-room shack had a mattress on the floor, an old kitchen on the other side, and a tub and toilet with a curtain as a door. He covered his mouth and slowly ran his hand down to his chin.

I crossed to the desk across from the mattress and pulled open the drawer. Inside was my mother's journal, and next to it was an old Polaroid. I slid the picture into the journal and then glanced at the bookshelf. I chose three books, the vase that she and I had made in one of the pottery places in the next town over, and a mason jar filled with change. When I turned, I nodded, and he turned off the lamp. I pointed my chin towards the six-pack of Gatorade by the door. I stowed the meager items on the passenger seat floor and then crossed to meet him at the front of the truck.

I handed him the drink and opened mine, then downed it. I waited for the flip in my stomach to stop before I capped the empty bottle and set it on the truck.

"What's the plan?" Tom asked without looking at me.

"I figured if we both blast it, our combined power will close it." I peeled off my right glove and took his hand with my left one.

"I've never been able to control my angel fire," Tom admitted as we stepped into the middle of the clearing twenty yards from the breach.

I let out a nervous laugh. "I've only suppressed it, so I'm not very versed in control, either."

"Aren't we a pair?" he said with a smile. "Here goes nothing."

We tightened our grip on each other, and aimed our palms toward the crackling light. Flames licked my hand, but that was it. A small ray of white light sputtered from his. We both stared at our hands as if they were impotent tools.

I pulled my hand out of his grip. I nearly torched my face before I closed my hand. He fisted his hand before the angel fire shot into the stratosphere.

His eyes looked like wide anime eyes. I imagined I carried the same expression. We both turned and faced the breach.

"Let's try that again," he said, and the moment our hands opened, white and blue flame shot from our hands.

The moment it hit the breach, it was as if a thousand souls screamed. But it wasn't screams of pain; it was screams of joy. The breach opened wider.

"Jesus Christ!" Tom closed his palm and took a shaky step back. "We weakened it! Fuck!"

I screamed, pushing more power into my fire. The gap widened, and bodies started pushing through. Panic bloomed as the first charred figure fell through the breach. Its red eyes turned towards us and it smiled.

"God damn demons," Tom muttered.

I aimed my palm at the thing. Once they were on this side, they had no defense against the force of a human blowtorch, but that didn't help us. The minute I torched him, two more tumbled out.

"I'm coming for you," a voice carried through the breach. A voice I recognized, but my singular focus wouldn't allow me to draw a name.

Tom's face went deathly pale. "Give it everything you have."

I concentrated, grinding my teeth as more demons fell onto this side of the breach. When blue eyes peered out through my wall of fire, I gasped and renewed my effort, letting the overwhelming panic fuel the fire.

Lucifer was coming.

I threw not only flame, but force behind it. Force strong enough to rival category five hurricane gales, so those that broke through had to be strong.

A storm brewed overhead.

"You know what you have to do," Tom said, stepping close.

"No!" I screamed, using the grief that had snuck up on me as more fuel.

"You have to," Tom whispered. "It's either him or you, and I'm betting on you."

The roar of the wind surged around us, and I stared into Tom's eyes.

He tore his shirt open, revealing Raphael's sigil on his chest, and pointed at the breach. "If Lucifer gets through, I'm dead anyway."

"I can't." My throat tightened at the thought of eating a human heart. "You should have killed me that first day."

His gaze hardened. "Never think that. Ever. You understand?"

I nodded, feeling the full force of Tom's impending death even more than the loss of my mother. This was my fault.

His gaze flicked to the disturbance between worlds, and then he closed his eyes. Clenching his jaw, his skin broke open like a scalpel running down the length of his chest.

I gasped in horror. I couldn't imagine the pain, but the shake in his tight fists gripping his shirt conveyed it, anyway.

He cried out as bones snapped, and his rib cage ripped through his skin, giving me a clear view of his innards.

"Take the grace," he said, and his lungs inflated and deflated with his labored breath.

The fact he'd cracked open his own sternum terrified me, and the hold I had on the portal waned. Fire spit like crackling embers from my ungloved hand.

If I failed, Lucifer, along with the entirety of Hell, would be let loose on earth. The chaos and destruction would be unimaginable. Tom knew what kind of massacre would happen if my father got loose. He was willing to sacrifice his life to give me the only source of power that could stop it.

I reached into his chest with my gloved hand and grasped his heart. The beat of the muscle continued, and tears clouded my vision.

He met my gaze. "Do it," he commanded.

I screamed as I yanked his heart from his chest, and the fire flared brighter. I had no choice. If I didn't ingest his heart and absorb Lucifer's grace, my power wouldn't be strong enough to repair the rift. My father was already halfway through. If he made it to this side, mankind would perish.

My fire was the only thing keeping him from reaching this world.

I closed my eyes and shoved the still beating muscle into my mouth, then bit off half of it. The chewy consistency and warm blood made me gag, but I forced the bite down and kept eating until it was gone. I wouldn't let Tom die in vain.

He had once described what it was like to absorb grace, and he was right. With blood still dripping down my chin, my entire form went rigid as the grace of two angels and every ounce of Tom's gifts fused in my cells.

Memory upon memory clenched my muscles. Pain radiated outward, causing a chain reaction. I screamed but still held fast, blasting the portal with all I had.

I had no idea if Tom lived long enough to see my transformation. But I got a good view of it in the reflection of the cottage windows. Wings of fire formed on my back, burning into my skin before they turned as black as the void. The fire flowing from my hand tripled in strength, turning into white-hot angel fire, annihilating the rift between worlds and anything in its path.

When the searing agony abated, I was left with only sparks in the air, the closed portal, and Tom's dead body at my feet. My chest constricted, and I dropped to my knees. I pressed his hand to my lips as my tears drenched his stiff fingers.

"Just remember to keep your promise," Tom's voice rang in the clearing.

I looked up and blinked at Tom's ghostly figure. I nodded, trying to get a hold of the power snaking through my form. Lucifer's grace was darkness personified, and it wanted to rule in my blood. Tom had carried this massive responsibility around for the last fifteen years, and I felt the weight of it smothering me. I had promised Tom that I would always reject the darkness, no matter how seductive it seemed.

"I will remember," I whispered.

Tom smiled and faded into the smoky mist surrounding me.

I didn't know how long I kneeled next to Tom and cried. But when my mind finally kick-started back into order, I glanced at what he had done to his chest. I couldn't bring him home looking like this, so I closed my eyes and tapped into what he had given me. Tom's repairing of the living room window came to mind, and I wished his chest closed.

Sweat broke out on my forehead as I envisioned his ribs back in place, and his skin fused together, unbroken. When I opened my eyes, his chest still lay open.

"Damn it," I whispered. I let go of his hand, placed my palms on the skin on the outside of the shattered ribs, and pushed. They collapsed in with a sickening crack. At least his chest was no longer open, but I had no clue how I was going to get him into the truck.

I climbed to my feet and took hold of his ankles. Dragging him to the truck took more energy than I thought I had, but somehow, I found enough reserves to get him to the side of the truck.

I struggled to get him over my shoulder to get him in the back. Tears heated my face with frustration and grief. I didn't realize I was sobbing until I got him into the truck and closed the back door.

I buried my face in my hands and fell to my knees. What the Hell was I going to tell them? That my bright idea nearly cost us the world? That it did cost Bridget and April their world?

"I knew this was a one-way ticket," Tom's voice echoed in my brain. "They knew it, too."

His words didn't help the devastation riding hot waves through my veins, but it gave me the strength to get to my feet. I wiped my face, and my gaze landed on the smoldering pile of bodies under where the rift had been.

Nothing moved at first, and then the pile fell away. One charred body rolled towards me. Blue eyes peered from a blackened face.

I gasped.

I knew those eyes.

Those were the eyes of my father.

The End

Continue reading FIRE CURSED TRILOGY on
the following page with book two in the trilogy:
HOMECOMING

Homecoming
Chapter 1

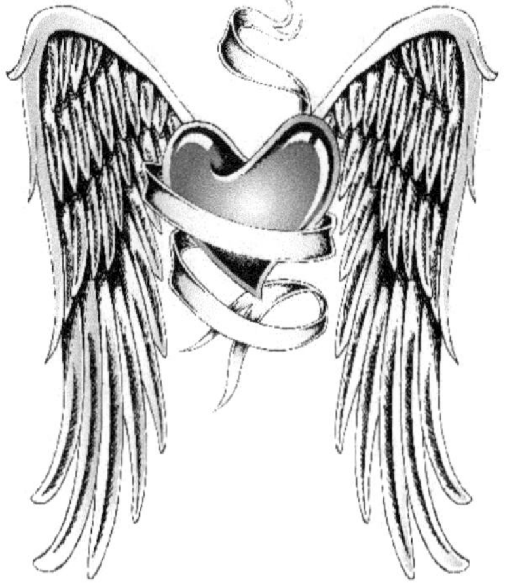

DRIVING WITHOUT A LICENSE with a dead body in the back seat probably wasn't my brightest idea. I didn't give too much thought to my current predicament until the flashing lights and siren filled my rear window.

I swallowed the last bit of spit, and it felt like I was trying to ingest a handful of spikes. I glimpsed my face in the rearview mirror. There was no wiping the amount of blood smeared on me away. If the officer pulled me over, I would land in jail, and I was still way too close to where Lucifer was to take that chance.

"You aren't chasing me," I whispered, wishing it to be so.

The police car changed lanes and flew by me.

I uttered a high-pitched laugh. I wasn't sure if that had resulted from my words or just dumb luck, but either way, I would take it. I wasn't going insanely fast, like Tom had driven up to the cabin. But I wasn't going the speed limit either.

I wanted home.

I wanted Alex's arms.

I wanted someone to tell me what I did was okay.

I didn't know if I would get any of those things.

My vision blurred.

I wiped away my tears and focused on the road. Pushing the pedal to the floor was tempting, but that was a surefire way to land in a world of trouble.

I glanced at the body lying prone on the back seat. Tom Ryan had died to save the world, but it had been all for nothing. Lucifer still got out before I could shut down the breach between our world and Hell.

Instead of wallowing in growing despair, I focused on what had happened the moment I ate the last of Tom's heart. My stomach lurched, and I swallowed back the bile. I had no idea what would happen if I vomited now. I certainly couldn't do it at eighty miles per hour.

Tom's memories swarmed in my head. But it wasn't just his memories. It was so many others going back thousands of years to a time when archangels walked among us. My hands trembled with the sheer volume in my head. It rivaled the aching power pulsing just underneath my skin.

I didn't have the first clue of how to use the arsenal I now had. I quickly realized that when I tried to close Tom's chest, and nothing happened. But I sure felt every ounce of the power inside me. I thought my fire power was strong. This little infusion of angel magic made all my cells hum.

I reached the town of York at a little after midnight. My muscles ached with the tension tightening my body. I drove past Tom and Bridget's house. I couldn't face either Bridget or his Tom's daughter, April, right now.

A lump formed in my throat, and I couldn't swallow. By the time I rolled up to the keypad at CJ's gate, my entire form shook, and tears blurred my vision. I didn't even have to roll my window down. The gate opened at the same time as the front door, and the blindingly pure light of CJ's aura shined on the front walkway, making me squint.

I pulled into the driveway, put the truck in park, and engaged the parking brake like Tom had taught me. That small activity brought the sobs back while I climbed out of the car. I made it two steps before I dropped to my knees on the walkway and buried my face in my hands.

"Where's Tom?" CJ asked, and his voice carried worry that I couldn't deal with.

I pointed at the truck. All I could do was shake my head.

CJ stumbled to his knees next to me. "He's dead?"

His words pierced my heart, along with his raw emotions. I felt the loss as if I were CJ, and it was crushing. I glanced up to see a stream of tears rolling down his face as he stared at the truck.

"We failed," I squeaked out between sobs. "It was all for nothing."

His gaze jumped to mine and widened.

A blur of motion came towards me, and then arms wrapped around me. It took a second to realize Alex had been the one to hug me, not CJ, but his presence didn't stop the tears. It didn't stop the churn of my stomach or the heat building inside me at my failure.

Alex helped me to my feet and led me towards the front door, leaving his father kneeling on the brick pavers.

There was no consoling CJ. His emotions flowed over me like a suffocating wave of fire. Even as Alex sat me on the couch and brought a wet towel to wipe my face, I couldn't climb out from under the weight of CJ's despair.

Alex cupped my chin and lifted it so I would meet his gaze. "Are you hurt?" he asked, and then glanced down at the soiled cloth in his hand. His worried blue-eyes waited for an answer.

I shook my head, unable to articulate while I studied Alex's aura. Light still shined, but it was much duller than CJ's. My heart constricted in my chest, and the horror of what I'd unleashed prickled my skin.

His brow creased as he lowered in front of me. "Uncle Tom?"

"He..." My throat tightened, and I couldn't say the words. How could I tell Alex that I'd ingested his uncle's heart? That he was dead, and even with Lucifer's grace riding my blood, we hadn't won? How could I tell him he was now in real danger of becoming the devil's vessel?

He glanced outside. "Where is Uncle Tom?"

"In the backseat."

He stood, but I grabbed his hand, shaking my head.

"Don't," I said.

"I'm okay. And if you are okay, I think I need to help my father." He gave me a soft smile. "I guess there are some benefits to being nearly soulless."

I nodded. His father's emotions were still pounding into me like the waves on the rocks outside. But there was very little emanating from Alex. He left me. A few minutes later, he brought his father inside and sat him on the couch.

"Should I call Aunt Bridget?" Alex asked.

CJ looked up at his son and then over at me, his face scrunching as a new set of tears tracked down his cheeks. He wiped them away and took a shaky breath. "I'll call her." He stood and headed upstairs.

Alex resumed cleaning the blood off of me. His gentle touch kept drawing new tears.

Overwhelmed. That was the only thought that surfaced. I was not handling this very well, considering I had watched cancer kill my mother.

But I was not the cause of my mother's cancer. I caused Tom's death and probably of all those who surrounded me here. All that I loved would be destroyed because I wasn't strong enough to keep Lucifer in his rightful cage.

"Show me," Alex whispered.

I shook my head. The time jump had caused the breach before. I couldn't guarantee another one would break open if I did it again, and I did not want to be responsible for Hell's army being released. It was bad enough Lucifer had survived.

"Were you able to close the breach?" he asked.

"Yes." My voice shook as if I had a teeth-clacking shiver. "But he still got loose."

Alex searched my gaze, and then slowly sat down on the coffee table in front of me. He closed his eyes, and his thoughts swarmed my head.

I didn't need to tell him the horrifying truth. He already knew.

"Well, then." He opened his eyes. "I will need to be extra vigilant."

I nodded, and a fresh wave of tears heated my face. "I can't even protect you," I whispered.

"Don't you have Uncle Tom's gifts now?"

"I have no idea," I said. "I tried to close his chest with whatever this is turning my bones to jelly inside me, but I failed at that, too." I hung my head.

"What exactly happened?" CJ asked from the stairwell.

The room twisted out of focus and I tried to stop the time jump from happening by clamping my eyes shut, but it was out of my control. When I opened my eyes, we were all outside the little cottage.

I glanced up at Alex as hot panic welled up in my blood. I did not want them to actually see Tom's death. It had been so brutal, so awful. My stomach did a slow roll, and I swallowed the sour bile that crawled up my throat.

"WHAT'S THE PLAN?" TOM asked, looking at the ground.

"I figured if we both blast it, our combined power will close it," she said.

I stared at my likeness and shivered. It was strange seeing myself, and now I understood the unease of both Tom and CJ when they'd witnessed my time jumps.

"I've never been able to control my angel fire." Tom said, and they stepped into the middle of the clearing twenty yards from the breach.

Her nervous laughter filled the tense air. "I've only suppressed mine, so I'm not very versed in control, either."

"Aren't we a pair?" he said with a smile. "Here goes nothing."

They aimed their palms toward the crackling light. Flames licked her hand, but that was it. A small ray of white light sputtered from his. They both stared at their hands with open mouths and creased brows.

She pulled her hand out of his grip and nearly torched her face before her fist closed. He closed his hand before the angel fire shot into the stratosphere.

Their eyes looked like wide anime eyes, and they both turned toward the breach in unison.

"Let's try that again," he said, and the moment their hands opened, white and blue flame shot from their palms.

Seeing us in action was spectacular and humbling. My chest squeezed because we should have been able to close the breach with our separate powers, but the opposite happened. The hole stretched, and screams of joy filled the air from the other side of the breach. That same sick feeling that had blanketed me at my cabin gripped me again.

"Jesus Christ!" Tom closed his palm and took a shaky step back. "We weakened it! Fuck!"

She screamed, and the flare from her palm brightened and only served to increase the gap. Bodies started pushing through the portal. Her face turned red with the effort, and tears tracked down her cheeks.

The first red-eyed demon smiled as it fell onto the earth, despite the shower of fire Faith aimed at it, but it finally charred under the blast.

"God damned demons," Tom muttered.

The more demons she torched on this side of the portal, the more broke through.

A voice carried through the breach. "I'm coming for you."

Tom's face went deathly pale. "Give it everything you have."

Her lips pressed together, and her eyes narrowed. The fire coming from her palm turned blue with white flares. The hottest color of fire, but blue eyes still peered out through her wall of fire. She screamed, and wind accompanied the fire rippling the demon's clothing before fire charred it.

A storm brewed overhead.

"You know what you have to do," Tom said, stepping close to her.

I wanted to stop the time jump. I didn't want them to see what I had to do to close the damn breach, but I couldn't pull this back. I screamed at the same time as my image, and Alex wrapped his arms around me from behind. Even his touch didn't stop the vision.

"No!" she screamed.

"You have to," Tom whispered. "It's either him or you, and I'm betting on you."

The roar of the wind surged around them.

He tore his shirt open, revealing Raphael's sigil on his chest, and pointed at the breach. "If Lucifer gets through, I'm dead anyway."

"I can't. You should have killed me that first day."

His gaze hardened. "Never think that. Ever. You understand?"

She nodded, her chin trembling.

His gaze flicked to the disturbance between worlds, and then he closed his eyes. Clenching his jaw, his skin broke open like a scalpel running down the length of his chest.

My image wasn't the only one who gasped. CJ shared the same horror I had, and his hand covered his mouth.

Tom's arms shook as he gripped his shirt. He cried out as bones snapped. His rib cage ripped through his skin, giving her a clear view of his innards.

"Take the grace," he said, and his lungs inflated and deflated with his labored breath.

Fire spit like crackling embers from her ungloved hand. She reached into his chest with her gloved hand and grasped his heart. The beat of the muscle continued, and tears streamed down her cheeks.

"Do it," he commanded.

She screamed as she yanked his heart from his chest, and the fire flared brighter.

Lucifer was already halfway through the portal.

Her fire was the only thing keeping him from reaching this world.

She closed her eyes and shoved the still-beating muscle into her mouth, then bit off half of it. She gagged, but continued to eat through her sobs until the heart was gone.

My stomach rolled, and I swallowed the bile lining my throat.

With blood still dripping down her chin, her form went rigid. Wings of fire formed on her back, burning until blackened. The fire flowing from her hand tripled in strength, turning into white-hot angel fire, annihilating the rift between worlds and anything in its path.

When the fire faded to only sparks, she dropped to her knees and pressed Tom's hand to her lips.

The ghostly figure of Tom materialized next to her. "Just remember to keep your promise." His voice rang in the clearing.

"I will remember," she whispered.

He smiled and faded into the smoky mist.

She closed her eyes, and a crease of concentration along with a layer of sweat broke out on her forehead. When she opened her eyes, her lips turned down in disappointment.

"Damn it," she whispered, and let go of his hand.

She placed her palms on the skin outside of his shattered ribs and pushed. They collapsed with a sickening crack.

She sat back on her heels and wiped her face as she stared at his prone form. With effort, she

If Tom had just been unconscious, the scene
would have proven to be comical, but the fact I
was struggling to put his dead body in the car
created a solemn atmosphere.

I BLINKED, AND WE were all back in CJ's family
room. Alex's expression hadn't changed, but
CJ's was tight, like he was trying to hold
whatever he had eaten earlier this evening
inside. His cheeks bloomed with patches of red
over the green hue that had colored the rest of
his face. He walked to the bathroom around the
corner and the sound of retching reached us.

I couldn't say I blamed him. I wished I could vomit, but I kept my stomach in check. I still didn't know what throwing up Tom's heart would do. From what I'd gathered from his memories, he'd had the same struggle and the same conclusion that something bad would happen if he didn't digest the muscle fully.

"So, you now have Lucifer's grace," Alex said, breaking the silence.

I nodded. "And I can see auras, and I saw his ghost, so I guess I got some of Tom's gifts. I don't know what is what, but my skin feels like it is going to fly off in a million directions at any moment."

The toilet flushed, and CJ came out just as car lights pulled into the driveway. He closed his eyes and took a deep breath, wiping his face.

He glanced at Alex. "I need wood in the backyard."

"Why?"

CJ sighed and tilted his head. His mind broadcast two words, and I shivered.

Funeral pyre.

Homecoming
Chapter 2

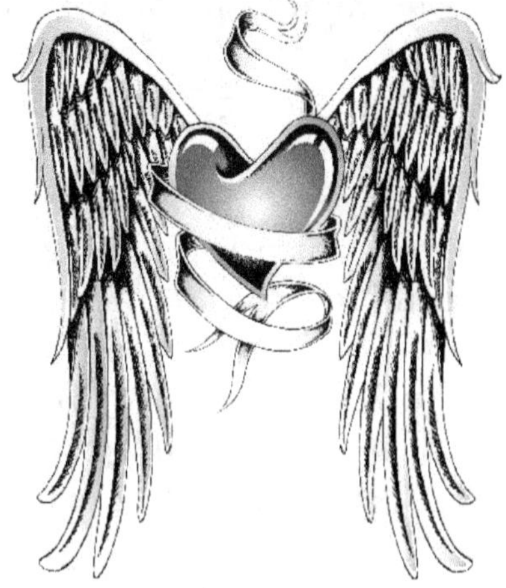

I WENT WITH ALEX into the backyard lit by the floodlights on the house, unable to face Tom's family. Unfortunately, I was no longer buffered from their emotions. I had a hard time standing on my feet, but focusing on building what was asked helped.

Alex must have known I wasn't coping well, because he didn't say a word. When he handed me wood, he made sure to touch my hands and meet my gaze. When we had a pile of wood that was four feet high and at least six feet long, I stepped back and stared at what looked like a cord of wood. The top was indented for the length of the pile.

"I think it will be a while before he comes for us," I said, thinking of Lucifer's charred form.

Alex nodded. "Did you want to clean up?"

"Not yet." I didn't want to traipse through the house at the moment. Besides, I had no clothing here, and from the inappropriate thoughts swarming Alex's head, it would open up a situation I wasn't ready to be in.

"Should we try to bring Tom back here?" Alex asked.

I didn't know if we could manage Tom's six-foot, two-hundred-pound dead weight on our own, but it would certainly mean CJ wouldn't have to get him on the pyre. Of course, CJ probably could just move him with his mind, but he was still battling the crushing loss.

Alex raised an eyebrow, waiting for my answer.

"He's really heavy." I shifted my weight and bit my lip.

"You got him in the truck on your own," he said, hooking his thumb over his shoulder.

Heat filled my cheeks, and I shrugged. I was hopped up on adrenaline at the time. My muscles were just starting to ache from the exertion of moving Tom and then moving close to a cord of wood. I wasn't sure I had it in me to move him to the backyard. But if it meant CJ and Bridget wouldn't have to, I could suck it up and help.

I nodded.

He took my hand in his and led me around the house. The truck still sat shrouded in darkness. I shivered at the thought of touching Tom's lifeless form, but Alex didn't seem fazed by it at all.

We opened the back door of the truck and stared at the empty, blood-smeared seat. My eyes widened, and I glanced toward the front door. I couldn't imagine them bringing his bloody body into the house, but perhaps they did.

We closed the door and headed inside.

"Dad?" Alex called as we stepped into the foyer.

CJ came around the corner, the crease between his eyes broadcasting his concern just as much as his mind. "Tom's not in the truck?"

We shook our heads. My heart thundered. If CJ didn't bring his body inside...

My breath wheezed in my chest as I spun on my heels, racing outside and around to the passenger side of the truck. Lights over the garage blinked on, bathing the area with brightness. CJ and Alex skidded to a stop behind me. A trail of blood and matted grass led toward the burned-out Andreas lot.

Both CJ and Alex muttered, "Grace."

"What the Hell would she want with Tom's body?" I said before the truth hit.

And it hit hard. Lucifer. If he had a body to inhabit, even one with his chest cut open, he would heal much faster than the burned husk I'd left at the cabin in Northern, Maine.

"Bridget and April are here, right?" Alex asked.

"Yes." He took a deep breath. "The last time he was injured, he powered up on angel blood."

I gasped. "Do you think Grace would sacrifice her family?" They were the only angel descendants not at CJ's house.

"I don't know." CJ shook his head and glanced at Alex. "I didn't think she would turn on us the way she did, either. So, I just don't know."

"What about Austin?" Alex asked.

CJ huffed, turned, and jogged toward the house. His mind was unreadable, but the fluttering of colors through his aura told me enough. I didn't need to hear his thoughts.

Paige and Austin trusted Tom. If Grace had stolen Tom's body for Lucifer, and Tom's likeness showed up at their door, they would let him in.

I stepped into the kitchen with Alex and CJ. Bridget and April sat on the couch. April's aura shined like the rest of the angel descendants, but Bridget's aura was so muted that it surprised me. Then again, all I had seen since I came back with Tom's gifts were angel offspring, so seeing a normal human aura was jarring and welcoming at the same time.

Bridget looked up, and a lump formed in my throat. Her pain was as acute as CJ's, bringing fresh tears to my eyes. At least Alex had cleaned off my face, so I wasn't covered in her husband's blood like I had been when I arrived.

She stood and crossed, then wrapped me in her arms. "Thank you for bringing him home," she whispered in my ear.

I closed my eyes, and tears burned my throat. "You might not want to thank me yet," I squeezed out. "I didn't lock the truck when I came inside."

Bridget pulled away and studied my face. Then she turned as CJ walked into the room with his cell phone to his ear.

"Tom is dead." CJ's gaze snapped to mine. "Get Austin away from him, now. Use magic. Use whatever the Hell you need to. That is not Tom. It's Lucifer."

Bridget gasped and looked at me.

"Grace," Alex interjected.

Bridget closed her eyes and brought me into a hug. "I'm so sorry you had to go through that, sweetheart."

The screams coming from the phone line echoed in my head, and I held CJ's gaze. Fury filled his eyes, and he squeezed the phone enough to crack the screen. The laugh that followed chilled me to the core.

I broke free of Bridget and crossed, putting my hand out. He blinked at me, like he didn't understand, so I snagged the phone from him.

"Next time, you won't be so lucky," I said into the phone.

A chuckle filled the line. "Are you sure about that, little girl?"

I met CJ's gaze. "Yes. Because of you, I lost the closest thing I had to a father. I will end you."

Silence filled the line. "You don't want to reunite with your dear old dad?"

"Why? So, you can rip my heart out?"

"From what I understand, it seems Grace may have already done that."

"You have been poorly misinformed."

"I have made a deal with that wild tiger. She can either deliver your heart to me, or your boy to me. Either way, I will deliver his soul to her." He paused. "Unless, of course, you would like to bring me the boy yourself."

"I will see you in Hell before I do that."

"So be it."

The line went dead.

I handed CJ his phone and turned, heading into the living room where no one was gathered. Three people had died today because of me. Guilt bit at my skin, creating an uncomfortable tightness in my chest. I sat on the stairs and covered my face.

Warmth radiated near me, and then a hand landed on my back as a body settled on the stair next to me. Silence prevailed. No thoughts came through, and I finally glanced over.

April sat next to me, her eyes red and puffy.

"I am so sorry about your father," I said with an unsteady voice.

She wrapped her arms around me in a tight hug. "You need to find that knife. It's the only way. Otherwise, the world will burn."

"Why me?" I whispered in her ear.

"You are the only one now. My uncle won't be able to. Not when Lucifer is wearing family." She pulled away and stared at me.

Her words chilled me more than seeing the empty truck seat. I shivered. I wasn't sure I could do what she was asking, no matter how sure I'd sounded on the phone.

"I failed once already," I said. "And now people are dead."

"I know. But I've seen the alternative..." She shook her head slowly.

I caught a glimpse of whatever vision April had seen.

Walls painted with blood. Bodies torn to bits. Smoke-filled air. Fanned red hair draped over a chair.

It took me a moment to realize it was *my* hair. In April's vision, I was laid out like a sacrificial lamb, with a hole in my chest the size of a man's fist.

Homecoming
Chapter 3

"I DON'T KNOW," BRIDGET said.

"You should stay here," CJ said.

Valerie nodded with eyes as haunted as CJ's. "He's already killed Austin and Paige."

"I know." Bridget glanced at April and me sitting on the couch. "It's just that..." She closed her eyes and took a breath. "I need to get our things," she said after a moment.

"We will help," CJ said.

"Really?" Annoyance crept through Bridget's grief, giving her voice a hard edge.

"No one in this family is going it alone." CJ crossed his arms.

Bridget moved the truck over to the side of the garage so CJ could access their cars. I piled into the back seat of Bridget's car, and Alex rode with me instead of the rest of his family.

He laced his fingers with mine as we sat in the dark of the back seat. Bridget didn't speak as she drove to the house. When she pulled into the driveway, she slammed the brakes and gasped.

A figure sitting on the steps looked up into the bright headlights and smiled in a chillingly familiar manner. His chin was still smeared with blood and his hands were painted crimson.

"Tom?" Bridget whispered and threw the gear into park.

I was out of the car before either she or CJ could step foot on the asphalt. I shut the door before Alex could follow. He was in more danger than anyone else here. He banged on the window, but I ignored him.

My senses were on high alert. I peeled both gloves off and slid them in my back pocket. Rage seeped in, turning my blood into liquid fire, and I balled my hands into fists to control the storm.

I caught motion out of the corner of my right eye. I raised my hand and opened my palm without looking away from Lucifer. A blast of angel fire streaked across the front lawn.

A yelp of pain followed, and the stench of burned fur filled the air. I didn't take my gaze away from Lucifer in Tom's form. I had the feeling if I did, someone else would die.

"Why did you come here?" I asked in a voice I barely recognized. It was raw and shaking with fury.

"I need more fuel to heal the wounds you inflicted on this body." Lucifer stood and waved to his bloodied chest.

I stepped to the front of the car, putting myself between Lucifer and those I cared about, and raised my hand.

"Tsk, tsk. You wouldn't want to annihilate your boyfriend's soul, would you?" He picked up the silver chain around his neck and swung the glowing orb at the end of it back and forth.

Damn him.

"I will kill you," I said, but I couldn't bring myself to open my hand to do just that. Not with the promise of Alex's soul dangling in front of me.

His smug smile burned.

I couldn't harm Alex's soul, but I could do enough damage to make it difficult for him to get around. Instead of blasting him full-on, I lowered my hand enough for his smile to disappear.

I splayed my hand and suppressed the angel fire, opting to only shoot my natural fire instead.

He dove out of the way, but he wasn't fast enough. The side of his jeans closest to the house caught fire, and I closed my hand. He rolled on the ground, trying to douse the flames. When only smoke trailed from him, a blur of fur flew from behind the house, grabbed him by the collar, and carried him into the woods before I could take another shot. The last thing that registered before they disappeared was the blackened streak across the tiger's side.

The trees beyond where he had been standing caught fire. I sighed. Creaks of multiple car doors pulled me around to face my family.

"Why did you lock us in?" CJ said, approaching me. Valerie and the girls were still in his car.

Alex came to stand by my side as Bridget and April ran for the front door.

I blinked at him and glanced at the cars before I shrugged. I hadn't consciously prevented them from leaving the vehicles.

"I couldn't even override whatever you did," he said.

"I wasn't aware I was doing anything." I turned towards the building fire. "I need to help get our stuff out before the house catches fire."

"It won't catch fire. I'll make certain, and I'll also make sure they don't come back." CJ leaned against the car, crossed his arms, and closed his eyes.

The power rolled through me, and I caught my breath. I could actually see the protective barrier grow to encompass the cars and the house. It sparked with raw energy.

I didn't want to know what would happen if someone inadvertently ran into it. I turned with Alex and ran into the house to help Bridget and April pack their things. I wished the skies would open up and drown out the fire and the house wouldn't be harmed, but I couldn't focus on that. Instead, I grabbed the shopping bags stowed in my closet and dumped all the clothing we had purchased a few days ago into them. In the bathroom, I did the same thing. The sum of my belongings fit into two large bags and my backpack.

Alex took those down to the car for me, and I stepped into April's room. She had two suitcases out on the bed and was standing in front of her closet like a lost deer.

"Show me your favorite outfit?" I asked.

She turned to me, blinking as if I had just pulled her from a stupor. This time, when she turned to the closet, she grabbed three dresses and two pairs of sandals and dumped them into the suitcase. I grabbed a pair of bright cowboy boots that looked awesome with jeans and put them next to her suitcase.

April gathered her favorite outfits from her drawers and at least a week's worth of undergarments and stuffed them into the suitcase. The pile was so high I doubted she could close the thing, but she managed to. Then she did the same with the other one. Since she already had two overstuffed bags, she grabbed her little overnight bag and went into the bathroom to pack up her toiletries.

Instead of waiting for her to finish, I trotted down to Bridget's room. She sat on the edge of her bed in the same near-catatonic state I had found April in. I crossed toward her and took her hand. Whatever had clouded her mind cleared as she met my gaze.

Her chin trembled, and she bit her bottom lip. "He offered me a life with Tom's likeness..."

I swallowed hard at the longing in her eyes. "At what price?"

A tear crested and slipped down her cheek, and she squeezed my hand. "He said he would spare April," she whispered and reached out. Her hand covered my heart as another tear slipped down her cheek.

"No!"

We both turned toward April's harsh tone.

She glared at her mother. "That would be against everything Dad stood for, and his sacrifice would have been for nothing. Put the knife down. Now." April's hair blew in a non-existent breeze, and thunder cracked outside the window.

My gaze snapped to Bridget's other hand. A sharp butcher knife gleamed in the light.

Bridget glanced at it, too. For the first time since I'd stepped into the house, Bridget's thoughts and emotions bubbled up to the surface, where I could hear them.

I tried to pull out of her grip, but she held tight and raised the blade. Heat engulfed my hands, and I clenched my free fist so the fire wouldn't get away from me.

She cried out, but didn't break her grasp.

I didn't want to hurt her. Despite the conflict in her eyes, I knew she didn't really want to hurt me, either. She wasn't in control, and I had a fleeting moment to wonder if perhaps Grace was being manipulated by the master puppeteer himself.

"Mom, stop!"

I put my arm up to block the blow, but before the metal hit my flesh, the knife flew out of her grip and embedded into the wall.

Another clap of thunder sounded. I ripped my hand from Bridget's, closing my fist as flames licked my fingers.

Alex stood beyond April, his eyes as wide as hers.

Bridget slumped down on the bed and her mind went blank.

I turned back to her and then looked at Alex and April. "Get her to the car. I'll pack some things for her."

They both hustled across the room and did as I directed. I grabbed the suitcases in the closet and packed some things for Bridget. I stopped and stared at the laundry basket. The flannel shirt Tom had worn a couple of days ago sat on top. After a moment, I grabbed that and added it to the mix in the suitcases.

Alex met me at the top of the stairs and took the bags from me. Without a word, he led me outside, threw the bags into the car, and then slid into the driver's seat. CJ headed back to his car.

I stopped. Rain poured on the driveway a few feet away from where the cars sat. I was perfectly dry, and so was the walkway to the front door. I turned toward the road, and rain bounced off the pavement. I glanced at CJ, and he shrugged.

The sky had been clear when we arrived. So clear that I could see the Big Dipper as we drove across town. I glanced towards the woods that had been burning when I went inside. Steam rose from the dampened fire.

I opened the passenger door and climbed inside the car.

The minute CJ's barrier came down, rain pelted the cars, but by the time we turned the corner, the rain stopped. I glanced out the back window at the solid curtain of rain and then the clear sky out the front window.

A sensation tickled my mind, and I turned back. The rain trickled to a stop as if someone in

Heaven had turned off the faucet. I blinked and settled back in the seat as we followed CJ back home.

Bridget stirred as we pulled to a stop outside the garage, but her thoughts were just static, like an old car radio out of range from any signal. I didn't know if her mind was still compromised. I grabbed my bags from the trunk and made my way into the family room with Alex and April.

Bridget was the only one under CJ's roof who wasn't of angel blood, and that made me uncomfortable. Especially considering her warped thought process just before she'd tried to kill me.

"Is it okay if I clean up?" I asked CJ and Valerie. I stood near the cracked garage door with my bags.

"That's fine." CJ looked from me to Alex. "Put her in your room. You'll sleep downstairs with the girls."

Alex took my bags and headed upstairs. I followed as Bridget stumbled into the house, looking like my mother had after she'd had too much to drink.

"What happened?" she asked, rubbing her eyes.

"You tried to kill her, Mom," April said.

I didn't wait to hear the rest, not with the tears stinging my eyes.

Alex put my bags down and wrapped his arms around me. He kissed my temple and held me at arm's length.

"How did you do all that?" he asked.

"Do what?"

"The cars? The rain? The knife at Bridget's house?"

"That wasn't me," I said, but even as the words escaped my lips, doubt laced my mind. Hadn't I wished for rain to douse the fire? The cars were just a protective reflex. I couldn't explain the knife, except I knew I didn't want to hurt Bridget.

Alex let go of me, crossed his arms, and raised a skeptical eyebrow.

"If it was me, I have no idea what I did. Where are the towels?" I asked to change the subject.

"The closet in the bathroom has bath towels and different shampoos inside."

I turned and headed into the bathroom, then closed the door on any more conversation. I found the towels and set a couple on the floor near the tub before I peeled my tacky clothing off and piled it neatly on the closed lid of the toilet. Then I stepped into the tub.

The first spray of water was frigid, and I clamped my mouth closed on a yelp. I forced myself to remain under the stream and was rewarded with the slow warming of the water. When it was hot enough to sting, I dialed it back a fraction to a comfortable heat and just stood under the spray until the water at my feet ran clear. I didn't realize how much blood had seeped under my shirt.

I scrubbed my skin, trying to reconcile all that I had seen tonight. The shower lulled me into an exhausted stupor. By the time I finished, the pads covering the bites I had gotten from Grace a few days ago were soaked through. After I lathered my hair and rinsed, and then just stood under the water until I was sure I would collapse if I didn't get out and get to a bed.

With my hair wrapped in a towel and my body dried the best I could, I wrapped a second towel around my chest, tucking it in place. The drenched gauze over my stitches peeled off easily, and I threw them away before I picked up my soiled clothing. I stepped across the hall into the room, ignoring the chatter downstairs.

The hall light illuminated the room, and I crossed to the desk and placed my bloodied outfit on the chair. Alex had laid out a nightgown and underwear on the bed, and the rest of my clothing was neatly stacked on the desk.

For someone without most of his soul, he sure was a sweetheart. I towel dried my hair and grabbed the brush he also had put on the desk. I ran the brush through my hair, wincing at the new aches and pains coming to the surface now that every ounce of adrenaline had been tapped.

"You need help?"

I hadn't heard him come into the room. I hadn't even heard his thoughts among the din filling my head.

Alex closed the door and crossed to me, then took the brush from my hand.

"You did all this?" I waved at my unpacked belongings.

"I figured if I didn't, you would just do a faceplant on the bed in a towel."

He wasn't wrong, but the fact that I was only in a towel and he was less than two feet away from me heated my skin more than the shower had. When he stepped behind me and gently ran the brush through my hair, I thought I was in heaven for a moment.

"Why didn't you kill him tonight?" he asked after a few minutes of bliss.

"He was wearing a necklace that contained your soul."

His gentle stroking stopped, and he stepped to my side, hooked his finger under my chin, and turned my head so I met his gaze. "Next time, even if he is wearing my soul, you take the shot. Understand?" His blue eyes blazed through me.

I glanced away.

"Faith."

I looked back at him and pointed to the rest of my matted hair. He obliged, but this time, his strokes weren't nearly as gentle.

"Are you mad at me?" I asked as he continued to take his frustrations out on the knots in the tangled mess on my head.

He didn't answer until he finished and set the brush on the table. He moved in front of me and cupped my shoulders tenderly.

"Yes, and no." He glanced down at the towel between us and reached for the edge that was tucked in.

I covered his hand, acutely aware of the desire brewing inside him. "I'm not ready."

He stepped closer and leaned down, then pressed his lips to mine.

Damn. The boy's kiss clouded my judgement enough for my hand to loosen, and the towel slipped between us. His arms wrapped around me, turning us so the back of my legs pressed against the bed.

He broke the kiss and slipped my nightgown over my head with a crooked smile. "While I'd love to take advantage of you right now, I know you'd kick my ass in the morning." He reached over and handed me my underwear.

Then he busied himself with hanging the towels over the back of the chair while I slid my panties on and straightened out my nightgown.

"What do you want me to do with these?" He pointed at the ruined leather.

"They can't go in the washing machine." The leather glove incident at Bridget's taught me enough about leather and normal washing machines.

"I'll ask my mom how to get them cleaned because I have a feeling you will need your kickass outfit again really soon."

The warmth he had created evaporated with those words. I didn't want to think about my next battle. I obviously was unprepared for any of this, and I needed to figure out how I'd made things happen today if I had a prayer of defeating Lucifer.

"I am going to need to find that knife that Fate mentioned. April thinks that's the key to getting rid of Lucifer for good." I met his gaze.

Any hint of a smile faded. "That means you have to get within his reach to do any damage." He shook his head. "I'd much rather you stay as far away from him as you can."

I closed the distance between us and pressed my palm to his cheek. "I am okay with getting within his reach if it means I can erase him from existence."

A crease appeared between his eyes. "Does erasing him from existence mean he never existed? Or does it mean from this point forward?"

"It doesn't matter. If I don't, the world will burn."

Homecoming
Chapter 4

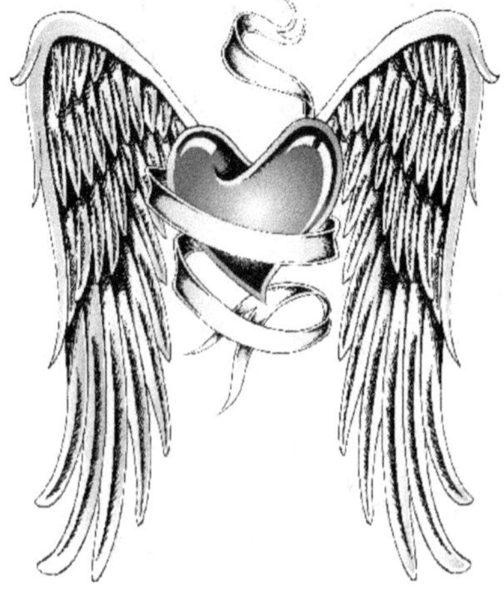

MY SCREAM ECHOED OFF the walls. I sat up in a dark room as the nightmares chased me awake. The bedroom door slammed open, and light framed a man in the doorway. I shivered and pulled the blankets tighter around me.

"What's wrong?" the shadow asked.

I blinked and then looked at the man again. "Alex?"

"Who else would you think would be at your door?" He stepped inside and closed the door before switching on the overhead light.

I squinted from the sudden brightness. "I thought you were downstairs with your sisters."

He shook his head. "Bridget is down in the basement on the couch, and Dad's downstairs in the family room. After what happened at the house, they all thought it was safer for everyone. April is sleeping with Amber and Ariana in their room, and I'm in the guest room down the hall." He hooked his thumb behind him.

He crossed to the side of the bed and took a seat next to me. "Are you okay?"

I didn't know how to answer him.

The nightmare still lingered, and I didn't know how to articulate it. Blood. Smoke. Fire. And endless screaming. But it was the last image that had brought my scream to the surface.

And that image remained like a sick joke— Grace bent over a table with Alex screwing her as the glowing necklace that Lucifer had worn bounced against her chest in time with his thrusts. My dead eyes had stared on as blood seeped out of the hole in my chest.

My stomach rolled, and I covered my mouth, willing myself not to empty the contents all over the bed. I pushed him aside and launched myself towards the bathroom. I made it to the toilet just as hot, bitter bile spilled over between my fingers. The plume of liquid was vile, and I gagged again.

When I was certain there was no more, I flushed the toilet and washed my hands before I rinsed my mouth and cleaned the taste out with toothpaste. My legs wobbled as I crossed back into the bedroom.

Alex still sat on the edge of my bed, and I was so thankful he hadn't followed to witness the bloody gore that had come from my stomach. I crawled back under the sheets, and he tucked me in, scooting me to the inside before he stretched out on the covers next to me.

He ran his fingers through my hair, and the silence of both his mind and his mouth unnerved me. I glanced over my shoulder at him. He smiled and continued to comb my hair with his fingers.

"You're going to get into trouble," I whispered.

He lifted his shoulder in a shrug. "I'm not under the covers with you, and you left the door open. This way, I will actually get some sleep. Before, every little creak of the house made me jump, thinking something might happen to you."

"Really?"

He nodded. "Bridget wasn't the only one who that bastard was trying to manipulate." His lips pressed together in a hard line. "She's just the only one he was able to get control of."

I stared at him as his meaning sank in. "He tried to get into your head?"

He nodded. "He tried to manipulate April, too."

The nightmare came back in full force, and my stomach clenched again. This time, I was able to get a handle on it. "I thought you were more vulnerable than Bridget."

He chuckled low. "No. I'm not vulnerable to being controlled. I think it's the angel blood that gives me a little more willpower than someone without it, despite the loss of most of my soul. And I'm not interested in what Lucifer has in mind."

"What's that?" I asked.

"He wants the perfect archangel bloodline mix." He met my gaze. "He wants this specific form because he already has the one bloodline that I don't possess under his thumb."

I swallowed a line of creeping bile, shivering at the nightmare. "That's what the nightmare was. You and Grace... together..."

His gaze softened. "I'm in love with you, Faith. Heart. Mind. Soul. Or at least what's left of it is yours. I know it's not much." He traced my lips with his fingers. "I'm still smart and resourceful, even if I no longer have a filter."

His smile was so endearing that I rolled onto my back and pulled him to my lips. Ridged surprise gave way to a gentle kiss. But it soon transcended into something wild that I didn't want to stop. I wanted to erase my nightmare with something real and tangible. Something no one could take from either of us.

The door swung closed, and Alex pulled away, glancing at it. When his gaze came back to mine, it was downright carnal. He grinned.

My heart thundered at the look in his eyes, and as he came closer to kiss me, I blurted, "I don't want her to be your first."

He stopped and pulled away, tilting his head. "Her?" Confusion creased his forehead, and then it smoothed out into annoyance. "That nightmare really did a number on you."

I bit my lower lip and nodded.

"And that's why you want to do this?"

"Does it really matter what my reasoning is?"

He licked his lips and stared at mine before meeting my gaze. "I wish I could say no, it doesn't matter. Well, *I* can say that." He smiled. "But in the light of day, you will regret making a rash decision based on a nightmare, no matter how amazing I might be in bed."

Heat filled my cheeks. I knew he was right, but in this moment, I was willing to find out just how amazing he was. I pulled him to my lips, and he fell into the kiss as fully as I did. Before I knew it, his shirt was off, and he was under the covers with me pinned under him.

"Damn," he whispered as he broke the kiss. His hips circled against mine, and the warm flannel of his pajama pants created such heat between us. His hand caressed me through my shirt, and he leaned forward and nipped my earlobe. "I can feel your heartbeat," he whispered in my ear. He licked a line down my throat, then sucked the spot where it seemed to pulse in a wild beat. "I want to taste you."

A loud knock on the door stopped Alex's downward progression. He glanced up at me with wide eyes and an open "oh shit" mouth.

"Alex?" CJ's annoyed voice echoed in the hallway. "Open the goddamn door."

CJ could open doors with just a thought. The fact he couldn't open Alex's bedroom door chilled me, and I blinked in shock.

Alex had just enough time to crawl onto the covers and drape his arm over me before the door exploded inward. CJ stood in the hallway with a sleepy glare. His gaze went to the bright overhead light and then to us.

"She had a nightmare," Alex said.

The sarcastic laugh that escaped CJ didn't calm my heart, and his glare pierced me.

"I'm not sure I would categorize her thoughts as a nightmare. And the fact she blocked me from opening the door again..." He pressed his lips together and put his hands on his hips. "You can't stay in here." He turned his sharp glare at Alex.

"Please," I said before I could stop it. Some images from the dream flashed through my mind, and I wrapped the covers tighter.

His brow creased, and he wiped his face and then pointed. "The door stays open, young lady."

I agreed emphatically.

He looked at Alex.

"And you get your sleeping bag and get on the floor."

"Yes, sir." Alex rolled to his feet, grabbing his shirt from the end of the bed and strategically used that to hide whatever excitement remained in his blood. He rolled the sleeping bag out and slid his T-shirt back on before he crawled inside while his father watched.

With the sham pillow under his head, he gave his father a nod.

CJ turned off the light and pointed at the two of us before he headed towards the stairs. I caught some of his grumblings and turned toward Alex with a smirk. The man wanted to be with his wife, but instead, he was trying to sleep on the lumpy couch in the event that Bridget went off the deep end again.

"Your dad is mad because you might be getting a little action and he isn't," I whispered.

"I heard that!" CJ's voice barreled up the stairs.

Alex snorted. "Well, I'm now in the same boat as he is and understand the aggravation." He winked and rolled on his side, facing me. The humor faded. "Would you have really said yes?"

I stared at his blue eyes reflecting in the hall lights and decided not to answer him. If we had gotten that far uninterrupted... I sighed just thinking about the way he felt molded to me. I wasn't sure I would have stopped him in my current state of mind, but I had the feeling he was right. I would have regretted being so rash in the morning.

"I love you, too," I said after a few moments.

He smiled and closed his eyes.

I watched him fall into the slow cadence of sleep and then rolled and stared at the ceiling. Doubts started layering over my thoughts. Doubts about whether I'd made the right decision on not blasting Lucifer back to Hell when I'd had the chance regardless of the form he took or the lure he had dangling around his neck.

If I had taken the shot...

A shadow passed by in the hall, and CJ stepped into the doorway.

"You can't do that to yourself," he whispered. "Second-guessing your actions will not prepare you for what's coming. And while I know Alex is okay with you taking the shot while Lucifer has his soul as ransom, I'm glad you didn't. It means there is still a chance for him. Besides, I am not sure I could watch my brother die a second time today."

A lump welled up in my throat, and I nodded. "Thank you."

"You do know I will need to take him out eventually, even if he is in Tom's form."

He nodded. "We need to get your powers under conscious control." He covered a yawn. "Tomorrow, we start those lessons." He disappeared again, and the stairs creaked with his weight as he descended.

His directive turned my nerves on edge, and I stared at the ceiling, wondering what absolute disaster would rear its ugly head.

Homecoming
Chapter 5

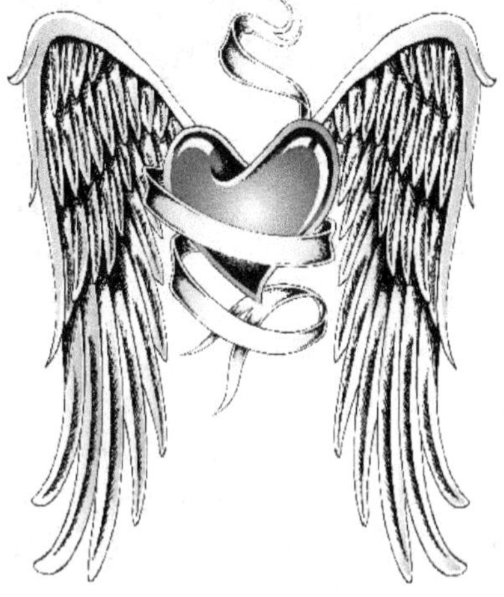

"AGAIN," CJ DEMANDED. HIS barrier covered the entire backyard right up to the back door, where Alex sat within his father's protective dome.

The rest of the family stood just inside the glass door, watching me stumble my way through the power control gambit. It was laughable. The only thing I had succeeded in doing was reducing the funeral pyre to ash. My natural talent and the added bang of angel fire worked in my haphazard way, but that was the extent of it.

All my attempts at moving things with my mind utterly failed. As did anything remotely similar to what my subconscious had manifested last night. I couldn't control matter or minds, no matter how hard I tried.

I got so frustrated that I burned a patch of lawn all the way to the rock wall, and my hands were in a constant state of flame. I was surprised I didn't spontaneously combust.

"Douse the flame," he ordered as he approached me.

I stared at my clenched hands and slowly opened my palms. A bead of sweat rolled into my eye, and the sting caught me enough off guard that I almost rubbed my eye while my hand was fully engulfed.

CJ grabbed my forearm.

I stared at the flames near enough to my face to feel the heat, and the shock of it sent a chill through me. The fire doused, and I looked beyond my hand at CJ's concerned stare.

"Let's try something different."

"Okay," I said, relieved when he led me to the lounge chairs and took a seat on one, indicating for me to sit on the one next to him.

"We are going to isolate the grace within you. You have both Lucifer's grace and Raphael's grace. I've got Michael's, Gabriel's, and Uriel's grace. I'm going to pull Michael's into my hand, and I want you to pull Raphael's out, okay?"

I was glad he hadn't asked me to pull Lucifer's because I wasn't sure I could without causing major damage at a cellular level.

"Think of your hand as a magnet and the grace as a cluster of steel pieces inside you. First, close your eyes and imagine those pieces pulling together into a tight ball in the center of your being."

I closed my eyes and concentrated, using each inhale as a sweep of more pieces of the fragmented light blazing in the center of my body. With each breath, I could feel that mass growing, solidifying into a power source all on its own.

"Now the magnet," he said.

I put my hand over my chest, and I arched into the pull. The orb inside nearly flew out of me like a grenade launcher. Heat fanned my hand, and I opened my eyes. The bright glow of grace radiated from between my hand and my chest.

I glanced at CJ and the equal ball of light trapped between his hand and his body. He grinned.

"Now push it back in." He pushed the light back into his chest, and light radiated outward from his skin before settling back into his usual aura. His quirky grin matched Alex's.

I repeated his actions, and the same anomaly occurred. My skin shone like a beacon before fading back to my normal hue.

"That looked pretty effortless for you." He glanced across the expanse of the backyard at the can of beer he had placed on the rock wall and tapped his palm. "Magnet." He aimed his palm at the beer. "Aluminum." The beer can flew across the yard and into his waiting hand.

I got the concept that he was trying to teach me, and I glanced at the partially melted Gatorade bottle sitting on the rock wall. I put out my hand, hoping I didn't make the thing explode or something just as embarrassing as the rest of the day had been. The power I'd used to pull the bits of grace into a ball flared, and I tapped into it, imagining my hand as a powerful magnet.

The bottle trembled on the rocks, then burst into flames and fell into the ocean at the far side of the wall. I stared at the spot as my mouth popped open. I hadn't shot a flame over the distance. I had envisioned it coming to me the way his can had come to him.

CJ pressed his lips together. I couldn't tell whether he was aggravated or suppressing a smile. "Well. That was certainly interesting."

I closed my hands into fists. "I tried..."

He put his hand up, and I quieted.

"I know you tried. But the opposite of what you wanted happened. What happened was what you actually hoped wouldn't. I think your underlying expectations are sabotaging your powers."

I huffed and crossed my arms. "Don't psychoanalyze me."

I yawned. All this work was making me tired, and I had no idea why I couldn't just do things as easily as Tom considering I'd absorbed his power.

"You need to master this shit," CJ said. "Because a storm is coming that I don't think you'll be able to weather without using these powers." He sighed and rubbed his face.

"My dad is right," Alex said, moving my legs to the side so he could sit on the chair with me. "You need to figure out why it worked yesterday with the car doors and again with my bedroom door. Once you figure out why it worked in those situations, then maybe you'll be closer to the key." He took my hands in his, and the heat in my palms cooled.

I squeezed his hands. If only I knew what I had done in each case.

I met his gaze as the truth clicked. "*You* are the common denominator."

Alex laughed.

I pulled my right hand out of his grip and pointed my palm towards the wall, wishing for the bottle to come to my hand. When the blackened plastic catapulted across the lawn like a stray bullet, my eyes widened.

It crashed into my hand, and the sea water still coating the plastic sprayed us. I stared at it and then dropped it like it was still on fire. My heart pounded in my chest. I couldn't have Alex with me when I faced off against my father.

I looked at CJ. His expression matched my horror.

I pulled my other hand out of Alex's and met his gaze. "You can't be near me when I try to take down Lucifer."

"Faith," he started.

I shook my head. "No. I will not let him get his filthy hands on you. Understand?" My nightmare flooded back, and I shivered. I swallowed hard and got up, then walked across the blackened grass to sit on the rock wall. I crossed my legs and stared out at the ocean towards the lighthouse where Tom and I had dumped my mother's ashes.

I needed my mom. Tears tugged at my eyes.

"Faith." Alex's hand landed on my shoulder. "I can hold my own against Lucifer."

I glanced up at him and then over to where we had been sitting. CJ had left us alone, but I already knew his thoughts on the matter. He knew better than anyone here. He wanted Alex as far away from the devil as humanly possible. And I couldn't have agreed more.

"No, you can't. Even with all the power your dad has, he still got duped by Lucifer, so you haven't got a prayer against him. And if he gets his hands on you..." I shook my head and glanced out at the ocean again. "I can't let you walk into the devil's lair with me."

He sat next to me and tilted my chin so I would look at him. "If you go, I go."

I went to speak, but he covered my lips with his. The kiss muffled my thoughts. By the time he pulled away, my mind was swimming with the connection between us.

"If you go, I go." There was no leeway in his tone, or the tight set of his jaw. "If you die, I die," he added softly. "I don't want to be left here without you. I'm still me when you are around."

He had said that before, but this time, I was privy to his thoughts, his fears. He wasn't kidding. The small amount of time I was away with Tom, he had lost the capacity to feel emotion. That was only hours.

I caressed his cheek. "I can't have you with me. I can't chance it."

His gaze grew hard, and he stood up. Before he could march back to the house in anger, I grabbed his hand. He stared down at the connection and then at me, unswayed by my physical contact.

"If Lucifer gets you and possesses you, I die. I've seen what April has seen, and it's horrifying." I blinked back the sudden sheen of tears and looked away. "I know you're scared. I feel it every time you are near me, but I... I can't." I swiped at my hot cheeks and met his gaze. "I care too much about you." Both desperation and a darker component of the grace inside gripped me like an icy vise.

"I resisted him at Bridget's house, so what makes you think I won't be able to do that again?"

"I locked you in the car."

He laughed and looked out at the water. "He didn't coerce me when I was in the car. It didn't happen until I was in the house just far enough away from my father that he chanced it." He pulled his hand out of mine and crossed his arms. "We aren't ever going to agree on this."

I fisted my hands, frustrated with his lack of understanding. I wondered if he would be this way with his soul, and deep down in my core, I knew soul or no soul, this is who he was. He would never let someone protect him from harm.

"Damn it, Ty," I whispered.

He froze in place, and the smile that appeared flashed in one of the memories I'd downloaded from Tom. Another gift, along with the transference of his powers. Alex looked exactly like his grandfather had. I did not know whose memories I possessed, but that grin and the impish light dancing in his eyes was a mirror image.

His reaction was immediate, and he stepped close. "You really shouldn't use my given name unless you mean it," he purred in my ear and then licked a line down the side of my neck.

The sudden switch from anger to seduction spun my head and warmed my skin.

"Alex." The sharp call from the house interrupted whatever had ignited.

A cloud of irritation passed over his eyes, and he turned, staring at his father in the doorway. The tight set of his jaw was back, and he headed towards the house in that funky, aggravated mood again.

"What am I going to do about you?" I whispered, staring at his back. My gaze lowered to his tight pants. I looked away, but not before the urge to ravage him surfaced.

I stood and started across the yard, but the motion from the property next door made my heart pound. I turned and raised my hands.

"Don't. It's Naomi," CJ snapped, and I closed my hands.

I didn't feel like talking at all, so I bypassed CJ and the crew in the family room, including Bridget, and headed down into the quiet of the cellar.

Before I could slump on the couch, Alex grabbed me around the waist and backed me into the computer room to the farthest corner where access to their panic room resided. He pressed the code and maneuvered me into the dark room before I could drum up an argument. The door closed, encasing us in blackness, although Alex's aura was bright enough for me to see his face. He navigated to the far wall and pushed me down on the couch.

His aura was in chaos, dark and light pulses. Reds predominantly swirled, announcing his mood like a wild tribal beacon. He ripped at my shirt, tearing buttons off as often as unthreading them.

"I need you," he whispered against my lips, and then crushed down in a kiss that was part passion and part desperation.

I had a door into his mind, and heat filled every inch of me with his explicit thoughts. Moments flashed like an iconic movie in my mind, bringing with them the embarrassment of walking in on someone, but also the heat of the greatest love story this side of Heaven.

Would our story be as brutal? Would it be full of a love so deep neither of us could breathe without the other?

I gasped as he kissed my throat and moved lower and lower, peeling off clothing as he went. I couldn't reconcile the ancient memories with the insistence of Alex's hands and mouth. It all blended into one blinding moment when Alex penetrated me, claiming me, making me nearly cry out in the dark. His irises nearly glowed, and the colors threading through his aura heated as much as I did.

We moved like we belonged together, frantic at first, then languid as if we had all the time in the world. His kisses became soft and as loving as his caresses.

"I need you, Faith," he whispered. "Even more than I love you." His voice squeezed tight and his arms followed. "Oh, Christ."

Everything inside me exploded into an array of lights, blinding me. I clenched my fists, praying. For what, I didn't know.

Not to harm Alex, not to forget this heavenly feeling, not to burn the house down. But most of all, I prayed I would experience this magic again.

Homecoming
Chapter 6

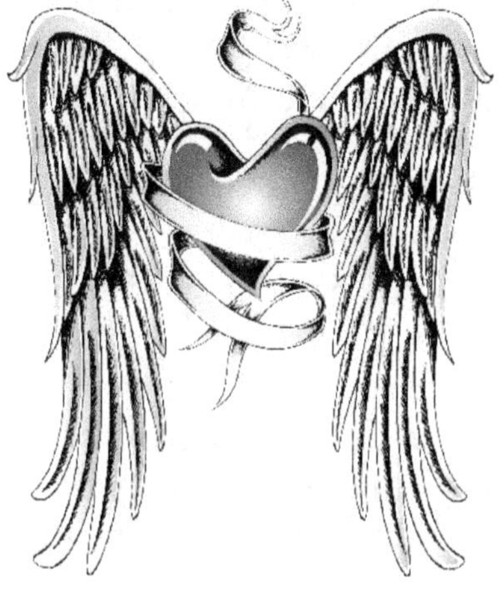

ALEX STAYED ON TOP of me, just running his fingers through my hair and tracing my lips. He sighed. "I wish I could see your face."

I put my hand out over the open space and willed my flame to lick my fingers. The soft glow lit up the room, and he glanced at my hand and then smiled at me.

"I forget you can do shit like that."

He had no idea that I could see him throughout. His rapture, his absolute bliss, washed over me like a gentle wave. I was sure I would have never hit that plateau that had reached almost a religious experience without him.

I couldn't speak. I was too choked with emotion. I hadn't expected our first time to be so frantic and beautiful at the same time. I also knew we were in a ton of trouble.

Alex traced my lips, his eyes tracking his motions, and he sighed, meeting my gaze. "My dad knows, doesn't he?"

It wasn't totally framed as a question, so I shrugged. I didn't want to run into a lecture right now. I just wanted to feel him against me for just a little longer.

"Are you okay?" he asked after studying me.

"Yes and no," I whispered, and closed my eyes at the concern that bloomed in his gaze and the thoughts galloping through his head. "I would have said no if I didn't want this, Alex," I said, my voice snippy at the direction of his thoughts.

Worry bled from him, making his shoulders sag with relief. "So why aren't you okay?"

My chin quivered. "Because now that nightmare is so much worse." Tears blurred my vision, and I bit my lower lip. "There is no way in Hell I'm letting you anywhere near either of them." I kissed him, silencing whatever argument he had lined up.

I sobbed with the kiss, and he hugged me, pulling us into a sitting position with my legs still wrapped around him. I closed my fist around the flame lighting the room.

"I want to see you," he said.

I glanced towards the light switch, wishing I could reach. Lights flooded the room, and I looked up at the ceiling and back to him.

"That is really handy when it works," I mumbled.

He ran his hands through my hair, pushing it away from my face before he got a clear look at my chest. His blue eyes glistened with interest, and when he glanced back up at me, he tilted his head to the side. A slow smile spread across his lips, accentuated with deep dimples.

"Say my name again," he whispered in the huskiest of tones.

"Ty Alexander Ryan," I replied slowly.

His look smoldered in a way that was way too raw, too powerful for a sixteen-year-old.

Enough!

I winced at the volume of CJ's voice in my head. From Alex's tightened grip on my hips, I knew he heard it, too. Any heat between us fled with the anger in that single word.

"No. It's not enough," Alex growled under his breath and met my stare.

His hips circled under me, but I was too terrified at the ramifications of not listening to his father to respond in kind. I climbed off him, frantically gathering my clothes.

"Shit," Alex mumbled as he looked at the couch. He glanced at me and ran a hand down his face. He nodded towards another door. "You might want to clean up in the bathroom," he said, his cheeks blooming as red as the thin streaks on my legs.

I felt like I should've been embarrassed, but there was something completely disarming about Alex's half smile and shrug. He was totally endearing. I crossed to the bathroom, glanced in the small pantry for a washcloth, and then cleaned myself up.

My shirt hung on my frame. Half the buttons were missing, and I stepped out into the room, holding the soiled towel. The couch had no sign of a stain, and I cocked my head at Alex.

"I turned the cushion over. I'll have to clean it up at some point, but not right now. Right now, we are going to get reamed. But it was worth it." He came to where I stood and cupped my face between his palms, then kissed me with the same bravado as he had earlier. "Marry me," he said when our lips parted.

I laughed. I couldn't help it. We were only sixteen. There was no getting married and having a happily ever after, at least not yet.

"You don't want to marry me?"

"Someday I do."

Then why did you laugh? His thought filled my head as he searched my eyes.

"We are only sixteen."

"Then marry me on my eighteenth birthday."

"Ask me on your eighteenth birthday, and then we can have this discussion. My wedding day will not be on either of our birthdays." I pulled out of his arms and headed towards the door at the far end of the room. There was no door handle. Keypad tones rang, and the door whooshed open.

CJ stood on the other side, his arms crossed so tight I thought his shirt was going to rip. His eyes blazed, and when they landed on his son's barely concealed grin, I thought CJ was going to slug Alex.

"Don't give me that look. You lost your virginity when you were my age." Alex crossed his arms. His cocky gaze was enough to set anyone over the edge, and I wasn't sure he realized just how close his father was to flying off the handle.

"Not under my roof."

"No. It was under her parents' roof," I blurted as the memory barreled from the mental file cabinets. I blinked and threw my hand over my mouth.

CJ glared at me.

I could feel my eyes widening despite my attempt at playing it cool. Memories were just coming forth willy-nilly. It was irritating that I couldn't clamp down on my mouth in response.

Alex burst out laughing. "Really?"

I nodded and more information poured out. "He got caught, too."

CJ's face reddened, but it wasn't from embarrassment. He grabbed both our arms and hauled us back into the room. The panic door closed behind us, locking us inside with him.

If I hadn't been scared before, I was when the sofa cushion flew across the room.

CJ pointed at Alex. "You are going to clean that up. Understand?" His teeth clenched so hard that I thought they might crack.

"Yes, sir," Alex said, but his amusement hadn't abated.

It was as if my mouth and his expression were tied together. I couldn't stop the facts from pouring out as soon as they came forth, and Alex couldn't stop smirking. The next set of images flashed forward, and I gasped.

"Put your gloves on, Faith," CJ said. This time his voice was cautious, like he was talking someone off a high-rise ledge.

Alex stepped behind me, and before I realized what was happening in the present, his hands wrapped around mine, closing them into tight fists.

"Tom didn't have a tongue?" A litany of memories assaulted me, blinking off like a gruesome slide show. The things my father did were awful, but this family had been through much more at the hands of humans.

"What's happening?" Alex asked, his voice strained and very far away.

"She has too many memories in her head. All the way back to the beginning, when Damian was born. Thousands of years. And she is time jumping from one to another to another," CJ yelled over the din.

"They're fucking everywhere," Alex said. "And she is shaking so hard I don't know if I can hold on."

Time jumping.

Those two words pulled air into my lungs, and I blinked back into the room with CJ and Alex. My breath wheezed, and then everything went black.

Homecoming
Chapter 7

I WOKE IN THE bedroom tucked under the covers with a cool, damp washcloth on my forehead. Valerie sat next to me, holding my wrist as she looked at her watch. She still wore her doctor's coat.

She looked from her watch to me, and the tightness of her lips told me enough. I reached up and moved the cloth over my eyes so I wouldn't have to be subjected to her overwhelming disappointment, but the cloth didn't hide her feelings. They pummeled me like a battering ram, and it was worse than when CJ had lost his brother because this time it was aimed at me.

"I know you're awake."

I lifted the cloth and looked at her. She cocked an eyebrow, and heat filled my cheeks.

"No protection?" she asked.

I stared at her and glanced at my hands, which now had my gloves on them.

She rolled her eyes. "Not talking about your hands, girl."

My eyes slowly widened at what she was referring to, and I gasped. "No, ma'am."

"Next time, make sure my son has a little bit of his head on his shoulders. Even if his soul is gone, his common sense should still be in there somewhere." She took the cloth off my head. "What's done is done." She sighed. "Now, let's talk about the seizures."

"Seizures?" I knew it was ridiculous to repeat her, but I couldn't get my head wrapped around that word. It had medical connotations, and I didn't need any complications beyond Lucifer.

"I have seen CJ have enough seizures after his first pummeling from Lucifer to understand what he described. Your brain couldn't handle the volume of information, and it shut down, leaving your body to deal with after effects it really can't handle." She took a deep breath. "In your case, it is much more dangerous than ending up in a vegetative state." She picked up one of my gloved hands to make her point.

I pulled my hand away from her and slumped down in the covers. "I'm sorry."

Valerie smiled at me. "No need to apologize. They are as much in your control as your time jumps are, and we need to fix that." She leaned back in the chair. "I want to hypnotize you so we can put up some organizational barriers in your brain so this doesn't happen at a critical moment, okay?"

The thought terrified me more than the barrage of memories. Allowing someone inside my head, playing with my psyche while I was not in control, just freaked me out.

"I'm a doctor," she breathed. "I will not take advantage of your vulnerabilities, and I won't make you walk around and cluck like a chicken. I promise."

I blinked at her a few times, and then her attempt at humor seeped into my befuddled brain.

"If you take a closer look, you would know that." She tapped her temple. "It's how I knew you had the best of intentions with us. Chris sees it, too."

"I am just learning," I mumbled. I didn't want to pry into others' heads. Except for Alex, I hadn't looked closer at those around me. "Besides, it just doesn't feel right to go sneaking around other people's thoughts without their permission."

She nodded a little. "I used to agree. However, just a peek into someone's thoughts can mean the difference between life and Death. I have saved more lives with this than with the healing ability. Consider the teenager who is thinking about suicide. Or the kid with a gun under his mattress at home who is angry with the world. When you encounter someone so deep in that hole, you offer your hand and pull them out of the darkness. This is the blessing of this power, and to not use it isn't right either."

"But isn't that... snooping?"

Valerie sighed. "Yes. I guess it is, but if it helps someone or protects the ones you love, isn't it worth it?"

I couldn't argue with her logic.

"Try it," she said.

"You mean, right now?" I didn't know if I could at will. I knew I could hear people's thoughts when I wasn't trying, but I sort of blocked it out. Well, except for Alex. I wanted to know what was in his head, but even so, there were some times I could only hear static or nothing at all.

"Everyone in this house knows how to create static in their minds. It makes reading thoughts impossible. But out there?" She pointed to the window. "If you are getting static from someone that isn't within our little circle, you give them a wide berth. No thoughts usually mean psychopathic at some level, or they are an investigator of sorts and have to look at things like a complex three-dimensional puzzle, which requires multiple trains of thought at the same time. Anyone creating static out there should be avoided at all costs."

I glanced at her skeptically, then closed my eyes and tried to get inside her mind. It was like walking into a warm and welcoming home. I completely understood what she had been talking about. Her intentions were pure. I shivered at the thought of what a mind with ill intent felt like.

She smiled as I opened my eyes. "Do you trust me now?"

I was sure she already knew the answer, but I nodded anyway. "Yes."

"Okay." She reached over to the desk, picked up a metronome, set it on the baseboard shelf of the bed, and turned it on. "Keep your eyes on the peg," she said. "When you are feeling sleepy, raise your finger."

I thought hypnotism was more than just falling asleep to a metronome. When I couldn't keep my eyes open any longer, I lifted my finger. Valerie's voice seemed distant as the constant clicking of the instrument filled my head.

In my mind's eye, I saw myself organizing a room full of papers, using a large file cabinet to arrange them in chronological order by person and then dates. Each person had a drawer in the file cabinet, and some drawers held more than one person's memories.

When I finished, I wiped my hands on my hips and then glanced at the key between my fingertips. An old skeleton key that looked like it fit in the cabinet lock. Sure enough, it did. I slipped the key on a chain and clasped it around my neck, then tucked it under my shirt before I glanced around the immaculately clean room. Even my memory box was neat and shiny.

Relief swept through me, and I blinked my eyes open to Alex's bedroom and the metronome keeping time. I yawned and glanced at Valerie. Dark circles stood out under her eyes. She looked even more tired than I felt.

"What time is it?"

"Seven in the morning." She rubbed her face and then turned off the instrument. "But I think we are all set for a while."

My brain was still stuck on the time. Alex had cornered me in the panic room downstairs in the early afternoon. I wasn't sure how long I had been out before Valerie hypnotized me, but I didn't think it was that late when we'd started.

"We've been at this for almost twelve hours," she said. "It took that long to get some organization in your mind." She covered a yawn. "I need some sleep." She stood and wandered out of the room.

I stretched and turned on my side to get some rest, but sleep didn't come. Instead, a vision of that file cabinet shaking under the pressure gripped me. It was only a matter of time before the metal holding it all together gave.

Homecoming
Chapter 8

VOICES PULLED ME OUT of the stupor I had fallen into. It sounded like a gathering that had turned into a brawl downstairs. I crawled out of bed and made a beeline to the bathroom before I investigated the noise.

When I had finished relieving myself and polishing my teeth, I climbed down the stairs. The moment I came into sight, the conversation near the stairs stopped. It looked like the same gathering that had been in Bridget's living room before Tom and I had ventured out to close the breach.

My gaze landed on Fate, and her honey golden hair shined in the streaks of morning sunlight piercing the family room. Her aura wasn't fluid, like a normal aura. It seemed to be stuck, as if someone paused had it like a video.

Movement next to her pulled my attention. A boy who looked like he was our age stood next to Fate. His eyes were as striking as Alex's, but he had no aura, unlike almost all the people in the room sporting the brightness of angel blood.

He gave me a nod and put his hand on Fate's shoulder, calling her attention to me.

She crossed to the bottom of the stairs and looked up at me. "We need to talk."

No one wanted to hear words like that from an entity like Fate. Me least of all, and I turned to go back upstairs. I didn't want to hear that I needed to confront Lucifer again. I already knew that. I didn't need to hear how many lives were at stake.

"Faith."

Her sharp tone stopped me in my tracks. I hung my head and took a deep breath. What I really wanted was Alex and his warm arms around me, but I hadn't seen him in the madness that was CJ's family room.

"I'll talk with her, Julia," the boy said to Fate and passed her. He climbed the stairs behind me and waved for me to lead the way.

"Who are you?" I asked.

He gave me a cockeyed smile. "I'm Nick." He waved me up the stairs again.

"You don't have an aura," I said, hesitant to move any farther. I couldn't hear his thoughts, and when I tried to read his intentions like I had with Valerie earlier, I got a blank slate.

He sighed. "No. I don't suppose I do anymore. But I'm not here to collect you. I'm here to talk, and having this conversation is going to be difficult enough. We don't need an audience."

"Who are you?" I asked, crossing my arms at the ever-increasing alarm budding inside me. I had to clamp down on the fire because my body was going into protection mode, as if I'd walked into a death zone.

Nick looked down and chuckled. "Well, technically I am Death, so your sudden nervous energy isn't unusual."

My legs lost the ability to hold me up, and I sat down hard on the step.

He reached for me, but I flinched.

"Is there somewhere we can talk that is a little more private?" He shoved his hands into his pockets.

I still couldn't get my head around the fact that I was having a conversation with the Grim Reaper himself. A big German shepherd came barreling up the stairs and stopped at eye level with me. A low growl in his throat caught me off guard.

"Levi, go play outside." Nick pointed down the stairs. "She's not going to hurt me."

The dog glanced at him, and then the growl ceased. He didn't move from his intimidating spot, though.

I stared at it, trying to read its chaotic aura. I hadn't seen a dog since I'd returned from closing the breach, but this was not what I would have guessed one looked like. I envisioned them having the same light as an angel descendant. Before I could stop myself, I reached out and touched its fur.

Shock filtered through me. It was like touching a giant lizard and not a fur-covered creature. I pulled my hand away and scuttled up the stairs, meeting Nick's bemused stare as he followed me.

This was not how I envisioned spending my evening. What I really wanted was another spell alone with Alex. Not a conversation with Death. I stepped into Alex's room, and Nick closed the door behind him.

"We came last night," he said. "Whatever happened to you fractured the barriers between Purgatory and here. We understand there were some bigger cracks created in Hell." He took a seat in the desk chair, and his dog sat beside him.

I sat down on the bed and just stared at him. "Excuse me?"

"There are at least a hundred tears in the fabric between this plane and beyond. Some big enough to let things through. Others are just ripples in the air, but with persistence from the other side, they will weaken and tear." He crossed his arms. "You need to shut them down. This takes precedence over going after Lucifer."

Gooseflesh rose across my arms, and I rubbed them. I didn't think there was anything more imperative than bringing Lucifer down.

He wiped his face. "Normally, I would agree, but there are now things out there that don't care about the order of things. And if things go out of whack, like too many people die who aren't supposed to, then earth becomes a battleground for the gods. Heaven and Hell will flood this land, and if you think Lucifer's end of times is bad, this is infinitely worse." He pulled a list out of his pocket and handed it to me.

I chewed on his words and took a deep breath, unfolding the sheet of paper. Locations were listed, including longitude and latitude coordinates. Dozens of locations worldwide.

"Does Lucifer know about this?" I waved the list. If he did, then everyone here was in danger.

Death shrugged. "I don't know, but if his minions have gotten out of Hell, it won't be long before he does."

There was absolutely no chance I was going to leave Alex in the line of fire, but I didn't know how safe closing the breaches would be. I also needed to find that stinking knife.

I glanced up at Nick. "Do you know where the knife that was built using Heaven's light might be?"

His jaw tightened as he looked out the window. "I know the area where it was lost, but I'm not sure that is the best course of action."

"Why?"

"Because none of us know how that thing works. It was never used. But the lore is that it will wipe someone or something out of existence. No more. No Heaven, no Hell, no Purgatory. As if they never existed. So that begs the question that I know you have already entertained. Is it from a point in time forward, or does it wipe the thing out from all existence?"

I picked at a hangnail and nodded.

"If you use it on Lucifer, and the worst case happens, Hell no longer exists as it does today. Lucifer's lineage disappears, and that includes you and the Ryans." He snapped his fingers. "Gone in an instant. The question that comes after that is what is the world like without Hell or the devil? Does evil even exist? The world may be better off at first glance, but it also could have been destroyed eons ago. There is no way of knowing what will happen, so I am very hesitant to point you to its location."

I ran my hand through my hair. "Fate said…"

"I don't care what Julia said. She has no clue of what that knife will do either. Even her book of those Fated to die doesn't give her a clue. Usually she can see the alternatives…" He stood, glancing out the window at the ocean. "There is already an out of balance now that people have died that weren't supposed to." He sighed. "More will die because of the breaches, and Lucifer will continue to wreak havoc. So, the prescribed course of action is to close the breaches and *then* stop Lucifer."

"And what if I cannot beat Lucifer with angel fire alone?" I asked.

He turned back to me. "Then I will bring you the knife myself."

Homecoming
Chapter 9

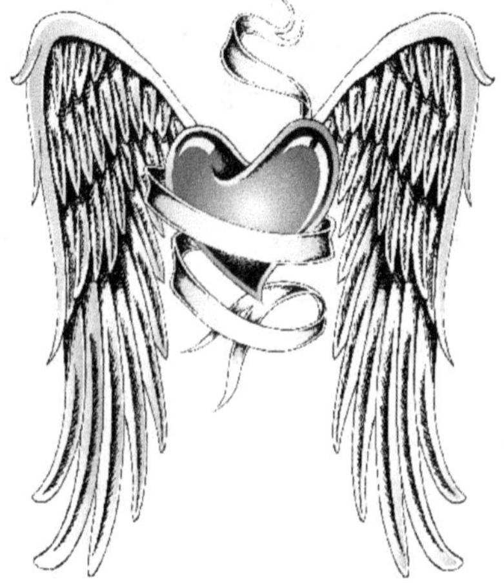

I SAT ON THE bed, stunned by everything Nick had told me. I had to leave soon, and I was not prepared for a nomad's existence. Tom's journey to close Hell's portals had taken him ten years. I stared at the paper in my hands, the map to all the breaches my little time jump seizure had created.

A throat cleared in the doorway, and I glanced over, right into Alex's inquisitive gaze. A hollowness spread through my core, and I folded the paper in my hands and stuffed it into my pocket. Nick had said Alex couldn't come with me, that it would be too dangerous for someone without powers or special skills.

I didn't know how to tell Alex I was leaving him again. And leaving for a significant amount of time, not just a handful of hours. He stepped into the room, and my gaze lowered, landing on his bandaged hands.

I scrambled to my feet. "What happened to your hands?"

He glanced at the bandages and shrugged. "My touch wasn't strong enough to stop the flames when you were freaking out with the time jumps. But at least I stopped you from doing any damage to the house." His smile seemed strained as he moved closer, kicking the door closed. "I understand we're going on an adventure?"

The hopeful lilt of his voice tugged at my heart. It would have been easier if I had just slipped out without seeing his pleading eyes.

I inhaled deeply and let out a slow stream of air. "I don't know about we..." I dropped my gaze to the floor.

"Please," he whispered, and it filled the room with an uncomfortable silence.

When I didn't look up, he crossed and stood close enough for my focus to fall on his chest. He tilted my head up with one of his bandaged hands, and while he tried to hide it, his wince of pain did not go unnoticed.

"Don't leave me here." This time it wasn't a plea—it was a demand. The anger dancing in his eyes made me take a step back, right into his desk.

"It's too dangerous." I repeated what I had been told, but it just felt empty.

He laughed. "And staying here isn't?"

I couldn't disagree with him. Being here was just as fraught with danger as being with me, but I doubted either of his parents would let him go galivanting all over the globe with me. Not when I was walking into dangerous situations every time I approached a breach.

"If anything were to happen to you…"

He stopped me with his lips. "If I stay, something is sure to happen to me, and you know it." He pressed his lips harder against mine.

I opened my mouth to protest, but that just gave his tongue access. Any coherent thought of mine disappeared. When he finally pulled away, I had to shake the fog out of my head.

"You don't have any special abilities," I said.

"No. But I am a blackbelt, and I can take care of my own unless I'm hit with a tranquilizer." He lifted his bandaged hands. "And I apparently can stop fire, so don't give me that shit about not having special abilities. Just because I can't shoot fire or move things with my mind doesn't make me helpless."

"But your hands are burned," I said. "You are hurt because of me."

He closed his eyes and crossed his arms. His silent countdown echoed in my mind. When he got to zero, he opened his eyes. "I'm alive. I will heal. And if my mom doesn't have time to fix me, I'll suck it up, because it's only temporary."

"And what happens if the next time it isn't something temporary? What happens if it is a fatal wound because I couldn't react fast enough?"

"I am going with you."

The door opened. "You are not going with her," CJ said. He filled the doorway, and his gaze was darker than I had seen it since I'd arrived in town.

From the look in Alex's eyes, I knew this wasn't the last word on this subject, but I was happy for the interruption. I was also more tired than I had been when I woke.

"Kylee and Michael have agreed to go with you," CJ said.

"Doesn't Kylee have a kid?"

"Yes."

"If it's too dangerous for Alex, it is way too dangerous for a helpless child." I crossed my arms. As much as I didn't want Alex in harm's way, I would rather have him with me any day over a child.

"Levi is accompanying you."

"What the Hell is a dog going to do against demons?" I asked, and then a memory swam to the front of my mind. One of Tom's memories, to be precise. I gasped at the image of the dog turning into some hideous dragon-like monster.

"Leviathan," CJ said. "And he likes to eat demons."

I laughed. That would explain the leathery quality of his fur. "If that's the case, then I'd rather go with Alex and Levi than relative strangers."

"It's not a field trip, Faith. Or a backpacking trip across Europe. You've got serious work to do, and Alex will be a distraction."

"Don't I have any say in this?" Alex asked, exasperated.

"No." CJ glared at him. "Say your goodbyes, because she needs to pack. She is leaving in the next half hour."

I balked at CJ. All I wanted to do was crawl into bed and sleep for the next twenty-four hours.

Alex glared at his father, but nodded. "Fine," he snapped between tight lips. "The least you could do is leave us alone," he added when his father didn't show any signs of budging from where he stood.

CJ cocked an eyebrow.

Alex looked at the floor. "If I can't go with her, I need a goodbye that will keep me sane. And yes, that means what you think it means." He glanced at his father and jutted his chin out in defiance. "If you won't allow me to say goodbye in my own way, I cannot hang on to what little humanity I have left."

His words were so soft and full of anguish that my heart squeezed in my chest. I needed Alex as much as he needed me, and I couldn't fathom being away from him for as long as it would take to close the breaches. Even if each one took minutes to close, the traveling to each location would take months.

"You are not sleeping with her under my roof again."

Alex threw his arms out, and his face reddened. "Then I might as well just waltz into wherever Lucifer is and let him take me, because by the time she gets back, there will be nothing left."

Anger welled up in me, and before I could catch myself, I slammed my fist into Alex's cheek.

Alex stumbled and caught himself on the desk. One of his bandaged hands flew to cover the ever-reddening spot where my fist had connected.

"Don't you dare threaten that!" I pointed at him as every fiber of my being sparked with fury. My exhaustion magnified the indignity flowing through my veins, and my vision clouded with a red hue.

"Ow," he muttered and stared at me. His eyes widened, and he stepped back. Fear etched into his face, and he put his hands up. "Calm down, Faith," he said softly, belying the sweat that broke out on his brow.

"You want me to calm down after that senseless threat?"

"Yes, I do." He straightened, swallowing hard enough for me to see his Adam's apple bob. He stepped towards the closet and swung the door open so the mirror on the back was directed straight at me.

I stared at the fiery wings spread out from behind my back. It was the same thing I had seen in the reflection of the windows when I'd closed the portal. My anger diffused, leaving my muscles feeling like pudding. The wings faded.

Tom turned into the spitting image of Lucifer when he got blindingly mad. I turned into a fiery winged being. Great. Just what I needed right now. I raked my hand down my face and glanced at the door.

"Just let us have a few minutes," I said to CJ. "Please."

He glanced between the two of us and nodded, closing the door.

"Don't ever throw that out there so callously. You understand? It's not a joke, and it certainly isn't a bargaining chip." Hot tears blurred my vision and burned my throat.

He reached to run his fingers through his hair and stopped short, staring at his bandaged hand. He dropped his arm and sighed. "I'm sorry. I was aggravated, and it just came out."

It was more than that and he knew it, which was why he was totally avoiding meeting my gaze. I crossed to him and wrapped my arms around him, squeezing him tight until his arms encompassed me. He kissed the top of my head.

"I don't want to go, either, but it is my fault. My responsibility."

"What if you have another seizure?" he asked against my ear.

"I don't think that will happen. I was able to pull Tom's memory of Leviathan without falling into a time jump." I snuggled against his chest, listening to his heartbeat. It lulled me into false comfort, enough so that when I pushed away, I had a momentary flood of panic that I would never see him again.

He unraveled the bandages from his hands and dropped them on the floor before tenderly cupping my cheeks with his reddened palms. "Lock the door," he whispered, searching my eyes.

I pushed onto my tiptoes and planted a kiss, but I didn't lock the door. When he started leading me towards the bed, I pulled away and shook my head. I was not going to blatantly disobey his father's wishes.

"I need something to motivate me to hurry back home," I said.

"I need..."

I covered his mouth with mine, shutting off his words. I knew what he thought he needed. I knew denying him wouldn't make him happy, but I also knew if I let him have his way again, I would not be able to leave.

I peeled out of his arms and headed towards the closet.

He grabbed my arm and spun me back into his grip. My hands slapped onto his chest, and I looked up at him in surprise.

"I'm not always nice." He pushed me against the wall. His entire body molded to mine as his kiss boiled heat in my veins.

Good lord, how I loved the way he kissed me. It was brutal and sensual and full of everything we didn't seem to be able to articulate. It was pure and dirty at the same time—if there even could be such a contradiction like that—but it was there, living in the motion of our tongues.

And it lit my soul on fire.

It took everything I had to break away from him, but I did and danced out of his reach, gasping for air while my heart pounded in a tribal mating beat.

"Alex." I splayed my fingers toward him. "I can't." The words felt foreign on my lips, especially since every cell was crying out for me to step back into his arms.

He leaned against the wall and stared at the ceiling. That mental countdown began again, as he counted his way into control. This time, it took him three counts to finally lower his gaze to mine. He nodded and turned, leaving me alone to pack up the shattered remnants of my life.

Homecoming
Chapter 10

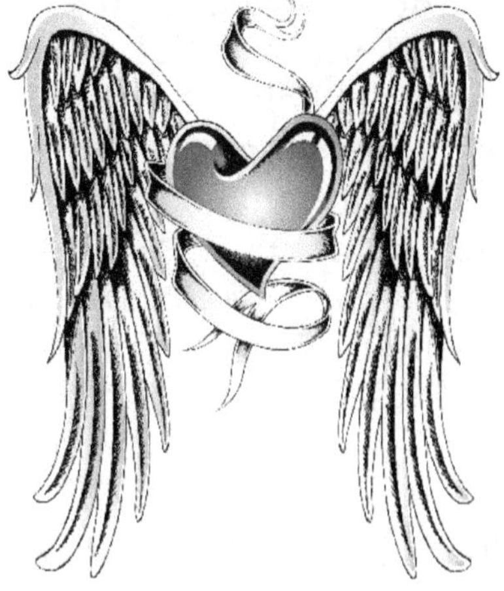

I SAT IN THE back seat with a baby between me and Levi. Michael drove while Kylee studied the map Death gave me, plotting our course on her tablet. The silence in the car was maddening. I glanced out the window, wishing it was Alex on the other side of the car seat.

He hadn't even said goodbye. He had just stared at me with his arms crossed from the farthest point of the room. He'd purposely blocked me from any of his thoughts. It was a harsher punishment than anything he could have done to me. I imagined it would be on par with tearing my heart from my body.

The whine from the other side of the car pulled my attention. At first, I thought it was the baby, but she was sleeping peacefully with a pacifier in her mouth. That left one other being. I met Levi's sad-eyed stare.

Do not fret. The boy loves you.

The deep and very ancient-sounding voice filled my head. I pointed at the dog.

Who else would it be?

My mouth popped open, and I snapped my gaze out the windshield while the silent communication sank in. I slid my gaze in his direction and thought, *You can read minds?*

The dog's mouth opened, and his tongue lolled out to the side in a weird canine grin. It was as creepy as his faux fur had felt.

I shivered. It was unnatural, and I didn't want to discuss Alex, even though the creature was trying to ease my mind. Alex had left me with a cold certainty that whatever we had shared yesterday hadn't meant a thing to him.

Stop with the overdramatic teen angst!

"Get out of my head," I muttered and turned away from the monster dog.

"Did you say something?" Kylee stretched around the seat to look at me. Her blonde hair hung in a wave between the seats.

"No, just talking to myself." I swore Levi was laughing at me.

Kylee glanced at the dog and back at me. "How are you holding up?"

I glanced out the window and shrugged. "I don't know. Honestly, I'm exhausted, and Alex didn't make leaving easy at all." My stomach muscles tightened at the thought of his brooding expression, as if I had taken his last piece of special candy away. It was childish and so very effective at hurting me.

She let out a small laugh. "It must be a trait of that name. My husband used to give me that look when I left for a job without him."

"You were married?" I asked.

Michael's gaze flicked to mine in the rearview mirror before he looked back out the windshield.

"Yes. Alejandro, or Alex, for short. That's what I called him for years. He was Alexis's daddy." She turned back to the front of the car, but even her profile announced her sadness. I didn't need to be a mind reader to feel it fill the car.

"What happened to him?"

She didn't answer at first, and suddenly her mind went to static. She was purposely blocking me, and she glanced at Michael. Her hands seemed to wrestle with each other as she looked over her shoulder at me.

"You did the right thing by leaving him behind." She offered a grim smile and turned away.

"If this is so dangerous, then why are you taking me? You have a daughter, for God's sake."

"Because I have an arsenal of ancient weapons that will help you. And I'm a seasoned fighter. I was the best choice in that room to help you do this quickly. Michael is going to watch over Alexis for me when we get to San Diego, which will ease my mind. Leaving both of them in York was not an option. No one but Fate knows where I live, which means both Michael and Alexis will be safe while I'm gone."

"You are leaving your daughter?" My voice cracked as I asked the question.

Kylee glanced back at me and nodded. "Yes. It won't take us as long as you think to do this job. Not with the map and a privately chartered jet that will take us to our destinations."

As if on cue, Michael turned off the highway and headed towards signs announcing Berwick. He navigated the roads until he pulled into a small private airport.

We climbed out of the car, and Michael grabbed the suitcases in the back as Kylee let Levi out of the car and unhooked the car seat. I stood next to the car waiting for them because I didn't know what to do. I had never flown before, and the only experience I had with airports was what I had watched in movies. This little stretch of tarmac followed nothing I had ever seen before.

Levi came over to my side of the car and nudged my hand with his nose. I glanced down and then realized that both Michael and Kylee were heading towards a plane that was waiting for us. We didn't go inside the building, and we didn't have to pass through any metal detectors like I had seen countless times in movies I'd watched.

I followed and climbed the stairs after the dog. The interior of the plane looked like a high-end living room. More posh than even the Ryans'. I was waved to a seat by the pilot.

"Hello, I'm Josh. I'll be your pilot." He glanced at the paper in his hands. "It looks like I'll be your pilot for quite some time based on the schedule here." He smiled, but it didn't reach his eyes. "First stop is San Diego." He turned and closed the door.

I glanced around the fuselage, and my heart picked up in my chest. I rubbed my hands on my jeans and tried to shake the building unease in my belly. Levi jumped up on the seat next to me and stretched out, laying his head on my lap. He glanced up at me with eyes that reflected the same amount of unease riding my blood.

The monster was just as afraid of flying as I was.

Kylee and Michael strapped in with the baby between them and smiled at me from across the plane.

"By the time we are done, you two will be seasoned air travelers." Kylee smiled. "That doesn't mean the unease of being sealed in a tin can ten thousand feet in the air goes away, either."

I noticed how tightly her hands gripped the arms of her seat and couldn't help but grin. "So, this flutter of fear is normal?"

Michael chuckled. He seemed to be the only one that was completely relaxed. "I don't know why you are so afraid of flying," he said to Kylee. "It beats driving across the country."

"I've never gotten used to it," she muttered. "It's unnatural."

I started stroking Levi's head despite the weird leathery feel of him under my fingers. He sighed heavily.

"I've never been out of Maine," I said as the plane started moving.

"Well, you're going to get to see the world over the next couple of weeks," Kylee said.

I had seen the list. I didn't think it was possible to close all the breaches in a couple of weeks. "What's the plan?"

Kylee's knuckles turned white, and I glanced out the window as the plane sped up. My heart lurched into my throat and my skin heated, but not in a scary way. It was thrilling, like driving the car at eighty down the empty highway. I grinned, excitement mounted, and when we left the ground, my stomach dropped. I giggled as I watched the houses on the ground get smaller and smaller.

"That was... exciting." I turned back towards Kylee and Michael. He had the same silly grin I supposed I sported, but Kylee was white as a sheet and trying to smile back at us.

She shook her head and gulped. "The plan is to go get my arsenal and start closing breaches." She pulled out her tablet and handed it across to me. "We need to get the bigger breaches first. We'll be flying back to New York and work our way west until we are finished with the first round. So in order of breach size: New York, Texas, South Pacific, New Zealand, Ireland, and then back home. Five major breaches. The minor ones can wait until after you deal with Lucifer."

"Won't the minor ones become major if we don't do anything about them?"

"The major ones are breaches to Hell. They seemed to be the ones that punched through completely. The others are to Purgatory, which really isn't a risk at all, or they are minor breaches in Hell that are nothing more than a shimmer in the sky. Most demons won't even notice those, so they are much less of a risk, and we don't need to concern ourselves with them right now." She sighed and rubbed her face. "As far as the bigger breaches, there is already evidence of some serious escapees across the globe. New York is the biggest problem and the one we have to fix as soon as possible."

"So why are we going to San Diego? Why not New York directly?"

"I need my weapons." She looked down at her sleeping daughter. "And I needed her safe before I could focus on this mess."

I couldn't argue with that logic. My ears popped, and I swallowed, relieving the pressure.

"If you don't mind me asking, what happened with Alex?" Kylee asked.

I took a deep breath and let it out slowly. "He wanted to say a proper goodbye, and I wasn't going to aggravate his father any more than we already had."

"Proper goodbye?"

I stared at her and then raised my eyebrows when she didn't seem to get it.

"Oh," she finally said. "Aren't you two a little young for that?"

"We're sixteen." I crossed my arms as my defenses riled up.

She laughed. "Sixteen is really young for that kind of responsibility, don't you think?"

Michael shifted in the seat and glanced out the window. His barely concealed smirk piqued my curiosity, and I used my newly found mind-reading abilities to tap into him.

"He was fourteen." I pointed.

His eyebrows shot up. "You can read minds now?"

The last time he'd seen me was when Tom was alive, and I wasn't sure how much information CJ had shared while I was laid out.

I nodded. "I have everything that Tom had, but I have very little understanding of how to use it all."

"Really?" He crossed his arms. His blinding aura flared with a string of purple and green.

I found it weird that doubt showed up as such vibrant colors, but then again, he obviously didn't know the entire story. "What were you told?"

"That Lucifer has Tom," Michael said.

"And to run if Tom approached us," Kylee added.

I raised an eyebrow. "Tom is dead. He died while we were trying to stop the portal from opening. He gave me his heart." My voice cracked. "And with it came everything. Powers, memories, and the strength I needed to close the breach. Except it wasn't enough to stop Lucifer from getting through, so Tom's death was a waste of a good man's life." My chin shook, and I bit down on my lower lip to stop the tide from bursting. When I had control, I continued. "I brought him back to the Ryans' house, but your sister took him to Lucifer."

Michael leaned back in the seat with horror written in his expression.

"So, Lucifer has Tom's body. But he really wants Alex's. And I'm on this godforsaken journey to close all the breaches when the guy that I'm in love with is fair game to fall into Lucifer's hands."

"What does Lucifer want with Alex?" Kylee asked.

"He wants his DNA. Alex and Grace have all the archangel bloodlines between the two of them, and Lucifer wants an army. What better way to build an unstoppable army?"

Michael paled. "And Grace wants Alex." He ran his hand down his face.

"Yes. And she seems to be willing to turn on anyone to get what she wants."

Kylee closed her eyes and leaned back in the seat. "No wonder why everyone was so subdued. I thought it was just because Lucifer killed Paige and Austin."

"He's trying to power up on what's left of the angel descendants," Michael said. "Damn." He glanced at Kylee and narrowed his eyes. "Is that why you want me in San Diego?"

She shrugged. "I need someone I trust to stay with Alexis. And yes, I've become quite fond of you, so keeping you safe from his radar is an added bonus."

A soft smile appeared on his lips. That was the first time Kylee had ever admitted to caring about him as more than just a traveling companion. It made me shift in the seat, feeling more like a third wheel as opposed to a partner in this crazy voyage.

Homecoming
Chapter 11

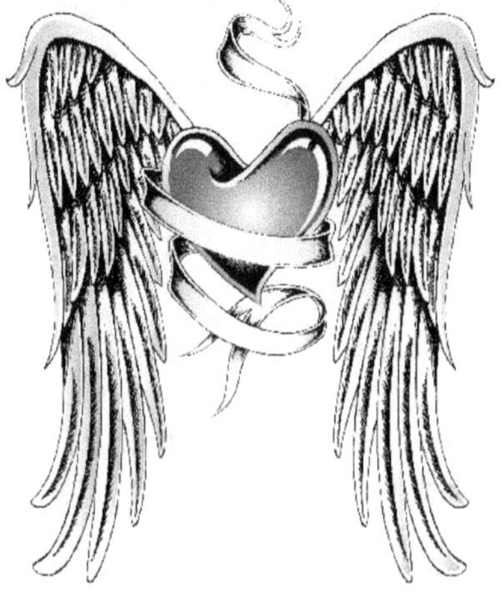

ARSENAL WAS AN UNDERSTATEMENT. I stared at the growing pile of weapons, from daggers, to tridents, to sabers and pikes. It was overwhelmingly amazing. I picked up a blade, and it vibrated in my hand. Power snaked up my arm and infused in my cells, making me feel invincible.

"That's Solomon's knife," Kylee said.

The tremors in my hand passed through my entire body.

"Not everyone can handle it." She stepped towards me and unwrapped my fingers from around the hilt.

The moment it fell out of my palm, I gasped. "Holy cow."

She handed me a different pair of knives. "These might be more your speed."

I didn't know how to fight with a knife, but I pulled the snake-like blade from the sheath. It was beautifully crafted copper and steel. I put it back in the holder and handed them back to Kylee.

"You keep them." She pushed my hand back toward me.

"I don't have the foggiest idea of how to use a knife outside the kitchen." I held them out to her again.

"You will learn." She turned back to her weapons room and gathered a few more ancient artifacts, then dumped them all into a pair of duffel bags. She handed me one and shouldered the other.

The bag was heavy, and I nearly stumbled. I adjusted the strap over my head, and it was a little easier to handle.

We climbed down the stairs to Kylee's open living room and kitchen area, and I stared out at the Pacific. It looked much more formidable than the Atlantic coast of Maine. The bright midday sun bounced off the waves, creating an energy on the air. It buzzed in my head, and I glanced at Kylee, wondering if she felt the same connection to the ocean.

Levi sat next to me, looking out at the sea with a wistful expression.

"Do you miss playing in the water or something?" I asked.

The dog looked up and gave me that crazy, tongue-lolling grin again. He didn't need to say anything in my head. I knew it just from his expression.

"You know dogs can't speak," Michael said.

I glanced at him. "Yes, but Levi isn't a dog."

He rolled his eyes at me and shoveled another spoonful of baby food into Alexis's mouth. He turned his attention to Kylee. "If something happens..."

"Nothing will happen." She leaned up and pecked his cheek. "Thank you for taking care of her while I'm gone."

He just nodded and glanced at me. *I'm counting on you.*

His thought echoed in my head, and I nodded. Everyone was counting on me. It was a lot to shoulder, but I would do my best to keep Kylee alive. She didn't seem the type to sacrifice herself for a virtual stranger, so I didn't foresee the same ending that Tom had met at all. Besides, she didn't carry angel grace in her bloodline.

We left and climbed into the little sporty coupe that was a totally impractical family car and sped off from the house. The drive back to the small airfield was cramped with Levi at my feet. I was happy it was quick, or otherwise I would have been sore for the flight.

Neither one of us said anything until we hauled our duffel bags onto the plane and stowed them in the back near the bathroom.

Kylee's tension filled the small fuselage. For someone with so much experience, I found it funny that flying put her on edge. The pilot wasn't on board yet, and as we waited, she seemed to tighten up even more.

After a half hour of waiting, Josh climbed the steps, looking more refreshed than when we'd left Maine.

"New York next, correct?" he asked.

"Yes." Kylee nodded.

"And you need a car, right?"

She glanced down at the tablet. "That would be helpful."

"We should touch down in a little over four and a half hours." He turned and entered the cockpit.

This time, he left the door open so I could see all the instruments.

He glanced back as if he knew I was looking the space over. "When we get in the air, you are more than welcome to come up and take a gander." His gaze moved between the two of us, lingering more on Kylee than me.

"I might," I said, feeling very self-conscious, as if the invitation hadn't really been for me.

He grinned. "I'll let you know when it is safe to pop in." He turned back to the controls and readied the plane for takeoff.

I traded a glance with Kylee as my heart jumped with the rev of the engine. That internal rush took over, and I kneeled on the couch to get a look out the window. I felt like a two-year-old in a toy store.

Some of Tom's memories filtered in. He knew how to fly a plane, and I grinned, glancing at the cockpit. I had his skills, his experience to tap into.

I could fly this plane.

"Why are you grinning like that?" Kylee asked. Stress layered over her sweet voice, making it sharper than she probably anticipated.

"I know how to fly a plane." I winked.

She cocked her head, and I tapped my temple. My smile was so wide that my cheeks hurt. I really wanted to fly the plane, too, but from the paleness in Kylee's cheeks, I wasn't sure she could deal with a teenager taking control of such a large toy.

"Please don't do that. It will give me a heart attack," she said.

I laughed, feeling giddy as we started to speed up on the runway. Blood pumped in my veins, heating my skin with a pleasant warmth. The sudden lift off dropped my stomach for a moment, and all I could do was smile. This was so out of the ordinary that I couldn't understand why Kylee was so afraid.

Levi crawled over to her to find some comfort since I was all about this rush. It was parallel to what making love to Alex had been like. Surreal.

The sudden reminder of Alex cooled whatever enthusiasm I was feeling, and I slumped in the chair.

"He really got under your skin, didn't he?" Kylee asked.

"Yeah," I said. "He was so angry with me." I looked down at my hands. "I just couldn't. Otherwise, I wouldn't leave."

"He is having a rough time of it, isn't he?"

"Yes, and I had a shot at Lucifer, and I didn't take it because he had Alex's soul stored on a chain around his neck. I hesitated and my opportunity vanished. He was angry at me for that, too."

"The things we do for love aren't always the best or the brightest."

"Tell me about your Alex." I wanted to change the subject.

"Alejandro." She sighed. "He died on a job, and if the thing we were hunting hadn't killed him, I would have had to put him down." She met my gaze. "He heard my siren's song, and that is a death sentence for a human unless they can kill the siren themselves."

"A siren?" I cocked my head. "You mean a mermaid like Ariel?"

Kylee burst out laughing. "No, sweetheart. Sirens are most surely not like the little mermaid. They are more like a horrific swamp creature that drives people into murderous rage with their songs."

"Oh." I glanced out the window. There was so much I needed to learn about this world and the supernatural creatures that I might be facing. "Can you teach me about the things out there?" I hooked my thumb towards the window. "I need to know what we might face at the breaches."

"It depends how deep the breaches go. I think we may only be dealing with demons, but if there are more things getting loose..." She let out a low whistle. "I certainly hope that's all, because if the breach goes deep enough, I can't fathom what could get loose."

I waited.

She rubbed her face. "Jinn, vampires, witches, soul eaters, sirens, bicorns, shifters, wendigos, banshees." She took a big breath and shrugged.

"What, no Frankenstein or mummies?" I asked, trying to stifle a smile. I had read the romanticized versions of a lot of the creatures she'd listed, and my mother's hand-me-down books hadn't educated me beyond the monster's basic need, like blood for a vampire, or wishes for a genie. So, I had zero frame of reference outside of the soul eaters I had experienced with Alex, and they had scared the crap out of me.

She leaned forward and narrowed her eyes. "This isn't a joke. If those things get out, who knows how many will die? It's bad enough if demons and hellhounds get loose."

"I'm sorry." I bit my lip and tried to figure out a way to erase the fiery anger in her gaze. "What if I tell you what I know, and you correct me when I go down the wrong path?"

She nodded and rolled her hand for me to continue.

"Vampires survive on blood and can't go out in the light?"

"Yes. Their venom is poison to a human. And most of the ones I ever encountered were mindless. They drank until their victim was drained. And if the victim got away, the poison would kill them within a day."

I shivered at the thought.

"Jinn or genies grant wishes?"

The bark of her laugh filled the plane. "That is partially true. Humans lose their life force to the jinn. Each wish takes a piece until there is nothing left. In that way, they are like soul eaters, with one exception. They don't leave the people alive. Because people are greedy beings, they always come back for more than one wish. There have only been a handful of people who have walked away from a Jinn before the third and fatal wish occurs."

I didn't really want to hear more. I would assume the rest of the pack was equally as horrific as the vampire and the jinn, but I pressed forward.

"Shifters turn into animals?" I asked, afraid of the answers.

She nodded. "They have a healthy taste for human flesh, as do all carnivores. However, these aren't as easy to distinguish from the other monsters. Some refuse to eat humans. They have laws against it, but there always seems to be one in the pack that rebels. Those are the ones that are in Hell. And yes, they can turn into almost any animal they choose."

"You told me about sirens, and I have dealt with soul eaters. So, what does a bicorn do?"

She licked her lips. "They feed on virtue. They steal souls and keep the victims as their slaves." She glanced away. "Wendigos eat humans, and banshees are a little like sirens, except they don't drive you mad. You just go blind and then your brain hemorrhages."

"What about witches?" That was the only being she rattled off that she hadn't covered.

"Witches are a little like shifters in that they aren't always evil, but they can certainly hex you to death if they are one of Lucifer's minions."

"Well, okay, then," I muttered, now more uneasy about this endeavor than I was before. I just thought I had to worry about demons, which were bad enough, but now I had to worry about all these other creatures.

The weight of that responsibility pressed on my shoulders. I slouched under it. "Can my angel fire kill these things?"

She nodded. "I believe so. The only concern I have is with a siren or a banshee. I don't know if either of us is susceptible to their calls. If so, we are screwed unless we kill the source. I think the only other being that might make things difficult is a witch. The rest we can take down before they have a chance to hurt us as long as we have each other's backs."

"Do you have my back?" The words slipped out before I could stop them. The only thing I knew about Kylee was she used to be a siren. I stiffened in the seat as a memory started taking shape. I closed my eyes, forcing it back, but it was too late.

The area between the seats faded out of focus, and Kylee's eyes grew wide. I wished the door to the cockpit closed while beyond the forming vision, the door actually swung closed before the pilot could witness this little time jump.

IN THE SHIMMERING VIEW, Tom shook his head, and he said, "I've had my fill of demons, vampires, and ghosts. You're the first siren I've ever met."

Kylee's voice rang through the air as if she were speaking, but her lips didn't once move. "I am no longer a true siren. Yes, I still hold the capability of siren song, but what you see today is what Fate turned me into after I escaped from Lucifer with my brother. The brother I was later commanded to kill. I'm enslaved by Fate, obligated to hunt down creatures that escaped from Hell during a breach. But, as I learned recently, I am only obligated to hunt down those that cross the line. Therefore, my contract will truly never end. I'm bound to Fate's whims for eternity."

Her face reddened, and her fists clenched. "This was not my choice. I'm the best at what I do, but it is not my choice to live an eternity alone. You asked about Alex. I made the mistake of letting him in, and he died because of it."

CJ, Valerie, and Tom stared at Kylee.

"I see ghosts. I never asked for that," Tom said, and bitterness threaded through his voice. "I never asked for my tongue to be cut out or my dead wife's to be sewn back in. I never asked to choose between my best friend and my daughter, either." He gave me a shrug. "Unfortunately, neither my daughter nor my best friend survived. So, you'll find zero sympathy from me." His hard gaze locked with hers.

Kylee climbed to her feet and started towards the door.

CJ stepped into her path, stopping her.

"Move." Her hands moved fluidly in sign language. "You don't need to be part of my shit show."

"Sorry, not happening," CJ said.

Kylee jumped into the air and spun like those old kung fu movies, but her entire body froze with her foot just an inch away from CJ's face.

I gasped and covered my mouth.

The Kylee on the plane with me rolled her eyes at my reaction.

"Are you quite done with your little show?" CJ asked and pushed her leg away.

Whatever suspended her in the air released, and she crumpled to the ground next to the couch.

"I can't stay."

"Yes, you can. And there is a way to fix this," CJ said.

Kylee clenched her hands in frustration.

The soft expression on CJ's face hardened, and his focus moved away from Kylee's face in an arc. A blade made of pure light slashed through the cords, Kylee fell to her knees, and Valerie clamped her hand over Kylee's mouth.

One of the ghosts thundered, "No!"

Kylee in the image passed out.

However, the Kylee on the plane with me had her gaze locked on the handsome ghost. "Alejandro," she whispered from the other side of the time jump vision.

A host of ghosts with broken tethers rose above her as she sank to the ground, and then her body shook. The ghost threaded his hand through hers in a tight grip while the rest of the dead were ushered out of the room. His severed tether waved in the air above them.

"You're killing her!" the ghost yelled, his ghostly essence turning red with aggravation.

"No, we're not. We're trying to save her," Fate said as she stepped through the door.

Death waited on the back lawn with a very unsettled Leviathan, pacing back and forth.

"You want to bring her back to Hell!" the ghost argued, trying to block Fate's advance, while he clung to Kylee.

Tom stepped in front of Fate, blocking Alejandro from her. "Trust me, we are trying to save your wife and child, but we need your help."

"You're out of your fucking mind!"

"Alejandro, I know she never trusted me. Not fully, but I never wanted to hold her to the insane contract she signed. I had no choice. If I don't deliver her siren to Hell, I will be in breach of contract. You don't want that on your head," Fate said.

"I don't give a damn. I'm not letting you take her." He squared up in front of Kylee without letting go of her hand.

"I do not want to take Kylee. The angels gave me a way to save her. It's a little unorthodox, but it will make it so none of us are breaching the contract," Fate said, articulating carefully with her hands out like she was trying to calm Leviathan instead of the ghost of Kylee's dead husband.

Alejandro stared at her. "You're serious."

"Yes. I need her siren. Now, will you help me save your wife?" She held a small glass bottle out to him.

He gazed down at Kylee with a nod and took the vial in his hand. "I don't know how to do this," he said. "Fate, the one before you, yanked it from her throat."

"That bitch didn't take her siren. She took her voice. It's different. The siren is actually a part of her. It was used to anchor all those soul tethers. You need to pull it out and shove it in that container."

Tiny worry lines formed around his eyes. "What will happen to her?"

"She will become mortal."

Alejandro's eyes widened, and he looked at the cluster of tethers floating above Kylee's head. "Mortal?" His mouth worked around the word. He licked his lips, glancing back at Fate and then at the only other person in the room who could see him.

Tom nodded. "It's not going to be pretty, but she will survive."

"You can guarantee that?" Alejandro asked.

Tom pointed at Valerie. "She will make sure of it."

Valerie glanced up at him with a tense smile.

Alejandro crouched down next to Kylee and unclasped his hand from hers. He swept the lot of tethers into his hands as close to her head as possible.

He looked over his shoulder at Tom. "What happens if she lets the siren loose before I can get it out?"

Tom gave a nervous laugh. "Then I think we are all doomed." He shrugged. "The key is to not stop once you start. No matter what."

Alejandro gave a nod and took a deep breath, wrapping the tethers around his fist until they were taut. The muscles in his arms contracted. "Here goes nothing." He yanked.

Kylee's body jerked. Her eyes flew open, shimmering like a true siren, and the tethers pooled together to form a scaly gray circle on her forehead.

"Hold her!" Alejandro said, trying to rise to his feet with the tethers grasped tight. The muscles in his back and neck flexed.

The ghostly bellow that followed made me shiver.

Tom's hand shot out, grabbing the tethers below Alejandro's hand, and he added his strength to Kylee's husband's.

The sound of wet flesh bursting filled the room.

"Jesus Christ," Alejandro cried, but the vial disappeared behind his ghostly essence.

Tom stumbled backwards, catching the edge of the couch with a bloodstained hand. Alex turned, giving Tom a full view of Kylee's body and the hole in my forehead. Valerie's lips landed on a clean spot next to the tear in her skull, and light danced across Kylee's form, pooling around the gaping wound.

Alejandro shoved the vial at Fate and then fell to his knees next to Kylee. "I'm so sorry, baby." His hands cradled her face and his lips brushed hers. "I'm so sorry."

The light surrounding Kylee faded, and her ragged breath evened out. Valerie checked her pulse and glanced up at Tom.

"She seems to be stabilizing," she said.

"Good. I will be right back. I have a siren to deliver." Fate gave Tom a nod before she disappeared.

THE IMAGE FADED, AND Kylee stared at the spot the ghost of her husband had occupied a few moments ago. Then her gaze swiveled to mine. Mixed emotions lived in her eyes and in her mind. She fought to remain calm.

I braced myself for another weird onslaught, but when nothing happened, my tightly coiled muscles relaxed.

"I'm sorry," I said when I thought my voice wouldn't crack.

"What are you?" she whispered.

"I'm Lucifer's daughter," I said. "And these stupid time jumps are what opens breaches." My chin trembled. "I don't know how to control them," I whispered and put my face in my hands. Hot tears dripped onto my palms.

Levi's head pressed onto my lap, and an arm wrapped around my shoulders.

"I'll help you figure this out," Kylee said in my ear. "And as far as your question, I do have your back. Tom had it, so I need to trust his judgement."

I looked up at her. "Tom sacrificed himself, and it was all for nothing." I swiped at the tears heating my cheeks in drizzles, but I couldn't staunch the flow.

"Men do that sometimes," she said with a sad smile.

"Really?" I sniffled.

"Yeah. They can be royal idiots."

Somehow, her wildly inappropriate comment made me want to laugh despite the building turmoil inside. It made me trust her the way I trusted Tom. I knew he had my back when he was alive. I just didn't want to be the cause of another senseless death.

Homecoming
Chapter 12

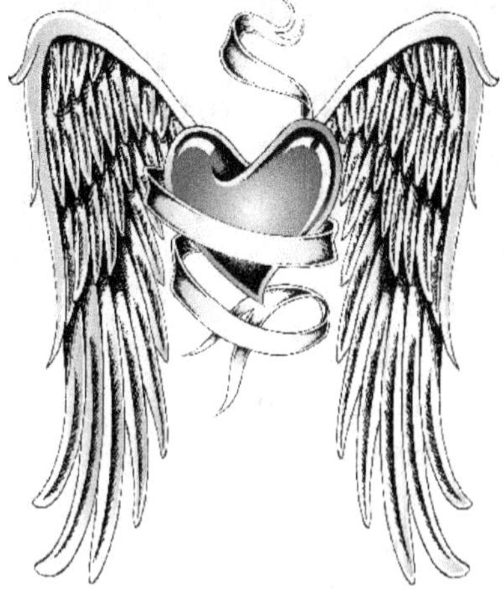

THE PLANE LANDED, AND I stretched to get the stiff ache out of my limbs. Kylee did the same from the couch near the back. Levi did an upward facing dog followed by a downward facing dog. It was the damnedest thing to see a dog doing yoga, but there it was.

I headed back to the bathroom to freshen up a little. The washroom was a little bigger than mine at Tom's house. The plane itself amazed me with its luxury. Of course, I didn't know any different.

When I came out, Kylee took her turn.

She came out a few minutes later and opened one of the duffel bags. From within the canvas, she pulled out an oversized tote and dropped some weapons inside before shifting it to her shoulder. She stood and glanced around the interior as we slowed to a full stop.

"This is the way to travel." She smiled when the cockpit door opened and Josh stepped out.

He looked at the sheet in his hands. "I am going to get some rest before our next jaunt. The plane will be here in this hangar for whenever you are ready." He looked at Kylee. "You have the number to contact me if the plans are changing, correct?"

"Yes. I do. I don't know how long this will take, but we will let you know when we are on our way back," Kylee said.

Josh folded the paper and slipped it in his shirt pocket before he undid the door and unfolded the stairs. He stepped aside and smiled as we passed by.

Just outside the hangar sat a town car, and Kylee led me to it and opened the door for me. I slid inside and scooted over so she could get in.

"Freedom Tower, please," Kylee said, looking at the coordinates on her phone. She glanced at me and sighed.

Just from her expression, I knew this would not be easy. I opened my mouth, but she shook her head and sent a wary glance at the driver. I got her meaning immediately. No talking about the mission in front of strangers. The drive from the hangar at LaGuardia took a little better than a half hour.

I climbed out of the car, awed by the tall buildings that strained my neck when I tried to see the tops. Glass and metal monsters surrounded us, and I didn't know where to look. It was as magnificent as it was scary.

Kylee smiled as she caught me staring. "Never been to a city before?"

"I've been to Augusta," I said, louder than I anticipated. The massive din of strangers' thoughts assaulted me all at once. I focused on Kylee, and the rest of the world faded into the background.

She snorted a laugh. "Honey, that's not a city. *This* is a city." She waved her hand at the hustle and bustle around us. "And this is calm compared to midtown."

I scanned the crowds. It was more people in one place than I had ever seen before. Both discomfort and excitement drilled through me. If I didn't remain focused on Kylee, I wouldn't be able to think straight.

I prayed I could block out the noise around me because I had a feeling I would need to concentrate to close whatever breach was here in the city.

Kylee led me toward a stairwell that went down. On the side of the railing was a sign for a subway. When she continued down the stairs, I stalled at the top, and the noise overwhelmed me. The idea of going underground really threw me and the echo of voices just left me cold.

She stopped halfway down and looked up at me as people passed by me with little more than glances, even though their thoughts, emotions, and auras screamed annoyance.

"It's okay," she said, too soft to hear above the din, but I heard her in my head. She adjusted the bag on her shoulder and turned back toward the underground path.

I inhaled and tried not to shiver, focusing only on Kylee yet again. The thought of releasing my angel fire in such a constrained place scared me. I could almost envision... I stopped and closed my eyes, stifling any possible preconceived notions. I didn't want to be responsible for the next televised disaster.

When I got to where Kylee had been standing, the stench of the subway hit. Sweat, pee, and grime combined to create a smell that I wanted to avoid at all costs. I covered my nose with my hand and forced my feet to continue moving until there were no more steps.

I looked up, and my heart leaped into my throat at the sea of people. No wonder I nearly could not drown them out of my head. Their auras melded together into swirls of color. I could tell those who were upset in some way from those who were content just through the pulses in each person's aura.

"Faith." Kylee's voice broke through my momentary panic.

I turned to her, and she ushered me through the turnstiles and down another set of stairs, bringing us deeper into the bowels of the station where the scents were riper, and the sea of people thickened.

I froze at the subway platform, freaked out by the crowd.

Kylee touched my arm, and I turned, catching sight of her in the tight space beside the stairwell. She nodded for me to follow, and I gladly slipped into the darkness with her, going away from the crowd. She glanced at her watch in the dark, following whatever directions that kept sputtering on the screen.

When we reached the end of the ramp, she muttered under her breath and turned to me in the darkness.

"We need to go into the tunnels." She sounded exasperated, and she ran her hand through her hair, staring into the blackness.

Her natural turquois and purple aura had threads of navy pulsing through it. I didn't need to be a genius to see she was nervous. Hell, I was shaking at the thought of going into that blackness, too.

"We need to be very cautious and try to stay close to the walls. Hopefully, there will be places to slide into if a train comes."

"And if there aren't?"

She glanced over her shoulder at me and just shook her head. "I just hope this thing isn't on an active track." She pointed to the red dot on her watch.

The display showed we still had a way to go in these underground tunnels to reach that red dot. I swallowed hard. The minute we dropped onto the tracks, one of the indicators turned green.

"What does that mean?"

"It means we are at the right depth for the location of the breach."

"Fabulous."

She pulled out a flashlight and glanced at her watch. Thankfully, she headed away from the subway ramp we'd come down. "Don't touch the tracks." She jumped over the one nearest and crossed to the other side, where the tunnel opened up into multiple tracks.

We crossed into a section between tracks wide enough that it looked like it was meant to be a walking path. Kylee's shoulders relaxed, and she exhaled loud enough for me to feel the tension melt away.

I nearly jumped out of my skin when a train barreled by on the track to my left. Kylee looked back at me.

"We are lucky there is a breezeway between tracks here, but up ahead, there aren't any. And it looks like the breach is at an intersection of three tracks, so be prepared to dodge trains as well as whatever is escaping."

"I don't know if I can do this," I said over the sound of another approaching train. "I am not sure if what I need to do will compromise this." I waved at the iron surrounding us.

She slowed down and glanced at me. Genuine fear reflected in her eyes and her mind.

"I could bring it all down on us." I swallowed and wished that Alex were with me. At least if he were here, I had more of a chance to do this right rather than create a world-class disaster.

Kylee closed her eyes, and when they opened, a hardness appeared in them. "You can do this." She seemed to be willing me not to think the worst. Willing me to man up according to the words forming in her mind.

I bit my lip and nodded, because what else was I supposed to do?

"I'll take care of whatever obstacles are coming at us. And you take care of closing the damn breach. You're a Nephilim. Embrace that shit."

I stopped short and narrowed my gaze at her. She was trying to make me angry. She was trying to get me to take control of the situation. I hated to admit it, but the way she spoke the word Nephilim—it worked. She had an aggravated and reverent tone, and I needed to start to live up to my heritage. I needed to be badass, as Alex had put it. Like I had been in Maine when I closed the first portal.

"Then let's get on with it." I waved for her to continue. As she turned away, I caught a hint of a smile.

The sureness in my step faded as the walkway we had been traversing ended and dual tracks sat side by side with very little space between them or on the outer edges. If two trains came at once, we would be mush, unless one of those man-trap alcoves was within reach.

"Damn it," Kylee whispered.

The dot on the map on her watch was still far enough away to dry the spit in my mouth. We exchanged a glance. She dug into her pocket and pulled out her phone. She attempted to pull up the subway schedules, but she had no service this far below ground.

"Left or right?" She looked at me.

Both were equally daunting, but on the right, I saw a dim yellow light on the wall. The left side was bathed in black.

"Right," I said, pointing to the light.

Kylee nodded and then hopped over the electrical rail that emitted a constant buzz. I followed her. When we got to the wall, she gave me a nod.

"Keep an eye out for a train," she said.

The closer we came to the light, the more it looked like the small area near the tracks that we were walking widened. It almost looked like a deliberate walking path, like the one we had left behind. But it wasn't nearly as expansive as the one between the tracks had been. But at least in this small section of track, if a train came, we could press our backs against the wall and not be hit.

The ground started to shake underneath us, and Kylee sprinted toward the dim yellow light. I followed, with the tremble of the earth below my feet and my heart pounding with the same velocity. I really didn't know if either of us would make the safety of what I assumed was an alcove.

The tunnel lit up from behind us. Kylee turned and grabbed me, then slammed me back first against the wall. She dropped her bag between us and pressed against the wall next to me. The fear in her eyes had me holding my breath. I didn't dare move.

Within a blink, a silver bullet of a train passed by within inches of us. The force of it pushed me harder against the wall. My heart thundered as loud as the howl of the train cars passing.

Vertigo gripped me as I stared ahead at the endless progression of silver and slot, silver and slot, silver and slot, barely making out the connections between the subway cars, forcing the wave of dizziness away. If I passed out now, I was a dead girl.

The roar continued. Then the train in front of us passed, but a train going the other way still lumbered in the other direction.

Kylee picked up her bag with a shaking hand and glanced at her watch again before continuing in the same direction we had been going. She took a few steps and then stopped. She turned towards the tracks and leaned forward, vomiting on the ground.

She wiped her mouth and stood and then started walking like nothing had just happened. I sidestepped the splatters and followed without comment. My stomach was still in my throat, and the adrenaline was still pounding my veins. I was sure as soon as all this was over, I would probably do the same.

But for now, my entire form was a live wire as deadly as the third rail. The power snaked along with the adrenaline, warming me into a tacky sweat. I itched to take my glove off, and that feeling of being electrified increased.

Kylee stopped and pressed us into a tiny alcove. We faced each other as she held up her hand, showing me her watch. We were so close. Close enough that it could be around the next bend.

"Stay here while I check it out," she said, low enough for me to catch sound, but not pick up her words.

If I wasn't psychic, I wouldn't have had a clue of what she was saying, but I heard her in my head as if we were in a quiet library and she was shouting. I nodded, and she handed me her bag.

I faced the direction she headed. It was increasingly lighter, and Kylee disappeared.

I almost stepped out to follow her, but a train barreled towards me. I shrank into the alcove. I closed my eyes and reached out with my mind, ignoring the people on the train. My mind finally found what I needed to loosen the knots in my back.

Stay cool, just stay cool. Kylee's internal mantra continued for the length of the subway cars.

It was easier to deal with in the alcove as I had been plastered to the wall, but my heart still jumped with tension. As soon as the train disappeared again, I poked my head out in time to see Kylee doing the same in the dim light. Instead of staying put, I trotted up to where she had been hiding.

The closer I got to the corner, the more my hands itched. The hair on the back of my neck stood on end, and I knew without looking that the breach was around the corner.

Kylee pressed her lips together, her eyes blazing before her hands started moving a mile a minute. I stared at them, trying to figure out just what in the world she was trying to say.

I told you to stay! Her voice barreled in my head.

I pointed to the alcove she had just been in. For some reason, I kept quiet. Maybe it was the air surrounding us. The stale, dusty, electrified air in the tunnel was better than that of the station, but it still had a greasy, uneasy stench that I would forever recall with the terror of a train blowing so close that a stray eyebrow hair could have been ripped off.

I closed my eyes and let the hum of the third rail fade. That's when the air surrounding us turned sinister, like evil had a particular smell beyond brimstone. I took her hand and glanced at the dots. Us and the breach. All that stood between us was the bend in the tunnel.

I peeled my gloves off and shoved them in my back pocket, then fisted my hands so they wouldn't spark. Nerves stung my skin, prickling against me as if I had walked into a wall of a thousand needles.

I needed to release this before it turned on me. Instead of being patient, I ran towards the corner.

"Keep watch for a train," I said, and my voice echoed on the walls.

I took the corner too fast and skidded to a stop at the sight before me. A handful of demons were crawling through the breach. More ran down the train tracks. One to the side turned to me with wide eyes. She was striking, and something made me hesitate. While the rest of the escaped crew took the tunnel to my right, she dodged down the left tunnel alone.

I raised my hands, undecided whether to blow both tunnels and eliminate all the demons or take out the breach and only concentrate on the path where a majority were going.

"I've got that one," Kylee said, deciding for me. She took off, following our lone demon.

I inhaled deep, concentrating on all the power inside me, coiling it, letting it feed off itself until I thought my entire form would burst wide from the strain. I aimed my clenched fists, palms toward the breach and the opening where the majority were fleeing.

I opened both hands.

A massive flamethrower would have looked like a little lighter compared to the angel fire that leaped from my palms. Screams filled the tunnel as I pushed the power, incinerating the creatures in my path to dust. I walked forward, moving my right palm to join my left, concentrating on closing the breach. I vibrated with the power, focusing all my energy as the breach mended. It looked like a giant needle doing ancient stitchwork while blasting everything behind it.

The right tunnel matched the left in its endless blackness since my blast had turned it to ash, but the opening where three tracks converged was lit up like a bright, sunny summer day. I screamed, pushing myself harder, willing the breach to mend faster.

The ground trembled, and the light increased. I moved forward, hoping I would not pick the wrong track. I prayed the oncoming train wouldn't come between me and the breach because I was sure the entire thing would turn to dust the way those beings had.

If I stopped now, the breach would double or triple in size like the one at my mother's cottage had. I couldn't risk it. I had to keep going, and I couldn't check to see how close the train was.

My brain registered a triangle-cut patch of gravel big enough for a person to safely stand on right smack in front of the breach. If I could get there before the train made minced meat out of me, I'd be able to close the breach. If not, then the passengers would have one hell of a view and know there were things in this world that didn't belong here.

I got over the maze of rails and stepped close enough to see inside. To see what Hell looked like from the outside. Beings were strapped in various forms of torture, but no one was there to do the vital deed. The stench of brimstone overshadowed the awful smell of the subway tunnel.

My internal alarms were going haywire. I couldn't save those poor, lost souls. Deep down, I knew they had to have done something bad to land in Hell, but seeing them strapped to those tables with all the sharp instruments of torture laid out next to them... My stomach tightened.

I could not save them.

I could not lose my nerves.

I could not lose focus.

If I didn't close this portal, who knew what would escape? Neither of us knew what or how many had already escaped. I refocused my efforts, and being this close to the portal made it much easier to mend the rip.

Movement to my left pulled my attention away from the open gate. Kylee came around the bend, huffing, as if she had just finished a marathon. She stopped short, and her eyes widened.

I turned back to the portal in time to see an arm reach through the fire. Whatever it was grabbed my arm. Its charred hand hurt against my skin. I tried to pull away, but it was strong enough to pull my arm through the breach. My fire sputtered with shock, but then flared brighter. I pulled so my hand was in the tunnel again. I sent a bullet of flame into the portal, turning everything in that room to ash, including the rest of the body that had a grip on me. The rest of the charred arm fell on the ground next to me, and I renewed my quest to close this god-forsaken breach.

The minute the breach blinked out of existence, I stopped the flames. The fact that I could gave me hope. My legs wobbled, and I leaned against the wall, out of breath. My arm scalded where that thing had grabbed me, but I would live.

Kylee crossed the rest of the distance and leaned beside me while I pulled my gloves back on.

A pair of trains barreled through the opening, making us both jump. I started to laugh as the wind whipped our hair around in the small alcove.

"Did you catch that one?" I asked after the trains passed and nodded toward the tunnel that she had chased the demon down.

"No. She got away." Her voice remained strained. "By the way, you are a hell of a sight to behold." She huffed a laugh. "I've never seen wings of fire before."

I remembered the reflection in the cottage. It was scary as hell. "I'm just glad I closed the portal before those trains passed. That would have been really hard to explain if someone had seen me."

She glanced down at the burn on my arm. "I'm glad whatever grabbed you wasn't at full strength, because I wouldn't be happy jumping into Hell to save you. And a chase through the underworld isn't on my to-do list."

"You've been there?"

She nodded. "I was one of Lucifer's pets before my brother and I escaped." She shrugged. "I don't know how far the next subway platform is in either of these tunnels, so did you want to head back the way we came or white-knuckle it down one of these offshoots?"

I hoped like Hell there wasn't a subway platform near this intersection, or otherwise I had toasted a lot of people when I took out those demons. My dread was more acute than my curiosity.

Either way we chose, we would be white knuckling it.

"The beast you know..." I shrugged, pointing the way we'd come.

"Yeah, at least we'll know when we get to that middle path where we'll be safe until we get to the platform."

We started the dangerous trek back to civilization.

Homecoming
Chapter 13

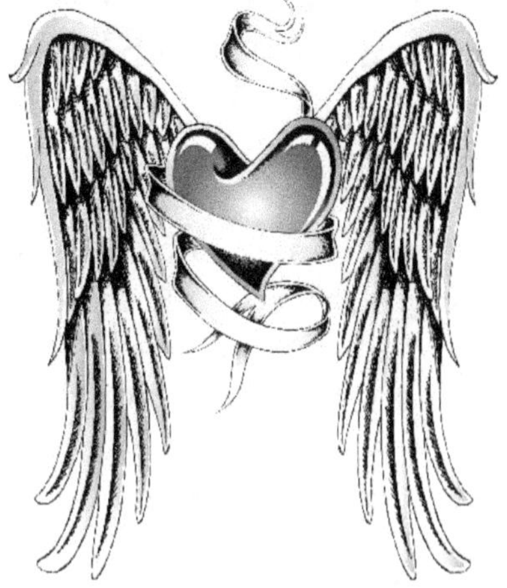

WE COLLAPSED IN THE seats on the plane, exhausted. Levi glanced up from his station on the floor with a curious glance before he lay back down. I was glad we didn't have him with us today. I couldn't see trying to get him to stay flush against the wall, and he could have seen the trains as play things. His true form was gigantic enough to take one of the cars in his mouth like a chew toy.

His tail thumped on the ground.

"You would have done that, wouldn't you?" I teased him, and his tail thumped again. He probably would have been able to catch the escaped demon, but I had a feeling he would have gone for volume. I wouldn't have been able to toast all those demons in the right tunnel with him chasing them.

His tail thumped twice more.

Kylee was leaning back in the seat with her eyes closed. Her chest still labored with each breath.

I cleared my throat, and she glanced over at me.

"I hope none of the other breaches are underground," she said.

"I hope we never have to take a subway. That place smelled worse than Hell did."

She broke out in a smile.

Josh, our friendly pilot, boarded the plane. He looked more refreshed than I felt.

"Texas next, right?" he asked as he looked at the itinerary.

"Yes, please," Kylee said.

He smiled and secured the door before he took the pilot's seat.

I pulled my phone from my bag and sighed at the powerless device, then plugged the charger into an outlet and waited until I could turn it on. By the time it had enough juice, we were taxiing down the runway.

I had over a hundred texts, and every one of them was from Alex. I closed my eyes a second before I started reading. What started as apologetic turned into aggravation and then escalated into furious.

I hadn't even looked at my phone since I boarded the plane.

I'm sorry, Alex. My phone died, and I didn't get your texts until now. I had my first subway adventure today, and I didn't screw it up either. I closed the breach, but I really never want to be in

I pressed send and held my breath. I wasn't sure what kind of response I would get. When my phone rang, I traded a glance with Kylee and answered it.

"You're okay?" Alex's worry traveled over the phone line like a thick, suffocating blanket.

"Yes. I am fine. We are on our way to Texas right now." The plane accelerated, and I glanced out the window. "I do like flying, though."

"Uncle Tom liked to fly," he mumbled. "He used to rent planes over in Wolfeboro and take us flying. It was cool."

The tension between my shoulders released, and I closed my eyes and put my feet up on the couch, laying back. "We could get our pilot's licenses when I get back."

"Really?"

The hopeful lilt in his voice made me smile. "I think it would be fun."

"Totally. But I think we will need our driver's licenses first."

"Probably." I wished I could see him.

He gasped, and my eyes popped open. I stood in his bedroom. He hopped to his feet, wide-eyed, and before my brain could comprehend anything, his arms were around me and his lips were planted on mine.

I melted into the kiss, savoring it.

When his hand ran over the burn, I gasped and sat up in the seat on the plane. The transition jarred me. Alex's voice called from my phone still in my hand. I put it to my ear.

"What the Hell just happened?" I asked softly, hoping not to disturb Kylee.

"You just projected yourself to me. My dad can do that and so could Tom." He laughed lightly. "So you don't really have to stay away the entire time."

My head could not wrap around this. It was more bizarre than the time jumps. "I left the plane?"

"No." He was still laughing. "You were in both places at the same time."

"Stop laughing," I muttered. I knew there were memories relating to this, but I just didn't want to open Pandora's box and pay the price.

"What were you thinking just before you appeared here?"

I wiped my hand down my face. "I wished I could see you."

"Well, all you need to do is wish again, and you'll show up. Try it."

I closed my eyes and concentrated on wishing to see him again. When I opened my eyes, nothing happened. It was similar to my attempt at making the Gatorade bottle come to me from the rock wall. A big nothing.

"It's not working," I said after a few moments. I had no idea what had triggered it before. Maybe a combination of his emotional state and an unconscious wish to wrap my arms around him. It was much more complex than a simple wish.

Alex remained quiet for a moment, and all I heard was his breath on the line. "I hope I get to see you again this way. I can't wait until you close all the breaches. I'm going insane." His voice was as soft as the clouds looked out the window of the plane.

It filled me with a sense of foreboding. "You will be fine." I stretched out on the couch again. "I need to go. I'm not sure I can be on the phone while we are up in the air."

"Are you on one of the Beaumont jets?"

"I think so."

"Then you can talk while you are flying. At least we always did." His voice changed, and I knew he was lying on the bed again. "Unless you don't want to talk to me."

"I do, but I am so tired. I'm not sure I can stay awake much longer, and when we land, I'll have to close another portal."

His internal debate on whether to keep me on the phone or let me rest came through the line, and I didn't interrupt him.

"I don't want to be the one that puts you in danger." He sighed heavily. "As much as I'd like to talk to you until the sun rises, I know you need your strength. Just don't wait so long to tell me you are okay."

"I won't," I promised. "I love you. I swear I'll do this as quickly as humanly possible, but you have to promise me not to go crazy in the meantime. Okay?"

He chuckled softly. "I promise now that I know you are okay. I love you, too. Goodnight."

"Goodnight." I ended the call.

Levi came over to me and put his head on my stomach. His soulful eyes read my mood and he sighed heavily.

I glanced over at Kylee, her breathing slow and steady as if she were asleep.

I started petting Levi, imagining fur instead of the leathery quality of his natural form. I yawned and closed my eyes, hoping that our adventure in Texas was less fraught with danger than the New York subway system.

Homecoming
Chapter 14

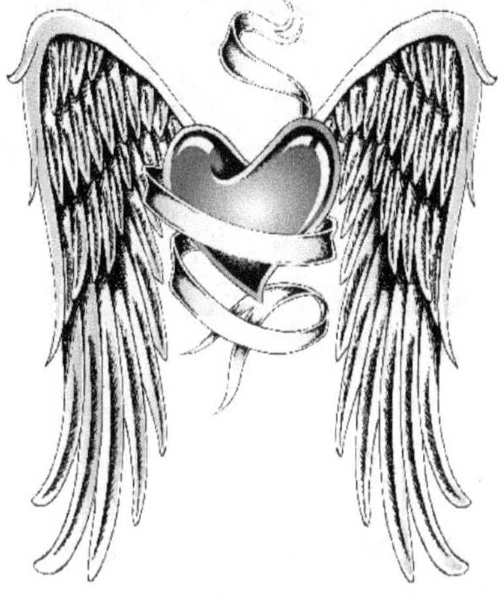

I JOLTED AWAKE AND blinked at my surroundings. I glanced out the window as the forward pull of brakes registered. The green I saw outside the window made me scratch my head. When I thought of Texas, I thought of tumbleweeds and dust storms.

Kylee stretched in the seat and glanced around. "We're here already?" she asked through a yawn.

"I think so." I stumbled to my feet. After relieving myself in the bathroom, I splashed cold water on my cheeks and rinsed my mouth out. I stepped back into the main cabin as Kylee dashed past me.

I opened my suitcase on the couch and pulled out a change of clothes.

Josh cleared his throat, and I turned. He nodded towards the sweater and jeans in my hands. "You might want to rethink that. It's supposed to get up to eighty-five today, and it's humid out there."

I glanced at my clothes and pulled out a short-sleeved shirt, trading it for the sweater. "Thanks."

"There's a full shower in the back, too. If you want to do more than wipe a paper towel over yourself," he said.

"I'll take you up on that after we return. I have a feeling we both will need to clean up after today."

"What do you two have going on?" He glanced towards the bathroom and then back at me.

I shrugged. "She's the travel planner." I hooked my finger over my shoulder. I didn't know how much the pilot knew about the Ryan family or the dark things that lurked out there, and I would rather not freak out our ride.

Kylee stepped out as if on cue.

Josh brightened up. He actually seemed to stand taller when she stepped out. I wanted to dig into his mind to see what his intentions were, but it just didn't feel right. I turned back to my suitcase and closed it just as Valerie's lesson came to mind. I sighed and closed my eyes, turning my mind towards him.

It was easier than it had been with Valerie. I got a distinct taste of honey in my mouth. While he thought Kylee was the most beautiful woman he had ever seen, he knew his job relied on him being discrete. He had a very high regard for the Ryans and would never do anything to compromise the business deal they had with the family.

I turned and headed to wash up and change, satisfied with his intentions. I still felt like I'd violated his trust, but if he was going to be flying us all over the world, I had to know where his mind was at.

I stepped out with my dirty leather outfit in my hands.

"Just leave that on the couch, and I'll get it dry-cleaned for you today," Josh said. His gaze moved to Kylee. "Do you need anything cleaned?"

"No, but thank you for asking." Kylee glanced at me. "You about ready to roll?" She shouldered her bag of weapons.

"I'm as ready as I'll ever be." I reached over, grabbed my cell phone, and slid it into the side pocket of my jeans.

"Come on, Levi." Kylee patted her leg.

Levi was up and out the door before either of us got to the top of the stairs. He stood on the tarmac with his tail wagging, waiting.

As soon as we stepped out of the cool interior of the plane, the heat hit. Josh wasn't kidding. It was already hot enough for my brow to break out in sweat. I was glad I waited on the shower, but I was sure I would need to clean up tonight.

When we started down the stairs, Levi jumped into the open door of the car waiting for us.

I couldn't help but laugh at his enthusiasm. I guess he really wanted to eat a demon or two. We slid into the car after him.

"Grasslands Nature Trail on Padre Island, please," Kylee said as she settled in the car. The dot on her watch blinked.

"Yes, ma'am," the driver said with a sweet drawl, then turned back toward the windshield.

I stared at the back of her head and reached out with my mind, checking her intent. There was nothing dark or dangerous in her mind, but she was worried about her sick daughter at home and unsure her husband could take care of things. They needed the money, or otherwise, she would have given the job to someone else.

I glanced down at Levi and patted his head, then settled in for the drive.

The landscape differed greatly from Maine. It was flatter. What people would consider hills here were what I called a speed bump back home. I stared out at the sparse scenery as we puttered along. A little over an hour into the ride, the driver pulled into the parking lot that donned the sign for the Grasslands Nature Trail.

Our car was the only one in the lot, and in the distance, a dark cloud hung over the land, blocking some of the hills.

"It looks pretty nasty over there. Are you sure you girls want to do this today?" our driver asked. She hoped we wouldn't go. It would make her work day quicker.

"We will be fine, but I suggest you lock your doors and don't let anyone in. That also means keeping your window up even if a police officer wants your attention, understand?"

She cocked her head.

"That's not a normal storm. There could be... fallout," Kylee added. "And it might affect anyone who comes in contact with it."

The woman paled and turned her attention to the cloud. "Am I safe in here?"

"Yes. As long as you don't get out or open any of the windows, okay?" Kylee opened her door to get out.

The driver nodded and the thousands of questions swarming her mind hadn't started coming out her mouth yet.

But that would change unless I did something.

"We have a special lotion that we wear that will keep us protected. And the fallout doesn't affect dogs," I said, trying to ease her fears. "I'd offer you some, but we left it on the plane." I gave her the right expression for embarrassed and humbled.

Kylee gave me a look. I didn't need to hear her mental question. That look said it all. Thankfully, the driver hadn't caught it, or otherwise she would have gone back to contemplating just leaving us out here like she had been. Kylee's little impromptu acting really had unnerved our driver.

"Is that where we are headed?" I asked after we closed the car doors.

Kylee rolled her eyes as Levi bounded towards the dark cloud.

The closer we got, the more solid my answer. I didn't need to see the dot on her watch getting closer, not with Levi's behavior and the hair on my arms standing at attention.

The cloud worried me. It cut down our visibility, and neither of us knew what hid in the gloom. I glanced over my shoulder and could no longer see the car. I hoped our driver would still be there when we came out. I wasn't sure what our condition would be, and from Kylee's tightened muscles and Levi's slow, cautious gait, I knew they were equally unnerved.

Levi glanced back at me and huffed. He transformed from the beautiful shepherd to his natural form, which reminded me of the dragons I had seen in movies. He was bigger than what I thought a tyrannosaurus rex would have been, but smaller than Godzilla. Either way, he was a force to be reckoned with.

When he crouched down, I glanced at Kylee.

"Get on," he said with a voice that rumbled like thunder. "I will keep you safe from these pests."

Ride a dragon. Check! Well, technically Leviathan, but still, the same principle applied.

I didn't hesitate the way Kylee did. I was on his shoulders within seconds and smiling down at Kylee. She sighed and glanced around before she climbed up behind me.

I grabbed the edge of his collar, and Kylee grasped my waist. When we were settled, it was as if Levi knew we were ready to go. He took off. I nearly lost my grip on the collar, but after a moment, I got the hang of his gallop.

When the path turned, Levi kept going straight, right into the belly of the fog.

The mist was thick enough to tighten my throat and make breathing hard. From the sound of it, Kylee was having the same issue.

What in tarnation could cause this? My answer came as we barreled around the nearest hill.

"Damn witch," Kylee whispered.

I stared at the wrinkled man wrapped in a cloak. His bony hands were flowing through the air, conjuring the choking smoke as beings fell from the breach. I couldn't tell if they were demons, witches, or other dangers to humanity.

Levi didn't slow one bit. He darted towards the mage, dodging the spells that the witch was throwing at us. The beast never slowed, never stopped, and gleefully tore the witch's head right off his body as he passed by. The others in the area had no chance. When Levi stopped a few paces in front of the breach, he lowered his head, giving me a full view of the portal.

Beings stared out at Leviathan, and every one of them registered fear. The spell holding the fog and smoke over the area faded. If it disappeared while we were riding on Leviathan's back, the driver would flee like she had seen the end of the world and it was coming for her.

I peeled off my sticky gloves and wiped my hands on my thighs, concentrating on building the power. I splayed my fingers with my palms both facing the portal and pushed out with everything I had. Without demons trying to escape, the breach closed quickly. Almost as quickly as the cloud cloaking us faded.

I didn't have much time left before people could see this bizarre scene. I tried harder, crying out with the exertion, depleting every ounce of energy.

Levi shrank under me until he was lying on the ground between my legs, growling at what was left of the breach. When the last stitch mended and the breach blinked out of existence, I turned, looking for Kylee. She had let go of me pretty quickly once I'd committed to closing the breach.

I stumbled and landed on the ground. My muscles trembled as I propped myself into a sitting position.

"Where's Kylee?" I asked Levi.

He looked over his shoulder and then trotted to a lump on the ground just below the high grass line. He licked her once and then again. She woke, batting his snout away.

I forced myself to my feet, crossed toward her, and then collapsed on the grass next to her. I glanced up at the clear sky above us and then at Levi.

Kylee sat up and rubbed her head. She scanned the carnage. "We can't leave this here." She looked at me expectantly.

I slowly sat up and looked at the bloody mess Leviathan had left. She was right. We couldn't leave these things here, but I had no idea what she was asking me. I glanced at Levi, hoping he had an answer of what to do with the bodies.

"Bedtime snack?" he said in my mind and cocked his head.

"And where do you think we are going to store them? If you want to eat them, be my guest." I waved towards the bodies.

"That isn't what I had in mind," Kylee said. *You could have turned them to ash.*

I stared at her. Even though the air was humid and the ground moist, my fire could cook this entire island whether or not I wanted it to. I slid the gloves back on as a sign the conversation was over. Besides, I was too exhausted to control it.

My stomach rumbled. "I need to eat, too. I haven't had anything since we left." And if I didn't eat soon, I wouldn't be able to function for days.

We turned our attention to Levi. Only his head transformed, and he made quick work of getting rid of the bodies. It was gross and intriguing at the same time, and I had to look away. When he finished, he transitioned back into a dog and let out a gargantuan burp. He wagged his tail.

We climbed to our feet and headed back toward the car. As soon as we rounded the hill into the view of the parking lot, Levi bounded ahead, his tongue lolling out the side of his mouth. I stumbled and Kylee grabbed me, helping me stay on my feet.

By the time we got to the car, the ground was spinning, and I collapsed in the back seat. Our driver gave us an arched brow in the rearview mirror.

A craving for barbeque ribs like my mom used to make hit. She would get those prepackaged ones from the local country store whenever they had them, which wasn't very often. Saliva filled my mouth at just the thought.

"Is there a barbeque rib place on the way back to the airport?" I asked.

"I know the best barbeque place in southern Texas," she said with a grin. "Mustang Sally's. It's near the airport."

"That sounds perfect," Kylee said, and we leaned back in the seats, enjoying the flow of cool air coming from the vents.

I pulled the phone out and sent a text to Alex. *Two down. Five to go. And I got to ride Leviathan.* ☺

Epic! Call when you get a chance. I need to hear your voice.

"He's a little needy," Kylee muttered.

I hadn't realized she was looking at my phone. I gave her a glare and pocketed the phone, not acknowledging either her comment or Alex's neediness. Instead, I glanced at Levi.

She isn't wrong. His thought filled my head.

"I know," I whispered and glanced out the window.

Despite what anyone said, Alex was my responsibility. I had opened the portal that let Lucifer loose. If that hadn't happened, so much of the destruction and death wouldn't have happened.

Sure, Grace would have still been jealous, but I doubted she would have let a soul eater nearly destroy Alex if Lucifer hadn't poisoned her with promises of a future with him. Of course, Lucifer's idea of a future was him possessing a soulless body, but Grace couldn't see past her own wants.

I glanced back at Kylee and shrugged.

"You aren't responsible for him," she said. "I know you feel you..."

I raised my hand, stopping her from trying to placate me. "I know you are trying to make me feel better, and I know he seems needy to you, but with the loss..." I stopped talking because there was no separation in the car and our driver didn't need to be privy to the details of what happened to Alex. "But with his recent loss, I seem to be the only one who can ground him. I guess I make him feel like he was before his loss." I shrugged, trying to explain without making it obvious. "There's enough of what he was left for him to know the difference, so he leans on me."

She nodded. "If you say so."

I narrowed my eyes. "What about your Alex? You felt responsible for him just as much as I do for mine."

"That's different. I caused his issues."

I crossed my arms and raised my eyebrows. My stomach even decided to pipe in with a hefty growl.

Kylee sighed and leaned her head back.

The rest of the ride was quiet, and when the driver pulled into the rib joint, I was nearly out of the car before she put it in park. I paused and turned back, then knocked on the driver's window. She rolled it down.

"Can we get you anything?"

Her mind filled with thoughts of bringing home a nice rib dinner for two with sides of slaw and potatoes, but she shook her head politely, like she was trained to do.

I just smiled and headed inside with Kylee.

"Do you have any money?" I asked while we stood at the counter.

Kylee grinned. "Yes. More than enough."

"Do we have enough to get our driver a meal, too?"

Kylee nodded as she scanned the menu. "And enough to get Josh something."

"Can I help you?" a waiter asked from behind the counter.

Kylee waved for me to proceed, and I stepped forward. "I'd like a barbeque rib dinner for two with potatoes and coleslaw in one bag and another double rack of ribs in a second takeout bag."

"Any sides with that double rack?" he asked.

"No, but I'll have a large orange soda, if you don't mind," I said.

"Will that be all?"

"No." I waved Kylee forward, and she placed an order for the rib dinner for two as well.

Thankfully, the bags were labeled, so when we got to the car, I put the dinner-for-two bag on the front passenger seat with a smile. "I hope you don't mind."

I sipped my drink and settled into the back seat with my bag on my lap, trying not to tear into it before we got to the plane.

Ten minutes later, we were on the jet, sitting at the table with Josh and our meals. Josh seemed to be the only one of us with manners, and he chuckled as he watched us devour our meals on the fine china stored in the back cabinets.

I sat back in the seat with a plate full of empty bones and licked my fingers. I could have had two more helpings and still been hungry, but I knew if I overate, that would come back to haunt me just as much as not eating at all.

Now I needed a shower and a nap, but I wasn't sure which should come first.

Josh cleaned his hands with a wipe. "Thank you for the meal. I didn't expect that. I replenished the refrigerator and freezer for the next flight. We have a jaunt to Hawaii and then a quick fill-up, and then we should be landing in American Samoa about seven hours after we fill up. So, expect to be landing at your destination in about fifteen hours from takeoff. The shower is available in back, as I mentioned before." He looked at me. "And then just relax. If either of you want to come up and learn about flying a plane, let me know. I'd be happy to show you."

"Thank you." Kylee cleaned off her hands.

"Do I need to wait until we are in the air to clean up?" I asked.

He glanced at his watch. "That's up to you. We aren't due to take off for another half hour."

I stood. "I'll clean up before we go." I grabbed my suitcase, hauled it onto the nearest bench, rummaged for the things I needed, and disappeared into the back room.

I stopped at the entrance. The back room was a full bedroom, and the bathroom beyond it was as big as mine back at the Ryans' house. It certainly made the restroom up front look tiny.

"Towels are in the cabinet under the sink," Josh called after me.

I closed the door and made a note that the bed wasn't neatly made. I wondered if this was where our pilot was sleeping while we were off on our breach-closing adventures. Instead of mulling that over, I focused on cleaning the grit and grime off my body and out of my hair. I pulled the wet bandages off my neck and looked in the mirror at the stitches.

I pulled out my phone and sent a text to Alex. *Can you ask your mom what I need to do with the stitches?*

I hadn't thought to ask before we left.

Mom said they will dissolve on their own. Just be cautious because they are probably still tender enough to rip if you overdo it.

Now they tell me. I studied the stitches, and they were all still in place. There was no extraneous blood oozing from any of them. I slid the shirt on and glanced at the soft flannel. Alex must have shoved this in my suitcase while I wasn't looking. It even smelled like him.

I closed my eyes and inhaled. That deep-seated longing took hold, and even before I opened my eyes, I knew where I was going to be. His room was dark, and Alex stepped inside, seconds after I opened my eyes.

He closed the door quietly and crossed to where I stood, half dressed in his shirt. "I had a feeling you might come." He ran his finger along the edge of the shirt, pushing the fabric back far enough to get a glimpse of my lack of clothing underneath.

When his gaze came back to mine, his eyes shined with interest. He slid his arm under the fabric and pulled me against his chest. I breathed in his kiss, letting it warm my soul. I had no idea how I got here without any sort of connection beyond his scent on the shirt, and I didn't really care.

The soft groan in the back of his throat thrilled me as much as the caress of his hands. His kiss broke and his lips trailed down my neck and then to my ear.

"I need…"

The bang on the door shocked me back into my body. I inhaled, glancing around the room. My phone rang at the same time Kylee asked if I was okay.

"I'm fine," I said to Kylee and answered my phone. "Hey. Can I call you back in a few minutes?"

"Can you come back?" he asked, his voice rough with the same heat that was making it difficult for me to concentrate on anything else.

"Not sure," I said. "Just hang on while I get dressed and let Kylee have the bathroom." I put the phone on the counter and pulled on my clothing as quickly as I could. With my dirty clothes, my brush, and phone in my hands, I stepped out of the bathroom and gave Kylee a tilted smile.

"I guess you lost track of time," Kylee said.

"I did, and I'm sorry I took so long."

"That's okay. I'll catch a shower once we are in the air." She led the way through the bedroom and closed the door as we took seats in the main cabin.

I dropped my dirty clothes in my suitcase and then sat down to brush my hair.

Alex called my name, and I put the phone to my ear. "Sorry, I was just getting settled for takeoff."

"Are you going to come back?"

"I don't know. I might, but I was thinking I needed some serious sleep. It took everything I had to close this one, and I was running low on energy even before I got to Texas."

"I need you."

His whispered confession struck deep inside, but not enough to pull me to him like last time.

"Me too." I said under the rumble of the engine. "What are you doing tomorrow?" I asked, hoping to change the subject away from us.

"Dad wants to take a ride to New Hampshire."

I stared out the window. "Paradise Cove?"

Silence blanketed the line. "Yeah."

There was only one reason to go to Paradise Cove. "He wants to talk to Tom?"

Alex chuckled in a way that chilled me. "No. He wants to talk to Michael. He figures if Lucifer could come back after what happened, so can the rest of the archangels. He wants them to help us stop Lucifer."

"He knows they can't leave the cove, right?"

Alex got quiet again. "He thinks they can. He also thinks his father can, too."

A sharp pain behind my eye drew a hiss from my lips. The memory box in my head started pounding, and I closed my eyes, clamping down, controlling it, and turning the imaginary keys to the locked position in my mind. I couldn't have another seizure. That would delay us from closing the next breach and keep me away from Alex for much longer than either of us wanted.

"Faith?" he asked.

"Mm-hm?" I replied when I had control over the file cabinet of memories.

"Are you okay?"

"Yeah. Just tired." Exhaustion ripped at my muscles, and I leaned back in the chair, watching the scenery fly by as we accelerated down the runway yet again. The blur of the scenery was appropriate. It felt like everything else in my life since my mother had died.

"Get some rest. We can talk after you've had some sleep." Although his voice was steady and full of compassion, the only thing bleeding through the line was his disappointment.

And as much as my body craved his touch, I was just too damn tired to make the transition now.

"Love you," I whispered.

"Back at you," he said, and then the line disconnected, along with whatever aggravation was brewing in his blood.

Homecoming
Chapter 15

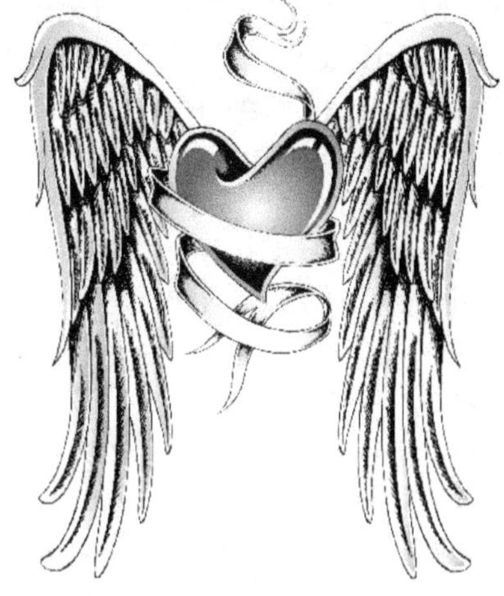

"Faith?"

Hands shook me.

I blinked my eyes open to the white ceiling of the plane. "Is something wrong?" I glanced around at the bright sunlight filtering through the windows.

"Yes. It's time to get moving."

"Huh?" I looked at Kylee, confused. It had been dark out when I closed my eyes.

"You slept through the stop in Hawaii. We've landed in American Samoa. I've gone out and gotten us breakfast and chartered a boat and bought us the proper hiking clothes." She waved toward the table.

I stared at her outfit. She reminded me of Steve Irwin right down to the hiking boots, and an identical pair of clothes sat on the table for me right next to a breakfast plate of fruit and crepes.

I struggled to my feet and headed to get the awful taste out of my mouth, then change into the ridiculous safari outfit. The thing fit and was surprisingly light, and much more comfortable than it looked. I tied my new hiking boots over the thick but weirdly cool socks before heading back into the cabin. I sucked down every bite of what was on my plate and then stood and stretched.

"Where's Levi?" I asked.

Kylee nodded toward the bedroom. "Levi is going to stay and keep an eye on the plane while we are gone. Josh needs sleep before we head to New Zealand, and I didn't think the rainforest was the place for Levi, anyway."

"He was really good to have around in Texas," I said.

"I know, but he's staying here. Besides, it should only take us a few hours once we get to the island."

Her smile made me uneasy. I wasn't quite in agreement with leaving him here. There had to be more to it than what she was telling me. Instead of extracting the information from her mind, I decided to ask.

"What happened? Seriously?" I glanced at my phone. There were more texts from Alex, but the battery was low enough for me to plug it in instead of pocketing it. When I looked back at Kylee, she was glancing outside and biting her lip. "Kylee?"

"We ran into some Kapua when we landed."

I stared at her, thinking that Kapua must be some sort of bird or animal of some sort. "If we hit some birds, is the plane okay?"

She started laughing. "Kapua aren't birds or any sort of natural animals." She presented me with a knife with sigils carved into the steel. "Please accept the protection of this knife."

I took it from her despite the odd way she gave it to me, and inhaled at the weird hum that came from the metal. I slid it into the holder she handed me and clipped it to my belt, just like she had done with hers.

"You see anything coming at us that isn't normal, use the knife."

Her command threw me. "What exactly is a Kapua?"

"It's a Polynesian monster with an elongated snout, razor-like teeth, and deadly claws that can decapitate a man in one swing." She turned away and slung a backpack over her shoulder, taking the time to actually strap it on. "I haven't seen one of those things in years." She stopped at the door and glanced back at me. "We need to hunt them down and kill them once we close the portal."

"Excuse me?"

Her gaze jumped from me to the bedroom door and back. "When we finish closing the breach, we need to let Levi loose to do his job here." She pointed at the floor in front of her.

I narrowed my eyes. She was still keeping something from me. When she looked at the bedroom door again, I crossed to it and turned the knob.

"Faith," she said sharply.

I ignored her and opened the door. Both Josh and Levi were lying on the bed. Levi opened his eyes, but Josh didn't stir.

Josh's chest was bandaged, and it was moving up and down in enough of a cadence for me to guess sleep. I scanned his mind just to make sure it wasn't something deeper, and he was just entering the stage of sleep where dreams were forming.

Levi's side had an ugly gash, and he moved to get up. I put my hand out, stopping him. I moved my gaze to Josh and then back, and Levi nodded, understanding my silent command to stay and protect.

I closed the door and looked back at Kylee. Obviously, something major went down when I was sleeping. She pulled a remote out of her pocket and aimed it at the stairs.

"Get ready to move," she said. "I think Levi and I took care of the ones here, but we've been here long enough for the bastards to call in reinforcements."

She gripped her knife and nodded for me to do the same.

"Whatever we do, we can't let anything get into the plane." She pointed her chin at the knife on my belt.

I peeled the glove off my hand.

"Um. Not anywhere near the plane," she said, turning pale.

I pulled the knife out of the sheath with my ungloved hand. As nervous as I was, I was also surprised that my hand didn't immediately engulf in flame. "I got it."

She didn't look convinced, but she waved me next to her right in front of the stairs. "Fast. We have to go very fast." Sweat broke out on her forehead. She took a breath and pressed the button for the stairs.

The outer shell opened, and the stairs unfolded in what seemed like slow motion. She pocketed the remote and took the lead, nearly jumping the entire way. I scrambled behind her. The minute she landed on the concrete, she turned and pushed the button. I jumped the rest of the way as the stairs started to fold back up.

Movement out of the corner of my eye made me spin in that direction, and my brain stalled. She hadn't described the thing very well. They had elongated snouts, and their teeth and claws were frightening. Their eyes were like shark eyes, black and dead. My heart jumped in my chest, and I ducked as the thing's arm swung in my direction.

I lunged under his swing and buried my knife in his chest. It howled and then blew into a ball of dust. I turned toward Kylee in time to see her battling another one of these creatures. It had one hand on the ladder, hanging from it and swiping at Kylee. I launched the knife, pushing with my mind. The blade cut straight through the beast. I caught a quick view of it buried to the hilt in the first seat on the plane after the monster exploded in a shower of ash.

The stairs finished folding, and the door clasped shut. Kylee grabbed my wrist and ran towards the beach. I got a quick glance at the cluster of homes, and my blood ran cold. There were bodies in the street. Bloodied bodies. Bodies of children and adults alike.

Rage filled every cell. I peeled off my other glove, shoving it in my pocket as we approached a beached power boat. Kylee sheathed her knife and started pushing the bow, sliding the boat into the ocean. I blocked her, facing the island as she pushed our vessel free from the sand.

When one of those things charged, I let out a targeted jet of fire. It struck with precision, carrying my fury with it. The thing didn't blink out in a cloud of dust like the ones that met the blades. No, this one screamed in a way that made me cringe at the same time I felt the true hand of justice.

"Come on!" Kylee called, and I turned, waded into the water, and climbed into the boat.

When a second charged from the woods, I let out a growl, accompanied by another shot of fire. Satisfaction at its scream fanned the darkness inside me. I closed my hand into a fist and looked down at the bottom of the little boat. I needed to rein in this anger.

When we were out far enough from the island, Kylee slowed the boat down, circling around the island until a smaller one came into view on the southeastern side of the one we'd landed on.

"I don't expect anyone to be alive." She wiped her face with a shaky hand. "Do you think you can close the portal by razing the entire island?"

I let out a laugh, and then it faded at her stark stare. "You're serious?"

"Afraid so."

I turned towards the small island. I could see end to end and shivered. The thought of an island full of those things didn't settle with me at all, but there was no way I could close a breach at this kind of distance, especially when I struggled at close range.

"What if someone lived?"

"If no one was alive where we landed, I doubt anyone is left here."

"Then who made the crepes?"

"I did." Kylee accelerated. "We're beaching this boat on the north shore, which is the closest point to where we need to go. I think we can still land safely there.

I gripped the wood plank I sat on as she plowed forward through the open waves. Our little dingy wasn't made for the open ocean, and we both white-knuckled the ride, while my heart banged in my temple.

I was ready to stand on land when we cut the engine and let the tide roll us onto the sandy beach. Kylee hopped out and pulled the boat behind an outcrop of rock, then staked the line in the dry sand beyond the rocks. She glanced at her watch and turned towards the hill on our left, ignoring the no trespassing sign.

"Looks like the flats first before we get to the basin of red lake." She led the way.

"Where did you get these clothes?" I asked, as everything hit me.

"At an outfitter near where we landed."

"I thought you said they were all dead."

She turned and gave me the kind of look that made me want to dig right into the sand and hide.

The store existed, but the people no longer did.

My stomach flopped with the breakfast I had eaten earlier. She'd cooked for us after her adventure defending the plane and getting us outfitted for this. I was grateful for the clothes and the boots, but it still made me feel sick.

We didn't encounter anything as we climbed through the rainforest. Once we crested the hill, a lake sat to our right. Kylee turned the opposite direction, towards the thickly covered hill. She stepped onto a sandy patch and sank like it was water. Deep water.

I reached out for her and grabbed the back of her collar. Unfortunately, her weight knocked me off balance, and I stepped onto the sand as well, sinking right along with her.

Stop!

The command barreled through my brain, and our downward progression halted. I breathed through the shock and exertion of tapping into Tom's power out of panic. I had stopped us from sinking farther. Now I just needed to get us out of the quicksand.

I met Kylee's wide stare. Up?

The thought was weak and timid and made me cringe. It didn't have the same power as the original command, which thankfully hadn't failed. Yet.

I was in the sand to my waist, Kylee to her chest.

I laced my fingers together and put them on top of the sand. "Can you put your foot in my hands?"

She shook her head. "I can't even lift my arms."

The flare of panic reared again. "Up!" I commanded aloud. Whatever power I had obeyed the command. We both popped up out of the sand and into the air. Straight up, and as we started down towards the sand again, I screamed, "Stop!"

My heart thundered as sand filtered over my feet. Kylee was at the same depth. Both of us lunged back on solid ground.

It was good to know panic honed my skill much better than practice. It was almost as good as having Alex's hand in mine.

This totally explained the no trespassing sign we'd breezed by. I glanced at the surrounding area, along with Kylee. Sand patches covered most of the area. There were a few green patches of earth, but they were sparse.

Kylee dropped her backpack at her feet and unzipped it. She pulled out a rope and tied one end around her waist and handed me the slack. "Tie the end around your waist. This way, if one of us falls in while we are trying to get from one patch of land to the other, at least we have a fighting chance."

I did as she said and studied the pattern. We would have to jump together because the rope was not long enough to cover some gaps.

She hooked her elbow in mine and marched us back far enough to take the first leap. "Once we start, we keep going, because if we stop, we have no runway to go from one to the next." She pointed at the order, and I studied the pattern and nodded. Any other way wouldn't end with us on the lush green earth that led up the hill at the far side of the sand marsh. "Ready for this."

I laughed. I was so not ready to die by quicksand. But I also knew if we didn't get over this hurdle, we would lose time and daylight backtracking to a more reasonable route. And who knows how many of those things were still on the island.

"I'm ready," I said when my laugh wound down.

"And go!" Kylee shouted, pulling me with her until I found my stride.

We launched at the same time, and landed at the same time, then pushed off for the next one to our left and then the next to our right until we successfully reached the bottom of the grassy knoll.

She unhooked her arm from mine and made quick work of untying and stowing the rope as I caught my breath. We both looked up at the hill, wondering what in the hell would be waiting for us up there.

"This is going to be a nightmare." She unsheathed her knife.

I couldn't disagree. The heat here, away from the constant breeze of the ocean, was downright oppressive. Drawing air felt like someone was forcing water into my lungs, and I nearly coughed each time I took a deep breath.

Sweat soaked my back, and I wished I had braided my hair. I needed to get it off my neck, so I twirled it into a tight but messy bun like my mother taught me to do before we took treks in the woods. The times I hadn't, my hair inevitably got caught on a branch. I did not want to be caught by a tree while I was battling one of the Kapuas.

I could just see me walking into Alex's house with half my hair chopped off. I smiled.

"Something funny?" Kylee asked as she hauled her backpack on again.

"No, nothing outside my own head, anyway."

"Try me. I could use a laugh." She started up the hill.

"When my mom and I used to go on hikes in the woods, if I didn't put my hair in a bun or a braid, it used to get caught in tree branches," I started, and then had to dodge one of the limbs Kylee had released. "I was just imagining what would happen here if I got caught in the trees and one of those things came. Explaining that I lost half my hair to Alex would be humorous."

Kylee snorted a quick laugh and then stopped, putting her fist up.

Movement to our right caught our attention, and I clenched my ungloved fist tighter. A bird took flight, and we watched it disappear. I wasn't convinced that colorful fowl was the reason we had stopped.

Kylee went to take a step, but I pulled back on her shoulder and shook my head. The hair on my arms had already risen, and my fingers tingled. I didn't know which direction the thing prowling around was, but its intent was clear.

We were food.

I scanned the branches above us, uncertain if the thing was in the air or on the ground. Or both.

That last thought chilled my blood, sending a slithering shiver up my back. For a moment, I wanted to spray the surrounding forest with fire, but I kept my hand clenched. *We* were in the forest, too.

"Bats are the only thing that live on these islands besides birds," Kylee said. "This thing tracking us is neither of those. There's a regular knife in the middle pouch of the backpack." She turned her back to me. "Just be careful you don't cut yourself rummaging around in there, okay?"

I unzipped the pack and gingerly felt around until I hit steel. I followed the cool metal to a rough handle and pulled it out. It wasn't a knife. This thing was a machete. I grinned at her as I held it in my hand. The weight if it was perfectly balanced, and I wondered how it hadn't sliced through the backpack. I handed it to her for a moment so I could zip up the pack.

When I was done, she handed me the machete and started moving forward again. I followed, thinking about the force field CJ had instituted around the backyard while I was practicing the other day. I wasn't sure if Tom had something similar, but considering his mojo came from CJ, I wondered if I could do something like that to keep us safe.

I put my hand on her shoulder and she stopped.

"Keep going. I want to try something, and I have a feeling that I will need some sort of connection with you to do it," I said.

Her brow creased.

"Force field," I whispered.

"Oh." She started forward again, creeping with slow progression.

I imagined a net surrounding us that consisted of a thousand volts. I concentrated on the electrified protection shield hard enough that the light sweat on my back turned into a tacky river. My skin tingled with the effort, and the air surrounding us let off occasional sparks.

An explosion behind us broke my concentration. We spun around in time to see a very charred four-legged being flying backwards. Contact with my force field didn't turn the creature to dust, but whatever it had been was clearly no longer among the living. Smoke radiated from it, and when the breeze shifted, the stench was godawful.

"I guess it worked," I said.

"I guess so," Kylee snickered, and we continued our slow trek to the top of this rainforest hill.

I tried to re-establish the force field, but I couldn't seem to tap into the power in the same way. I kept an eye out on the area surrounding us, but I didn't have the same overwhelming feeling of being watched as I had before that thing had attempted to attack us.

When we crested the hill, the forest thinned out, revealing a bowl-like clearing with a lake at the bottom. The breach was above the middle of the lake.

A screech echoed in the distance, and I jumped.

"Shrieking eels." Kylee pointed to the lake.

"Like in *The Princess Bride*?"

Kylee grinned at my reference.

The terrain and position of the breach created a new challenge. At least in the subways, I was only three train tracks away from the breach, but here, it was far enough away for me to doubt my ability to close it.

We descended the hill, and that weird itch between my shoulder blades took hold. "We're being watched."

"I know. But I can't figure out from where. Nothing's coming from the breach, either."

I followed her gaze. No beings were trying to escape from this corner of Hell. Which meant whatever was held there already had escaped. Who knows if they'd made it to islands beyond American Samoa at this point.

"I need to get as close as possible to that opening." I surveyed the landscape. Where the breach was and the angle it was facing would not help me at all. It was facing the farthest shore.

I might actually have to walk into the lake.

Another shriek filled the air. My mood soured at the sight of an eel cresting the surface of the lake. They weren't nearly as big as the ones in the movie, but they were still unnerving to see, even at this distance. I couldn't imagine those things swimming around my legs.

The closer to the shore we got, the more active the eels seemed to get and the more my hair stood on end. I handed Kylee the machete and ungloved my second hand, then secured the charmed material in my pocket.

I clenched and unclenched my hands, focusing on the power inside me, sharpening it like a blade, letting it build until I thought my entire form would explode. I led the way to the edge of the water with Kylee covering my back.

Sparks tingled over my skin as I held on to the growing ball of flame within my form. I was shaking when I waded into the lake. Water bubbled around my feet. I didn't want to hurt the wildlife in the lake, so I threw my first burst of fire at the tear, sending everything I had in one major blast.

Any doubt that I could close a portal at this distance evaporated along with the breach and half the trees across the lake. I took a shaky step back and fell to my knees. My reflection in the water startled me. It wasn't just my wings that were flaming, but my entire form radiated fire. The flames faded, and nausea rolled in. I had never unleashed that much power at once. Hell, I didn't even know I could release something as devastating as what I'd just witnessed.

Every muscle trembled from the release, and my stomach lurched. I swallowed bile and crawled ashore, then collapsed at Kylee's feet.

Kylee kneeled down and pressed her fingers to my neck, feeling for a pulse.

I turned my head. "I'm alive," I whispered. "Just drained. Give me a minute."

She stiffened. "You don't have a minute."

With an effort that left me dizzy, I lifted my head. Kapua lined our escape route. Rows of monsters at least five deep crept towards us from all sides except the side of the lake I'd torched to a crisp, which was on the other side of the eel-infested waters.

Kylee helped me up, backing us up into the lake. "Now would be a good time to put up that force field again."

I had nothing left. My hands weren't even sparking, and I was on the verge of passing out. I didn't even know if I could make it to the other side of the lake that Kylee was dragging me towards. I couldn't even conjure up panic.

I stumbled alongside her.

"If you can't put up a barrier, you better be prepared to fight," she whispered and offered me the machete.

Don't let them see that you are drained. They saw what you did, so use that.

Her thought thundered in my head. I shook my head at the machete and straightened, extending my arms out wide enough to encompass both ends of the massive group of monsters. I kept my hands fisted with my palms facing them.

They halted, and a thrill kicked at my adrenaline, sparking something inside me. These weren't beasts with a choice of who they were. They also did not have a sense of humanity in them. No morality, no compassion, just killing machines. As the assessment of these things flowed through my mind, so did the darkness inside me, powering the inferno.

The shrieking eels grew closer, sending another tendril of fear to my core. But I couldn't worry about what essentially was a water snake, not when I had an army of things with sharp teeth and claws that could cut us in half.

Kylee screamed and dropped down on one knee, hacking at the water. Blood rose to the surface. Scales wiped against my leg and I wanted out of this mess. Now. Hot panic flowed through my body like lava, causing a wave of pure destruction that crashed out in every direction around us, annihilating Kapua and eels alike. When the dust settled, we stood in an empty crater that had been the lake surrounded by a wasteland of ash.

I took a shaky step away from Kylee, and then the world went black.

Homecoming
Chapter 16

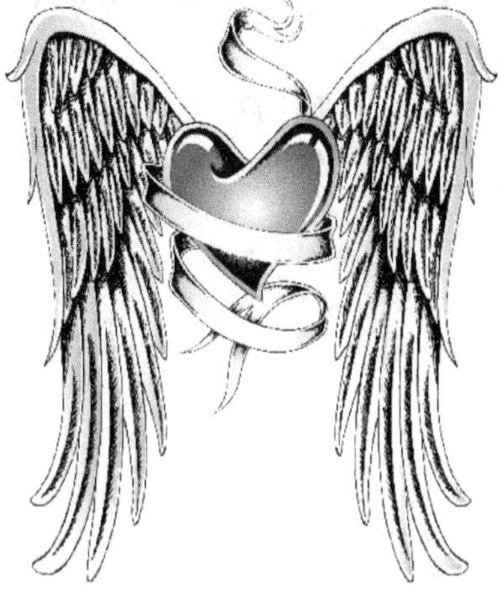

A DULL HUMMING WHINE filled my head. I turned, pulling the covers over my head. I just wanted the noise to stop. I wanted the pounding pain biting my temples to go away.

I cracked an eye to find the source and destroy it, but I wasn't in our little cabin in the woods. Even the bed I was lying in was foreign to me. I forced myself to sit up, and the room spun, sending me back onto the mattress.

When a dog's head popped up next to the bed, I jumped back. He looked as worried as I felt.

I glanced around again, trying to think beyond the pain threatening to shut my eyes again. The whirring sound continued.

The plane.

Those two words opened the flood of memories, and I stared at the dog. *Levi.* And on the heels of the dog's name, Kylee.

"Is Kylee okay?" I asked. My voice croaked with sleep.

Her calf was torn up pretty bad, but she'll live. Which is more than I can say for those vile Kapuas.

Levi's thoughts whispered in my mind, like he knew just how bad my head was pounding. His tongue dangled from the corner of his mouth in what I understood was his way of smiling.

"How long have I been out?"

"Two days." The answer came from the doorway.

I turned. Kylee leaned against the doorjamb, looking exhausted.

"Two days?" I gasped and threw the covers off me.

Kylee put her hand out and limped across the room to the side of the bed. "I already called Alex for you. I told him you were okay, but we had a setback."

My eyes widened. The last setback I'd had opened all these breaches.

Kylee seemed to understand my train of thought. "You didn't have a seizure like you did at their house. You just expended all your energy. I mean all of it to the point you were having difficulty just maintaining your breathing. Valerie told us what to do. And they stock these planes with medical equipment." She smiled. "We got you hydrated, and that seemed to get everything else in order, and then we let you rest." She waved at the bed.

"And what about you? The last thing I remember was you screaming."

Kylee shrugged. "An eel took a bite out of my leg just before you went off like an atom bomb. I'm just glad I wasn't swept away with the rest of the island."

I stared at the bedcovers. "How did we get back?" I asked after a few beats of silence.

Kylee glanced away and sighed. "I dragged you to the beach on the other side of the crater and got back to the dingy from there. I wasn't playing with the quicksand again."

"But the beach we landed on was isolated between a bunch of rocks."

Kylee smiled. "I had to decide on whether to leave you on the beach while I got the boat, or try to make the swim with you and come back for our gear. I'm a strong swimmer, but I didn't think I could get you to the boat, so I left you with the gear. I didn't think you'd be in danger considering you leveled the entire island, but it still left me on edge until I got the boat onto that shore."

"And when we got back to where the plane was?"

She chuckled, and Levi slinked out of the room. "Leviathan did not wait for us to get back. He convinced Josh to let him out. When we got back to the island, there weren't any left. Josh was pretty freaked out by what he witnessed. He's no longer clueless to what is out there, and he forced me to tell him what we were doing. What this trip was all about."

"Did you tell him about me?"

"I said you were special, like the Ryans. He seemed to understand that more than I expected. But I didn't explain who your father was. I think that might be a little too much for his mind to wrap around."

I burst out laughing. I could relate. It wasn't easy for me to digest either. "Thank you," I said, still laughing.

She nodded. "I didn't tell him what I was, either."

My stomach growled loud enough to be heard over my laughter.

"Come on. There is food in the pantry in the main cabin." She handed me a bathrobe that had been hanging over the end of the bed.

I slipped it on over my grubby skin and climbed out of bed slowly. She offered me her arm, and I took it. I wasn't steady enough to make this trip on my own. Once I was settled at the table, Kylee whipped up a breakfast that had my mouth watering. Eggs, bacon, toast, and a side of strawberry-filled crepes.

"Just eat slowly." She put a plate and a glass of orange juice in front of me.

I heeded her warning and savored the meal, choosing the proteins before the sweets.

She carried a plate and a steaming cup of coffee to the cockpit and knocked before she entered.

Josh looked over his shoulder at me as he took the offerings from Kylee. He sent me a smile and a nod and turned back to the task of flying us to our next destination.

Kylee sat and pulled out her tablet. She stared at the location and then put her head back on the seat. She looked as defeated as a prizefighter who'd lost the match after making it to the very last round.

I swallowed the last bite of my food. "What is it?"

She sighed. "Think you're up for a little mountain climbing?"

I stopped drinking my juice. "Excuse me?"

She glanced between her watch and the tablet and then turned it towards me. The red dot was far enough in the mountain range for me to swallow hard. I mean, I had hiked in the hills around the cabin I grew up in, but that didn't compare to true mountain climbing. I guess I should've been glad we weren't heading for Mount Everest.

I looked over the tablet at Kylee. "Are you going to be able to do that?"

Her wry smile, followed by a half-hearted shrug, told me all I needed to know. I might need to do this one on my own.

"Levi will come with this time," she said. "Just in case we need a sled ride down the mountain."

"I'm not a sled dog," he said from his station on the floor.

The fact he spoke aloud really screwed with my mind. Josh glanced back and after he looked at the talking dog, his gaze found mine. His nonchalant demeanor brought home just how odd things were getting.

"You're talking now?" I asked.

"I no longer have to hide my ability to communicate within this... thing." He huffed and laid his head on the ground.

I cleaned up my plate, stowed it back where Kylee had gotten it, and then headed into the cockpit.

"Do you mind?" I asked, pointing at the co-pilot seat.

"Not at all." He took a sip of his coffee.

The blue expanse of ocean stretched out before the window. I studied the view, noting how the colors differed. I guessed that had to do with the depth of the water at different points. It was mesmerizing.

"So, Kylee explained what you two were doing on these..." He waved out the window, clearly unsure of whether to categorize them as adventures.

"They are adventures, in a way," I answered. "Just not the kind of adventure I ever thought I'd be tackling."

He laughed. "I'll bet."

His mind swarmed with questions, but he didn't seem all that surprised that I had read his mind. Instead of shooting question after question at me, he glanced at me. "You really know how to fly a plane?"

I blew out the air I had just inhaled. "I've never flown, but Tom did, and when he died, I inherited his gifts and his memories. So I know the motions based on his memories, but honestly, I'm not sure I could mimic them."

"Gifts like whatever magic he used to get us from Europe to the US in the time that even a fighter jet can't do?" He glanced at the control panel.

"Yes." I didn't deny it. Since he was in as much danger as we were, as evident by the attack in American Samoa, I thought he deserved the truth, however disturbing it might have been. "But I have some of my own, too."

He just grunted and finished what was on his plate, then washed it down with coffee. He wiped his mouth with a napkin.

"Well, if you wouldn't mind manning the cockpit, I'm going to clean this and hit the head." He smiled and didn't wait for me to say yes or no. He unbuckled and left me to monitor the autopilot.

I did not expect that. As my gaze jumped from instrument to instrument, I rubbed my palms on my bathrobe. With my heart beating in my throat and a silent mantra telling me I had this, I reached for the control wheel. I hesitated before I plowed on and touched the yoke.

I knew I shouldn't worry since autopilot was on, but that didn't lower the sudden sense of responsibility I had for the other three living beings on the plane beside me. I wished Alex were here to hold my hand and calm my nerves.

The pull started, but I resisted. I couldn't let my spirit leave. Not while I had this kind of obligation. The yank back into my form was jarring, and I twitched, knocking the yoke. My gaze jumped to the control panel to make sure I hadn't done anything, like disengage the autopilot. When everything registered as status quo, I leaned back in the seat with an exhale.

"It isn't really that stressful." Josh took the pilot's seat.

It is when you almost leave the plane.

I just smiled up at him. "I think I'm going to go clean up and put on some clothes."

"Sure. I just have one more question. What are you and what are the Ryans?" He stared at me.

"I'm a Nephilim. The Ryans are descendants of Nephilim."

"Nephilim." He said the word like he didn't know what it meant, and the crease between his eyes along with his thoughts confirmed his confusion. "I'm assuming that is good?"

I smiled. "A Nephilim is the offspring of an archangel and a human. My mother was human." I turned, leaving him to digest the fact that archangels existed.

I picked up my phone and suitcase and slid into the bedroom to find clothing and take a shower. Just like the last time, the hot shower felt good. When I finished, I pulled out layers to wear. Underwear and bra went on first, followed by leggings and a tank top, and then I slid my jeans on and chose one of the thick sweaters Alex had picked out and pulled it over my head.

I pressed the familiar number on my phone and put the speaker to my ear.

Alex picked up on the first ring. "Faith?" His question was framed with a rough voice that I didn't recognize.

"Alex?"

Quiet hung on the line, and I got nothing from the connection beyond silence. "No, it's Chris."

"Oh. Is Alex around?"

More silence. "He's out with Valerie," he said after a moment.

"You're not with him?" My heart thundered. I didn't think the stilted conversation resulted from being half a world away.

"No, I'm with the girls." This time his tone was reasonable. "I can have him call when they get back." His offer sounded hollow, almost like he was going through the motions.

"Mr. Ryan?"

"Yes, Faith," he said.

"Where is he?"

"I told you where he is." This time his tone was clipped.

A burn started under my skin, accompanied by that low-grade internal alarm of mine. My breath quickened. "Why are you lying to me?" I barely whispered.

"Because you have a job to do," he said.

Panic bloomed and within a blink, I stood in the Ryans' kitchen, staring at CJ's back. He slowly turned, and my heart plummeted. CJ looked like hell. Like he hadn't slept in at least twenty-four hours. Bridget sat on the couch with her arms around Valerie. The entire room screamed tragedy.

"Where is Alex?" I said through clenched teeth.

He just shook his head as his cheeks reddened. "We don't know."

I let go of the connection and sat down hard on the bed on the plane. "What do you mean you don't know?" My voice rose to a high pitch. I had a hard time swallowing.

"Head between your legs," CJ said from the other end of the line. "And a panic attack right now won't help anyone."

"Where's April and the girls?" My voice cracked. I folded in half and concentrated on breathing.

"Downstairs watching a movie," he said.

I could tell the difference between the tone when he was telling the truth and when he was lying. This time, he was telling the truth.

"Look, I don't know if he hopped on a plane to go to you, or if..."

That sentence was definitely delivered for placation. "Don't coddle me," I hissed.

"You have to finish what you are doing," he said. "And then we can look for Alex. If you don't, the ramifications are bigger than you can comprehend."

"But if he has Alex..."

Silence and a little of CJ's devastation flowed through the line. "I know," he whispered.

I ended the call. I couldn't listen to CJ's reasoning, not with my chest hurting under the pressure. If Lucifer had Alex, I was doomed. My nightmare came back, and my stomach clenched. I made it to the bathroom in time for my breakfast to come up hot and fast. Acid lined my throat, and I gagged again.

I leaned against the porcelain as stinging tears bathed my face. I didn't know how long I sat on the floor crying. I couldn't stop the fountain, and every thought of what I might have to do stabbed into me as sharp as a knife penetrating my skin.

Kylee poked her head in, and her questioning gaze turned to concern. "Are you sick?" Her worry bled into her aura in a sickly yellow arc.

"No." I wiped my face and forced myself up on shaky legs. I took the time to rinse my mouth and splash my face before I turned to her. "Alex has disappeared."

Her face paled. "I'm so sorry."

"CJ said I needed to finish what we were doing before…" I couldn't finish the sentence. I doubled over and fell to my knees.

Kylee was by my side in a flash, and she wrapped her arms around me. She didn't say that things would be okay. She didn't say that everything was all right. She didn't say anything. Instead, she just held me and rocked me because she knew words wouldn't heal the hurt.

I finally stopped crying and wiped the snot and tears from my face with tissues she offered me.

"Now, think you can get your head in the game for this?" she asked.

I gawked at her. How? How was I supposed to do this?

"This is what heroes do. We allow only a moment to fall apart, and then we move on and do what we need to before we get to do what we want to."

"I'm not a hero." I stood, dusting my knees off, and crossed to the bed. I kept repeating that in my head while I made the bed. The linens stretched into a clean spread that was worthy of a bed made by a soldier.

I stared at the perfect corners, still lost in my hurt. But I could breathe.

I concentrated on breathing and glanced up, meeting Kylee's gaze. "I. Am. Not. A. Hero."

She chuckled and raised her brow.

Sparks lit off my fingertips, and I grabbed the gloves off the side table and slid them on before my irritation flashed into fire.

The loudspeakers squawked on. "Ladies, we are approaching the airport. Please stow your weapons under the bed in back and make sure you have your passports."

Kylee disappeared and came back in with her bag.

"I don't have a passport," I said, then swallowed hard.

Kylee tossed me something, and I caught it. I stared at my picture and my information. Of course, while my first name was correct, the last name typed in the passport had Paradox instead of Kennedy and an address in San Diego, not Maine.

"Fate," she said.

"Fate deals in fake passports?"

"She knew we were short on time, and she also didn't want our friend to track you." She lifted the bed and picked up the suitcase that sat underneath.

I was about to ask her what she was doing when she pulled the corner of the carpet away from the edge and pulled on an eye hook. A compartment opened under the carpet, big enough to fit both duffel bags. She closed it and set Josh's suitcase back in place.

She glanced at me and pushed the bed back down on the compartment. I didn't question why there was a secret compartment in here. I didn't want to know. I focused on the passport in my hand as she led me back into the main cabin.

I fanned through the thing. At least it didn't look new, and it had some stamps already. Mostly Canada and Mexico, along with a couple of the islands in the Caribbean. The expiration date was the following year, too.

"You're my little sister." She nodded at the papers in my hand and smiled as we sat down and strapped in for the descent into Christchurch International Airport.

"We just need to be cleared by customs here before we head over to Hokitika, which is closer to Mount Cook. I also want to do a flyby so we can see what you are in for. But I'm not sure how close we can get with the weather over that area."

I didn't want to see where we were going. I didn't want to see what type of challenge this was. All I wanted was to know Alex was safe.

I pulled my phone out of my pocket and scrolled through the messages from him. Tears threatened again at the increasingly frantic tone and then the once-again calm after Kylee had called. His last message was to tell me he loved me and that he'd talk to me when I woke up.

I held the phone to my chest and closed my eyes. I missed him, and now that he was missing, I was itching to get this over with. This brief stop was necessary in getting to the other side of the island, but the fact we had to stop and not just go to our destination ate at my nerves.

The jerk of the plane on the runway brought me back to our present situation, and I glanced out at the gates as we passed. We rolled to a stop in front of a group of hangars. A truck was waiting, and the minute Josh powered down the plane, the car doors opened, and official customs officers stepped out.

Levi hopped on the seat next to me and curled up, putting his head in my lap. He looked up at me.

I can't eat them, can I?

I pressed my lips together against a smile and shook my head.

He huffed, and I stroked his head, glad for the interruption and his successful attempt at making me smile.

Josh opened the hatch and let the stairs down. Two customs agents and a large dog came aboard, but the minute the dog saw Levi, he backed up on the stairs whining. They tried to drag him on, but he refused.

"I can put Levi in the back room if you need me to," I said as Levi chuckled in my head.

I grabbed his collar and led him into the bedroom, where he immediately jumped onto the bed and curled up with his tongue lolling out the side.

"Be good," I said, pointing at him.

When I turned back around, their search dog calmed and came onto the plane, sniffing around, but he wouldn't go near the back room.

Josh extended his hand, and Kylee put her passport in it. I added mine when he turned to me and he handed all our passports, along with papers he'd grabbed from the cockpit, to the customs agents.

"You don't have papers for the dog." The customs agent with the papers shuffled through them again while the other walked around the room with the dog as it sniffed for contraband.

Josh looked over at Kylee. Concern registered in his gaze.

I got the feeling this needed to be fixed, and fast. "He's my support dog. I've had him since my mother died. He can sense if I'm going to have a seizure and warn me." I had read a book with a support dog in it, but I had no idea if they would need paperwork relating to that or not.

"We are going to have to put him in quarantine until we get this sorted."

I huffed a laugh. "I don't think so," I said before I had the good sense to shut my mouth.

The agent with the papers narrowed his eyes at me as both Kylee's and Josh's mouths popped open in surprise.

"What's in the back room?" The second agent opened the door to the bedroom, and his dog pulled back on the chain.

"Beg your pardon?" the one with the papers said to me, but my attention was torn between him and the agent in the bedroom.

I heard enough of their thoughts to bite my lower lip. The one at the bedroom door suspected what might be inside Levi, because there had been others who tried to smuggle things into the country inside their pets. Although his dog used to go right for those with smuggled goods, not display this kind of fear. When the custom's dog slipped his collar, ran out the door, and down the stairs, the agent traded a glance with his partner.

Suspicion painted both their faces red.

"I think we would like you to step off the plane with your dog. He needs to be quarantined, and we need to search this vessel."

My heart thundered. "I'm sorry, but I'm not comfortable leaving him in quarantine, especially if we are going to try our hand at mountain climbing. He could be the difference between me making it down the mountain or not." I shifted my stance, realizing the more I spoke, the more I dug us deeper into trouble.

I closed my eyes, nearly growling my disdain at their darkened thinking. When the one near the bedroom put his hand on his weapon, I sighed, resigned to getting us out of this mess.

"We have the proper paperwork. Everything is in order," I whispered, hoping I was using Tom's gift right as I pushed the thoughts outward, targeting the two customs agents.

I opened my eyes, and both guards paled for a second and then blinked.

The one with the paperwork shuffled through it again and smiled. "My mistake, miss. It seems we *do* have the paperwork here."

Josh traded a glance at Kylee and then stared at me.

"Everything seems in order." The guard handed a couple of the forms back to Josh. "Don't forget to send payment before your departure." He started down the stairs.

The second agent followed and grabbed the scruff of his dog's neck.

As soon as they were on the ground, Josh closed the door and locked it. He spun on his feet and stared at me. "What the Hell did you do to them?"

I tapped my temple, and my lips formed a cocky smile. "Another one of Tom's gifts."

He glanced at Kylee and then back at me. "Just which archangel are we talking about?"

My smile faded. "Does it matter?"

"Yes. It matters a great deal."

"My father does not define me," I said. "As a matter of fact, when we are done closing these damn breaches, I have to find that bastard and kill him because he wants this world to burn."

Josh's face lost all color. "You're the antichrist?"

"No. She isn't," Levi said as he strolled into the room. "As young as she is, she is the one who's destined to save the world. But even that is not guaranteed."

"And I should believe an ancient monster?" He waved at Levi. His aura was full of doubt—the awful eggplant color weaved through the calm blues and greens and bright yellows.

"I am not a monster. I'm Death's faithful companion." He practically pranced over to me. "I've been tasked with protecting Faith on this journey."

"You're not helping the situation," I said to Levi. "Look, there are very few of us left because my father gets his kicks out of killing angel descendants to get a little of their grace. It doesn't matter if they are his offspring or not. They serve a purpose. To either fuel the bastard, or to sire his ungodly army."

I glanced at Kylee, and she shook her head. In her mind, she was begging me to shut up.

"He deserves to know. He's on this mission, too, whether we like it or not." I dismissed her and returned my focus to Josh. "CJ Ryan was the first trilogy ever born. He had a mixture of Raphael, Uriel, and Lucifer's bloodlines. His children have the blood of four archangels, because his wife is of Michael's bloodline." I wiped my face. "Tom's best friend, Damian, was Gabriel's son, and he married a woman who had Michael and Raphael's bloodlines, creating the next trilogies born."

"And you are Lucifer's daughter," he said, still coming to terms with that.

"Yeah. That's not something I'm really keen on advertising. But that is not the end of it. Damian's daughter did some things to CJ's son, and now we think Lucifer has him. And when I say 'has him,' I mean Lucifer is wearing him." My chin trembled, and I pressed my lips together, trying to blink the hot tears away. Instead, they slipped down my cheeks. "And when this is all over, if I can't save Alex..." My voice trembled, and I couldn't finish.

"She may need to kill the vessel to kill Lucifer," Kylee said it for me. "And she is in love with Alex."

"Alex Ryan?" Josh said, looking between us.

I nodded. "He went missing the night we got back from the island I leveled." I sniffled and wiped my nose with the back of my hand. "I know you're freaked out."

He laughed and ran his hand through his hair, leaving it in disarray. "You can't even imagine."

I looked out the window, trying to grapple with all the facts I had at my disposal, and how to frame them so he would understand. "My mother died two weeks ago, and before she got sick, I thought I was the only freak out there." I took my glove off and let the flame lick my fingers before I doused it and put my glove back on. "She told me who my father was just before she took her last breath. Imagine dealing with that on top of seeing cancer kill your mother." I offered a sad smile and blinked the sting of tears away. "After her funeral, I was supposed to go into state care, but that's when Tom Ryan changed the course of my life, and I found out I wasn't alone. That I wasn't the only gifted one out there." I glanced at Kylee. "I didn't know monsters existed. I didn't even really believe in the devil two weeks ago, so when I say I know what you're going through, I do." I wiped my face. "I still can't quite comprehend it all. I mean, even in my worst nightmares, I couldn't fathom the things that are out there." I pointed out the window. "I didn't ask for this. I didn't want this, but it looks like I'm the only one who can stop Lucifer."

The radio squawked, giving us permission to approach the runway for departure. Josh took a seat in the cockpit. His hand shook as he picked up his headset and plugged it in.

"Roger," he said into the microphone and started the engines. Then he turned the chair around and stared at me.

I pushed the urge to jump into his head and filter out his thoughts, and I tried not to listen to them. This was his issue to figure out. His mind kept going back to CJ Ryan and the instructions he gave for this trip. Josh had spoken to him directly. CJ had said to take care of me. He had made it clear that I had to be on the trip home.

Josh turned back to the controls and started the taxi out. Before he got in the line, he reached back and closed the door.

I could hear a muffled conversation in the cockpit. I felt a jolt of surprise come from Josh, but I restrained from opening the door. I blocked his thoughts from my head. He needed to deal with this in his own way. I wasn't going to wipe the fear from his aura. Only he could do that.

I looked at Levi. "Really? Death's companion?"

"He called me a monster."

"Well, aren't you?" I crossed my arms, challenging him.

"I am an honorable monster." He crossed his paws, trying to look all regal. It was as humorous as it was sad.

We started our taxi to the runway, and the engines revved. The sudden lurch forward and rush of speed captured my full attention, and I let the adrenaline follow. This high was almost addicting. I could see myself flying a plane. It wasn't anything I had ever aspired to before, but now, it was a goal.

"You are a strange child," Levi said, eyeing me.

"Why?"

"You like this Death trap?"

I smiled and looked out the window as we lifted off. "Yes. I do."

Quiet settled on the cabin as I scrolled through Alex's texts again. The visit to Paradise Cove had been a bust. I was right. The angels couldn't leave the cove, and they did not recommend that they bring Lucifer there, not with how precarious things were. But on the upside, they got to see Tom.

Reading his recounting made me smile, and then sadness crashed in again like the wave of a tsunami. That same feeling of having my stomach punched out gripped me, and I turned off my phone. I needed to push that away, even though every single cell wanted to go save him now. I had a job to do, whether I wanted to or not.

Homecoming
Chapter 17

JOSH PUSHED THE DOOR open. "Ladies, we are approaching the southern Andes. If you want to get a look at your destination, I suggest you come up here to get the full view."

Kylee didn't give me a choice. She dragged me into the cockpit, nearly pushing me into the copilot's chair. I looked at the jagged mountains and the snow that covered most of everything in sight.

Josh pointed to the tallest peak sticking out of the cloud cover in the distance. "That's Mount Cook. When we land in Hokitika, I can see if they have either a helicopter or a smaller plane that can take us up to the plateau hut." He eyed the weather over the mountains.

"Us?" Kylee asked.

This was quite the deviation of attitude in him from when he closed the door.

"Yes. Us. I doubt anyone will fly you up there in that." He pointed at the cloud cover and then tapped the radar. "That's white out conditions, which is rare for New Zealand in the fall." He bit his lip and glanced at us. "They might not give us permission either."

I shivered at the thought of going up that high. Snow didn't bother me at all. We used to get several feet of snow every winter, and my mother always had warm snow clothing for us. Sometimes we would have to sleep in the ski pants when our firewood stock went low. But the heights and challenging terrain gave me pause.

Josh looked at me, concern flooding his features and pulling the corners of his lips down. "What kind of... things do you expect here?" he asked, trying to be all cool about it, but his heart was clanging so loud I could almost hear it. His nervousness came out in the tapping of his foot and made little green and red flares in his aura.

Kylee turned and took a seat in the jump seat behind him instead of answering.

I turned the copilot seat to face her because I had no clue either.

"I don't know. There aren't very many..." She struggled to come up with a proper word. "Stories in the area," she finally finished. "The most likely scenario is kahui-tipua."

The name meant nothing to me, just like Kapua had meant nothing. "What exactly is a kahui-tipua?"

"Simply put, ogres."

"Like Shrek?" Josh said, his voice lilting with hope.

"No. They look like a cross between man and beast. They are white as the snow and are built like rock. They have sharp teeth and retractable claws, but prefer to kill their victims through blunt trauma. They eat what they kill, and there is very little that can kill them." She glanced back at Levi. "They might even give Levi a run for his money."

"How do you know about these things?" Josh asked.

Kylee looked at me. "I had to take one down before."

I was learning her expressions. The downturn of her lips was enough to tell me she would not enjoy this expedition. She was actually nervous. She fidgeted in her seat and glanced into the main cabin where Levi lay quietly listening to us.

"How do you kill them?" I assumed it would be like the Kapua and there wouldn't just be one of them.

Her haunted gaze turned to mine. "Fire."

I glanced at the mountains again as we headed out over the flatlands near the shore. All that snow. I sealed my eyes and sagged my head. Fire could cause massive avalanches.

"We have to make sure there is no one below us." I glanced at Josh. "And that includes you. You can't stay on the mountain."

"But..."

"I'll have a radio, and I'll let you know where you can pick us up," Kylee said. "You'll do a quick in and out. Even if we have to jump from the aircraft." She gave him a hard stare, then went into the back bedroom and came back a few seconds later with her bags. She rummaged through the contents, exchanging things from her backpack with things in the duffel bags. "When we land, I'll go get what we need for the mountain climb. And you can go figure out a ride to the plateau hut, Josh."

"And we need to get there today," I added. I didn't want to have to hang out for another day or two. Not when Alex was gone, and I still had one more stop before I could get home and stop whatever Lucifer was planning.

"That's a very tall order." He glanced at me. "It's late enough in the day for most pilots to laugh at you." He unengaged the autopilot and took the controls.

Watching the landing from here was much more thrilling than watching it from the little side windows. My heartbeat drummed in my chest, and I gripped the seat arms. When we landed, I let out a laugh.

Josh grinned like a little kid. "Quite the rush," he said as we slowed down and turned towards the private hangars at the end of the thoroughfare.

The airport itself was small, with just a couple of commercial puddle jumpers from Jetstar and Air Chathams parked at the gates. There were several private planes, from the small scenic ones to a couple like what we were in down in front of the hangars.

"Can I sit up here when we take off to go to Ireland?" I asked as he pulled to a stop in the farthest hangar and powered down the plane.

"Sure," Josh said, and then stepped away to help Kylee get off the plane to go get our hiking gear. He sat back down without voicing the 'assuming you are conscious' that fled through his mind. "I'm sorry for judging you earlier." He rubbed his hands together.

"You talked to Mr. Ryan?"

He let out a laugh and glanced at me, nodding. "I'm amazed I didn't crash the plane into one of the other jets on the runway."

"He showed up." That explained the sudden shock I had felt, but then nothing else had come through. I should have known CJ would do something like that.

"He told me everything you said was true. And he said you should have kept your damned mouth closed." He smiled. "He also said you had a good heart. An honorable heart. Those were his words." He looked out the window. "He said to get you back as quickly as possible after you take care of this thing here and the one in Ireland."

"So, all it took was CJ Ryan telling you I had a good heart for you to believe I'm not like my father?"

Josh rubbed his face. "No. He showed me what evil looked like and asked me what my intuition was saying about you. It was my conclusion, not his." He put his hand on the armrest.

I covered his hand with mine and squeezed. "Thank you."

He shrugged and pulled his hand away. "The only time I ever second-guessed someone was Tom Ryan. I was the one who flew him home with his dead daughter in his arms." He shook his head. "I questioned that for years, but my boss kept telling me that the Ryans were complicated, and our business is to be discrete." He chewed on his lip. "I never said anything because I knew there was more to the story than what I saw that night, and I now know what happened." He glanced at me. "It's nice to know that my intuition has never been wrong."

I had no idea where he was going with this conversation.

"You aren't evil. You're just a kid that's caught in the crosshairs of a much bigger war." He sighed. "So, I'm in. I'm here to help with whatever I can, like Kylee."

I opened my mouth to tell him Kylee was different, too, but I stopped myself, closing my mouth before I screwed up his view of her as well. Thankfully, Josh was looking out the window and not at me.

"I get why you have Levi, but I don't get why you'd bring Kylee into this?" he asked.

"She has a very extensive collection of ancient weapons that can take these things down. Plus, she's a paranormal investigator, and she's an expert at hand-to-hand combat. She knows how to use the weapons."

"That little thing?" He hooked his thumb over his shoulder.

"Yeah. That little thing is deadly." I grinned. "I'm glad she's on our side."

"I would have never guessed, but then again, I never looked in the duffel bags, either." He glanced at them spread out on the couch, with

Levi lying at the foot of them like a lonely sentry. "What's his story?" He pointed at Levi.

"He's really Death's sentry. Death told him he had to watch over me." When I looked back at Josh, the deep crevices in his forehead was all I needed to see. "Death is real. His name is actually Nick, and he's... I don't know. I guess he's married to Fate. Her name is Julia, and she is actually really sweet."

He kept blinking, like all his synapses were not firing properly.

I chuckled. "Mind blown. Right?"

He met my gaze. "Totally." He got up and looked around. "Man the plane while I go figure out our transportation." He trotted down the stairs and out of sight.

My smile faded as I glanced out the window. I just prayed nothing would happen to any of my little band of warriors. If this trip turned bad, I wasn't sure I'd be able to follow through in Ireland.

April's morbid vision threatened to overshadow everything. Even if I succeeded in closing these portals, the likelihood of her vision coming to fruition seemed inevitable.

Homecoming
Chapter 18

KYLEE CAME BACK WITH some serious winter wear. The cleats on the boots were enough to make Levi's claws look tame.

"Where's Josh?" she asked as she set everything down on the bench.

"He went out a while ago to get us a ride to the mountain."

Kylee sucked her bottom lip in. "You don't think he took off on us, do you?"

I hadn't even considered that, but given the same set of circumstances, I might have bugged out, too.

"Don't be ridiculous," Levi scoffed at us.

As if on cue, Josh entered the plane. "Get your gear on. We have a tiny window." He crossed to the cabinet. He grabbed a handful of protein bars and a couple of water bottles and dumped them in the backpack that Kylee had left on the couch.

We just stared at him.

"Get your gear on." He pointed at the pile. "I got us a chopper with a not-so-sane pilot, but he was the only one willing to take us up the mountain. No one has gone up there since the storm blew in."

I didn't need to be told a third time. I slid on the snow pants and tied the boots tight before I put on the coat and pocketed the hat and gloves.

Josh grabbed his jacket for the ride and handed Kylee the backpack. We all followed him off the plane, and he pressed the remote that closed the bird up nice and tight.

He jogged down the line of hangars until he reached the last, most rickety-looking one. Inside sat an old helicopter that reminded me of the ones I saw in old movies about Vietnam. When the pilot stepped out and gave us a toothless grin, I had a moment. It looked like Kylee did as well because we both drew up short.

Out of self-preservation, I scanned the pilot's mind. He was a lunatic but not homicidal, and he was the best pilot in the entire country. At least, that was his opinion of himself.

Josh climbed into the copilot seat and nodded toward the back. Our toothless guide took the pilot's seat and waited for us. Kylee put on the backpack and clasped it, glancing at me.

"Go on," she said.

I climbed in, and Levi followed, leaving the seat next to the door for Kylee. As soon as she was in and the door latched, the pilot engaged the engines.

"You might want to belt up," he said. "We are guaranteed to be in for a bumpy ride." He glanced back at us and cackled.

Josh looked back at me and shrugged. At least he had controls in front of him as well.

"Stetson requesting takeoff," the pilot said into his radio. "Just a sight-seeing jaunt over the mountains." Another pause. "Will do." He flipped the monitor off. "Mission control says to stay clear of the storm." He laughed like a crazy man.

He flipped on a radio, and Jefferson Airplane's "*Somebody to Love*" came piping out. I felt like I had just been transported back in time. My mother and I used to dance to this song whenever she played it on her old record player.

"Let's rock this ride!" Stetson shouted over the engine.

We rolled out into the open air and then lifted off, leaving my stomach on the ground. This was very different from a plane. I gripped the edge of my seat as we rocketed toward the black cloud.

The closer we got, the more erratic the helicopter behaved, and the more animated Stetson got. He whooped and hollered at the wind and the snow swirling around us.

Josh had his hands around his controls, too. I wasn't sure who was flying the helicopter, but Josh's tight jaw and sweat on his brow told me it was more him than Stetson at the moment.

"God help us," he muttered under his breath, and his raw fear radiated in his aura and in my bones.

I closed my eyes and dug my fingers into the seat, imagining a bubble around the helicopter that buffered us from the weather. It also cut a path though the storm, giving the pilots visibility to get us where we needed to go.

"What the Hell?" Stetson said.

I opened my eyes, still concentrating. Josh glanced back at me and gave me a nod. His silent thank you was worth it, but I didn't want to tell him I couldn't guarantee that I could hold it long enough to get them out of there.

The rest of the ride was smooth until we got close to the Plateau Hut. The view of the snow under our lights looked like it was painted red.

"What the actual fuck?" Stetson said.

"Do not land!" Kylee yelled from the back. "Just hover and we can jump."

"How many were stuck up here when the storm rolled in?" Josh asked as he circled to find a flat surface for us.

"There were at least two large parties up here, but we all figured they hunkered down in the bunker."

Levi started growling in the back seat, and Kylee swung the door open even though we were too far up to jump without major injury.

Something white was coming at us from the side. Levi launched. The minute he was clear of the helicopter, he transformed. His jaws caught the white flurry, cracking it in two.

I caught sight of the breach, and my heart lurched. It was bigger than the other three combined.

"Take us down below the hut," Kylee said. "Levi will provide the distraction we need."

Josh didn't hesitate, but it also meant jumping into the blood-streaked snow. He found a spot and hovered ten feet above the ground. Poor Stetson was staring at the battle of the monsters like he was on some sort of acid trip.

Kylee jumped out and landed in the perfect crouch.

I laid my hand on Josh's shoulder. "I'll hold the bubble as long as I can. You'll know when we've closed it," I said, and then flung myself out.

I landed hard next to Kylee and sunk down to almost my waist in the snow.

The helicopter veered up high in the sky and headed back the way we'd come. I prayed they got out of this vortex before my powers failed.

I crawled out of the hole I had made and climbed to my feet. My face was already numb and so were my hands, but I needed them free of fabric. I peeled the warded gloves off, and shoved them in an inside pocket, and let the fire form on my fingertips. I glanced over my shoulder, and I could no longer make out the helicopter, even though the sound of it still carried through the howling wind.

Kylee and I exchanged a nod, and then we sprinted towards the melee on the upper plateau. The one we had to run the length of to get to the portal. At least a dozen ogres were now in battle with Levi, and for the first time, I feared for our beast.

Toss them this way!

Levi tossed the first ogre in our direction. Before he landed, I blasted it with a shot of mixed fire. The thing let out a piercing scream that made me want to cover my ears, but I refrained. Unfortunately, my incineration of the ogre caught the attention of the rest. They split their attacks.

Kylee and I sprinted towards the breach and skidded to a halt when another half dozen appeared between us and the portal to Hell.

"Shit," Kylee said.

I opened my palms, holding one towards the breach and the other towards the ogres sprinting towards us.

"Get down!" I yelled. The command was for both Kylee and Levi. I didn't wait to see if they obeyed. I tilted my head back and screamed, letting both angel fire and my natural-born fire torch through the entire area.

I spun in an arc, obliterating what was close, and then positioned myself with one hand aimed at the portal and the other where Levi had been. My heart lurched at the empty field with only burning embers left. I closed my fist and turned back to the portal, then blasted it with everything I had.

Kylee kneeled by my feet. She was okay, but I couldn't see or feel Levi. I swallowed hard.

The crunch of snow yanked my attention. I didn't have time to raise my hand before the full weight of a charging ogre hit me. It felt like I had been plowed by a wrecking ball.

I sailed through the air and landed with the thing on top of me. I couldn't draw air. His fangs snapped at me. My palm was wedged against its chest, and I let my powers go in a fit of panic.

It was as if I shot him from a cannon. A cannon filled with fire. He went sailing right into the face of the mountain. The impact shook the ground. I got up and caught Kylee's eyes. We were both at the same distance from the portal.

An avalanche rumbled, pushing snow and rock with it. I sprinted towards the only logical exit where we had a chance to survive. Kylee understood, and she followed my lead. I dove through the breach, wondering just what in the Hell I was thinking. Kylee followed, and as I spun to close the breach from the inside, a shepherd leaped through the opening.

I lifted my hands. "Send a text to Josh to meet us in Ireland, Kylee." Then I blasted the breach closed from the inside. I prayed he got the message as the last of the opening closed with a pop.

Kylee sat on the ground, breathing as hard as I was. The text she had typed blinked on her phone, and then she met my gaze.

I glanced at Levi and threw my arms around him. "I am so damn glad you are okay."

"I wouldn't say any of us are okay. We're in Hell, and we have an awful lot of ground to cover to find the last breach." Levi stepped out of my grasp.

I blinked and glanced around us as the situation fully sunk in. We were actually in Hell. H E double hockey sticks. Hell.

Homecoming
Chapter 19

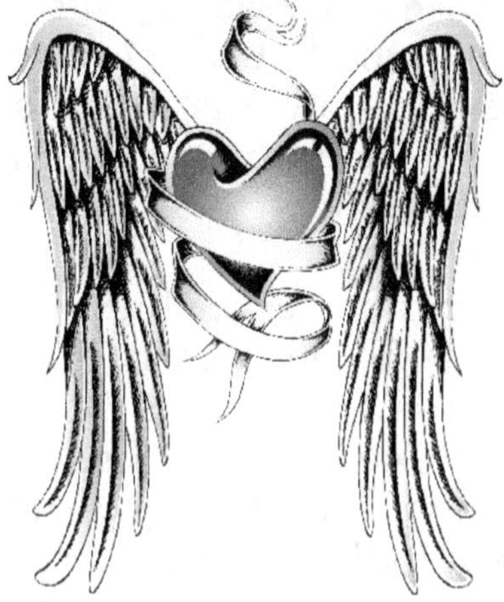

"IF WE CAN GET to the entrance, I can get us into Purgatory," Levi said as we walked down the mountain path from the breach. It was so cold, and I was glad I had the snow suit. I didn't know if we were lucky or not, but we didn't run into any ogres.

"What good would that do us?" Kylee argued. "Purgatory is still in the land of the dead."

Levi muttered under his breath, but conceded.

"We need to get to that breach." Kylee undid her gloves and peeled one off, then pushed her sleeve up far enough to see her watch. She pulled up whatever program she had on there, and a red dot appeared on a map.

She raised an eyebrow and met my gaze. "At least we are going in the right direction, but we have a long way to go."

She showed me the watch, and I slowed to a stop. The black dot of the one we'd just closed was so close to where the green dots showing our location were, and the red one looked like it was a half a world away.

I swallowed hard. What had I done to us? How many territories of Hell did we have to get through to get to the breach in Ireland? How many monsters did we have to battle?

Kylee ran a hand down her face. "The only good thing is *he* isn't here," she said very softly. "There probably will be some animosity between the kings and some internal power struggles. At least there used to be every time he used to take his leaves. Of course, that's if there are any left. Those that tried to take the helm were destroyed." She glanced at her watch and sighed. "I just never thought I would set foot in this place again."

"Can you get us to where we need to go?"

She shrugged. "We'll find out." She unclasped the backpack and pulled out weapons, then clipped them to her legs and handed me a couple as well. "I know you have your angel fire, but we probably shouldn't use it unless we have to. Same with you, Levi. You can't transform unless it's the only way to get us out of here."

"So, I'm just supposed to be vulnerable in this form? I would much rather have a demon buffet." He sounded disappointed.

"We are going to try to blend in, so when we get to that wooded area down there, we are going to ditch these snow clothes. Demons don't get cold, and we can't be bundled up like this walking through the main domain."

I chewed my lip, remembering the demon that escaped in the subway tunnel. She was wearing what I would call normal clothes, so my jeans and sweater that I had on underneath would fit in. Although if this cold persisted throughout the rest of this place, I would die of frostbite before we got to the other side.

So far, Hell didn't look that much different from the mountainside we'd left behind the void. I wondered if Hell mimicked the earth.

"I don't think it does," Levi said.

"Does what?" Kylee asked, looking at him.

"Hell doesn't mimic the human realm."

"Some parts do, but most of it is desolate. The topography has some similarities, like the mountain we're climbing down, but the rest of it is very different. You'll understand when we get to the woods."

When we approached the woods, Kylee found a fallen log for us to sit on and strip the ice spikes from our boots.

"Are you sure you want to do that?" I asked. "Because sharp spikes on my boots sounds like a fantastic idea to me."

"You can't run quick on spikes." She pulled her boots off before she dropped her ski pants and winter coat. She yanked her boots back on and laced them up. When she finally stood, she was weaponized to the hilt, and she handed me a bottle of water and a protein bar from the backpack. "It may be a while before we get a chance to eat again."

After I strapped the knives she gave me to my thighs, I put the gloves in my back pocket and finished the protein bar and bottled water.

She took my empty bottle and stuffed it in the backpack along with hers and then handed me the backpack. "You can carry that. I need to be agile if I have to take down demons, and it will protect your back."

I raised an eyebrow.

"Kevlar." She gave me a smile. "I'm always prepared for the worst."

I slung the straps over my shoulder, and she stepped forward, clipping it together.

"If it's clipped, it can't be easily torn off." She glanced at Levi. "You need to walk with us and not bound forward all willy-nilly."

I swear Levi rolled his eyes, but he didn't argue, even when she pointed to the spot between where we were standing. He grumbled and stepped in line with us.

A chill ran down my back as we stepped into the woods. A few steps in and they swallowed us up. Kylee was right. This wasn't the kind of woods I was used to. The trees were black as melted tar and looked just as appealing. The bushes looked like blood with sharp prickers. She steered us clear of those, but now and then, my jeans would catch on a thistle.

At least the ground looked like normal, hard packed dirt. I kept my eyes on the narrow path, looking for any gnarled roots that might trip us up. Eventually, the path opened up so we could walk together instead of single file.

"It looks like someone poured hot tar all over the trees," I said.

Kylee glared at me. *Zip it. Eyes forward and walk like you know where you are going.* Her thoughts echoed in my head.

I stared forward again, focusing on the path ahead of us, wondering just how long this would take us. I didn't have the luxury of time. Not with Alex missing. I tried to think of how many miles it was from New Zealand to Ireland. I knew the world was roughly twenty-five thousand miles around, and we were a tad less than half a world away from Ireland. My brain stalled. If I were calculating correctly, it would take us something like six months to walk halfway around the world if we walked night and day.

Kylee gave me a sideways look. "Chill," she whispered.

I didn't realize my breath was wheezing. But I couldn't imagine what would be left of Alex if Lucifer possessed him for a month, never mind a year.

Levi whined softly and nudged my knee. It was his way of comforting me. I dropped my hand to his head and gave him a pat, but my nerves were as frayed as they had ever been.

I forced myself to breathe normally, but that didn't stop my heart from galloping away. Especially when the woods thinned and offered me my first view of Hell proper. A barren red desert as far as the eye could see.

"Shit," Kylee muttered and stopped in her tracks. She looked at her watch again before glancing at me. "This isn't good." She sighed and scanned the sand. "We aren't even at the right level." She wiped her face. "I am such an idiot."

Numbness set into my limbs as I got the gist of her thoughts. This wasn't Hell proper. This was the monster realm of Hell. She should have connected the dots when all that attacked us at the mountain were ogres. We were much farther from home than she'd initially thought. And demons don't go into the monster realm.

Only Lucifer dared to walk into the monster realm.

My eyes widened.

"Um, Levi." Kylee cleared her throat. "I think we could use your true form to get across that." She pointed at the red sand. "And you have permission to eat whatever tries to stop us." She looked at me. "Feel free to use your fire, too," she added with a nervous smile.

Levi leaped into the air and turned into his natural form. His tail nearly plowed us over, it wagged so hard. He lowered his shoulder for us to climb up, and I took the forward seat.

Kylee unzipped the backpack and pulled the rope out. She threaded it through Levi's collar and then tied it around both our waists and back again. She wrapped her arms around the bag securely hooked around me.

"This time, neither of us is going anywhere, and you have some leeway to use one of your hands if needed," she said. "So, hold on tight. This is apt to be a Hellish ride. No pun intended."

"What's in the sand?" I asked.

Before she could articulate an answer, Levi took off, yanking us both backwards. If Kylee hadn't tied us in place, we would have tumbled off. He bounded like an overexuberant dog on a clear stretch of beach.

I held on to his collar with both hands as we bounced on his iron-like skin.

Movement to my left drew my attention. I gasped at a scorpion that was scrambling across the sand. It was as big as a car, but then again, Levi in his natural form was as big as a cargo plane, dwarfing the creature. Before I could blink, another half dozen of the things were racing towards us.

Levi let out a joyous laugh and picked up speed.

The wind nearly blew us over. If I didn't have my feet hooked under Levi's collar, we probably would have been bouncing at the end of the rope like two insignificant rag dolls. I was sure by the time we got off this wild ride, I would have a bruised tailbone for the next decade.

"Duck," Kylee yelled in my ear.

I folded forward with her pushing me down. Thankfully, it was just enough as a creature sailed towards us.

Levi snatched it out of the air. His jaws crunched its exoskeleton to a pulp before he tossed it aside. Without breaking stride, he went through the pod of scorpions like a wrecking ball, laughing as he dismembered and discarded them.

"I'm glad he's on our side," I said to Kylee.

She chuckled. "It is scary as all get out to be chased by him. Been there, done that, and somehow lived to tell about it because of Michael Andreas."

I glanced over my shoulder, and she smiled.

The scorpions stopped attacking. They kept a sufficient distance, but they paced us, flanking either side like they were waiting for Levi to tire. These things had intelligence.

A shiver caught me unprepared.

They were biding their time. Studying us. Waiting for the right moment to attack us en masse. It was eerie to the point I couldn't *not* shudder.

"Light them up," Levi said as he kept up his brutal pace.

Kylee and I sat up, and I opened my arms wide, pointing my fists at the clans in the distance. I tilted my head back and closed my eyes, calling on the fire within me. A hum filled my ears as I collected strength until it pooled in my belly, coiled and waiting.

My eyes and hands snapped open. Jets of fire shot out of my palms with the precision of a marksman. The screeches of the scorpions filled the air. By the time I got to the front of each pack, a few of them bugged out, but mostly, I left a black scar of giant and very dead scorpions.

I closed my palms, pulling the fire back into the box in my mind. Shutting it until I needed it again.

"You're getting better with that," Kylee said in my ear as we continued to gallop across the barren wasteland that reminded me of the pictures from the Mars rover.

"Every time I use it, the power seems to grow." Each time I used the powers at my disposal correctly, it flared like a battery renewing tenfold. Same with the mental stuff. Each time seemed easier than the last. I knew from experience that tapping myself would incapacitate me for longer than we had time for, so using these quick bursts that built strength was helpful.

"Ten degrees to the north," Kylee called out. She pulled her sleeve down over the watch and buried it in the space between my back and the pack she clung to.

Levi adjusted his trajectory.

"Watch for sand serpents!" Kylee called.

Levi nodded, continuing to lumber at a speed which belied his size. Sand spit behind us with each thrust of his hind legs. I wished I could see him running at a distance. I could envision him running like a cheetah, but with a much more feral, reptilian face and a tail that could crack boulders with its power.

In his natural form, Levi reminded me of a dragon from a JRR Tolkien movie. Except he didn't have wings, and he didn't breathe fire. Basically, he was this deadly prehistoric lizard the size of Godzilla, but he was deceptively agile and much smarter than most people I had come in contact with, the Ryans included.

Levi's chuckle rumbled across the sand.

And then there were times like this when he was more like a little kid with his choice of toys. Here he was in his element. I didn't know nearly enough about Levi, other than he was Death's sidekick.

"I was chained in Purgatory for thousands of years until Nick set me free," Levi said. "That is why I am loyal to the boy."

I patted the side of his neck. Leviathan was honorable. Who would have thought?

He glanced over his shoulder at me and cocked an eyebrow.

"Look out!" Kylee pointed in front of us.

A giant worm shot up from the sand. Its mouth had a thousand razor-sharp teeth in row after row, and it was heading straight for us.

Adrenaline shot through my veins in a hot pulse. My hands were up in front of me before my brain caught up. The blast exploded the thing outward into a million tiny bits. A bloody mist hung in the air, and when Leviathan ran through it, the mist coated my skin, making me gag.

Kylee coughed from behind me, but I didn't dare look back, not when Leviathan's gray coat now was a gross mixture of red and green. I would have preferred to ride through raining ash than whatever that had been.

Leviathan's tongue swathed his face. "Yum." He grinned and kept running.

"That was gross," I said, looking for a clean piece of clothing to wipe my face, but there was none.

A zipper sounded, and then Kylee handed me a washcloth. "I grabbed a couple of clean cloths just in case we needed them on the mountain."

I didn't question her preparation reasons. I was just thankful she had the forethought to think of these things. I wiped my face and neck, then tried to get what I could off my hands, but the cloth was already dripping. The thought of squeezing it out just made my skin crawl.

"What do I do with this?" I held the cloth out to my side like it was diseased.

"Toss it."

I glanced back at her. I didn't want to litter, even if this was Hell.

"Something will eat it."

"But..."

"It's cloth. It won't hurt a monster."

"That's like saying eating a sock won't hurt a dog."

"Oh, for Heaven's sake." She grabbed the cloth from me and flung it out into the sand. "I can't put it back in the bag and contaminate everything in there with worm guts. These creatures don't have the same digestive issues that we have on earth. Their stomach acid will disintegrate that thing."

"Oh." I faced forward again, feeling a little small and stupid, more from her tone than her words.

Levi slowed his pace at the first signs of something other than red sand in the distance. And it wasn't another mountain range.

A spewing volcano reached into the mass of black clouds that looked even more daunting than the ones over Mount Cook. But that wasn't what made us pause.

It was the sea of monsters and demons fighting at the base.

"Double fuck," Kylee whispered.

"That is how we get to the demon realm?" Levi asked.

"Yup." Kylee said.

"We should have kept the cleats," I said, looking at the volcano instead of the fighting.

She huffed behind me.

The surrounding sand rumbled. Levi bolted towards the ruckus. He ran straight for it, thundering down on the monsters and demons alike with claws and teeth bared.

Scorpions and sand worms barreled down on us from behind. A few of the fighters on the outskirts turned towards us, their eyes widening at the sight of Leviathan.

There were too many blocking our path. The fiends following us were just as menacing. Levi's ferocious roar sent some of the group running, but those with weapons turned from fighting each other and focused their blades in our direction.

Leviathan was a behemoth even here. I guess from a distance Levi didn't look all that formidable, but the closer we got, the more the masses scattered. It was like seeing King Kong take New York, but even King Kong could be taken down with a well-placed strike.

The minute his feet hit solid ground, the earth shook with each of his bounds. The scorpions stood in a line at the edge of the sand, snapping their claws and raising their stingers in the air.

Levi trampled a path from the edge of the sand to the side of the volcano, leaving a trail of broken limbs and decapitated bodies. He leaped into the air, and I grabbed his collar, straining to hold on. His nails dug into the side of the volcano, cutting trenches as he hauled us towards the heat above.

Kylee hissed loud enough to catch my attention, and I turned to see her pulling an arrow out of her arm. Another one flew by my head. I reached around her and opened my palm, aiming directly for the demon with the bow. Before he could let the next arrow fly, he turned to dust under my white firebolt.

All the other demons froze in wide-eyed terror.

Their only task was to not let the monsters escape.

That was their only job in Hell, and with the breaches in both realms, the demons were losing the battle to keep the status quo.

I almost felt sorry for them, especially with the renewed determination of the monster clans now that Levi plowed a way through.

I scanned the monsters, and my chest tightened as I realized just what kind of mistake we had made in approaching this way. My gaze moved to the scorpions lining the sand, and I knew there was no other way across that desert than bounding across on Levi.

If we didn't get the last breach closed, our world...

The thought hung in my mind, and I turned forward in time to be swallowed by the black clouds.

Homecoming
Chapter 20

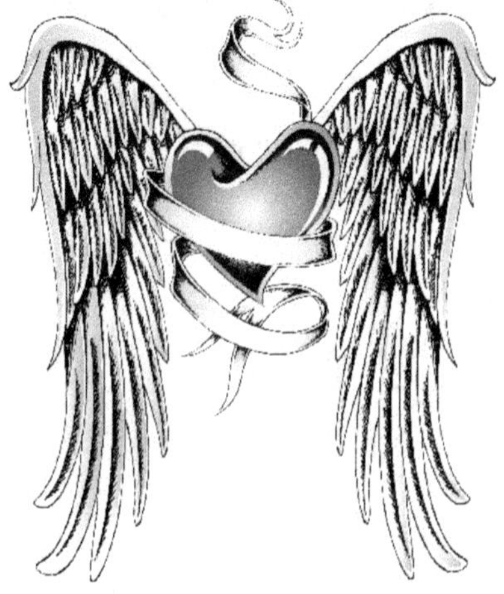

LEVI PUSHED ON, HIS head hanging low against the pressure of the cloud. Kylee and I clung to Levi, both leaning forward to make out anything but the cloud surrounding us. Even letting the fire burn on my fingertips provided no penetration. There was no visibility, and all I could think of was stepping off the ledge and falling into the hot lava rumbling in the belly of this beast.

Thunder rumbled around us. If we were at ground level and not riding Leviathan, I didn't think we could have broken through into the cloud at all. Every step of his seemed impossible, and he punctuated every motion with a growl, like it hurt him to maneuver through the nearly impenetrable mist.

We broke through the cloud layer into clean air that filled my lungs and made me question whether or not we were still in Hell. Then the wind shifted, and a whiff of brimstone flowed down the volcano. I could almost see over the top of the thing.

"Levi, you need to shrink. Now." Kylee sliced the ropes holding us together.

I blinked and then landed on my ass, almost tumbling back into the cloud layer, but Levi grabbed my pant leg with his teeth.

Kylee was face-first on the mountainside, and she pushed up on her elbows. "You could have let us down first." She glared at him.

"You said now," he said.

I got to my feet and dusted myself off. "You did."

She climbed to her feet and glanced at her watch. Her eyebrows rose, and she showed me the dial. We were halfway between the black dot and the red one now.

"Now, follow my lead." She sauntered up to the crest with one of her knives in her hand, grumbling.

I followed with Levi on my heels, walking with a similar strut as Kylee. Levi walked close enough to rub against my leg. I placed my hand on his head as we crested the top of the volcano.

When I looked up, I had to check the sudden lurch in my chest and keep my face neutral. A sprawling city was situated across from the volcanic opening, and a narrow path crossed over the top, more like an old, crafted bridge than a death trap over a volcano. Halfway across, I made the mistake of looking down at the fiery pit below. I grabbed Levi tighter than I meant to as I stared at the bubbling arcs of flaming earth.

"Ow," he muttered, and I eased up, forcing the fear out of my grip.

A demon sentry on the other side gave us a cursory glance before looking back at the book in his hand and muttering, "Tough shift?"

I guessed being covered in worm blood and guts was a normal occurrence for the demons keeping the monster realm in check.

"Very." Kylee kept walking until we passed onto the street.

The streets were crowded with people. Demons, I guessed, and their similarities to us gave us the perfect camouflage, especially with our bloodied appearance. We blended in.

Now I understood why they didn't want to let the monsters loose in their realm. Their realm mimicked earth in many ways, and the monsters below would happily tear down their steel towers. The cold buildings seemed as appropriate as the black asphalt. No trees dotted the corners. It was all so sterile and without personality. The demons hustling from place to place either had blackened auras or no auras at all.

We weaved our way through the crowds, and each demon that crossed our path hurried away from us, giving us a wide berth and an almost respectful nod as we passed. As we neared the far side of the city, the buildings thinned, and beyond lay a black sea with ferries like I had seen as a kid that took folks up to Nova Scotia for the day. They lined up in neat little rows, sometimes three deep on a single dock.

Kylee headed for the dock that had only one ferry, and thankfully, it was sparsely populated with only a few passengers on board. We stepped onto the ferry, and she pointed to a row of seats that had the wall of windows as a backing. We sat, keeping an eye on the demons on board.

That was when another truth hit me. We were the only ones with any color. Everyone else was a variation of gray or white or black, and their clothes matched. We were covered in blood, which made us stand out on this boat.

It also explained why demons moved out of our way in the streets, but they didn't stare. It was as if being a guard to the monster realm had some weight. The boat lurched forward, and my stomach turned. I swallowed and tried to hide my grimace.

The ferry captain tipped his hat as he passed by us, and then he stopped and retraced his steps. He stared at Levi and pointed at him. "I thought dogs went to Heaven?"

Kylee glared at him. "He's a new breed of Hellhound. One that we designed to someday terrorize the human realm. Levi, do you want to show our captain your teeth?"

Levi's lips pulled back to normal canine teeth, and then he opened his mouth, revealing the razor-sharp layer of his own natural teeth, ballooning his mouth out almost like a cartoon dog. When he closed his snout, he seemed normal again.

The captain stepped back, gave us a nervous smile, and hustled away as if he had just seen the devil himself.

I patted Levi, and he licked his lips, glancing at the handful of demons on the boat.

Kylee looked over her shoulder at the fading cityscape and then out at the open waters ahead. "Light them up." She glanced at me.

My mouth popped open at her directive.

"We need the boat," she whispered.

"Can I eat them?" Levi asked.

They looked like people. Acted like people. Even had the mundane thoughts of people. I couldn't just roast them like flambé. "No."

Kylee closed her eyes. *I know they look like people, but these are demons. Demons loyal to Lucifer. Demons that would slit your throat on earth without issue.* She opened her eyes and met my gaze.

I knew it was probably stupid as sin, but I opened my mouth, anyway. "Hey, does anyone know when Lucifer is supposed to come back?"

"Why? Are his monsters getting restless?" A man sneered and crossed his arms. He shook his head in disgust. "No one knows when that bastard is coming back."

"Shhh," the woman next to him said while yanking on the arm of his coat. Her face was filled with the sort of worry that was distinctly human. I couldn't tell what color her hair had been in life, but it was black as night now.

I glanced at Kylee. These were not Lucifer's tribe, and I would not toast them. Not if I didn't have to.

His eyes narrowed as his gaze flitted from my hair to my face and back again. A crease appeared between his eyes, and he leaned down and whispered something in the woman's ear. Her gaze snapped to mine, her eyes wide.

"You had to open your mouth," Kylee whispered out the edge of her lips.

I shrugged and heat filled my cheeks.

The man's mouth dropped open, and he reached into his pocket. His thoughts betrayed him. While he wasn't going to kill us, he certainly was going to notify the authorities that there were intruders in their midst.

"Don't." I put my arm out with my hand fisted. Now everyone's attention was on us. "Please," I added softly, even though I knew it was futile.

He pulled his hand out and held a small contraption with a red button on it. His thumb moved towards the button, and I opened my hand. The plow of angel fire lit up the entire inside of the boat. When I closed my hand, no one but the three of us were left. Not even the captain.

Kylee hurried to the helm and took control, charting an alternative course in sync with her watch. I sat back down in the seat and covered my face. This felt so wrong. A part of me embraced it, but the other part, the one that loved Alex with every fiber, felt nothing but chilling shame.

Levi put his head in my lap. "I would have eaten them," he muttered, and I met his gaze. "They were demons. You don't get ushered to Hell for being a boy scout."

"So, what do you get ushered to Hell for?" I scoffed. The demons I'd killed didn't seem like cold-blooded killers.

"Mortal sin."

"Mortal sin," I repeated. "Like what I just did." I waved toward the cinders still floating in the air.

"Killing demons is not a mortal sin."

I stared at him. "*Killing* is. And every time I do it, I lose a piece of myself."

Emptiness surrounded me. I couldn't deal with what I had just done. I closed my eyes, letting the sudden flush of exhaustion that made my muscles feel as fluid as the black ocean we were on take over.

Homecoming
Chapter 21

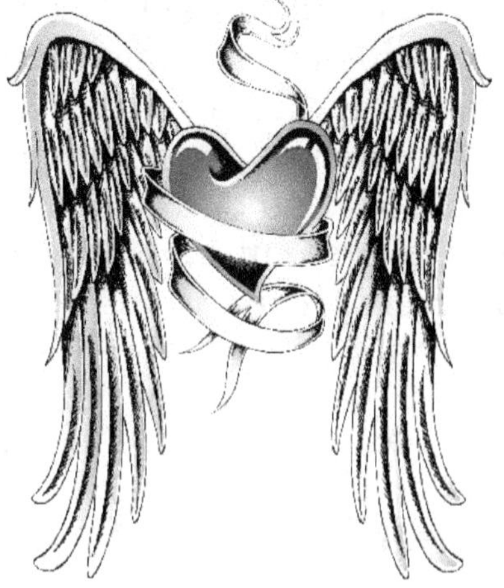

I BLINKED AND GLANCED around. Kylee was still at the helm, and Levi was sleeping in the middle of the floor between us, his paws twitching like he was running in his dreams.

"Where are we going?" I asked and cleared my throat.

The black ocean stretched out as far as I could see in every direction, looking more like an oil spill than water. The air pressed down, leaving a stale taste in my mouth that had more to do with where we were than sleep.

"To the inner circle." She tapped her watch. "We are close, which is the good news. The bad news is, this is where the demon kings live." She glanced over at me. "These aren't ones to play around with. They are just as depraved as Lucifer, so none of us can hesitate. Once we land, you shoot on sight. Understand?" She sent a glare in my direction.

I looked down at the floor and nodded. I was not ready for a kill-on-sight order. It was different when things were chasing us or putting people I cared about in harm's way. Then it was a defensive reflex. Even toasting the demons at the portal with Tom could be justified, but it still didn't make me feel any better about ripping someone's life from them.

"Assuming they didn't all bug out," she muttered under her breath, but it was her thought that left me shivering: *God help the world if they did.*

I moved forward and took the seat next to her. The sleeve of her shirt had been torn off, and a bandage applied to her arm where she had ripped the arrow out. I ran my fingers over the cloth.

She glanced at me, and I met her gaze.

"I'm sorry. I didn't even think to do a protective barrier around us." I dropped my hand and glanced out at the sea.

"Don't do that to yourself. You can't always protect the ones you care about." She bit her lip and scanned the horizon. "I don't even know how much time has passed up there."

"What do you mean?" We had only been down here a day or two at best.

"Time is different down here. Six minutes could have passed, or six months. I have no idea." She shook her head like she didn't even want to entertain the thought.

"What do you mean, it could be six months?" My heart lurched.

"It could be six years, for that matter." She rubbed her palms on her pants before gripping the wheel again.

"Everyone we know could be dead," I whispered.

She sucked her lower lip between her teeth. "God, I hope not." She stood taller. "Time to get your guard up."

Levi's head popped up from the floor. "I can eat this time?"

The hopeful lilt of his voice made my stomach sour, but I would be happier if he did the assassinations than if I had to. His tail wagged, thumping on the floor, and his tongue lolled out the side. Even in dog form, he looked a bit like a deranged cartoon.

His infamous eye roll cast in my direction, and then he got to his feet and padded to the front window, where he jumped his front legs up to the sill. Dotted lights flickered, and a dark energy rolled over the boat.

Nerves bit at me, and I realized my fingers were sparking involuntarily. I closed my fists. It wasn't long before Kylee pulled into a deserted dock. We tied off the ferry and hopped onto the wooden planks. The soft slosh of water against wood sounded around us, but the quality of the noise flattened like the malignant air absorbed it.

Kylee took the lead, creeping forward with knives in both hands. I unsheathed one of mine and held it in my left hand, keeping my dominant hand free to shoot fireballs if needed. Levi took the rear.

The quiet unnerved me. It was like walking through a ghost town, but one made of towering castles made for kings and thatched huts of those that served the kings. It was medieval in shades of gray and was such a stark contrast to the metal towers of the last area of Hell we went through. The vacant streets closed in on us, delivering the smell of blood and decay overlaid with undertones of brimstone. As we maneuvered towards the center of the dark village, I thought I could hear crying in the distance. Occasionally it sounded like a scream, but no sooner did the sound reach us than it dissipated to nothing.

We finally got to the green in the center. The ground looked like someone threw buckets of paint here and there among the tools of destruction. A guillotine here, a torture rack there, and many other devices that I didn't know the name of. The red scorched earth under them rattled me. When I slipped in one of the paint puddles, I realized it wasn't paint. It was blood. My stomach lurched.

We were walking on slaughter grounds, and right in front of where the gallows stood was the breach. I started towards it, but Kylee grabbed my arm and pointed at Levi.

Leviathan first.

As we neared, I could see the bright, sunny green fields on the other side. I wanted to get home, but I understood. They deserted this place for a reason, and who knew if someone was watching the other side. If we went through without caution, it could be the last thing we did.

Levi jumped, transitioning to his formidable self as he crossed over. A blade swung into view, lashing his side. He turned on the owner but didn't attack. In fact, his tail actually wagged.

Kylee stepped through with her blades at the ready, but they fell from her hands the moment she stepped on the grass. She nearly jumped off the ground towards whoever was out of sight.

I crossed over into the beautiful Irish countryside to see Kylee in Michael's arms and Josh standing next to him, both armed to the hilt and looking like some medieval knights coming to save the day.

I turned and aimed my hands at the portal, blasting it to oblivion within seconds.

"Where's Alexis?" Kylee asked as she pulled away from Michael.

"With CJ and his wife." He glanced at me and back to Kylee. "Some serious shit has gone down since you took your detour."

"How long were we gone?" I asked.

Michael and Josh exchanged a glance.

"Five months. We thought…" Michael ran his hand down his face. "I thought I had lost everything." He cupped Kylee's cheek and ran a finger over her lips. "I thought I lost you." He sniffled and stepped away, getting his game face back on.

"Five months?" My legs gave out, and I sat down hard on the ground.

"We've been doing demon detail for the last couple of months." He nodded to where the portal had been moments ago.

"Alex." I looked up.

Michael's eyes softened. He shook his head and looked away. "Lucifer."

The world swam. I placed my palms on the ground to get some order in my head. Lucifer had Alex, which meant Grace had Alex. I turned onto my hands and knees and dry heaved. The cramping went all the way from my toes to my neck, and I thought my head would just explode from the pressure.

A hand rubbed my back, and soft coos finally broke through the high-pitched buzz filling my ears. Anger enveloped me, and for a fraction of a second, I wanted this world to burn. Darkness dotted my vision as I glared at Kylee.

She kept rubbing my back despite the screams. Screams that I didn't realize were coming from me until this moment. That truth that I was screaming like a wild banshee shattered the darkness threatening to overwhelm me. I resisted because if I didn't, my fire would ignite and consume her and everyone around us.

My screams gave way to sobs, the kind that were reserved for loss and mourning. April had it wrong. I wasn't strong enough to kill Lucifer, not while he had Alex's face. I sobbed because deep down I knew... I knew that killing Lucifer now would kill everything good in me.

Homecoming
Chapter 22

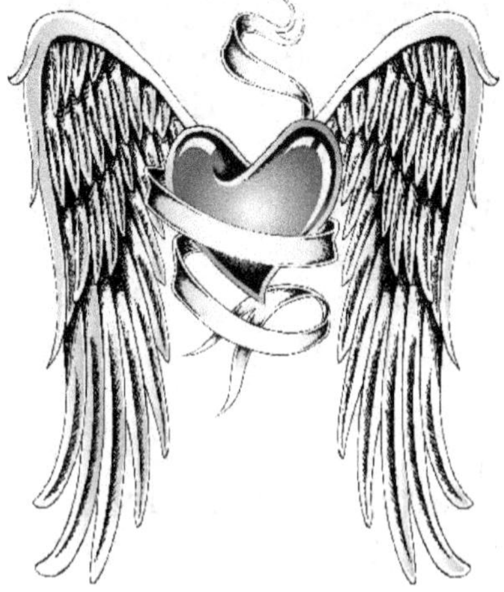

JOSH LED US ONTO the plane in Ireland. I went to the bathroom and just stood under the hot stream of water, trying to close up the open wound in my soul, but it refused to mend. I needed Alex for that. I pressed my lips against another sob. I couldn't continue this way. I needed to get a grip on my emotions. Now. Before we got home.

When I finally came out into the main cabin, I slumped in the seat and just stared at the floor. My insides were a mess, and when Michael offered me food, I shook my head. I couldn't stomach it, but I took the water he offered.

"Did you want to come up here for the takeoff?" Josh asked from the cockpit.

I shook my head. I had no interest in anything. I didn't even look out the window when the plane took off. I blocked everyone's thoughts because I didn't want to hear their worry. I didn't want to feel their emotions. Hell, I didn't want to feel mine either.

"Are you going to be okay?" Kylee asked.

I looked up at her, and the hollowness that had taken over the minute I'd stopped screaming bloomed in my chest. I gave her a nod to soothe the worry in her eyes.

"I need to clean up too," she said, "and then we can find out what happened when we were gone."

She disappeared into the back room.

When she came back all clean and shiny, she took a seat next to Michael. "Tell us what happened."

He wiped his face and leaned back in the chair. "Some of it is his story." He pointed at Josh. "I guess they had a hell of a time getting out of that storm without crashing. He didn't get Kylee's text until after he landed. On our way here, he told me he didn't leave right away. The storm had cleared, and the avalanche devastated some of the lower huts. Half the mountain crumbled down with the snow. He thought maybe you had been trapped, but I guess that's when CJ called and told him you guys had taken a little detour and that he needed to get to Ireland."

"When I got to Ireland, I actually looked in your bags, Kylee," Josh said from the pilot's seat. He had turned towards us. "Arsenal is an understatement." He laughed. "I hung out listening to stories of people being slaughtered in the area, and I knew there were some seriously bad things here, but I didn't know the first thing about battling them, so I called CJ again after two weeks had gone by and no word from you all."

I listened but kept my gaze on the floor, even when Levi climbed next to me and nudged my hand. I met his questioning stare and looked away. He whined and laid his head on my lap.

"My orders were to sit tight, but I wasn't in the mood to sit and do nothing." Josh turned back to the front window.

His statement broke through my numbness to tickle my curiosity. "What did you do?"

"I kicked some demon ass with some of Kylee's weapons," he said. "But not without getting myself into a little trouble. I guess that's when Fate sent along some vigilantes to help. I had a little time in the hospital, and when I was finally released, Michael was waiting for me at the airport." He nodded toward Michael and focused back on flying the plane.

I just couldn't see our kind, sweet, calm pilot fighting demons, but I guessed it was always the quiet ones who were the most courageous.

"While Josh was running around trying to be the hero, I got a call from CJ." Michael squeezed his hands together, and his jaw tightened. "My mom and brother went missing." He blinked several times and took a big inhalation through his nose, filling his chest with air, and then slowly exhaled. "I'm not sure if it was Grace or Bridget... Either way, someone coerced them to leave the safety of the Ryans and we have not seen them since." He closed his eyes. "Shortly after I got to the house with Alexis, April called her mother out on a few things. Including Alex's disappearance."

My entire body felt like someone had sliced me in half at the mention of his name. Pain tore deep, and I wrapped my arms around my mid-section to keep myself together. Tears blurred my vision, but I blinked them away.

"CJ told her to run. If she ever showed her face near his family, he would put her down like the traitorous dog she was." He wiped his face. "I've never seen him that angry. I've never seen a man sprout wings and look like Heaven's wrath had been handed to him." He shook his head. "He wouldn't allow her near April, and April didn't want to go with her mother, anyway. I'm not sure if she will ever regret that decision, but she didn't want to be on the side where evil reigned. She believed in the light and she believed in you." He pointed at me. "Well, Bridget ran. And so did we. We went to New Hampshire, to Paradise Cove." He glanced out the window. "To the place we were born," he said almost too softly to hear.

The box of memories shook in my head in response to his whisper. I clamped down on it. I had Michael's father's memories stored in my head, and they were the ones that blew my circuits to begin with. I didn't want another repeat of what had opened these breaches. So I brushed it aside and focused on Michael.

"Did you ever find out what happened to your mom?" I asked, wiping the tears from my cheeks.

He shook his head. "But the emptiness right here,"—he pointed to his chest—"that tells me one of my siblings isn't here any more, and if he's dead, so is my mother."

Kylee cocked her head at him.

"It's a triplet thing," he muttered.

Or just an accurate conclusion. Lucifer was a greedy bastard, and even if he was in Alex's form, he'd still kill them for the grace that resided in their hearts.

"So, I left Alexis with CJ and Valerie and came over here to wait for you." He glanced at Kylee. "I lost almost everything to Lucifer, but he wasn't in Hell, and if there is anyone who could successfully escape that place, it's you." He took Kylee's hand and squeezed.

"We didn't encounter much after we went back to the portal. And I didn't mean to hit Levi when he jumped out, but the thing shimmered like it had when demons came through, and I reacted," Josh said from the cockpit.

"It was just a flesh wound," Levi said from my lap.

Josh smiled back at the dog and continued to fly the plane.

The rest of the trip was quiet, and Kylee, Michael, and Levi fell asleep.

I took a seat in the co-pilot chair and stared out at the Atlantic. It was deep blue, like the mood threatening to overtake me. I had a moment where I thought we would all be better a thousand leagues under the surface, but Tom's words echoed in my head.

I closed my eyes. "Damn him," I whispered, unsure of whether I was targeting Tom, Alex, or Lucifer with the statement. Maybe all three.

"How are you holding up?" Josh asked after a few minutes.

"Not very well," I said. "What's Alex going to be like after five months of being possessed by Lucifer?" I glanced at Josh. "What am I going to be like if I have to kill him?"

Josh didn't have answers for me, but he covered my hand and squeezed.

My throat tightened with a lump.

Josh disengaged the autopilot. "Take the yoke." He nodded towards the controls in front of me.

My eyes widened. "What?"

"I want to see you fly the plane." He crossed his arms, and we started losing altitude.

"What the..." The voice came from the main cabin.

I grabbed the controls and steadied the plane before I sent Josh a glare. He smiled at me in a way that eased the aggravation. I scanned the gadgets on the dashboard, checking speed and altitude. Everything made sense. I looked back out the window as the thrill of flying the plane erased everything else in my mind. It was a temporary fix, but it drove the darkness away and replaced it with a rush, much like Alex's kiss.

"What if I can't save him?" I whispered.

Josh sighed. "I don't have answers. I've never fallen in love."

A profound sadness filled me. Everyone should feel the glow of love at least once in their lifetime. "You should."

He laughed and glanced over his shoulder. "Yeah, well, maybe destiny has other plans for me." He shrugged and met my gaze. "And I'm okay with that." He nodded towards my yoke. "Keep us steady and on course." He tapped the course heading.

I looked back at the instruments, adjusted our heading, and focused on getting us home in one piece.

Josh took over when we neared our destination and glided us into a smooth landing in Wolfeboro. I didn't know if he realized what he'd done for me by thrusting the responsibility of flying on me, but he might have saved me from a true mental breakdown.

He pulled us to a stop next to a town car outside a hangar. After helping us put our luggage into the trunk, he and Kylee, and Michael exchanged hugs before they got in the car.

Josh opened the back door of the car for me, and Levi jumped in without prompting.

I turned to Josh. "Thank you." I gave him a hug.

He returned it, squeezing hard. "Be good," he said.

I nodded and then slid into the back seat of the car with Levi. The ride to the lake was short and quiet as we all battled our own jet lag. The radio played softly in the background, and every song hit raw, exposed nerves in my soul.

When we finally pulled up to the cottage, the pull of Paradise Cove was almost overwhelming.

I wanted my mother to hold me and erase the pain in my chest. I wanted her to tell me everything I had done was not in vain, but I knew that was impossible. Only Alex could make me whole, but I had as much control over my situation as I had over the moon setting over the mountains across the lake.

Instead of running to the cove like I wanted, I headed inside with Kylee and Michael.

CJ stood from the couch when we walked in. He looked ragged, like he had aged ten years. His hair was as out of order as the papers on the kitchen table, and his welcoming smile did not reach his eyes. Frankly, he looked as shell-shocked as I felt.

It was close to two in the morning, according to the clock over the fireplace. No one else was up to greet us, so just CJ and the stillness of the house grated on me.

Kylee gave CJ a hug.

"Alexis is in the far room. There's a double bed in there for you," CJ said, and pointed.

"Thanks," Kylee said. She gave me a nod and headed towards the room with Michael clasping her hand.

I turned back to CJ, and another thing I noticed about him was how much he looked like Alex. I nearly crumpled on the floor.

"Awkward," Levi whispered next to me and I sent a glare to shut him up.

CJ approached me, but I couldn't do this right now. I didn't want a hug. A hug from him would open the floodgates again. Not when he and his son looked so painfully similar that my heart tore in two at the sight of him.

My chin trembled, but before I lost it, I turned and fled out the door, across the yard, and onto the soft moss of Paradise Cove. I fell to my knees as sobs crushed my chest. I couldn't articulate the pain ripping me to shreds.

I just wanted my mother.

A hand landed on my shoulder, and I looked up, expecting what I had wished for.

Tom squatted before me, and his sad eyes reached into the depths of my hurt. He placed a blue knife on the ground. It seemed to reflect light, even in the darkness. "Death asked me to give this to you."

I pushed him on his ass and stepped back, away from Heaven's blade. "No."

He shut his eyes and lowered his head. "It has to be done." When he looked up, tears tracked down his cheeks, sending prisms across them. He was breathtaking and devastating at the same time. "It has to be you."

I sank to my knees. "I can't. Alex is still in there. Please. Please don't make me do this."

Tom put his hands on his knees. "Life isn't fair, Faith. Sometimes you have to step up and take the hit for the rest of the world." He glared up at me. Frustration framed his face as he pressed his lips together. "You are not done yet."

At least he hadn't told me I was young, and I would eventually find someone else that would make me feel the same way Alex did. If he had, I thought I would have blasted him right into Hell.

It shredded my insides as if Leviathan had swiped his claws right through my flesh. I covered my face as a fresh wave of tears gripped me.

Leaves crunched, and I stiffened. No thoughts came through, so I looked up. CJ stood at the entrance with his gaze locked on the knife. A single tear rolled down his cheek as he met my stare.

His pain hit, nearly doubling me over. He wasn't capable of doing what was necessary. He might have found the courage to kill Lucifer if he had still had Tom's likeness, but his son... He would sooner die than bury a knife in his son's heart.

I squeezed my fists tight and screamed my anguish to the Heavens. When my voice failed, I reached forward and picked up the knife, resolved in what I had to eventually do.

But I wasn't going tonight, or tomorrow, or the next day. I needed time to steel my nerves and hone my skills before I took on the devil.

I climbed to my feet and headed back to the cottage with the father of the boy I was destined to kill.

The End

Continue on the next page with JUDGEMENT DAY the last book in the FIRE CURSED TRILOGY.

Judgement Day
Chapter 1

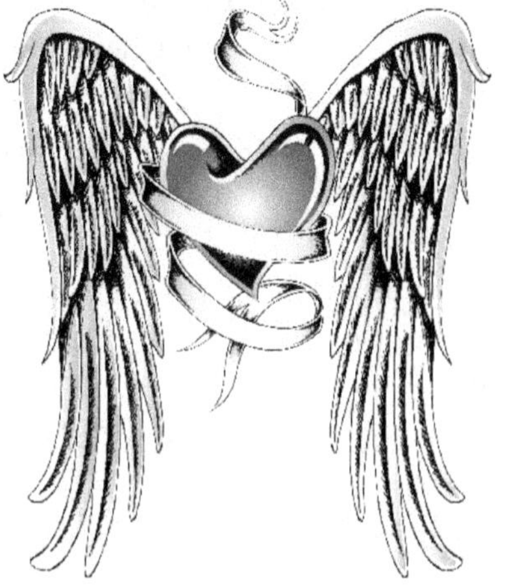

I STARED AT THE deadliest weapon ever to touch mankind's hands. It glowed, filling the cabin with a soft light that belied the danger it represented. Anyone I cut with the blade made of Heaven's light would cease to exist.

No Heaven. No Hell. Just poof. Gone.

It was a responsibility I did not want.

I wanted to smash it to bits. To erase *it* from existence. But the knife was the only thing that would stop Lucifer. Not even the combined power of angel fire, my natural fire, and Tom Ryan's powers could take out Lucifer. That would only serve to kill my boyfriend and send Lucifer's spirit back to Hell, where that bastard had the potential to escape again.

Plus, I didn't think I could burn Lucifer while he was wearing Alex Ryan.

So, this ungodly knife, forged in Heaven by Lucifer himself, was the only hope of mankind.

I still couldn't believe I was contemplating killing my boyfriend. Patricide was bad enough, but killing Alex... I just couldn't wrap my brain around that.

The worst thing about the knife—no one knew how it worked because it had never been used before.

There were two camps on the subject of what timeline Heaven's blade would destroy. The first group thought the knife would wipe the slate clean to the point before the person—or archangel, in this case—came into existence. The other train of thought believed it would blink someone from existence from the point when the blade sliced into flesh.

Either choice sucked.

Wiping the slate clean meant Lucifer never existed. No Hell. No monsters. No Ryans. And no me.

But what exactly would remain? No one had a clue. It could be far better or infinitely worse. The thought of me blinking out of existence, along with Alex, wasn't as awful as it should have been given the circumstances.

The second line of thought would mean I would kill both Alex and Lucifer in one thrust of the blade. Doing that would strip me of my soul. Anything good inside me would die with Alex. I was as sure of that as I was of the sun rising in the morning.

Using this knife on Alex would make me lose my sanity. And who knows, in that kind of state,

I could very well grant my father's greatest wish and turn the world to ash.

The monster wrapped in dog form on the ground huffed. I ignored him. I didn't need Leviathan's wisdom or his sarcasm right now.

I stood and crossed to the alcove at the window, then took a seat on the comfortable bench cushion. He followed and jumped up, curling up at the opposite end of the window bench.

"Just leave me alone."

"Not with your mind so clouded with darkness," he muttered and sent me a sideways glare.

I looked away. The lake outside the window didn't have the same calming cadence of the ocean waves in Maine. It only made my nerves more jumbled. This cabin stood on sacred ground, and a part of me knew I shouldn't be here. Not with Lucifer's blood raging inside me.

"Pft," Levi huffed at me. "The Ryans share Lucifer's blood, too, so you should not discount your inherent goodness based on who your biological father is."

It was my turn to scoff at him. I wasn't inherently good. I was a walking fire hazard, and now I had this crazy level of power that wiped out an entire island.

I climbed to my feet and left the cottage, closing the door on Levi. I needed to be alone. I needed to set my mind right, and I wasn't going to get there with him staring at me like I was a wounded bird.

I crossed to the gazebo and sat on the swing inside the wooden structure. The cabinet in my mind that Valerie had helped me lock up had many answers, but I was hesitant to open it. I didn't want to be overwhelmed with thousands of years of memories and open all sorts of breaches again. But I knew if I didn't look at the history I had, I wouldn't be prepared to battle Lucifer.

I needed to see his games. I needed to understand his strategies. I needed to know just how horrifying Lucifer was.

It was chilly enough outside for me to shiver from more than just the thoughts flitting through my mind. Instead of going inside to grab a coat, I figured the caress of cold air might be good. It would keep my fire in check.

I pushed off with my feet, letting the swing sway back and forth, and I closed my eyes, concentrating on shoring up my mind so this didn't go haywire. I envisioned the file cabinets we made to organize the memories and kneeled down in front of the one containing the oldest ones. The imaginary key appeared in my hand, and I unlocked the drawers that had the name Damian Andreas printed on the card.

Perusing his memories was a delicate matter. It was as if I had stepped back to almost the dawn of time when the earth was lush and the deserts hadn't fully formed in the Middle East yet.

I scanned through memory upon memory of Damian's, from vague images of his father, the archangel Gabriel, to the people who raised him. He even went to war with his comrade, but he was the only one to come back. His friend made Damian promise to take care of his wife, Athena, and his child before he died on the battlefield. Damian kept that promise, and Athena ended up being the love of Damian's life, or at least of that life, before darkness befell him.

And darkness came in the form of Lucifer because Athena was a Nephilim. She was Michael's daughter, and heartbreaking was the only word for what Lucifer did to her. He made Damian watch as he tore Athena's heart from her chest and ate it. Then he threw Damian into a pit of bloodthirsty monsters.

Athena's child had been visiting with family and survived to continue Michael's bloodline, and luckily, Lucifer did not know that Damian was Gabriel's son, or he would have suffered the same fate.

Still, being turned into a vampire wasn't exactly the most humane choice. Damian survived the pit, and Michael pulled him from that living Hell, giving him an ultimatum: keep his angelic bloodline safe or be smited on the spot. Obviously, he chose to be Michael's bloodline protector.

Michael was as fearsome as Lucifer, and until Damian met Naomi, he quaked every time Michael appeared.

Damian came across Lucifer many times before Naomi, but it was usually from the shadows as he plotted his revenge against the dark lord. Naomi was never meant to be someone he fell for. She was just something Lucifer wanted, and Damian was Hell-bent on destroying anything Lucifer coveted. Unfortunately, Damian didn't know she was one of Michael's descendants.

Naomi was fearless, and when Damian bit her, she bit him back, turning herself into a vampire in much the same way Damian had been turned. If she had ever been afraid of Lucifer, she never showed it.

I shook my head and refocused on Damian's memories, putting my assessment of Naomi aside.

Every encounter with my father was bloody and depraved. He certainly was a master at manipulation and torture. He wiped out entire families to get what he wanted. He wanted trinity blood to build an army. Well, now he had more than just trinity blood. He had the entire host of angels.

My stomach cramped with the thought, and tears covered my eyes. I blinked them away and leaned back, pushing the swing with my feet. The rocking sensation calmed my raw nerves.

Michael Andreas probably would love to have his parents' memories. Guilt bit at my insides, creating a web of bumps that spread over my exposed skin. I rubbed them away and ran my hands down my face.

Well, maybe not all their memories. Some of the more intimate ones heated my cheeks, and I shuffled them back into the drawers when I encountered them.

Valerie's name came up in Damian's history a few years before Naomi came into the picture. I took a closer look. Valerie was just a child when Damian met her. Unfortunately, after Naomi came into the picture, Lucifer learned of Valerie's heritage as one of Michael's descendants. She was also the reason the archangel Michael was vulnerable enough for Lucifer to strip his grace.

Valerie had a fierceness to her I was starting to identify.

Fierce bravery seemed to be something representative of Michael's bloodline. As much as I didn't want to put Grace in the same category, she certainly was fierce. However, I would not put her in the brave category at all. She was a coward of the worst kind.

Irritation bloomed like it always did when Grace crossed my mind, and I had to shake it away and focus back on Damian's memories. Unfortunately, she was a part of his history, so I couldn't ignore her like I wanted to.

But I still had some horrific memories to inspect before she came into their lives. Each encounter with Lucifer left me cold. He truly was warped and depraved, and the damage he was capable of produced a frightened shiver.

I wrapped my arms around me tighter.

I didn't want to see Grace's birth, but it was a significant day, one that was central to Tom and CJ entering the battle. It was also the first glimpse I had of Alex's grandfather's spirit. While I had his memories of when he was living, this was the first vision of him with his wings. Wings that matched those of CJ's when he got angry.

If Alex had an infusion of grace, would he end up with wings?

I shook the thought away and refocused.

Ty Ryan was even more intense than his son, CJ, and his expression as he glared at Lucifer chilled me. Ty's memories were in my head, too, and the resemblance to Alex was even eerier than his resemblance to CJ. When a cocky smile formed on his lips, it was so similar to Alex's that my chest squeezed.

I closed my eyes, blocking the image. It hurt just as much as seeing CJ had.

But this day was important to both the archangels and CJ's father. It was the day his father lost his ability to leave Paradise Cove, along with Michael and Gabriel. Lucifer made a grand spectacle for the audience watching. He came out from Paradise Cove, where the battle had started, with both Michael's and Gabriel's heads in his bloodied hands.

When Lucifer had his grace, he was more terrifying than anything I had encountered. I couldn't imagine going against him fully charged, but that's exactly what Damian and Alex's grandfather did. The minute Lucifer tossed the heads onto the newly fallen snow, both of them left the sanctity of the warded cottage.

Tom and CJ witnessed Lucifer tearing their father's head clean off. I had both their memories layered together, along with their emotions. The devastation CJ felt at watching his father decimated by Lucifer matched that of losing Tom.

I took a slow breath, trying to calm the building dread wrapping around me. How was I going to beat him? I was only sixteen and had no defense training. I didn't even know how to use a knife beyond stabbing with the pointy end.

I glanced at the house, and CJ stood in the bedroom window watching me. The knife glowed in his hand. I startled in the seat and then looked at the ground as heat filled my cheeks. I should have put that thing away somewhere, but I was too preoccupied with everything I needed to do.

He put the knife on his dresser next to him. When he turned away from the window, I exhaled at my stupidity. If one of the kids had gotten ahold of that blade...

I shivered and glanced back at the lake, resuming my inspection of their lives. I didn't need to see anything more of Damian's life. I knew how it ended, and again, it was related to the devil himself. I was tempted to sort through the cabinet that held CJ's father's memories, but I didn't have time for that. I needed dirt on Lucifer.

I locked up Damian's memories and moved on to CJ. While I was curious to see some things from his background; I didn't bother. Everything before they met Damian and Naomi was moot. I needed to see what kind of damage Lucifer had done to them. I still didn't have enough of a pattern to go by beyond his craving for destruction.

CJ's first encounter with Lucifer after the showdown with Damian left him in a coma for two years. But it was his next encounter that had me leaning forward in the swing with my hands clenched. Lucifer used CJ's image to torture Valerie. That wasn't the only time he used CJ's image to torture those closest to him. My mind shuffled forward to a memory of a warehouse in New York City. Lucifer did the same thing to CJ's father, and his father's mind had fractured.

With Tom, Lucifer used his wife and child to get in his head and try to coerce him to give up his soul. Tom lost both of them to Lucifer's wrath because he refused to play the game.

I closed my eyes.

Lucifer already had control of Alex's form. This was his favorite modus operandi, and he was sure to dangle it in front of us in equally tormenting ways.

He wanted to break CJ. That was a personal vendetta I was sure played into my father's motivation. He didn't need Alex to build an army, but it just made it much sweeter that Alex brought the missing archangel into the mix. It was a means to royally screw with CJ's head.

And then there was me.

The daughter who chose the Ryans over her own father.

Of course, my father just wanted me for a refueling station to get his revenge on the Ryan clan. I'm sure the fact that Tom gave *me* his grace in order to shut my father in Hell just made him angrier.

I was as much of a target as CJ, despite our blood bond. My father got off on torturing those he wanted to destroy, and I was now on his hit list.

How the Hell do I fight that?

I stood up and crossed into the only portal to Heaven on the entire globe. Paradise Cove. I licked my lips and glanced up at the sky.

"Damian?" I whispered.

The lake shimmered and fog rolled off it, creating an eerie atmosphere. A dark-haired man appeared. He looked like an older version of

Michael Andreas, and he crossed his arms as he stepped out of the fog and onto the moss of Paradise Cove. He stared down at me, waiting for me to speak.

This was the man who'd punched a hole in the devil's chest and ate his heart. I shivered at the power and will that had taken. I knew firsthand it wasn't easy.

"How do I beat him?" I asked, looking at the man who stole Lucifer's grace.

"Have you talked to CJ?" Although the timbre of his voice sounded like his son's, his Greek accent threw me, but it made perfect sense, given his upbringing.

"He can't deal with the idea of losing his son. Besides, he never truly beat Lucifer. He may have torn his head off and laid waste to his body with angel fire, sending him back to Hell numerous times, but he didn't kill him. Nor did he strip Lucifer of his grace, like you did."

Damian looked beyond me at the path, his expression brooding. When his gaze came back to mine, he nodded like he understood, and I suspected he probably did, considering recent events.

He looked out over the cove with a frown and a crease between his brows. He closed his eyes and tightened his fists, shaking his head. "I can't believe my daughter made the choice to hand everything over to him. She knew how hard we fought against him so that this day would never come, and yet she just..." When his eyes opened, they were covered with a layer of tears that he blinked away. "If I had known all the destruction that he would cause..." He wiped his face and took a deep breath.

I shifted from foot to foot, uncomfortable under the strain of his voice. "There wasn't anything you could have done," I whispered.

His bright gaze met mine. "You are his only obstacle left. Don't let him win," he added in a choked voice, and turned away.

Nothing he'd said answered my question. It only struck more fear in the pit of my stomach.

"But how do I beat him?" I asked again.

"You already know how," he said with his back to me. "Tom gave you the weapon. You just have to get close enough to your father to use it."

Judgement Day
Chapter 2

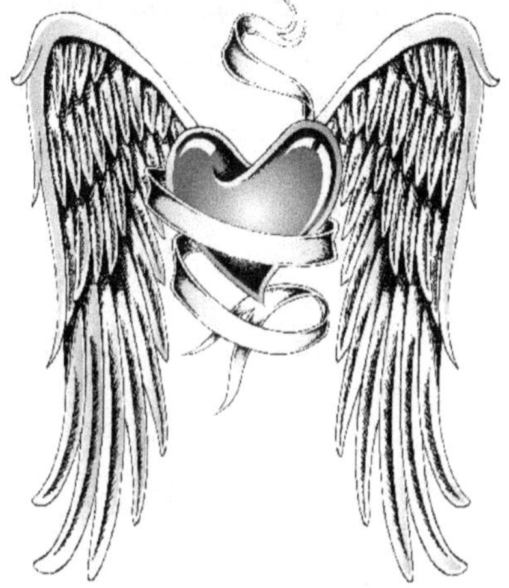

GREAT. JUST ANOTHER DIRECTIVE that left me with zero choice.

I sat back down in the gazebo. The lightening sky did nothing for my mood. A new day, a new problem to figure out. Life marched forward despite the misery surrounding us, and it irked me.

My phone buzzed. I pulled it out, staring at the unknown number blinking in my text messages. I pressed the button to open the preview. One word displayed. *Mine.* Along with a picture of Alex kissing Grace below the statement.

My hands burst into flame. Fire engulfed the phone, and I pitched it into the lake with a roar that echoed across the water.

A flock of birds took flight, swirling away from me like I was the evil one.

I wanted to burn the image from my brain. I clenched my fists, putting out the fire before I gripped the edge of the swing. I just wanted to scream, but I didn't want to wake everyone inside, if I hadn't already with my initial outburst.

I glanced at where the phone had plunked into the water, sending ripples out from the point of impact. My breath caught in my throat. I had just destroyed the only thing I had with Alex's texts on it.

I closed my eyes, and tears squeezed from the corners.

"Damn it." I put my head against the back of the swing and wrapped my arms around myself, trying not to lose it yet again, but it was too late. Hot tears slipped down my cheeks, and one pooled by the corner of my mouth, bringing with it a salty taste of failure.

"Why don't you come in?" CJ said from a few feet away from me.

I jumped. I hadn't heard him approach at all. He was like a silent ninja in that manner, and it piled onto my feeling of inadequacy.

I shook my head, wishing I had more control, but my tears wouldn't stop.

He took a seat next to me and put his arm over the back of the chair. The heat from him seemed to warm the back of my neck, loosening some of the tightness. His legs pushed off with mine, giving the swing a wider arc.

He sniffled. "You know, if you want your phone back, all you have to do is retrieve it with your mind."

"It's ruined," I said with a voice so full of sorrow that I thought I would choke on it.

"I could probably get the data off the memory chip." He kept the swing moving.

I finally looked at his profile. The corners of his lips dragged into a frown, and I caught a tear tracing the side of his face. It dripped down onto his T-shirt unchecked.

"You're not the only one he's taunting." His voice cracked. "He said the things he would do would make my father's transgressions seem like child's play, and he'd make sure it was caught on film so my son's face would be just as infamous as my dad's."

I huffed and looked out at the lake. "He sure knows how to push our buttons."

CJ let out a small laugh. His loss scraped over my skin like a dull razor.

"You've already written him off." I studied him again.

He lifted his shoulder. It wasn't a confirmation or denial. "He's no longer my son." He met my gaze. "And I've got four girls under my roof that are now his prime targets, along with my wife. I don't have the luxury of hoping for a miracle." He pressed his lips together. "Hope is not a tactic. We can't rely on it, or we will all die."

He rubbed his face and stopped the swing. "He's using my son's brains, too. Any time he pings me, it goes through so many goddamn servers that I can't find him. I'll keep trying to pin it down, but I have had no luck with that for the last five months." He closed his eyes and pinched the bridge of his nose. "I should have let him go with you." He stood and marched back to the house, obviously kicking himself for the decisions he'd made.

I couldn't let him take the burden of this. The breaches and Lucifer being topside were my fault and mine alone.

I followed him and stopped him at the door before he stepped inside. "I don't blame you for this."

"I know, but I do." He turned and headed inside.

"You didn't know."

"I absolutely should have known when Bridget tried to kill you." He spun on me with such ferocity that I stepped back. "I should have known she was compromised. If I had left her behind then, Alex would be here with us now."

"She just lost her husband; you couldn't have just sent her packing."

"He should have," a sleepy voice said from behind me.

I spun around to April standing in one of the bedroom doors. Her blonde hair was knotted and unruly from a night of sound sleep. She ran across the room and threw her arms around me. I held her tight and closed my eyes, letting Tom's love for her fill me.

I kissed the top of her head and opened my eyes. "Your father loved you so much."

I hadn't had much time with April after Tom's death and I knew our time was limited now, but

I wanted her to know just how much her father cared.

She smiled up at me. "I know. He's been trying to get me to forgive my mother, but I can't. Just like I can't forgive Grace for what she has done." She pulled away from my hug and propped her hands on her hips with an uncompromising pout.

"You know forgiveness is more for you than it is for anyone else," I said, and even CJ's eyebrows went up. "Holding onto anger... It just destroys who you are." I glanced at CJ and then back to April. "Don't hold on to it. Let it go."

She stared up at me as my words sank in, then dimples appeared in her cheeks. "Quoting Disney movies now?"

I couldn't help it—I grinned, too. I hadn't meant to quote one of her favorite movies of all time. But she embraced it, opening her mouth and belting the song out like a true thirteen-year-old diva. I looked at CJ, and then joined April, because I needed a little silliness after everything I had been through. Our singing woke Valerie and the girls, but I didn't care, and obviously neither did April.

And we sang the Hell out of the song. When we finished, we turned back-to-back and crossed our arms, claiming the power of Elsa. Power we sorely lacked at the moment, and it was rejuvenating.

CJ started a slow clap from his position against the bench. The half smile on his lips warmed me as much as it reminded me of Alex, and my heart ached.

"Are you two done with your little show?" He waggled his fingers at us.

"Why? Do you want to join us?" I asked.

April giggled from behind me.

CJ cocked his eyebrow as his girls came out of the room, rubbing their eyes. The sun's rays came over the mountain and bathed the room in warm spring morning light. He opened his mouth, and the first words to another popular Disney song came rolling off his tongue. His girls clapped with glee.

His voice was as mesmerizing as it had been on television. Full, with a beautiful timbre that brought gooseflesh to my arms and put Elton John's voice in the dust. He opened his arms and turned to the new day, welcoming it with the song like he was on stage and his audience consisted of more than a few birds and his own family. His entire persona switched into the entertainer I was used to seeing, and with it came that magical gleam in his eyes along with a full smile that reminded me so much of Alex that my knees weakened.

When he got to the chorus, we all joined in, and our harmony filled the house. Arianna and Amber's voices were just as rich as their father's. Just as rich and full as Alex's voice had been. April and I... Well, we weren't quite as mesmerizing, but at least we were on key.

Levi just stared at us from the floor like we all had lost our minds. Valerie leaned against the bedroom door with a sad, slightly haunted grin. She still wasn't quite herself, but at least there was a smile on her face.

The only ones who hadn't stirred were Michael and Kylee, but they had had a late enough night for sleep to overcome any noise at this point. I just hoped our singing euphoria hadn't woken Alexis.

Music soothed me as much as it seemed to soothe the Ryan clan. My heart actually felt lighter because of it, and from the looks of it, it seemed to break whatever depression had settled on the house since we had arrived.

I knew I'd pay for my all-nighter later today, but for now, I would hang on to this lightness even though I knew it was a farce.

Quiet fell on us as CJ whipped up some eggs for the family. We sat around the table eating with only the clang of silverware on the plates to keep us company. Smiles faded as reality crashed down on us. Even Arianna and Amber ended up falling silent.

"When is Alex coming back?" Amber asked after we finished the meal. She looked at me, not her father.

I pressed my lips together and shrugged. "I don't know." I glanced at CJ for help, and he stood and started clearing the plates.

"We don't know if he'll ever come back to us," CJ said, slamming the mood right into the toilet.

I wouldn't have said it in the same way. He didn't even try to soften the blow. I got up and walked out the door, leaving them all to deal with the fallout. That seemed to be my norm when I couldn't deal with the emotions surrounding me. This wasn't a new thing, either. I used to do the same thing with my mother when I was upset. Disappearing into the woods when things got heated was my way of pushing aside the unease itching at my fingers. It was either that or set the place on fire. So, I opted to remove myself. It was a good strategy most of the time, but it still felt like running away.

Instead of going to the swing again, I sat on the stairs on the dock.

Frustration burned under my skin, and I opened those drawers again, going straight to CJ's. Looking for how he'd beaten the devil.

"I didn't beat him." He took a seat next to me. "My father did, but as you saw, there was a price. There's always a price." He glanced over the lake. "I don't know whether to just hop a plane to Disney World and let the kids have as much fun as humanly possible until the gauntlet falls, or just sit tight to weather the storm."

"The knife. You think it will wipe us all out?"

CJ sighed. "I don't know. Maybe. I just can't see what's coming." He waved towards Paradise Cove. "I asked my father, but he has no clue, which I think is a load of crap because he knew enough to write Steve into his will long before he met the guy. But then again, he was alive at the time." He shrugged. "I even asked my older brother, but he's so damn cryptic about things it's enough to drive anyone mad." He chewed on his lip, shook his head, and quietly stared out over the lake. "I'm okay with never existing."

"I'm okay with that, too." I was. If annihilating Lucifer wiped us all off the map, it was far different from killing my boyfriend.

He gave me a soft smile. "I know you are." He pointed to the lake. "Bring back the phone."

I sighed. "I haven't had any sleep…"

"I don't care. We need to get you prepared, Faith. Tired or not. Sore or not. Unsure or not. You need to train your mind. You did well last night, shuffling through the memories in a controlled manner that didn't overload your brain. You need to learn to count on your power regardless of whether you're at your best or worst. If he gets the knife, you have to have the power to get it back without cutting yourself so you can end him."

His stern reprimand heated my face. "This is your son you're talking about."

He shook his head. "No, I'm talking about Lucifer. He is capable of putting you in a world of hurt if you underestimate him. I underestimated him more than once and paid for it. He stole two years of my life and left me a stuttering idiot for a while. I still battle that from time to t-time." He stuttered on the last word and closed his eyes. "See. I may be a trinity with all sorts of ungodly powers, but I'm not infallible. Neither are you." He pointed at the lake again. "Retrieve the phone with your mind." He barked the command.

"Fine." I stared at the water, ignoring the irritation creeping just under my skin. I never liked being ordered to do anything, but I understood what CJ was trying to do. It was much the same as what Kylee did for me in the subway tunnel.

I felt out the lake in the general vicinity where I thought the phone had gone, mentally searching the sandy bottom for metal that didn't belong. It didn't take me long before a strange scratch itched in my temple. I put my hand out, concentrating on pulling the phone to me from the depths.

A small ripple started on the surface, and my heart jumped into my throat. *I'm doing it.* As soon as the thought popped in, my connection failed. I closed my hand and shook the disappointment out of my head.

I opened my hand towards the water again and used sheer force of will until sweat dripped into my eyes.

I glared at CJ. "I can't do this." I went to get up.

"Sit," he commanded, and my body behaved, doing exactly as he'd said, regardless of whether I wanted to or not. "You were close the first time. Reconstruct that effort and don't get cocky in the middle of it."

Reconstruct. Who talks like that?

He huffed, giving me his evil eye.

I closed my eyes and inspected my memory as if it were a puzzle, trying to figure out why it worked the first time versus failing the second time. I had the mental connection to the object right up to the point I realized I was actually doing what he'd demanded.

That was the difference. And it was a vast difference.

So, I sent that mental radar out again. This time, I found the object a lot faster because I had a spot of reference. I concentrated on pulling the phone to my hand, leaving my eyes closed.

Wet metal drifted into my palm, and I opened my eyes. My phone dripped on the dock in front of me as I wrapped my fingers around it. I handed it to CJ since he was the one who'd said he could get Alex's texts for me, even with the water infiltrating the electronics.

He handed it back. "Dry it."

I reached for the hem of my shirt.

"Not like that."

His exasperation confused me. "Huh?"

"Manipulate the air to dry it off." He twirled his finger and then pointed at the phone.

"How?" Air wasn't a thing I could connect to. Not in the way he was asking me. I thought back to the witch conjuring the storm in Texas and then met his gaze. "That's not possible."

At least not without using pure magic.

"You made it rain. I think you can do a small breeze around your phone."

My heart clattered in my chest. I didn't know how I'd made it rain. All that had come to mind was putting out the fire before it moved onto the house from the woods. It was not a conscious decision.

He nodded towards the phone, unfazed by my unspoken narrative or my mounting panic.

I curled my hand that wasn't holding the phone to make sure my fire didn't get loose. I closed my eyes, thinking about the rotation of the clouds that the witch was manipulating, as well as how the wind worked in the whiteout on Mount Cook, which was more of a natural event than the witch's spell. In my mind, I attempted to harness that power and shrink it to the size of my hand. I opened my eyes and stared at the phone. It was still wet. However, a little dirt devil swirled at the end of the dock before it dissipated.

CJ smiled. "Close." He glanced over his shoulder and his smile faded, like something had opened the door to his emotions for just a moment.

"Why now?" I asked and stared at the phone. "There weren't any texts from him between the day they took him and today."

CJ pressed his lips together and sighed. "I think Lucifer had someone watching Ireland. I got calls from time to time, and I think he was just testing the waters to see whether you were alive. He knows you're the only one who can close the breaches. And once the last major one closed..." He shrugged and put his hand out for the phone. "I'll see what I can do with it. In the meantime, get some rest before we have another session."

He climbed to his feet, and I gave him the phone.

"Session?"

"Yes. You need to be one hundred percent reliable before I will let you go after Lucifer. I don't want to lose anyone else if I don't have to." He turned and headed inside.

I yawned, suddenly feeling every bit of lack of sleep. I stood and made my way inside. He pointed out the bedroom for me to use, and I collapsed on the bed. I think I was asleep before I even hit the pillow.

Judgement Day
Chapter 3

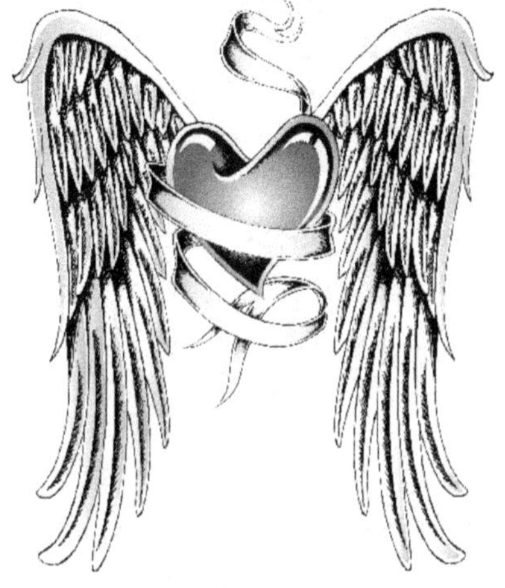

CJ LEANED BACK IN the recliner while the kids were all playing with their toys and Kylee was feeding Alexis in the kitchen. His jaw was tense, as was his grip on the chair arms. It was not CJ's normal lounging form. He had been more relaxed on the dock with me this morning. His mind raged with static and nothing else, so I had no frame of reference for his seemingly dark mood.

I took a seat on the couch, rubbing the sleep from my eyes. The sun was still up, and the sink was filled with dishes and the sweet tang of spaghetti sauce hung on the air.

"There's a plate on the counter if you're hungry," CJ said, but he didn't look away from the television droning on in the background. A stock ticker moved across the bottom of the screen as talking heads discussed the latest economic news.

I wasn't ready to eat yet. I needed to wake up first. "Thanks." I didn't move from my spot. I would eventually grab the saved dinner, but for now, I was content to watch the stock market stories.

CJ switched channels, restlessly looking for something else. The speed at which he channel-surfed was annoying. It reminded me of a flashing strobe light. How could someone actually digest the channel with one second or less of a view?

As if to prove me wrong, CJ's eyes widened, and he backtracked slowly until Alex's face filled the screen. CJ leaned forward.

My lungs tightened at the sight. Everything about him was familiar except his eyes. His eyes were not those of the sweet boy who was so concerned with my welfare. His eyes were cold and hard and gleefully dark.

The banner below the screen scrolled with Alex's name and some sensationalized wording to get viewers' attention. But that wasn't what clenched my stomach and made me glad I hadn't chosen to eat the offered dinner yet. My boyfriend's face riveted me to the television just before a chained Gabriel Andreas filled the picture. His body was black and blue and some other distinctly sickening colors that indicated the type of beating most people wouldn't live through. The camera panned enough to show Alex grinning like a maniac.

CJ paused the television. "Get the children out of here."

But Valerie's attention didn't waver from the picture of her son.

"Val!" CJ snapped.

Her gaze jumped to his and then what he said sank in. She ushered her girls and April outside, but before April stepped out the door, she cast a worried glance at me and the television.

Michael stood frozen in the kitchen with a drink in his hand. His face lost all color, and he, too, stared at the frozen picture of Alex and his brother's nearly unconscious form. The glass in his hand cracked.

"Take Alexis outside," he said in a low, strained voice.

Kylee didn't argue with his commanding tone. Personally, I wouldn't have either. She grabbed her daughter out of the highchair and ushered her outside with the rest of the family.

CJ glanced at me. "This might not be appropriate for you either."

"I need to take him down. Remember?" As much as I would have liked to disappear and not see what my father had done to Alex, I needed to understand the depths of horror he was capable of. Even though in my mind, I already knew. The fact he took the time to record it and send it to a news channel was seriously messed up.

CJ closed his eyes, and I actually felt the mental steel erect in his mind and around his heart. He exhaled through pursed lips and pressed play just before he opened his eyes.

Lucifer, in Alex's form, smiled at the camera. "You think my grandfather was warped, welcome to the new and improved circus of true depravity. Oh, and be sure to ask my father what we are when you see him." Then his fingernails dug into Gabriel's chest.

Gabriel screamed, and someone laughed in the background.

The snapping of bone followed, and the rest of Lucifer's hand punched through Gabriel's chest.

When Lucifer yanked Gabriel's heart free, Gabriel's eyes widened. His mind registered what he was seeing before his face turned ashen and his eyes rolled, showing only white. His body sagged even more in the chains as all his muscles gave at once.

A crazy cackling continued beyond the camera.

Blood dripped down Alex's arm, and he took a slow whiff of the beating muscle in his hand for his rapt audience. The smile that followed chilled me to the core.

And then the bastard took a bite out of the heart.

I could see thousands of people getting sick all over their living room floors. Hell, I knew what eating a human heart was like. My stomach twisted, and I put the back of my hand to my lips to keep it in check.

Lucifer closed his eyes as if he were eating a rare delicacy. He savored each bite until it was gone. A glow started around him as he swallowed the last bit, but faded almost immediately. When he opened his eyes, they shimmered a golden color before settling back to Alex's normal blue. He licked the blood from his fingers slowly for the benefit of the camera.

It was gruesome and deliberate. And the grin that followed nearly had me launching for the bathroom.

I controlled the roll of my stomach and swallowed the bile, unable to look away from Alex. I knew it was Lucifer doing these things, but seeing Alex's face made the hurt in the center of my soul flare.

I had no choice but to bury the knife in the bastard's heart.

Michael dropped his glass into the garbage and turned, heading outside without a word. Seeing his own brother's death numbed him. I glanced over the back of the couch and watched through the window. He sat down in the swing and just looked out at the lake with an expression that showed none of the turmoil inside him.

CJ still stared at the television, watching the newscaster speculate. The banner stated that the Ryan family couldn't be reached for comment and showed the abandoned home in Maine through the gates. His hands clamped tighter on the armrests, making them creak.

It was all too much to cope with. I didn't want to hear what the newscasters were saying about Alex Ryan. They likened him to his namesake, and I could almost see the steam rising from CJ's head. A red hue coated his skin, and I knew there was a slow simmering fury underneath his calm exterior. It blazed in his eyes.

I was done with the drivel for today, and the television blinked off. CJ turned his sharp glare at me but said nothing. He could have easily overridden my off command with one of his own, but he didn't.

Lucifer had just compromised any future Alex might have had. He was hedging his bets all around.

"That leaves one," CJ said with a growl.

I cocked my head and met his darkened gaze.

"He televised Bridget's Death, too. Beat her to a bloody pulp for the camera."

His growling answer left me shaking.

"When?"

He pressed his lips together. "You were asleep and everyone else was at the grocery store getting supplies when I happened to turn on the television." His hands curled into fists. "Thankfully, April wasn't here. I don't think she could have dealt with that kind of brutality. It was far worse to watch than what we just witnessed."

I had a feeling April had already seen what Lucifer was capable of in her visions.

CJ's gaze lifted to the path at the edge of the woods, and I knew where his mind was going. I was up on my feet, even before he was. I beat him out the door and sprinted to Paradise Cove. I was out of breath when I reached the moss.

"Bridget?" I gasped as CJ stepped from the woods behind me.

He just shook his head.

It took a few moments, but then it sank in. Bridget wasn't in Heaven. I nearly folded over like I had been sucker punched.

"Gabe?" CJ said.

The air shimmered over the cove, and Gabriel Andreas stepped out of the mist onto the moss between me and CJ.

"Where is he?" I asked.

He glanced at me, and his lips thinned. "I don't know where we were."

"And your mother?" CJ asked.

He shook his head. "She was the first one he killed, because just for a moment, she got through to Grace." He wiped his hand down his face. "That's when he chained Grace next to his goddamned throne. Shredded her clothes and fu—" He stopped and glanced at me.

His haunted gaze stripped me of my voice. I knew what he was going to say. The boy who'd made love to me in the panic room was gone, replaced by a warped exhibitionist.

"When he finished, he stormed over to my mother, whispered some vile things in her ear, and then punched a hole in her chest with his bare hand. He ate her heart right in front of her before she exhaled her last breath."

CJ's eyes welled up with tears, and he bit his lower lip.

"Grace didn't even react, and from that moment forward, anytime that bastard snapped his fingers, she would lean over the arm of his chair and spread her legs for him. She's lost it completely."

I closed my eyes and hung my head, collecting the shattered pieces of my heart and doing whatever I could to keep myself together. CJ put his hand on my shoulder, and the simple contact gave me an infusion of strength. Strength to handle whatever Gabe said next.

"What can you tell us about where you were?" CJ asked, his voice calmer than I expected.

"The building we were in was in rough shape. I'm talking condemned-building type of shape. The paint peeled so much it looked like fuzz on some walls. The space wasn't that big, maybe the size of your family room, but the wall we were chained to was rough like concrete blocks or exposed brick underneath the crumbling drywall. Most of the windows were boarded up, but a few were missing or splintered, so during the day it wasn't dark."

Leaves crunched, and we all turned. Michael stared at the ghost of his brother for a moment, and then he moved across the space and nearly tackled Gabriel in a hug.

When the hug broke, Michael asked, "Mom?"

Gabriel pointed toward the sky. "With Dad."

Michael's numbness broke, and with it came both anger and sorrow so thick I nearly gagged on it. "And Grace?" he squeezed out of his tight throat.

"She's batshit crazy," he said, not sugarcoating it at all. "Do me a favor and stay as far away as you possibly can."

Michael shook his head. "I don't know if I can do that." His hands curled into fists as he let the anger overwhelm the hurt. It was that crazy, fierce, brave side of the archangel's blood that was bubbling to the surface.

"Too many have died already," I said with a shaking voice, capturing Michael's attention.

He pressed his lips together, and his borderline glare held a promise of charging to his death without my permission.

"He has traps everywhere, and if you get caught, he has chains that will make you helpless." He looked at both CJ and me. "He's preparing for an assault from both of you."

"Is there anyone else there besides Grace?" I asked, pushing aside the brokenness inside me. Tom had said it best when he told me life wasn't fair and I had to take the hit for the rest of the world. I was ready, and I knew, despite the rage in CJ, he still wouldn't be able to kill his own son, no matter who was possessing his body.

"I saw at least a dozen different demons. I don't know if there are more."

I blew air from between my lips. I wasn't sure I could battle that many demons in a building that was basically fire tinder.

I wiped the thought from my brain and focused on Gabriel. "Is there anything else? Anything at all that you can remember that might help us find him?"

Gabriel looked down at the moss and drew his eyebrows together in concentration. "There was enough newer graffiti sprayed over the walls to make me wonder if it wasn't as desolate as I thought. Some of the garbage lying around made me think it might have been an insane asylum at one time. I think one of the decaying pamphlets had something about mental health on it, but I'm not sure. I was pretty much delirious half the time, first from the physical beatings, then from grief, and then from lack of food." He met my gaze. "If he hadn't killed me when he did, I probably would have starved to death. I'd bet my body is still hanging in the chains, just like my mother's. He left Tom and

Bridget's bodies where they had fallen, too, so the smell of decay has to be hideous." He glanced back at the moss. "The place may have been haunted, but I'm not positive about that. I thought I saw a few ghosts, but I was pretty delusional near the end."

CJ wiped his pale face and gave a nod. He turned and headed back towards the house. I shifted from foot to foot, unsure of whether I wanted to ask anything else or if I should follow CJ.

"What took you so long?" Gabriel asked, staring at me. His arched eyebrow announced the accusation as much as his tone.

"We jumped through one of the breaches to get out of an avalanche." I met his gaze and shrugged. "Kylee, Levi, and I had to traipse through Hell to find the last open breach."

His jaw dropped and his mouth formed a surprised O before he recovered and found his voice. "Seriously?"

"Afraid so," Michael said. "We camped outside of the breach in Ireland until they came out."

"I am so sorry we didn't get here sooner, but time didn't work the same way down there. We had no idea so much time had gone by when we finally jumped back through." I studied the moss at my feet.

"It wasn't your doing, Faith," Gabriel said with a sigh. He glanced at the treetops, like admitting that had actually physically hurt him. When he finally looked at me, his expression was torn between sorrow and frustration.

"If I hadn't caused the avalanche, we would have been home." I met his stare. "Then you wouldn't have been taken." Again, it was my actions that had almost wiped out an entire family. I swallowed that bitter pill hard.

"Sweet child," a voice from the water interrupted, and Naomi Andreas stepped onto the moss. She crossed to stand in front of me. Her warm hands descended on my shoulders.

I had an entirely new respect for her now that I had Damian's memories, and I understood her standing by her daughter the way she had. Even though her disappointment had been visible, it had still been her daughter. Saving her was Naomi's first instinct. Her failure to save either Gabriel or Grace reflected in her eyes, and I covered one of her hands with mine to ease some of her suffering.

"You know as well as I do what would have happened had you been home. None of us would have survived. Lucifer would have taken the fight to us, and you know how that would have ended."

Her sad dark eyes reached into my soul, and I bit my lip to keep from tearing up. I shivered, thinking of April's vision. I knew exactly how that would have turned out: the walls of CJ's house painted with the last of the angel descendant's blood, and my red hair draped over the kitchen table and my chest with a gaping hole where my heart had been.

I couldn't stay here anymore.

Not with the mix of emotions thickening the air.

Michael gave me a nod, as if he knew just how freaked out I was getting. I turned and left so he could have time with his mother and brother before they disappeared.

The girls were playing soccer on the front lawn when I stepped out of the woods. Valerie and Kylee sat on the dock stairs with Alexa, talking quietly. CJ wasn't anywhere in the yard. I glimpsed him through the big bay window and headed inside.

CJ had a map printed out in front of him and was placing dots on it as he looked between his computer screen and the paper.

"What are you doing?" I asked as I closed the front door behind me.

CJ looked up from his computer. "Mapping out the abandoned hospitals and asylums within reason from York that are in the same condition that I saw in that video."

"What's within reason?" His idea of within reason and mine could be vastly different.

"A four-to-six-hour radius."

I would have gone up to eight hours.

He raised his gaze from the screen for a second. He didn't even have to say it. I knew he had heard my thoughts, but he didn't respond beyond that intense stare that made me want to study the wood grain in the floorboards.

"Why not more?"

"Bridget disappeared and then returned within the same day. So, eight hours would be pushing it."

"Oh." I glanced out the window at the kids playing and wished I could be a kid again just for a moment. I wanted to be carefree like they were. It was something that I'd never gotten to experience.

CJ sighed, pulling my attention back to him.

"The last time I found Lucifer in an abandoned building, it was New York City." He wiped his face. "But I'm not sure he'd go back to the city again, although we can't rule it out."

"He seems to like the city. He had Naomi and Damian in an abandoned building in New York as well," I said, remembering some of Damian's memories I'd filtered through in the wee hours of the morning.

He nodded and jotted down the names of the locations at the bottom of the map, biting his lower lip. "There's nothing in New England that hasn't been converted or doesn't have public access. He wouldn't be somewhere that has regular foot traffic."

I agreed with his assessment. He had to be somewhere Naomi's and Gabriel's screams weren't able to be identified. Which meant a fairly remote area or deep underground, but deep underground didn't fit with Gabriel's description of the space.

CJ leaned back and stared at the list on the map in front of him. "We'll go here first." He looked up at me and tapped the one in western New York.

I glanced at where he tapped on the map and looked up at him. "We?"

"Yes. We. I am going with you. I just need to make sure Valerie has what she needs."

I crossed my arms. This was so not a good idea. "I don't think so. I will not lose another Ryan in all this. Besides, you heard Gabriel. He's set traps."

"Precisely." He pointed at me. "You need me."

It was funny how CJ could be reasonable and cocky at the same time. The same thing that endeared me to Alex frustrated me in his father.

"No." I reached down and ripped the list from his grip. I stared at the six names, four of which were in New York.

"We'll go to Willard first and then loop around to Pennsylvania, then track back from there." He traced the route he had mapped out, and it made sense to me. "We might need to break overnight at our penthouse if we don't find him before we hit Staten Island or Poughkeepsie, though."

"That's a good plan, but you keep saying *we*. You need to stay here and protect them." I pointed out the window. "Besides, I've got Levi, the demon-eating dog."

"I am not a dog," Levi grumbled from the living room floor.

I had almost forgotten Levi was still inside. I guess in our hurry to get some breathing room after Lucifer's on-air debut; we didn't think to let him out.

I threw my hands up in the air. "Okay, demon eating monster." I turned back to CJ's sharp glare. The more razor-like his look became, the more he knew I was right. "Besides, you won't pull the trigger," I mumbled under my breath.

His glare tightened. "I am going with you. Or we wait until you are strong enough to do this on your own." He crossed his arms in a silent challenge.

I didn't have a smart comeback, so I glanced out at the kids playing in the yard as the night started creeping in.

We didn't have the luxury of time. But we also couldn't underestimate Lucifer. If we did, that could be a disaster.

Lucifer was picking up his game. Destroying Alex's future seemed to be hot on his list, even though he was the one wearing the image. He no longer had anyone in his grasp beyond Grace. And all she had was time on her side, especially with Lucifer's end game of creating an army of trinities.

The longer we took, the deeper the hole he would dig for Alex. It was his M.O., his favorite game, and he knew just as well as I did it would flush us out of the woodwork. As much as I didn't want CJ to go with me, I couldn't exactly turn down the help, especially since I hadn't mastered this power searing my veins.

"Fine, but we can't leave them unprotected." I nodded toward everyone outside. "If you are with me, Levi stays here."

"I wasn't planning on leaving them unprotected." He stared me down.

It took a few seconds for his meaning to sink in. He could transfer power. He had done it multiple times before.

"Levi stays." I folded my arms, adopting my most intimidating stance because we both knew one protector wasn't enough.

"Don't I get a say in this?" Levi said from his station on the floor.

"No," both CJ and I said in unison.

"I have my orders," Levi growled.

I spun on him and pointed. "I am changing them. You are to stay here and make sure everyone in this house remains safe, along with whoever CJ deems suitable to have this kind of crazy power." I was certain I looked like a deranged teacher wagging my finger at a problem student.

Valerie stepped into the house, and Michael followed. Kylee had stayed outside on the swing rocking her baby while the three girls continued to kick a soccer ball around the backyard. The sun dipped below the horizon and daylight was fading fast.

"What the Hell are you thinking?" Valerie said to CJ, ignoring me as she crossed to stand close enough to encroach on his space.

"I'm thinking someone has to stop that madman, and she isn't strong enough to go it alone," CJ replied.

Valerie's hands clenched as she closed her eyes. "It is still our son in there."

CJ put his hands on her shoulders and sighed. "It's been almost six months."

"He's still in there!" She broke away from CJ and ran into the bedroom, then slammed the door.

CJ glanced at me and then at Michael. "I've got a favor to ask you."

"I'm going with you," Michael said.

"No, you aren't." He pointed out the window. "I need you to stay and protect them. All of them. Kylee and Alexa included."

The glare Michael sent was deadly, and his jaw tightened. "We are vulnerable here alone, and you know that better than anyone."

"Levi will stay to make sure nothing happens. And if you need to go to the store, you bring everyone. Including the dog. Understand?"

Michael crossed his arms. He looked more like Superman taking a pose against a threat than just a guy hellbent on running to his death.

"You can't go with us. You're the last one left," I said, and his piercing gaze swung in my direction. I swallowed hard at the fury in his glare.

"My sister is still alive." His teeth clenched. "As much as she has betrayed all we have stood for, she is *still* my sister."

"And she will not lift a finger when he punches a hole in your chest and rips your heart out," April said as she walked into the room.

We all turned to her. She had that glossy zombie-eyed quality that reminded me of when she'd had the vision at Tom and Bridget's house. She had passed out then, and when she swayed on her feet now, I moved. But Michael was faster. He caught April as she fainted.

Her words snuck under my skin, and I rubbed my arms against the goosebumps. CJ slipped into the bedroom to confront Valerie while Michael laid April on the couch.

Michael turned to me, and his face was less bright, less stubborn than it had been before. "I just..."

"I know. I want him gone as much as you do, but if I can save Alex, I'm going to try. You would take the shot without giving Alex a chance. That's if you got close enough."

"And Grace?" His lips pressed together.

That wasn't as clear-cut as Alex. I studied my hands for a moment. "If she doesn't get in our way…" I sucked my lower lip between my teeth and nodded. "I'll bring her back." I stopped short of saying alive, because that wasn't a promise I could make. "But if she attacks us…" I met his gaze.

He slowly nodded. "I get it," he said, and he seemed resigned to being the last Andreas standing.

Light flared under the bedroom door. I traded a glance with Michael before I bolted to the master bedroom. I swung the door open as the last of the light inside faded and Valerie took a large inhale of air.

"Why?" she asked CJ. Her voice shook and her wide-eyed gaze was glued on him.

"Because having angel grace is dangerous where we're going," CJ said. "And I know you'll give it back when I return." He leaned in and gently kissed her cheek. "It's safer with you."

"You gave her your power?" I asked as I looked between the two of them.

"I gave her enough to keep the family safe, but more importantly, I gave her the archangel grace for safekeeping." He glanced at me. "You should do the same."

My mouth popped open and my face heated. I knew I wouldn't have an issue with Raphael's grace, but I was certain that Lucifer's had bonded with me at a cellular level.

"I don't know if I can." My gaze bounced between the two of them as the rest of my skin heated. I clenched my fists to keep my fingers from sparking as nerves bit relentlessly.

CJ cocked his head, studying me. "You didn't have an issue pulling out Raphael's grace before."

"I'm not worried about his grace. It's Lucifer's that I don't think I can extract. I think I have the same problem that Tom did."

The lines in CJ's face softened. "I know you have the same issue Tom did. I was talking about transferring Raphael's grace," he said, his voice quiet and calm. "I'm tempted to have you transfer Tom's gifts as well, just in case the worst happens, but my gut is telling me you will need everything you have, especially if we are going to attempt to save my son."

I crossed close to Valerie. "I agree. And if something happens, I think you're right. I shouldn't walk into battle with more than just Lucifer's grace."

I put my hand over my chest and concentrated, remembering CJ's original instructions about imagining the grace as a power mass in the center of my being. I concentrated on sweeping the pieces into one large and separate power source in my chest, and then I imagined my hand was a magnet pulling the grace out of my body. When I opened my eyes, angel grace shined in my hand. Instead of putting it back inside me, I pushed it towards Valerie's chest. Her back arched, and her sharp inhale filled the room, as did the light dancing over her skin.

The absence of Raphael's grace left me shaking, and I took an unsteady step backwards. CJ grabbed my upper arm to steady me. I hadn't realized just how much Raphael's grace had balanced the darkness of Lucifer's. Without it, I struggled to push away the raw evil trying to take over every cell.

"Faith?"

CJ's voice seemed far away, and I shook the fog out of my head. "I'm okay," I said, but even my voice sounded strained.

How could angel grace be so tainted, so vile-tasting in my mouth?

I shivered and rubbed my arms. I wanted to ask for Raphael's grace back, because I wasn't sure if I could handle it. I did not want to end up as warped as my father.

The awe I had for Tom increased tenfold. He had carried around this malevolence for over ten years. I had no idea how the man didn't go dark. I now understood his insistence that I never give into it because it was as overwhelming as drinking poison.

"Maybe we should..."

I glared at CJ, and he stopped talking and just put his hands up, stepping away.

"You're the one with the doubts," he said.

I hated that he could read me so easily.

"If Tom could do it..." I inhaled. "I can do it." I brushed away my worries and focused on building a wall between my soul and the darkness assaulting it.

Judgement Day
Chapter 4

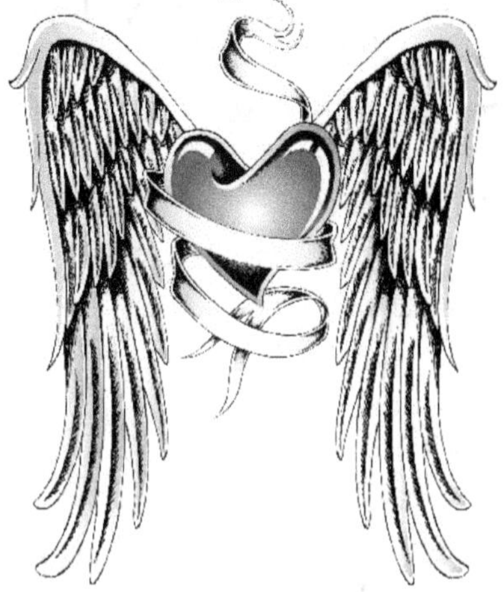

AT FIRST LIGHT, CJ knocked on my door. "Time to go."

I rolled away from the door and stared at the wall. Today would either end up in triumph, disappointment, or death. All things considered, I'd rather stay in bed, thank you very much.

CJ banged his palm against the wood. "Up. Now!"

"Fine. I'm moving." I rolled off the bed, obeying his sharp order.

By the time I finished getting dressed and throwing a few things in an overnight suitcase for our unwanted adventure, I stepped into the living room. Michael came out of his room and crossed to the kitchen. He poured a coffee and sat down on the couch without even a nod of acknowledgement to either me or CJ.

I guess he wasn't a morning person.

"Are you good?" CJ asked from the kitchen.

I bit my lower lip and nodded. "We need to have some sort of plan for Valerie to know if things go sideways."

"We talked about that last night. I promised to call or text her every hour." He turned to Michael. "If Val doesn't hear from me for more than three hours, something is wrong, and I need you to assume the worst. If that happens, you need to take them to Kylee's. Understand?"

Michael crossed his arms. "I'll send them all to Kylee's, but then I'm going after Lucifer myself."

CJ looked at the floor and nodded. "That's your funeral, but I need you to assure me you will make sure Val and the kids are safe before you barrel off to your death."

Michael's jaw tightened.

"I will make sure they are safe," Levi said from behind Michael, his deep baritone voice nearly shaking the walls of the cottage.

"Thank you," CJ said to Leviathan and then nodded for me to follow him outside.

"Maybe they should go west anyway," I said before he unlocked the garage and lifted the door.

CJ neglected to answer, but the dusty little BMW roadster took my focus away from what I had been saying, anyway.

"Are we taking that?" I pointed at the sporty little car, and a thrill of excitement raced over my skin.

The way he grinned reminded me of Alex, and my heart stalled in my chest for a blink before it resumed beating. His smile faded just as quickly. Sadness flared in his eyes, and he looked away, busying himself with toweling off the dust.

"This was Steve's car," he said, referring to the man who had adopted him and Tom. "When he died, we brought it here."

I stared as each swipe cleared off a crystal blue patch. When he finished with the outside, he reached into his pocket and pulled out his keys, then held them out to me.

"Can you move our van out of the way?" He pointed at the van blocking the garage.

"Sure." I took the keys and moved the van to the other side of the driveway behind Michael's car. When I stepped back into the garage, I asked, "Is this the only set of keys you have?"

He looked out from the passenger seat. "Hmm?"

"For the van. Does Val have keys, too?"

"Yes. We each have a set." He climbed out of the car and took the keys from me. "I need to charge the battery."

He dropped the dust-ridden rag on the workbench in the back of the garage and took a seat on the driver's side of the car. He moved the manual gear to the center before he made sure the emergency brake was tight.

He got out and held the door for me. "When I tell you to turn the car on, press the brake and turn the key." He pointed at the manual shift. "Don't touch the gears."

"Yes, sir." I saluted at the bark in his command.

"Don't be a wiseass." He closed the door on me and walked to the front, then popped the hood.

The air tingled around me, and I realized CJ was using his energy to charge the battery and not jumper cables. My mouth dropped open.

"Turn the car over," he said.

I turned the key, and the engine whined before puttering out.

"Turn it off again," CJ called from the front.

I could see a little of the engine under the hood opening. CJ's hands came into view a few times, and then that familiar twang of energy filled the air. I felt it hum through the car frame itself.

"Again," he called.

I turned the key, and this time the engine roared to life. The entire car rumbled with it and I smiled. CJ slammed the hood shut and came around to the driver's door.

"Let it run while I go pack a few things." He peeked at the gas gauge and then turned, leaving me to rev the engine like a race car driver at the starting line.

I studied the interior of the car. CJ hadn't done a very good job cleaning, so I reached over and opened the glove box, hoping to find a stash of napkins. What sat in the dark space made me sit up fast. A nine-millimeter gleamed in the small space. Underneath it sat a stack of white fast-food restaurant napkins, and I gingerly pulled out a couple.

I polished the dashboard and the inside of the windshield, wiping away the rest of the dust that CJ had missed, and then sat back, studying my more diligent work. My gaze dropped to the stick shift. I studied the gears tattooed on the shift head, memorizing where reverse was in relation to the rest.

Tom's truck had been an automatic, and so had my mother's car. I'd never driven a manual shift, and the thought filled me with both apprehension and exhilaration.

I closed my eyes and rifled through the cabinet of Tom's memories. Steve had taught both Tom and CJ how to drive a standard transmission when they were fifteen.

By the time CJ came out to the car with his bag and a few other items, I felt like I could implement the instructions I'd seen in Tom's memories. I guess CJ knew I had been looking at my stash again, because instead of taking over the driver's seat after he closed the trunk, he went directly to the passenger seat and belted himself in. He handed me a cell phone.

"Since yours is shot. I figured Alex won't mind." He nodded towards the phone. "The passcode is six-seven-one."

I stared at the phone, and my throat tightened. I slid it in my pocket while he programmed his with the first address we were heading to. When he finished, he lifted an eyebrow and waved towards the gear shift as if to say *be my guest.*

"Oh." I didn't expect him to really let me drive this car. "Really?" I asked after a tense second.

"Yes. Most kids these days don't have a clue how to drive a standard. It's a good thing to know, especially if something happens to me. You won't be stranded. So, go ahead. Drive."

I blinked, unsure of where to start. His approach to teaching me to drive was very different from Tom's. Tom had walked through every little thing. CJ just waved me ahead like anything he would say would fall on deaf ears.

He crossed his arms. "You were pretty confident you could do this. Besides, me repeating Steve's instructions would just irritate you." He taunted me with pursed lips, as if challenging me to say otherwise.

Unnerved by his honesty, I adjusted the seat and mirrors and took a deep breath. I pushed down on the clutch and brake, released the emergency brake, and pressed down on the gearshift, moving it down and to the right, mimicking the sign for reverse on the shift. The leather grips on the steering wheel felt foreign as did pressing something with my left foot. I released the brake and put my right foot on the gas. The engine revved, and I released the clutch.

The car lurched backwards, and once I was clear of the cars, I turned the wheel and pressed the clutch back in. I found first gear in the farthest left forward gear and did the same with the gas and clutch. Except this time, the car jerked and sputtered. The engine stalled.

Dimples appeared in CJ's cheek, and he looked away. "It's not as easy as it seemed, is it?"

"No." I wiped my face.

"There's a cadence between the clutch and the gas. As you are releasing the clutch, you press on the gas at the same velocity. Sometimes fast shifts like you just tried to do will stall the engine, especially between backing up and going forward again or vice versa."

His cocky tone made me want to wipe that amused smile off his face. Mensa or not, he could be annoying.

"Clutch in and turn on the car again." He waved to the keys.

This time when I released the clutch, I did it slower and pushed the gas at the same pace. The rolling start was smooth. Shifting to second was easy, too. I didn't stall out once on our way to the highway.

"Are we meeting Josh?" I asked.

"No, we're driving. I need the time to get my head around this." He glanced out the window, much more relaxed than Tom had ever been when I was in the driver's seat. He smiled at me. "In case you hadn't noticed, Tom and I have very different personalities."

"Yeah. You're cocky confident, and he was always second-guessing himself."

The mood in the little car sobered, and he nodded. "Tom was always more wild and daring than I ever was, though."

"And yet you went after Lucifer by yourself," I reminded him.

"Yep. I was young and stupid, thinking because I had all this power inside me, I could win against a graceless Lucifer. I never bet on him having an army of demons at his disposal."

"Do you think if it was just the two of you, you would have won?"

He stared out the windshield with his brow scrunched. He rubbed his right arm, shivering at his own memories. "I don't know." He glanced at me. "There are too many ifs there. If there weren't demons. If I had been able to use my power on his turf. If I had known I had angel fire in me. Way too many ifs to be able to give you any sort of intelligent answer beyond the fact that if Damian hadn't shown up when he did, I would have died."

My heart plummeted. If he didn't believe he could have won back then...

"Stop that." His glare shut down my thoughts more than his admonishment. His jaw tightened. "You need to learn to shut off access to your thoughts."

I concentrated on driving. "Why?"

"Because if you don't, Lucifer will know you are around. Some of his demons will, too. I know Valerie explained static to you. But I don't think she told you how to block someone from your thoughts."

"We were kind of more focused on getting the memories in my head sorted."

He let out a small laugh. "I guess that was a little more pressing," he conceded under his breath. "Well, think of this as another lesson in self-preservation." He rubbed his hands together.

"Should you be driving for this?" I asked.

"No. Concentrating on driving and thinking about multiple things will help. Thoughts are normally linear. That's why they flood our heads if we aren't concentrating on something or someone. I'm sure you've experienced the magnitude of noise assaulting your brain if you don't focus."

My mind drifted to the subway and the sheer volume of voices I'd heard in my head. Concentrating on Kylee had saved my sanity.

"Exactly. And I know you've heard nothing from me unless I've let my guard down, or I've been too overwhelmed with something to consciously create static."

I nodded. "Alex could do that, too, and it frustrated me not knowing what was on his mind."

"He's very good at blocking me. He's probably the only one who I can't break through his barrier when it's up, even if I wanted to. But then again, he is my son."

I sighed and scanned the traffic ahead of us. That hollowness inside me grew, and my stomach fluttered with angst. "How are we going to save him?"

"We have six hours to think about that before we get to Willard Asylum. In the meantime, you need to learn to cloak your thoughts."

"Think of multiple things at once?" I asked, and he nodded. I wasn't sure that was possible, but I concentrated on driving and tossing around how to save Alex and lamented about what he would be like if we did free him from Lucifer.

I glanced at CJ, and his lips formed the perfect scowl as he shook his head. "It's still linear."

"How do you think of more than one thing at a time? It's impossible!" My exasperation filled the small space in the car.

CJ drummed his fingers on the dashboard. "I don't know how to explain it beyond thinking about more than one thing at a time. I think it's just so ingrained in us that it's second nature." He wiped his face. "Steve used to say to treat your mind like a three-dimensional cube, and each side has its own thought track, all working at the same time but focused on different things. It's more like solving complex puzzles at the same time as having an in-depth political conversation where your focus is split between the two equally." He sighed and shrugged.

"So, if I constantly did mathematical problems, would that work?"

"Maybe. But you have to be thinking of other things at the same time as the math problem. Take the next exit." He pointed.

I changed lanes and took the exit without hitting anyone. The engine started sputtering as I slowed on the curve. I quickly shifted down, and it smoothed out. At least I didn't stall on the exit ramp. Heat filled my cheeks, and I focused on shifting through the gears as I quickly caught up with the flow of traffic.

"I was going to give this car to Alex when he graduated," CJ said as he studied the scenery passing by.

A lump formed in my throat, and I couldn't gulp it down. Tears blinded me, and I blinked them away. "He would have loved it." I choked on the words.

He just nodded, never looking away from the scenery.

The quiet of his mind left me to my own morbid thoughts I knew he was privy to, but I couldn't block them now that CJ had said his name.

I prayed we would be able to save Alex, even though deep down, I knew it was only a futile, desperate wish.

Judgement Day
Chapter 5

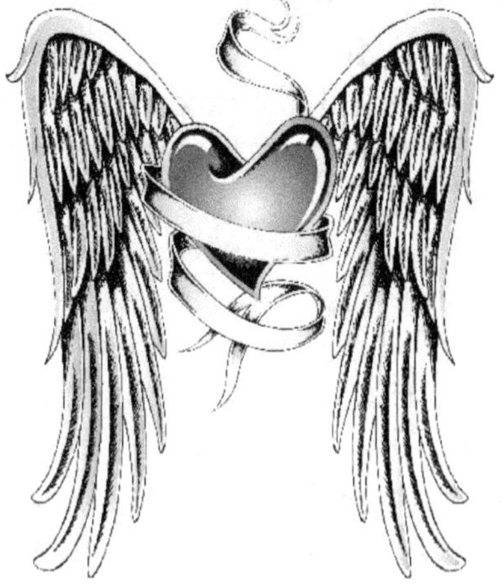

THE SIGN FOR A rest area in a mile caught my attention. I needed a break, and the gas tank was nearly empty. CJ had said nothing for a while. The only thing he did was send a text to Valerie to see how the kids were.

When I pulled off, he glanced at me.

"We need gas." I pulled up to the gas tanks and put the car in neutral, set the brake, then turned the car off and handed him the keys.

"First gear." He pointed at the gears. "Always put it in first gear after you turn it off when you are on a flat surface or going uphill, so it doesn't roll away."

I did as he asked and then headed inside to use a restroom. The scent of breakfast meats and home fries from the adjoining fast-food restaurant made my mouth water, but I went the opposite direction to the bathrooms.

When I came out of the restroom, CJ was leaning on the wall, waiting for me.

"I'm hungry. I figured you might need some fuel too." He nodded toward the food court and herded me into the line for exactly what got my stomach growling. Instead of taking our meals to the car, he took me to a seat near the window in a quiet section of the restaurant.

We ate in silence, and when he finished, he leaned back in the seat. "If Lucifer still has his soul in that necklace, we may have a chance."

I sipped my smoothie because I wasn't ready to discuss this yet. Every scenario I tried to work out in my mind ended with Alex dead. I couldn't see my way around this puzzle. Besides, if I started talking about it after eating two egg-and-cheese sandwiches and a mountain of home fries, my stomach would turn into a burning mess of anxiety.

"Fine," he mumbled under his breath, and collected the garbage. He left me at the table and threw the load of crumpled paper into the receptacle. When he returned, he stayed standing. "Before we leave this parking lot, you need to see if the boots I grabbed of Valerie's fit you."

I blinked up at him. "Why didn't you just grab mine?"

"Because yours doesn't have built-in sheaths for a sharp knife that could erase you from existence if you cut yourself by accident." He crossed his arms.

I had forgotten about the knife, and the reminder of it was just as unwelcomed as discussing ways to save Alex. I nodded and focused on the creamy coolness of my smoothie, ignoring his impatient stare.

When my drink was gone and I sucked air through the straw, I stood, dropped my empty cup in the garbage, and followed him out to the car. He reached into the back and handed me the boots.

I peeled off my sneakers and slid on Valerie's boots. They weren't an exact fit, but it was close enough, especially since the leather gripped my leg and the knife holders pressed into the side of my calf were snug enough to make the looseness in the fit around my foot moot.

The second boot fit just as well, and the blue handle peeked out from under the holder. When I zipped it up, the knife disappeared. It was a neat trick.

"Thanks," I said.

Relief flooded through me. The boots were nice, and they went with my jeans, but they would be killer with my leather outfit.

I stretched out and closed my eyes. "What did you mean if they still have his soul locked in the necklace we have a chance?"

"I was thinking maybe if we set his soul free, he could bounce Lucifer out of his body."

"Wouldn't that leave all of us vulnerable to being possessed?" I opened one eye and glanced at CJ.

"With a soul, you have to agree to let him in."

"So, he would possess one of the bodies, assuming they are still there?"

"That would be my logical conclusion. And that would make it easier for us to get close and end the bastard." The cruel smile that formed on his lips seemed foreign on his normally kind face.

"And what if it doesn't work? What if he can't bounce Lucifer out?"

The look CJ gave me said it all. If he couldn't bounce Lucifer out, he was as good as dead.

"Then we have to take him out," he said in a very soft whisper, like saying the words too loud meant they would come true.

I wasn't ready for this, so instead of bouncing around ideas, I leaned back in the seat and closed my eyes, attempting to rest my mind and loosen the knots that had formed throughout my back.

WILLARD ASYLUM WAS PROBABLY the creepiest place I had ever seen, and the nearby prison just exacerbated the issue. My skin prickled with anticipation. This was the kind of place I could see Lucifer holed up in.

CJ and I exchanged a glance over the roof of the car, and I came around the front to meet him. With the prison next door and the chain-link fence surrounding the asylum, I wasn't sure how we were going to breach the barriers without being detected.

"It looks like there is an opening over there." CJ pointed towards a break in the fence that I hadn't seen on my first pass.

He led the way, and when we stepped inside, the dust and decay eating away at the building churned my stomach.

When we crossed into the hallway, CJ pulled one of those big Maglite flashlights from the inside pocket of his coat, like a magician. He pointed it down the darkened hall and switched it on.

The floor had caved in down the center. There was no way I was going to try to teeter along the edge to get to the other side. My teeth ached at the thought of it, and I realized I was clamping my jaw too tight.

I licked my lips as CJ handed me the flashlight and played on his phone for a minute. I glanced over his shoulder at the blueprints displayed on the monitor. He swiped the screen slowly, studying the layout.

"There's another door farther down that we can take, and there's a stairwell that we can use to get to the next floor. Hopefully, we can get to the other side," he mumbled.

He traced his way back to the door, and once outside, I actually took a deep breath of the fresh air and felt some of my anxiety abate. Warmth radiated from the midday sun, baking the chill right out of my bones. We hadn't run into any traps and I didn't have that tingling sensation announcing any demons in the area, but that's not to say this next entrance would change all that.

The closer to the door we got, the more jumbled my thoughts became. I really wasn't ready to see Lucifer in Alex's form. My mouth went dry with apprehension.

CJ glanced over his shoulder at me with eyes that carried the same dread pulsing in my muscles. His jaw tensed as he reached for the door.

The second entry was even dingier than the fist. Even with the sky outside bright and cloudless, the light barely penetrated the building. The doors that stood open in the hall layered bright swaths of sunlight across the path. These bright beacons of light interrupted the dullness of the rest of the hallway. It was a strange effect and one that made the penetration of the flashlight not as deep as if it had been shrouded in darkness.

We inched our way down the hall, testing the floor with each step before we put our weight down.

As we looked in each room, I scanned the windows and stopped CJ halfway down the passageway. "None of the windows are boarded up."

CJ looked around again and huffed a laugh.

"This doesn't fit Gabriel's description." I stepped gingerly into another room where the floorboards had seen better days. Every window was clear of wood. The panes were dirt-ridden, but the sun still glowed through the grime.

The floor groaned in a more alarming way than the other creaks we had heard along this path. I turned, meeting CJ's gaze. Before I could leap to safety, the floorboards underneath me gave way, opening to a dark abyss behind me. My heart jumped into my throat. I reached my hand out as I started to plummet.

CJ's fingertips just grazed mine and then I was freefalling towards spiked debris falling below me. Echoing bangs sounded just as loud as my wheezing breaths. I didn't think I screamed, not with the rush of air whipping around me as gravity yanked me nearly three stories down.

"Stop!" CJ's sharp command filled the air.

My fall stopped just as suddenly as it had started, as if a rope had finally pulled taut around my waist.

I hung suspended in mid-air, held by nothing but CJ's willpower. I blinked up at the concentration written in the deep lines on his forehead as the strength of his powers pulled me back onto an intact spot by the door where he stood. He grabbed my arm and moved me to safety.

My temples pulsed with adrenaline as his concern turned to irritation. I inspected my arms to make sure I wasn't bleeding anywhere, and all I found were a few scratches. I glanced back at the cascading hole I'd fallen into and shivered.

"You could have stopped yourself," he said when I finished my examination, then he turned and stormed down the hall in the direction we had come.

I caught up with him, and movement at the far end grabbed my attention. I clutched CJ's arm. He glanced in the same direction and then looked closer at me with a crease between his eyes.

"You don't see them?" I pointed at the huddled group of people peering at us. They clung together as tightly as I gripped CJ. It took me a second to realize they weren't demons like I half expected to jump out at us at any moment.

And they weren't other haunted asylum adventurers like us.

They were ghosts.

Real ghosts. The kind that Tom used to exorcise from houses.

The only true ghost experience I had was when Tom Ryan died. I wouldn't categorize the spirits I saw at Paradise Cove as ghosts because they were solid to touch. The things at the end of the hall weren't solid. They were like wisps of smoke, which somehow made me even more nervous.

CJ closed his eyes, and that crease of concentration appeared between his brows. After a moment, he glanced at me. "I can't sense anything beyond fear from the ghosts, but keep an eye on them while we make sure..." He twirled his finger around.

I don't think he wanted to say Lucifer's name out loud, not with the group staring at us. Scratch that. Staring at *me*.

We inched down the hallway towards them. CJ turned me into a stairwell before we reached the surreal crew. The door creaked, and CJ climbed the steps, testing each one out as we climbed to the top floor.

We stood in one of the rooms that was as large as CJ's family room. Even though the walls had peeling paint similar to the video, the state of the floor wouldn't support multiple people, nor would the wall hold anything akin to a chain.

CJ shook his head.

I glanced around one last time before we went back down the stairs we had climbed. We probably only investigated half the building, but beyond the huddled ghosts, nothing else stirred.

"This place is a bust." CJ headed for the exit.

Judgement Day
Chapter 6

CJ TOOK THE DRIVER'S seat again, and I was thankful. Just as thankful as I had been when he indicated the all clear of Willard Asylum.

He wiped his face and sighed as he stared at the building. "This isn't it, even though it still doesn't feel right."

"I know what you mean." The hair on my arms was still standing on end. "Maybe it was the ghosts?"

He shook his head and looked in the rearview mirror at the maximum-security wing of the prison within fifty yards of Willard Asylum. "Maybe it's that place." He gestured with his thumb over his shoulder.

That made more sense to me. After all, a prison was certainly a place where evil existed, despite the mantra of rehabilitation.

I glanced back at Willard. "This place is too much of a hazard. I mean, I'm surprised only one floor gave out." I waved at the building as he started the car. "Thank you for saving me, by the way."

He chuckled and pointed at me. "You really need to master your powers. As far as the building, it would certainly deter anyone from entering the area, even Lucifer."

"Should we do something with the ghosts?" I wrung my hands at the thought.

"They were just watching, not engaging. They seemed harmless." He put the car in gear and started away from our first dilapidated asylum. We had five more to go before we regrouped and looked further.

I didn't know whether to hope we found them or not. If we didn't find them, it could mean they moved on, and it would be near impossible to find them.

"Do you think he's sending us on a wild goose chase?"

He remained quiet until we pulled onto the highway heading south. "I'm not sure. I have the same unease that you do, but considering he's preparing for us, I don't think he'd just disappear off the grid. It's not his style."

I glanced out the window at the thick trees lining the highway and let the scenery lull me. My mind wouldn't stop with the what-if scenarios, either. My stomach growled loud enough to capture CJ's attention.

"There are snacks in the bag behind my seat," he said.

I couldn't envision CJ putting together a care package like that.

"April put it together for us, so I'm sure it's all carbs and will leave us with a hell of a sugar crash. I just hope it doesn't come at the wrong time."

I reached over and pulled the bag free. One glance inside proved he was right. Snacks weren't the right term. It was more like a candy explosion. I pulled a bag of gummy bears out and offered it to him.

"I'm good." He focused on the road with his forehead creased in concentration.

WHEN CJ FINALLY TURNED into Letchworth Village, we both gawked at the number of cars in the parking lot. Beyond it, the number of people walking the paths between the buildings wasn't what we expected. Neither was the golf course bordering the village. It looked as if all the winter wallflowers had turned up for a pleasant walk between the actively used buildings and the boarded-up and crumbling monstrosities.

He parked, turned the engine off, and leaned back in the seat. "Lucifer isn't here." He sent a text to Valerie to let her know we had arrived at the second on his list, and that it was another bust.

I scanned the campus. "You don't think he'd be in one of the remote buildings?" I knew it was a long shot, especially with the number of people in the area, but I didn't want to underestimate Lucifer.

He slowly shook his head. "I can't sense a thing. Usually when I get near him, my chest feels like someone tightened a belt around it. My skin crawls with the evil in the air. And that isn't what I sense here."

"We should take a walk around just to be sure," I said, even though I knew CJ was right.

I didn't have any forewarning at Tom's house when we'd pulled in and Lucifer stood from the side steps. All I knew was my heart had suddenly lurched, sending a shot of adrenaline through every muscle. The portals were different. What CJ had described was exactly what I felt like when I approached one of the breaches.

CJ pocketed the keys and got out of the car. He spared giving me an eye roll, and instead gave me a curt nod and waved me forward. He was just going through the motions. So was I, to be honest. The longer we stayed here, the more time we had to get our minds wrapped around what we needed to do once we finally found Lucifer.

It took us a half hour to walk the grounds, and he was right. No demons, just a lot of people cruising the paths on a nice spring day. I stopped on our way back and stared at one of the older buildings where a few of the panels blocking the windows had fallen. Faces peered out at me. At least a dozen of them.

CJ stopped and glanced at the building before backtracking to where I stood. I felt the tickle of his mind invading mine, and then it was gone.

"They're just ghosts." He wrapped his hand around my wrist. "There's nothing we can do for them today." He pulled me towards the parking lot.

"Didn't Gabriel say he thought he saw ghosts?"

CJ sighed and glanced at the building again. "It's too close to the town hall for Lucifer to gamble his freedom on." He nodded at the building next to the boarded-up atrocity.

I gave the building next door the once-over. The lower windows were open to let in the warm breeze, and even if they had been closed, I was sure they weren't noise-canceling. Someone inside sneezed, and I heard it clearly enough to be skeptical. If this was the building, an awful lot of people would have heard the screaming coming from inside.

The ghosts still stared at me, and I shifted from one foot to the other and then turned toward the parking lot.

CJ said nothing on the rest of the walk until we got to the car. "I scanned the building while you were making up your mind." He slid into the driver's seat.

"Scanned?"

He tapped his temple like I should know what that meant and then brought up his GPS. With a few keystrokes, a dot appeared on the map and he set the phone into the holder on the dashboard.

I stared at the map. "Pennsylvania?" I asked. "Why not New Jersey first?"

A dimple appeared in his cheek. "Because I said we'd loop around and then backtrack, if you recall. That way, we would only really have one or two left to deal with tomorrow, depending on the time." He started the car. "There were many that I didn't even consider because of regular tours or ones that are now public parks or being renovated. I should have seen that this one was part of a greater village with buildings that were actually being used." He waved at the landscape in front of us. "If I had, I wouldn't have bothered."

He navigated us back on a southerly route.

I leaned forward and flipped on the radio. I was tired of the silence and the restlessness of my mind. Static filled the car, and I scanned through the available radio stations and finally settled on a rock station. I wasn't in the mood for ballads or country, and rap certainly wasn't my thing.

When a Bob Seger song came on, CJ started singing along. His voice lulled me into a trance for the next two hours. Song after song poured out in the little car, and he seemed to sit taller and more assured each mile we passed.

It was hauntingly familiar. Tom had reacted to music in the same way, although his voice was not a gift from Heaven like CJ's. But the growing confidence that came with each tune grated on my nerves.

I reached over to turn the radio off, but CJ grabbed my wrist.

"Leave it." He resumed singing.

I crossed my arms over my chest, fisting my hands while I glared out the window, unable to voice my irritation.

He stopped singing abruptly. "Whenever Tom and I would lift cars, we used to cruise around with the radio so loud the car vibrated. And we sang louder. It's a brother thing."

I raised my eyebrows at him. "You stole cars?"

CJ smiled and shrugged. "Tom did. It was part of his rebellion period. I went along with him to make sure he didn't wrap the car around a tree or something. But every time we did it, we got caught, and Steve would smooth it over and then ream the Hell out of us at home." His smile faded as he continued to drive. "I lost my brother. I can't lose my son, too."

I bit my lower lip and blinked the sudden blur of tears out of my eyes. I didn't want to lose his son, either, but that really wasn't up to us. That was a hand that had already been dealt, and all our bets were down. All that was left was to see the dealer's cards.

Judgement Day
Chapter 7

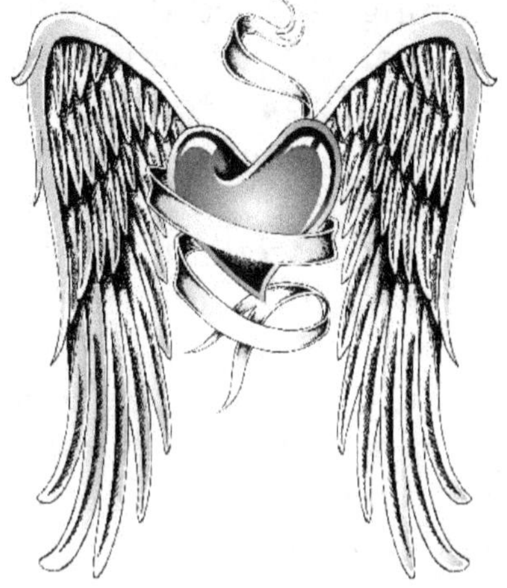

PENNHURST ASYLUM WAS AS creepy as I thought it would be. The number of brick building clusters left me on edge. We pulled onto the side of the road, and CJ turned off the car. He shivered as he scanned the campus.

"Ready or not..." He pocketed the keys and stepped out of the car.

I slowly got out. The hairs on the back of my neck stood on end, and I traded a glance with CJ.

He bit his lip. "There's a lot of darkness here," he said, and he flexed his shoulders as if he were trying to steel himself for what we were stepping into.

I nodded. My skin tingled with it, but it wasn't like the evil from the breaches. It was heavier, as if it had formed over years of neglect.

As we approached the closest building, the door opened, and we both stopped. A blonde woman in what could only be categorized as patchwork clothing climbed down the stairs and grinned at us, making the wrinkles around her eyes look as welcoming as her smile.

"We aren't open for tours today," she said.

"You have tours?" I couldn't help the surprise in my voice as I glanced at the buildings and over at CJ. I was beginning to think his research skills were faulty.

If he'd heard my thoughts, he ignored me.

The woman stopped halfway down the stairs, and her eyes widened. Her hand fluttered to her mouth as she stared at CJ.

"Are you..."

CJ's cheeks reddened. "Am I?" He smiled, and his eyes twinkled.

"CJ Ryan?" she whispered, turning red and fanning herself the way I would have envisioned my mother doing if she had ever had the opportunity to meet her favorite crooner of this century.

"Yes, ma'am," he said, and actually bowed and kissed the back of her hand.

I swear she was close to passing out from excitement.

CJ's magnetism and his stage persona manifested in a blink. And his easy smile was just as intoxicating as Alex's was. CJ could be a smooth-as-silk entertainer, but to me, he no longer was the voice that could soothe my fire. He had just become Alex's dad.

"And I'm doing a little ghost hunting with my niece here. Do you think we could look around?"

he asked, tilting his head in such an endearing way that I almost laughed out loud.

"Please, call me Kathy," she said demurely. Her back arched so her chest stuck out more, and she smiled in a way that made me want to vomit. "Well... I guess I could show you the place."

"If you have some place to be, we could explore on our own," he said, and winked. "I promise we won't disturb anything."

"Oh, but I know all the places people have experienced ghosts," Kathy said excitedly and turned back to the building, leading us inside.

CJ rolled his eyes at me, and I could almost hear his under-breath curses. Neither of us wanted a chaperone. Not if we had to fend off demons and other traps. Although with tours, my gut told me we shouldn't bother, but the heaviness in the air gave me pause.

I doubted Kathy had seen the news the day before. It had never even entered her mind beyond the fangirl reaction to CJ Ryan. If she had, perhaps the star power of being in his presence chased it right out of her mind.

The minute I passed through the doors, I knew this would not be pleasant. There were enough ghosts to leave me chilled and my hands itching to ignite even with the leather gloves warding my fire power. I tried not to make eye contact with any of them, but I thought they sensed me as much as I sensed them.

CJ sent a worried look over his shoulder at me and then beyond me, like he had seen what I had seen.

The walls inside were too pristine to be the ones in the video.

"Do most of the buildings look like this or are there some that are in more dire need of repair?" he asked as we walked down yet another hallway with at least a dozen ghosts loitering.

She glanced over her shoulder with a crease between her eyes. "Excuse me?"

"This place is actually in pretty good shape compared to some we've seen," he said. "But is all of it this well-kept?" He tried to backtrack and get the doubt out of her head.

"There are a couple of buildings that we don't let people go into because they aren't safe." Kathy continued walking down the hallways, explaining the different rooms to us.

But I wasn't listening. I was concentrating on being invisible to the ghosts, but it wasn't working. They followed as we passed, and I was afraid to look over my shoulder at the growing crowd. They didn't engage. Yet. I pulled my glove off my right hand, just in case. I didn't want to be the cause of the building burning down, but I also didn't want to be accosted by a mob of angry ghosts.

CJ stopped. *Put the glove back on. If they attack, I will take care of them.*

His thought barreled through my head. I slid the glove back on as we continued through the halls. We climbed another flight of stairs, and my unease grew as our guide explained that the section we were entering used to be for the criminally insane.

My heart picked up, and I swallowed hard as the door creaked open. I nearly choked on the malignant air that rolled out. CJ's hands curled into tight fists as the darkness washed over us.

As much as I wished Lucifer were here in this building, both of us knew the moment Kathy had mentioned tours he wouldn't be here. At least not in the buildings with access. But evil did occupy the buildings. The ghosts following us were not made of the same dark components as the wing we entered. I chanced a glance over my shoulder, but the collective of ethereal beings stayed on the stairway. Their faces reflected the same horror riding my blood.

The door closed on them, and Kathy droned on. I froze in place with the door at my back. CJ stopped as well and stepped closer to me. Finally, Kathy stopped and turned toward us, her head cocked like an inquisitive puppy.

I felt it before I heard it. From the end of the hall that was gated off to any foot traffic came a horrific howl. Both CJ and I turned. Just like the other floor we'd visited, there were several ghosts here, but they were darker, baring their teeth like a pack of wild animals. All of them reeked of malice.

And it was aimed squarely at us.

I took a step closer to CJ, and my movement seemed to set them off. They charged, their growls of derision rising until I wanted to block the sound. I couldn't get my glove off fast enough to blast them. Before any of them reached us, CJ lifted his hand. Angel fire shot from his palm, and eviscerated the ghosts with white light.

Their dying screams echoed in the hallway. I covered my ears. The darkness overshadowing this building faded with the screams, and warm relief swept through me.

The tickle present in my head disappeared as CJ met my gaze. It was only then that I realized he had been in my head, seeing what I had been seeing since we'd stepped inside the building.

We turned back to a very wide-eyed and very pale Kathy. Her gaze was still stuck on the last place the burning mass of ghosts had been. When she swiveled to us, CJ shrugged and smiled.

"You still have ghosts in the building, but they aren't dangerous like these were." He hooked his thumb over his shoulder.

"What are you?" she asked, her voice shaking as much as her body.

CJ crossed until he stood right before her. "You will not remember that," he whispered and exercised the same power I had used to influence the customs agents in Australia.

She blinked a few times, and then her sunny smile was back, along with the droning descriptions of the building we were touring. Whatever darkness had hung over Pennhurst when we'd arrived was gone.

"Is it possible to see the other buildings? The ones you don't let people explore?" CJ asked after an hour of exploring the buildings on the Pennhurst campus. "We'd just like to see them."

Kathy led us back to the stairwell we had come up, and when she pushed through the door, the sea of ghosts parted to let her through. I stood on the top step as she and CJ descended. They watched CJ pass with awe inscribed on their faces and then turned to me.

"You are free to go," I whispered.

"You can see us?" one of the younger girls asked.

I crouched down to look her in the eye and put my hands out. The girl placed her palms on mine. She stared at the connection of our flesh, and her wide eyes found mine again.

"I can see you." I smiled at her and then looked around. "All of you."

Kathy and CJ stopped on the landing below and stared up at me.

"What are you doing?" Kathy asked, her voice sharp enough for me to look away from the ghostly posse surrounding me.

"She's talking to the ghosts," CJ said.

Kathy's face paled. "Ghosts?" she asked, her voice filled with fear.

CJ glared at her to shut her mouth.

I looked back at the girl. "They aren't bad ghosts. They're just lost."

The girl smiled back. "No one has ever actually seen us," she said, and excitement filled her voice.

"Well, I'm a little special that way." I glanced around as an idea sparked. "Can you tell me if Lucifer is here at Pennhurst?" I figured these ghosts might know.

They shook their heads in unison.

"Is that a no you can't tell me or a no, he isn't here?"

"No one by that name is here," the little girl said. "At least not in this wing."

I didn't know whether or not to be disappointed. I shook the weird ambiguity away and focused on the ghosts in front of me.

Especially this sweet little girl whom I couldn't believe had been locked up in such a hideous place. "Thank you. You know, I might know someone who can help you get out of this place."

Every ghost's eyes widened with hope.

"Join hands." I moved one of my hands from the little girl's to the ghost next to me. I stood as they took hands until we had a full loop. "I promise it will be okay." I smiled reassuringly and looked at the ceiling. "Nick?"

The space next to me shimmered, and in a blink, Nick appeared next to me. Death in person was not intimidating in any way. Even if he put on a cloak and carried a scythe, he would still not be anywhere in the realm of frightening. And when he smiled like he was now, he looked like the proverbial kid next door.

The ghosts seemed to sense what he was and pulled back the way I had when I first encountered him. I kept my grip on their hands.

"Trust me. He is a cool guy, and he will show you some really cool places. You don't need to be afraid." I transferred the little girl's hand into his. "He will take you to a much nicer place than this one," I added, and Nick gave the little girl an even more dazzling smile.

"Faith is right," he said, and his voice seemed to soothe the tension.

I put the other ghost's hand in Nick's free hand, completing the loop. The connection flowed through every one of them, filling their ethereal forms with light.

CJ squinted up at the lights.

"Y'all ready for an adventure?" Nick asked, and the ghosts nodded.

Kathy swayed on the step, her face slackened in disbelief and her eyes rolled back in her head. CJ reached his arm out, catching our fearful tour guide. But his eyes never left the vision of the ghosts rising to the ceiling with Death himself.

Just before they disappeared, the little girl waved at me.

I waved back and turned to CJ, who held a limp Kathy with one arm and wore a smile of such awe.

"I've never seen so many leave so peacefully," he said. "Usually they are like the ones up there." He nodded towards the door behind me where the warped and evil ghosts had been.

I climbed down the stairs. "I assumed that bad feeling was them until they wouldn't cross the threshold on the upper floor."

CJ nodded. He turned his attention to the dead weight hanging over his arm and tapped Kathy's cheeks gently.

She blinked, and she nearly shot out of his grasp, her gaze darting from me to the stairwell and back.

"You fainted while you were telling us about the buildings out back," CJ said. His voice held concern as he looked at her.

The air rippled in the space between CJ and Kathy, and she started blinking.

"I..." She glanced around and then back at him. "I haven't eaten anything today, and all the excitement..."

"Well, if you don't mind us wandering the grounds, you should get something in your stomach so that doesn't happen again." His smile was warm, and she just nodded and headed back to the ground floor and out the door in the stupor that always follows having your mind bent to our will.

We followed out onto the front steps and watched her wander off.

"I hate doing that," CJ said after Kathy turned the corner out of our sight.

"It is unnerving, but I'm not sure we would have gotten out of here without the national media descending on us if you hadn't."

He huffed a laugh, and we turned and crossed the overgrown lawn to the rear buildings, which were far worse than what we had just walked through.

"I don't think he's here," CJ said as we stood in front of the dilapidated structure.

None of the foreboding I had felt when we originally arrived presented itself as we looked from one condemned building to the next.

"Gabriel said he set traps. Do you think the ghosts were a trap?"

CJ rubbed his chin and studied the structure in front of us. "Probably not, but I don't want to underestimate Lucifer, so I guess we're searching these after all. Just be careful where you step." He held the rusty old door open for me. "Calling Death was a nice touch, by the way," he said when I walked through.

"I figured they needed to move on." I stepped into the dark, musty space and held my nose against the need to sneeze. "And Nick owed me a favor."

CJ drew up behind me.

"He showed up pretty damn fast. I'll give you that."

The door clanged closed, encasing us in darkness. If it weren't for CJ's bright aura, I wouldn't have seen the crumbling floor in front of us.

I sneezed despite trying not to.

"Bless you." CJ went to step around me.

"Hole in the floor." I sneezed twice more.

"How can you see in here?"

"Your aura. It's bright enough to see a few feet in front of us." I pulled off my glove and let my fingers ignite, lighting up the rotted entry that we stood in, along with the gaping hole preventing us from going any farther in the structure.

He closed his eyes, and a pulse of power went through my body, searching the building like a sonar ping. The pulse returned a few minutes later, and he opened his eyes. "Nothing more than a few birds and rats are alive in this building, outside of you and me."

"Agreed," I said. I wasn't keen on trying to climb down the hole, but I would have if I had felt any twinge of evil, regardless of the danger. We also didn't run into any demons, so this couldn't be the place. I closed my hand, and we retreated into the sunshine.

We still did as much of a walk-through of the other questionable structures as we could, but they were in a similar state of disrepair as the first condemned building had been. Not one of them had fuzzy walls like what we saw in the video, either, although a few had moss growing, but that was the wrong kind of fuzzy.

We started back toward the car.

"You have a choice. Drive to Cedar Grove, New Jersey, or drive to Staten Island after Cedar Grove." CJ tossed the keys up and down in his hand as we walked.

"Can I just drive to a place to eat instead?" My stomach growled.

He glanced at his watch. "This took a lot longer than I'd hoped." He pulled out his phone and sent a text to Valerie that we had seen another place on the list, and while there had been ghosts and a very odd tour guide, it certainly wasn't where Lucifer would have stayed. He let her know we were heading to New Jersey after we grabbed food.

He tossed me the keys. "You're driving this leg. After we eat, I need a nap, especially since I know I'll have to use angel fire again before this day is over."

Judgement Day
Chapter 8

I WASN'T SURE CJ was happy when I pulled into a restaurant known for its pancakes. But I didn't care. The thought of a tall stack of sweetness covered in strawberry sauce and whipped cream had made my mouth water enough to turn the wheel. They had other items on the menu, but I already had what I wanted tattooed on my mind before they even handed me a menu.

"Pancakes?" CJ asked as the waitress walked away. His voice held the disdain echoed in his gaze.

"Yes. You don't see me mocking your dinner choice, do you?" I crossed my arms and sat back in the seat.

He wiped his face and leaned back. "Sorry. Just more stressed than I thought," he mumbled and smiled up at the waitress as she brought his coffee and my whipped-cream topped hot chocolate.

"I was actually hoping we would find him earlier rather than later," he said after the waitress left. "That way, I wouldn't have to continue to play different scenarios over in my head."

He tried to smile at me, but it didn't work. I knew exactly what he was talking about, too. The quiet times like this were when the what-ifs became darker and more violent, and the stretch of time only ate away at my confidence instead of bolstering it.

He chuckled and stared into his coffee. "You and I are alike in that manner." He lifted his gaze and shrugged. "The time allows us both to cultivate our doubts instead of building up our defenses."

I took a fingerful of whipped cream, but instead of sucking it off my finger, I flicked it at CJ. It was childish, but I didn't need him voicing my thoughts with his own spin on them. It stopped inches from his face, and his eyebrow rose. The glob shot back at me, heading straight for my forehead.

I couldn't help but laugh and caught the cream in my palm. I promptly licked it off my glove.

CJ grinned and nursed his coffee. "I get why Alex likes you."

"Thanks. I think." I wiped my hands on a napkin and glanced towards the kitchen where our waitress was gathering our plates. "I haven't had a second to really breathe and be myself since my mother died. It's just been one thing after another. So..." I shrugged.

"So, when you see a chance to be outrageous, you take it?"

I shook my head and flicked my gaze to the approaching waitress. She arrived before I could formulate an answer. She set my plate down and then CJ's.

"Thank you." I picked up my silverware, then dug into the tall stack.

CJ picked up his loaded burger, and we both devoured our meals.

"No," I finally said. "But I do take my chance to provide levity when it presents itself."

"You don't talk like you were raised off the grid." He wiped his mouth and crumpled his napkin.

"And you do talk like you were born with a silver spoon."

"You mean like a pretentious ass?" He smiled.

"I didn't say that. You did. Besides, Tom never talked down to me." I found myself saying more than I would have had we stayed holed up at the house with everyone around. Somehow, being alone with CJ made me a little braver in sharing my thoughts.

"But I have." He closed his eyes and hung his head. "You're only sixteen. So yes, I have treated you like a child because you are. I don't want to boost you beyond what you can do because it's unwise to make you think you are invincible. I'm trying to help you not repeat the same mistakes I've made."

"I'm not you, Mr. Ryan."

He leaned on the table on his elbows. "No. You're better than I am. You're almost as smart, too. So, I'm a little harder on you because of that. Just like I was strict with Alex. Between you and me, he's even smarter than I am, but I'll never admit that to my son." He looked out the window behind me. "Lucifer is smart, too, so the combination we are up against is formidable enough to scare the crap out of me. He knows we both want my son back." He bit his lip and met my gaze. "I'm afraid he may have already destroyed that possibility."

I recoiled in the seat. What CJ had insinuated left me cold and hollow inside.

"We have to be prepared for that reality. Both of us."

My gaze darted around the restaurant, and he took the cue, peeling off enough for the dinner along with a hefty tip. He led me out to the car, but instead of climbing in the passenger seat like I thought he would, he went around to the driver's side and put his hand out for the keys that I'd put in my pocket.

"Are you sure?" I hesitated with the keys in my hand.

"Yes. Dinner helped, and we have some things to discuss on the off chance we win this."

"Thinking optimistically?" I asked as I placed the keys in his palm.

"Well, I think we've beat the other alternatives right into the ground. Don't you?"

He was right. I had envisioned every awful scenario as we'd traveled down from Maine. I nodded and circled around to the passenger side.

He started the car. "Let's not talk about failure. If we by some miracle pull this off, we have to figure out a way to fix what those videos destroyed."

"How?"

"I have an idea, but I'm still figuring out if it will work or not." He sucked his cheek between his teeth for a moment. "But for it to work, there can't be a trace of the bodies. No bone, no blood, nothing to trace back to any of them."

"You want me to burn the place down?"

He glanced at me. "No. We need to purify it with angel fire. And then maybe burn the place down just to be sure, but I'm not certain that will be needed."

I thought about how I'd decimated an island in the South Pacific. "I'm not sure I have the angel fire thing under control like you do."

"You really leveled an island?"

"It was a small island," I mumbled under my breath, and looked out the window.

"Then I'll have to be the one who does the clean-up. We don't need you going nuclear and wiping out an entire town from the map."

"If Alex is holding my hand, I should be able to control it." I crossed my arms and cringed at the whine in my voice.

He nodded.

Silence filled up the car, and I fidgeted in the seat. "Is that it? That's your big idea?"

He chuckled and glanced at me. "The second part of my idea has to take place in Paradise Cove. But I have never tried to film a spirit, so I'm not sure it will even work. I asked Valerie to take some videos on her camera to see if they appear normal on film. So, we will know by the time we get to the next stop whether it works."

It was a brilliant idea.

Film Naomi and Gabriel with a timestamp at a later date than what Lucifer sent to the television stations would wipe out whatever damage Lucifer did to Alex's future if there was video proof of everyone alive.

My throat tightened. "You can't film Bridget."

CJ nodded. "That's the only gap in the plan."

"And how will you explain all of it?" I knew a later time stamp would show that they were okay despite the earlier videos, but what plausible explanation could he give to the general public to wipe those scenes out?

"Well, Lucifer provided us with that when he mentioned my father. My dad was one of the best editors out there. So, we just have Alex explain he was trying his hand at special effects and video editing and was attempting to produce a low-budget horror flick. The release to the news stations was meant to be teasers, and he didn't think about the consequences that went along with sending those blind."

"And what about the finished movie? They are going to ask about that."

CJ glanced at me. "Computer crashed and a fire at the place he was filming destroyed his equipment."

"You've thought this through."

"Between the darker outcomes, yes. I've put some thought into this. As you said, the only gap is Bridget. We can even show Tom if needed. I just hope it's enough."

I didn't want to think about the ramifications if we freed him, but couldn't exonerate him, so I focused on a more troubling issue.

"What do we do with Grace?"

CJ shook his head. "I don't know."

"What if she's... pregnant?" I squeaked out. If Grace was pregnant, it would be CJ's grandchild by blood. I knew how strongly Tom felt about family, and CJ was the same.

He was slower to answer this time. "I don't know how to answer that." His voice cracked. "If she is, it isn't Alex's child, regardless of the DNA. Sleeping with Grace was not what Alex wanted." He wiped his face. "Alex won't want anything to do with Lucifer's child." He glanced at me, and then his cheeks reddened. "Present company excluded." He stared out at the road ahead. "If she is pregnant, she would be carrying your half brother or sister."

My stomach clenched at the thought. Everything about this was wrong. I wrapped my arms around my abdomen and held tight, trying to reconcile what that would mean. My brain couldn't fathom it, and I concentrated on the passing scenery so the darkness wouldn't overtake me.

"We'll deal with all that *after* we save Alex," CJ said, closing the conversation.

He turned on the radio and began to sing along softly. The croon lulled me, relaxing the tightness of my muscles until my eyelids drooped. The last thought before I fell asleep nearly jerked me awake.

What if Lucifer had already destroyed Alex's soul?

Judgement Day
Chapter 9

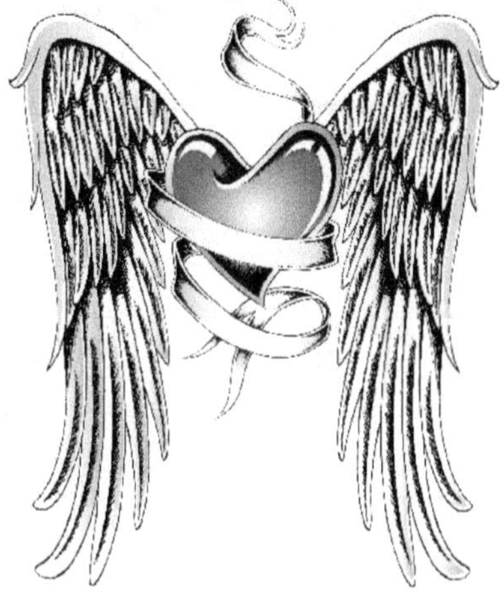

MY EYES FLUTTERED OPEN at the slowing of the car. I licked the dryness from my lips and swallowed the pasty taste of sleep from my mouth. The partially crumbled sign for Overbrook Asylum loomed before us. And beyond, large dumpsters piled with debris and construction equipment dotted the mostly cleared landscape.

"Your research sucked," I said in a raspy voice.

CJ pulled the car to a stop. "It seems so," he replied and pulled his phone from the holder, then texted Valerie. When he finished, he plugged the address of our next stop into the GPS and then turned the car off.

When he stepped out and stretched, I climbed out of the car as well.

"Do you want me to drive?"

"No. We have to drive through the city, and you're too new at driving to do that." He walked around the car and leaned on the hood with his phone in his hand.

"What are you doing?"

"Making sure the other places I had listed will not be a waste of time." He looked over his shoulder at me. "As much as I like road trips, I don't want to keep hopping from one to another to another that doesn't fit the profile."

I nodded. It was just a waste of time. Time we really didn't have.

"Did Mrs. Ryan get back to you about your idea?"

He put his finger up. "Hang on a minute."

I leaned against the car next to him and scanned what he was looking at. It seemed tours or construction did not rule the next few places on the list out. He flipped to his messages and pressed play on an attachment Valerie had sent. It showed Tom and April sitting on a blanket having a picnic. Light framed Tom. April was normal.

CJ sucked in his bottom lip and played the video again. "We might be able to fix the lighting," he said, but his voice didn't sound all that sure.

"At least Tom looks solid and not ghostly."

CJ raised his eyebrows and nodded before he pulled the GPS back up. "It's going to be another couple of hours before we get to Staten Island. I need to fill up the car before we hit the highway again. Did you want something to drink for the ride?"

"Sure."

He handed me a twenty-dollar bill. "You can grab me a coffee while you're getting something for yourself." He turned and got back into the car.

I followed and put on my seat belt while he spun us out of there and back onto the main road. He pulled into a gas station with a convenience store, and while he topped off the tank, I went inside to hit the restroom and then find something that struck my fancy to drink.

The drinks were easy, but it was the fast-food section that had me lingering. I stared at the chip selection with a coffee in one hand and a sports drink tucked under my arm. Nothing jumped out at me. I walked down the sweets aisle and stopped in front of the packages of frosted cream-filled cakes.

My mouth watered, so I grabbed one and headed to the counter. It was probably going to give me another sugar crash, but it looked too good to pass up on and nothing else had drummed up that kind of reaction.

When I climbed in the car, I handed CJ his coffee and put my drink into the cup holder. As soon as we were on the highway, I dug into the cakes, offering one of the two treats to CJ.

"Thanks. But I'm good," he said, but his gaze lingered on the chocolate.

"Are you sure?" I asked, waving the cake so he got a good whiff of chocolate.

"Yes, I'm sure." Dimples appeared in his cheeks as he focused on the drive.

I enjoyed every bite of the sweet confections and grinned at CJ after I licked my fingers clean.

I didn't bother with the drink yet. The chocolate lingered on my tongue, and I closed my eyes, relishing it.

"We are staying the night in the city before we hit Staten Island because I have a feeling that going into one of these places in the dark will be the Death of us." He glanced at me with serious eyes.

"Pun intended?" I asked.

"Yes."

"What? Are you afraid of the dark?" I didn't mean for that to escape, but it was out of my mouth before I had the good sense to shut my trap.

The hard stare he sent my way sent a rush of heat to my cheeks.

"Sorry," I mumbled. The lingering chocolate taste soured, and I opened my drink to wash it away.

"There is too much risk if we go after him at night. We don't want to get blindsided by anything. Demons, hellhounds, other monsters. Who knows what he has at his disposal?" He took a sip of his coffee, winced, and swallowed it as if it were bitter. "The traps Gabe talked about; those won't be fatal."

"How do you know?"

"Because Lucifer likes to be the one who delivers the Death blow." He glanced at me. "And he will only kill us after he's subjected us to the kind of torture that nightmares are made of. So, if it is all the same to you, I'd rather hit him during the daylight when I can see things coming."

I nodded dumbly in the seat. The one thing CJ was good for was cutting right to the point. Although right now, I would have preferred him not to be so brutally honest. I would have much rather just enjoyed my chocolate dessert and stared out at the uninspiring highway view.

WHEN CJ PULLED INTO a garage across from Central Park in New York City, I glanced over at him in surprise. He bypassed the attendant with a wave and drove to the top floor, then parked right next to an elevator.

"We own the penthouse." He put the car into first gear before shutting it off and yanking the emergency brake. He stepped out of the car and opened the trunk to grab our overnight bags.

I took my jacket when he handed it to me and followed him to the elevator.

"None of us have been here since..." The elevator doors opening interrupted CJ.

He didn't need to explain. I had Tom's memories. I already knew neither of them had been to the apartment since Lucifer had murdered their adoptive parents. So, us staying there was a big deal for CJ.

He glanced at me as the elevator ascended. When the doors whooshed open, I stepped out onto the landing. There was only one door, and I wondered how many people took that elevator, thinking it would bring them to their floor.

"The elevator works on either a key." He held up a key on his keychain, "or fingerprint." He waved his fingers at me with a dimple etched in his cheek. He shrugged. "It's part of being obscenely rich, like my father used to joke about. I never was sure if he was serious, and then he passed away and I got an idea of what we were worth."

"Yeah. I looked you up after Tom told me he paid for the hospital bills," I admitted, and my face reddened.

"I know."

Of course, he knew.

I followed him inside the apartment and glanced around at the barren living room. They had stripped it down to the subfloor and studs on the walls. Even with everything gone, Jennifer William's blood still stained the wood. What had been glass sliders was now just boarded over. The last of the setting sunlight colored the sky over the city through the oversized window next to the boarded sliding doors.

He stared at the spot on the subfloor for a long time. His jaw tightened, and he turned and headed down the hallway. He stopped short of the master bedroom and pointed to the right. "You can stay in there." He opened the door across from mine and headed inside instead of heading into the master bedroom.

I opened the door he had indicated, and no sooner had I dropped my backpack and suitcase on the bed than CJ came in with his arms full of sheets.

"The beds aren't made. Do you want help making yours?" he asked.

"I'm good." I took the sheets from him, and he turned to leave. "Are we supposed to go to sleep now?" It was way too early for me to go to bed.

"I'm tired. I didn't sleep much last night, so..." He shrugged. "Get some rest. I have a feeling we'll both need it tomorrow." He left me to figure out how to make the bed on my own.

After I put the sheets on the mattresses, I wandered around the apartment until I ended up unlocking the sliding doors and stepped out onto the balcony. The view of the city was incredible, and I took a seat in one of the lounge chairs. The air was warmer in New York than it had been up in New Hampshire. The leather jacket I wore provided almost too much warmth, but I knew the moment I peeled it off, I'd end up getting chilly.

My stomach growled. I wished I had thought to grab the snack bag from behind the seat, but I was too busy being overwhelmed by the city again.

When a bag landed on the lounge between my legs, I nearly blasted it with my fire. CJ crossed in front of me with two cans of beer in his hands and took a seat.

"There isn't anything else to drink in the apartment." He handed one to me.

"You could have just poured a glass of water." I glanced at the beer and then at him. "And I'm underage."

He turned the can around so I could read it. Non-alcoholic beer. "Tastes like piss," he muttered after taking a sip of his.

"In that case, I'll pass." I opened April's goody bag and scrounged around for a package of Skittles I thought I'd seen earlier and then offered the bag to CJ. "I thought you were going to go to sleep."

"This place doesn't have a lot of good memories for me. The last time I slept in this apartment was the night before I saw my father being tortured by Lucifer in a warehouse. The time before that, my father died in a warehouse. So... just lying in that bed brought some of those nightmares roaring back." He took a sip of his non-alcoholic beer.

"So, just as long as we stay clear of warehouses, you'll be okay," I muttered under my breath.

CJ spit the beer out in a spray that covered the distance between the chairs and the ledge wall. Coughing and sputtering, he glanced at me like I had just told the world's worst joke.

I peeked into the bag but saw nothing else I wanted. I dropped April's care package on the decking between our chairs and avoided CJ's blatant stare. Even though I wasn't looking at him, I knew his gaze was on me like a laser that jumbled my nerves.

When I finally got the courage to look over, he was squinting up at the darkened sky. His lips turned down, and he lowered his gaze to the city landscape before us.

"You can't see the stars here," I said as I followed the path his gaze had a moment ago.

"No. Even in the dead of night, you can't see the stars in the same way we can in Maine or New Hampshire." He sighed heavily and glanced over his shoulder at the boarded doors. "I should renovate this place and then maybe sell it."

"Why sell it?" I asked, but deep down, I knew. It wasn't a place Tom ever came, either. Not since Lucifer killed their adopted parents. He couldn't stomach coming here.

CJ just nodded. "Tom and I have way too many houses. And someone could be happy here."

"Why renovate? Why not just sell it as is?" It wasn't like he needed the money.

He huffed and nodded. "I should." But even his tone lacked conviction, despite everything he had said. This was the apartment his father had bought when he broke free from his stepbrother. It represented many turning points in his father's life, but most importantly, it was where CJ had been conceived. Despite his hang-ups about being here, it still held a sentimental place in his heart.

"If you were to renovate, what would you do?" I decided we should discuss something less ominous, and maybe it would wipe the frown that had formed on CJ's face away.

His bottom lip disappeared between his teeth, and his head tilted to the side. "I don't know. I might blow out the wall between the kitchen and living room and take that stupid divider between the door and the living room out, and I might make the sliders wider and floor-to-ceiling windows on either side. Put an island in the kitchen to separate the space." He shrugged and glanced at me. "It's not like I haven't thought about it. It's just that I'm not comfortable here."

"I know. Tom wasn't either."

"I would imagine he wouldn't be. Especially since it was his likeness that did the killing." He raised his beer and polished it off in one long pull. "I wish this was real beer instead of this crap." He sneered at the bottle. "There used to be a bar with all sorts of hard stuff, but I couldn't find any of the bottles in the kitchen."

"Should you really be drinking?" I didn't think a hangover would help us if we found Lucifer tomorrow.

"No. You are right. A hangover wouldn't help us, and I wouldn't have the same reaction time that I had today." He raised an eyebrow at me, and heat filled my cheeks.

I probably could have saved myself with the floor giving out under me, but I wasn't sure I could have done anything about the ghosts without setting the building on fire. I nodded my thanks, and a yawn crept up on me.

"Maybe we should try to get some sleep." He gathered his bottles and the bag he had brought out. "I think we're going to need it."

I couldn't argue with him. Suddenly, fatigue claimed my muscles and my eyes drooped from the absence of energy. It was like the sugar crash I'd expected hit with the power of a nuclear bomb.

He held the slider open for me, and then he shuffled to the kitchen while I headed down the hall to the bathroom to begin my evening routine.

Judgement Day
Chapter 10

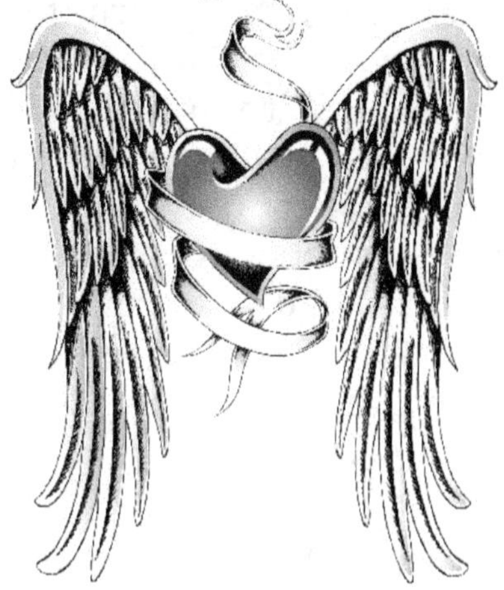

MORNING CAME FAST. OR should I say early afternoon. Both CJ and I slept much longer than we had anticipated. It seemed both our bodies needed it. Besides, we only had two places left on the list.

He had gone out to get breakfast while I cleaned up. When I came out of the shower in my jeans and T-shirt, he was already back, and his bags were next to the door.

"We can eat and then stow our suitcases in the trunk before we head out."

I put my suitcase and backpack next to his and followed him into the kitchen. The table had some pastries laid out along with wrapped sandwiches.

CJ took a seat and unwrapped the sandwich on his side of the table. My mouth watered at the sudden smell of bacon, and I sat and opened mine. Egg and cheese along with bacon poked out from between light and fluffy croissants that melted in my mouth with the first bite.

We didn't speak as we polished off every morsel on the table. With our bellies full and the garbage cleaned up, CJ glanced at me.

"Are you ready for this?"

I laughed and shook my head. "No. But I'm going anyway. Just like you are."

A dimple in his cheek appeared, and it reminded me so much of his son's expression that I sighed. I certainly hoped we could save him. If we couldn't, neither one of us would be the same, assuming we survived.

CJ was quiet as he grabbed the suitcases and headed to the elevator. I followed with my backpack slung over my shoulder. The locks engaged behind me as soon as I closed the front door.

"You're right, you know," he said as we stepped into the waiting elevator.

"How so?"

"No matter how much I want Lucifer dead and gone, I won't be able to kill him while he is possessing my son. I would have been able to do it if he was still wearing Tom's body, but that's only because I know Tom's already in Heaven." He shook his head in disgust. "But Alex..." He closed his eyes and leaned against the back wall.

The doors swished open, and he stepped out onto the concrete of the parking garage and headed towards the car. He opened the trunk and slung the suitcases inside.

When I went to throw my backpack in, he shook his head.

"You're going to need that." He closed the trunk. When he pocketed his keys and started down the ramp on foot, I stared after him. "I'm leaving the car here," he said over his shoulder, and led me outside to the sidewalk.

He raised his hand to hail a cab. A cab pulled up almost immediately. He opened the door and waved for me to get in.

"Whitehall terminal," CJ said after he settled in the back with me.

A cab ride in the city was about as harrowing as walking on the subway tracks had been. I gripped the door handle so hard I thought CJ would have to pry my hand off by the time we stopped. My fingers ached, and it had only been five minutes.

CJ laughed under his breath.

I sent him a scalding glare.

"I thought you liked adventure?"

"Pft. This isn't an adventure. It's just terrifying."

The cab swerved through traffic and honked too many times to count, and when he pulled up to the terminal, I nearly launched myself out of the vehicle. Instead, I pried my fingers from the handle and picked up my bag and coat. Stepping on solid ground gave me a fleeting sense of relief.

CJ ushered me into the terminal and paid for two round-trip tickets, then handed me one as we went to stand in line for the ferry. I pocketed the ticket and put my backpack on the floor in front of me while we waited. It didn't take long to shuffle onto the next ferry.

We went to the top deck and outside as far forward as we could get. CJ leaned on the railing and stared out at the water.

I put on my jacket and hoisted the pack over my shoulder. "Why did we bring this?" I nodded at the heavy pack.

CJ glanced at me. "There are only a few left on the list. It might behoove us to suit up."

I cocked my head. I already had Heaven's blade tucked away in my boot.

"You don't want to tip our hand by using that on anything we come in contact with. That should only be used on Lucifer."

"What's in the bag?"

"Proper outfitting for a battle, at least in Kylee's mind."

Now I really wanted to open the bag and inspect the contents. If she had packed this backpack, I'd bet she loaded it with her special weapons. Of course, I had no real clue of how to wield them, but at least I'd have more than just my fire to protect myself. And in an enclosed space, that seemed to be the more prudent option.

"Bathroom's in there." He nodded towards the weather-protected area.

I didn't need him to tell me twice. I headed inside and found a single restroom with a lock instead of a line of stalls. I dropped the bag on the counter and unzipped it. My leather kick-ass outfit sat on top of the pile, and below it was a note in Kylee's handwriting.

Be badass and take him down. I also have a couple of potion bombs in here for you that will stun anyone, including you and CJ, if you don't throw it far enough, so be careful with those. I am told it should work on Lucifer, too. Suit up, Nephilim. I'll see you when you get back. Kylee.

I glanced in the mirror at my ratty T-shirt and jeans. I hand combed my unruly locks and then braided them in a tight single braid, which made the black leather outfit I'd changed into much more intimidating. I pulled the boots back on, clipped the leg sheaths to my thighs, and slid the knives from the bag into them. Kylee also had a belt studded with Chinese stars. I tucked the potions in my coat pockets and stared at the last thing in the bag. I was not sure whether I wanted to take that out or not. I didn't have a license, and getting caught with a firearm was not an offense to take lightly.

I knew how to use a gun, though, so I took it out and inspected the pistol. It was small enough to tuck into the holster at the back of the star-studded belt, so I ensured the safety was on and tucked it in place before stuffing my clothing in the bag. I slipped the leather jacket over the ensemble and stared at myself in the mirror.

I looked like a cross between Lara Croft and The Road Warrior. Satisfied, I opened the door and ignored the stares as I walked back onto the deck to where CJ stood.

He smiled. "That's the best cosplay outfit I have ever seen," he said loud enough for the people staring at me to hear. The minute he uttered the word cosplay, people stopped staring as if cosplay was a norm in the city.

I'd have to remember that.

I dropped the bag and leaned on the railing as the ferry started its trek across the Hudson River. We passed the Statue of Liberty, and I gawked at it like a tourist. Someday I'd like to come back to the city and explore, just as long as I didn't have to go into those god-awful subways. But then again, the taxi was just as terrifying.

CJ leaned on the railing as well, but his mind was closed, transmitting only static. If I stopped concentrating on the quiet he projected, the noise of the crowd on the boat overwhelmed me. I turned back towards the magnificent cityscape behind us, wondering if this would be the last time I would ever see this view.

"Don't be so melodramatic," CJ muttered.

"I'm a teenager. I have the right to be melodramatic," I said, still staring at the skyline of downtown Manhattan, now with the Statue of Liberty in the foreground. I reached into my pocket and pulled out Alex's phone and snapped a picture before I pocketed it again.

CJ seemed to go into himself as he stared ahead. The crease of concentration between his eyebrows was the only sign I had that he was deep in thought.

I studied his profile, noting the similarities between Alex and his father. They both had dark hair and the bluest eyes. Eyes that you could fall into for days. The strong jawline was definitely the same, but Alex's cheekbones were less pronounced than CJ's. In that manner, Alex looked more like his grandfather than his father. CJ looked a little more aristocratic than Alex, but they both were fine-looking men.

CJ's cheeks reddened, and I realized he had picked up on my internal study of him.

"My son is not a man yet." He slid his gaze to mine.

"I beg to differ," I said, and then pressed my lips together and looked away.

"He's a teenager, just like you are."

I glanced at him. "In your world, when does one become a man? Or a woman in my case?"

"When you turn eighteen." He stared ahead. "Until then, you are children who need guidance and protection."

I started to laugh. "I don't think I need protection."

He slowly raised his eyebrow and looked at me in a silent challenge.

"I don't need protection, but I agree. I need your guidance with my gifts," I conceded. Until I had the same level of refined control that he had, I couldn't claim I didn't need help.

Those dimples I was getting used to appeared just before his smile. It reminded me so much of Alex that I locked my knees in place to keep me steady.

The ferry docked, and we waited for our turn to get off. I let the thoughts of the crowd assault me, blocking out any of my own thoughts as we slowly moved toward our destination. The auras distracted me as much as their thoughts, and those kept me occupied until CJ hailed a cab.

"Greenbelt Recreation Center." He pocketed his phone.

I refocused on him, and silence layered over the din. My nerves prickled. Something hung in the air that caused my hands to itch, and I stared at the driver. When he glanced in the rearview mirror at me, I sensed more than saw an animosity that I didn't understand.

I looked away and pushed into his mind like Valerie had taught me. Our driver disliked Americans, especially strong American women. In his culture, if I went out of the home dressed like I was, I would have been stoned to death in the street.

I pulled out of his hateful thoughts and glanced at CJ. His tight jaw and hard gaze were enough to convey he'd heard the man's judgements as well. While he was harmless to us, the darkness in me wanted to shoot him into oblivion.

"So, Uncle," I said loud enough to be heard over the obnoxious music the driver had playing on the radio.

CJ glanced at me and raised an eyebrow.

"I've decided I want to go to Harvard," I said.

"You're smart enough." He smiled. He knew I was trying to get under the driver's skin, and from the smile on his face, he approved. "And what exactly do you want to do?"

I thought about everything I had read and tossed up so many powerful careers. "I want to be a sex therapist." I smiled demurely.

I think if CJ had liquid in his mouth, he would have spit it all over the cab. The driver nearly choked in the front seat. And I'd accomplished my goal of shocking the bastard. I'd shocked them both.

"Either that or a scientist for NASA," I added.

"You can be whatever you want to be," CJ said, trying not to crack a smile, but the dimples etched into his cheeks told me he was barely containing it.

The driver pulled over after another ten minutes of fuming in the front seat. He let us out at an empty baseball diamond. CJ paid him and gave him a small tip. Much smaller than customary, and then the driver sped away.

"You really do latch onto anything that will provide levity," CJ said, letting his laughter finally surface.

I shrugged and refitted the backpack, clipping it like Kylee had taught me. With a Kevlar backing, I knew my back was covered.

His smile faded as we both looked down the hill. There were several people cheering on a soccer game. CJ pointed to the woods found on the far side of the baseball field, away from the crowd.

"Farm Colony is through those woods," he said.

That dark, ominous feeling that had preceded all the portals brushed against my skin and I shivered. The hair on CJ's arms raised, and we glanced at each other.

"Something's here," I said.

"A whole lot of somethings," he agreed as we stepped into the woods away from the families cheering on their kids.

Each step closer to the hidden buildings left my skin crawling as if a thousand spiders had taken root just under the surface. The itch left behind made me want to scratch every exposed piece of skin until it bled and I got rid of this festering feeling. Hell, I wanted to burn it out. My fingers sparked. I closed my fists, dousing the flames.

The air hummed around us, and my gaze snapped to CJ.

"Just in case," he said. "Just don't bolt after anything, okay?"

I nodded and inspected the shimmering air that moved a foot ahead of wherever we walked. The power in CJ's shield flickered occasionally. I wondered what would happen if someone ran into it.

"They would turn to dust," CJ said as we continued to make our way through the thick trees.

The afternoon sun broke through the canopy sporadically, leaving walls of light dotted through the darkening woods. It was like stepping into a fairy tale land or stepping through time.

The first building we came upon was half gone. The blackened brick crumbled, and what little glass remained were jagged, shattered pieces that didn't want to let go of the windowpane. With a clear line-of-sight right down into the earth and every area open to the elements, neither of us believed Lucifer inhabited the ruins. We didn't bother to navigate the precarious floors that were rotting and sagging with mold. Besides, it radiated nothing other than decay.

We stepped around the ruins and moved on towards the other buildings farther into the woods.

My senses heightened. Every snap of a twig made me jump, and that familiar tingle between my shoulders told me we were being watched. When we entered a grand courtyard with multiple buildings surrounding us, my steps faltered, and I stopped.

CJ stopped when he noticed I was no longer beside him. The shimmer in front of us disappeared as he spun around to stare at me, his wide eyes addressing the sudden panic radiating off him.

For a second, I didn't understand, and then it slammed into me. I nearly got toasted by CJ's force field. If he hadn't noticed I wasn't walking with him so quickly, our bid to take out the devil would have ended with my spontaneous combustion.

The buildings loomed around us, and I stared at the one right behind CJ. My mouth suddenly went dry at the host of spirits milling inside. They weren't kindly either. A cancerous malignance rolled from the building, and my breath caught in my throat.

A blur caught my attention, but before either of us could turn, it slammed into CJ, knocking him clean off his feet. The thump of his skull hitting the broken pavement echoed like a melon smashing.

The snap of bone followed. CJ didn't react.

I ripped the gloves off my hands, but before I could raise my palm to shoot whatever was mauling CJ, arms wrapped around me, pinning mine to my sides. Teeth sank into my shoulder, and I screamed at the flare of pain.

I twisted my hand and let the fire go.

The beast attacking CJ spun towards the pain-filled cry that left my ears ringing. It only took me a second to realize I was free. The monster in front of me charged. I blasted the thing back to Hell, but not before I got a good look at our attacker.

The thing looked worse than the Kapua that Kylee and I had run into in American Samoa. This was some type of cross between a man, and a buck, with claws like the Kapua and teeth like a shark. I shivered and ran to CJ's crumpled form.

Blood flowed from his head, and his arm was bent at an odd angle. The thing had taken a chunk of flesh out of his forearm after snapping it. I peeled my backpack off, grabbed my shirt out of it, and quickly wrapped it tight around where the thing had bitten him.

I straightened his arm and ripped a patch of denim from my jeans to help splint the break. A broken branch lay on the ground within reach, and I grabbed it to use as a splint. I closed my eyes, gripped his arm above and below the break, and took a couple of deep breaths before I snapped it back in place. My stomach rolled, but I swallowed the bile and ripped a second strip of denim from my discarded jeans to tie the splint in place.

After I finished, I leaned forward and put my ear to his chest. His heart remained beating, and I closed my eyes, saying a small prayer of thanks. Next, I tore a bigger strip of denim and inspected CJ's head wound.

I needed to stop the bleeding. I concentrated, making my finger into a cauterizer. A controlled jet of blue flame leaped from my fingertip. I pushed his hair back, staring at the deep cut.

"Sorry, Mr. Ryan," I whispered, and then ran my fire-laced finger across the cut, pulling it away just as quickly. The bleeding stopped instantly as the scent of scalded human flesh drifted on the air.

I closed my fist, dousing the flame, and wrapped the burn with the larger patch of denim. The hair on my arms stood on end. The whir of a blade sliced through the air. I threw myself on top of CJ. My protective instinct flared, and I spun in time to see a blade pierce a large demon that had snuck up behind me.

More than one demon surrounded me. I shivered at the half dozen that stopped when their leader fell to the ground as dead as CJ appeared to be. I snapped my head in the direction that the knife had come from, and my brain stalled.

The woman standing twenty yards away looked so familiar. I blinked at her long dark hair and her nearly golden eyes that reflected amber when the light hit just right. I blinked as her origin bloomed in my brain. She was the demon that got away in the subway system. The one Kylee couldn't find.

Another knife sailed past me, taking down another advancing demon. I made a decision that I hoped wouldn't burn me. I turned towards the demon horde and opened my palms. A combination of angel fire and regular fire shot out, annihilating the demons and leaving only dust hanging in the air, along with a few scalded trees.

I closed my hands and turned back to the woman. She had closed half the distance, and I put my closed fist up. She halted and put her empty hands in the air where I could see them.

"I'm not here to hurt you," she said.

"You're a demon," I growled, tempted to let my fire send her back to Hell. I hovered over CJ protectively. Demons could easily possess the unconscious, and I wasn't about to make that mistake.

She nodded and inspected me closer. Her eyes widened after a moment. "You're the one from the subway." She gasped and covered her mouth. "The one who freed us." Awe filled her voice, like I was the second coming or something equally as ridiculous.

I climbed to my feet, ready to let loose on the next thing that moved, including her. "And you're the one who got away."

Her cheeks bloomed red, and she nodded, averting her eyes. "And I am thankful."

The darkness inside me demanded that I end her, and I recognized where the order was coming from. Lucifer's grace commanded the sacrifice. I clenched my fists tight against the urge.

"Why?" I asked and waved at the two dead demons behind me still bearing her knives.

"I was actually hunting the wendigos." She nodded towards my wounded shoulder. "But they attacked before I had a chance to intercept them."

"And you knew they would be here how?" I still didn't trust her. Gabriel's words about traps kept coming to the forefront of my mind.

"Fate sent me. She said it was imperative that I stop the wendigos." She glanced at CJ, still unconscious on the ground. "Apparently, I did not get here fast enough."

"Fate?" I cocked my head. I forced my mind into the woman's and sure enough, she was telling the truth. Either that or she was very good at manipulating her mind into making me see what she wanted me to. Doubt still tainted my intuition.

She nodded. "As hard as it is to believe, yes."

"What does she look like?"

"Blonde little thing with chestnut eyes. No older than you." She nodded at me.

I lowered my hand and then glanced at CJ as what he'd said in the car resounded in my head. Demons could read me as easily as he had. When I looked back at her, I lifted my hand again.

She put her hands up in front of her. "Fate said I needed to help whoever I ran into here." Her voice shook with fear. "Please," she whispered, begging me with eyes as wide as saucers.

"You want to help? Get these bodies out of here while I call for an ambulance." I pointed at the two remaining demons.

I glanced at the nearest house, and every single ghost was staring out at us. The escaped demon pulled the blades from each dead demon and whispered an incantation. The bodies crumbled to dust.

Unease still scraped over me. I needed to search these buildings for Alex, but I couldn't leave CJ here alone. When the demon approached, I stiffened.

"I'm Phoebe." She stuck out her hand.

I stared at the offering and then glanced up at her. I couldn't bring myself to shake a demon's hand, not even one Fate had sent. She eventually stuck it in her pocket.

"I've never seen someone shoot fire before," she said with reverence. "I could sure use someone like you on my side."

"I don't think so." My voice was cool, and I was sure my stare matched it.

Who the Hell does she think she is? Phoebe crossed her arms.

I straightened at her thought and narrowed my eyes, wondering if I should play my hand. The scowl on her face clinched my decision. "I'm Lucifer's daughter. And I'm looking for him."

Her eyes widened in fear, and she stumbled backwards like I was the devil himself and not his daughter. Her entire body trembled, and her eyes darted around, likely looking for an escape. Her mannerisms didn't convey someone working for that bastard; rather, the opposite.

"He has something that belongs to me, and I want it back," I growled. "Where is he?"

Her laugh was too high, and she took another step back.

"Is Lucifer here?" I asked a little softer and waved at the buildings.

Her head shook back and forth in quick succession. "I would have never set foot on this land if he was here."

"But you're a demon."

"I escaped for a reason," she said. "He would drag me back kicking and screaming and then do to me what he made me do to so many." Her voice trembled with honest terror.

It flowed from her in waves that tightened my throat. Deep down where my never-failing intuition lived, I believed her. Now that all the demons were gone, I did not feel that dark presence overshadowing the land. Only the restlessness of the spirits inside the buildings.

"Go. Get out of here before I raze you and this entire village to cinders." I pointed, and she didn't second-guess my orders. She ran just as fast as she had in the subway tunnel.

I turned back to CJ and pulled out the phone. When Valerie didn't answer her phone, I tried to get CJ up onto his feet. His dead weight was as onerous as Tom's had been, but at least this Ryan was breathing.

"Damn it," I muttered. The swear felt so foreign on my lips. But CJ needed help. Now. I pulled out his phone and dialed nine-one-one.

When the dispatcher answered, I took a deep breath.

"What's the nature of your emergency?"

"My uncle was attacked by some sort of dog out at the Farm Colony. He's unconscious and his arm is broken, and the thing took a bite out of it."

"Your uncle has been bitten by a wild dog?"

"Yes. I've tried to set the bone and splint it and have wrapped the wound with a shirt I had in my backpack."

"When did he lose consciousness?"

"He hit his head on the pavement when he was knocked down and hasn't come to since." In the distance, I heard sirens.

"What's his name, honey?" the dispatcher asked.

I opened my mouth to tell her and then glanced around. "Chris Williams," I said. Neither of us needed the publicity, which would come with CJ Ryan being taken to an emergency room. I pried his wallet from his back pocket, dropped it into the pocket with the potion bag, and then shifted to sit near CJ's head. Closing my eyes, I built a wall of protection around us.

The air shimmered around us.

"The EMTs will be there in a few minutes. They are parked as close to the grounds as possible. Do you want me to stay on the phone with you until they get there?"

"No, ma'am. I need to reach my aunt," I said, and some of my nerves came through on the line.

"It's okay. We can contact your aunt for you if you'd like?"

"Thank you, but I think she would prefer hearing what happened to her husband from me rather than a stranger. But if you just want to stay on the line with me, that would be okay." I closed my eyes. CJ had scanned prior structures today, and I concentrated on doing the same to the surrounding buildings.

I sensed nothing. No living beings, anyway. I went deeper and still found nothing.

Frustration roared in my blood. I was tempted to light up all three buildings with angel fire just to be sure, but Phoebe's terrified face kept flashing before me. That was not manufactured fright.

I shook my head slowly and opened my eyes. If Lucifer were here, scrubbing the place would kill Alex. If Lucifer were here, something else would have attacked us. I was sure of it. But nothing came. I begrudgingly believed my intuition. That wayward demon had been honest with me. Lucifer was not here in this desolate, ghost-ridden place.

When the ambulance technicians breached the clearing with a stretcher, I let my protection barrier fall and followed them out of the woods and into the back of the ambulance, despite the strange looks I kept getting.

"Cosplay," I finally said, and heat bloomed in my cheeks. "Ghost hunting and all." I shrugged. "He refused to wear the Indiana Jones outfit I got him."

Their soft chuckles and evaporation of suspicion put me at ease.

The technician checked CJ's vitals and plugged them into a pad before he pulled off my make-shift bandages. "Definitely broken." He winced at the bite. "I've never seen a dog bite like this," he muttered and bandaged it enough to staunch the bleeding. After he looked closer at CJ's temple, he glanced at me. "Did you do this?" He pointed to the cauterized wound.

It didn't look as bad as the open gash had, but it was still gnarly.

I shrugged. "He was bleeding, and that was something I knew how to fix."

"Were you trained in doing this?" he asked and applied a burn salve to the wound. There was an edge to his voice.

"No. Why?"

"Because it was done as neatly as a professional." He glanced at me. "And you don't look old enough to have taken one E.M.T. course. Never mind the years this kind of precision requires." This time his voice carried envy, and I understood the edge. He considered himself one of the best in the area, and he would have never done as clean of a job as I had.

"I've had some practice." I waved at CJ. "How is he overall?"

"His vitals are good, but he took quite the hit in the head, so I'm not sure if he'll wake up tonight. You did a great job with the splint and the tourniquet, so I think you may have saved him some nerve damage, but he lost a pretty sizeable chunk of flesh, so I'm not sure whether that will have any lasting effects. He was lucky it was his forearm and not his hand." He nodded towards my shoulder. "I probably should look at that."

I glanced at the torn fabric of my leather jacket and frowned. "I'm okay."

"Take off the jacket," he said.

As uncomfortable as I was, I did as he asked and winced as I pulled the leather off my left shoulder.

He took a quick look. "Can you move your shirt so I can clean the cuts for you?" he asked. "They aren't deep, but they should be cleaned so you don't get an infection."

I unthreaded my arm from the shirt and pulled it so he could work on the wounds. The cleaning agent he used stung when he swabbed the cuts, and then he put some small bandages on them.

"Your leather jacket saved you from the same type of damage as your uncle," he said as he put the last bandage on. "You can put your shirt back on."

I threaded my arm back into my shirt, then slipped it into my leather jacket and sat back. I pulled CJ's phone from my pocket and dialed Valerie.

"Hello?" she said, out of breath.

"Aunt Val?" I asked over the sirens.

"What's that in the background?"

"There's been an accident," I started, and the immediate panic from the other side of the line filled me. "No one died," I added quickly. "It's just that Uncle CJ's been knocked out. He got attacked by a... wild dog."

"Where are they taking him?"

"Where are we going?" I asked the tech.

"Staten Island University Hospital in Midland Beach area."

"I heard him. We will be down there in a couple of hours. Just hang tight and keep him safe."

"I will. See you when you get here." I hung up the phone and texted her the name I used for him. "My aunt will be here in a couple of hours."

"Can you give me a little information before we get to the emergency room?"

I nodded.

"His name?"

"Chris Williams," I said.

"And where are you from?"

"New Hampshire." I couldn't remember the name of the town the cottage was in, but I remembered the name of the town the airfield was in. "Wolfeboro, New Hampshire."

"Do you know if he has insurance?"

"I really don't know." I shifted in the seat.

The technician checked his pockets. "He isn't carrying a wallet."

I bit my lower lip and shrugged like I didn't have a clue what he was talking about. But the weight of his wallet lay against my side, along with one of the potion bombs in my pocket. Thankfully, he hadn't said anything about the gun tucked into the holder on my belt in the back. At least not yet.

He sat back and stared at me. "Are those knives real?" he asked and pointed to the sheaths on my thighs.

"Yes. I couldn't pull Tomb Raider off without real blades." I rolled my eyes.

"And your uncle didn't have a problem with that?" He checked CJ's pulse again.

"He wasn't all that pleased," I mumbled and tried to smile. "A lot of good they did against the wild dogs. I completely forgot I had them."

He smiled. "Then how'd you get rid of the one that bit your shoulder?"

"I elbowed it in the ribs as hard as I could. I guess I spooked him, and then I ran towards the one attacking my uncle, screaming like a wild child."

He pressed his lips together to stop the smile, but it didn't work. "I'm impressed. Running off wild dogs and cauterization skills. If you were a few years older, I would ask you out on a date.”

The heat that encompassed my face was born of pure embarrassment, and I didn’t know how to respond except to look at the floor and pray CJ would wake up and save me from this awkwardness.

The ambulance pulled to a stop in front of the emergency room, and we were shuffled inside. They tried to tell me to wait in the waiting room, and I influenced their minds to let me stay in the same room.

When the nurse shoved me paperwork allowing treatment, I glanced it over and then looked up at her.

“I’m not authorizing you to do anything beyond dressing his wounds and setting his broken arm.” I handed the clipboard back to her. “His wife will be here in a couple of hours. Unless you are telling me he is in mortal danger, then I would prefer to wait for her.”

“The doctor won’t know unless we do a CT scan.” She shoved the forms back at me.

“Can I be in the room with him?” I asked, with my pen poised over the paper.

“No.”

I put the pen back under the clip and handed her the board. “Then the answer is not until my aunt arrives. I am only relaying what my aunt requested.”

Her lips pressed together in aggravation.

“Dress his wounds and set his broken arm, and then she will look at him when she arrives.” I crossed my arms. “My aunt is a doctor,” I added. "Besides, I'm not eighteen. I can't authorize care."

Her gaze narrowed at me. "The doctor will be in to take a look at him soon." She marched out of the room in a huff.

I lowered into the chair next to the bed and stared at CJ. Nothing came from his mind. I shifted uncomfortably.

I fished out his wallet, pulled out the wad of cash tucked inside, and zipped it into an interior pocket of my coat. I stuffed the wallet back and pulled out his phone, then sent a quick text to Valerie about when she would arrive.

The phone rang, and I answered it.

"We are less than ten minutes from landing and there is a car waiting, so a half hour at the latest. Is he okay?"

"Still unconscious, and they wanted to do a bunch of tests. I didn't sign the release for them to do a CT scan. Is that okay?"

"I'll check him when I get there," she said. "If my presence doesn't wake him, then we will have to do some tests."

The strain in her voice left me shivering with guilt. I should have seen this coming or been faster. I wiped my face, trying not to let this failure drag me down farther into despair, but I couldn't help it. Every doubt magnified. Without CJ, I wasn't sure I could do this, but I had to.

"You'll be fine for another thirty minutes?"

"Yes, but when you get here, I need to go."

"I'll have the car wait for you and bring you over to the apartment where everyone else is going."

"Okay. See you soon." I disconnected the call.

I had no intention of going to the apartment. I still had one more place on the list, and while I waited, I researched Hudson River State Hospital using CJ's phone. It looked like the place where my worst nightmares could come to life. It seemed even worse than Willard Asylum had been. I shivered and took notes on the address and places nearby because I did not want to be recognized by anyone, much less a cab driver dropping me off at the door of a place that ended up being torched.

Judgement Day
Chapter 11

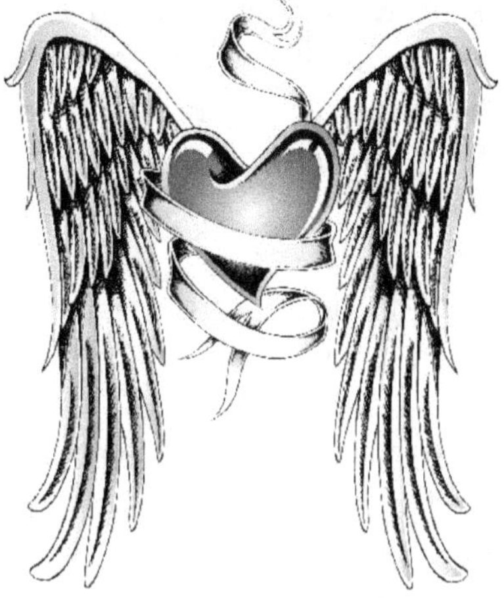

VALERIE STEPPED INTO THE room a half an hour later as the nurse was taking CJ's vitals. "How is my husband?" she asked, crossing and taking his hand.

The nurse narrowed her gaze at Valerie and then glanced at CJ, studying him closer. Her eyes widened.

"His name isn't Chris Williams, is it?" she whispered. She had already recognized them. Valerie had been on television almost as much as CJ, and her presence made all the wheels in the nurse's mind click.

"He is Chris Williams." I pushed my influence on the nurse harder than I intended.

The nurse stumbled back a step, and Valerie glared a warning at me.

"How is he?" she asked again, and the nurse blinked and glanced at her chart.

"His right ulna and radius are fractured, and a chunk of flesh was torn out of his forearm. As you can see, we have a partial splint to immobilize his arm so the open wound can be addressed." She waved at CJ still unconscious on the bed.

"What about the bandage on his head?"

The nurse looked at me. "Your niece cauterized his head wound in the field. I'll go get the doctor." She turned and left the room.

Valerie waited until the nurse was out of sight and then leaned over and pressed a kiss on CJ's forehead. The familiar light danced over him, and his jaw tightened, showing the first sign of a reaction since he fell.

I took that as my cue and handed CJ's wallet and phone over to Valerie. "I took the cash in his wallet in case I needed a cab." I pulled it out and offered it to her.

She waved my hand away. "Keep it. The car is waiting out front for you. We'll see you back at the apartment once we are released," she said softly as she watched for motion in the door.

I glanced back at CJ before I stepped out of the room. Color had returned to his cheeks, but I would bet that if they removed the bandage on his head, the burn mark would still be there. Valerie's healing power didn't penetrate injuries that my fire caused, just like her powers didn't heal me. It seemed my fire-born abilities and their results couldn't be wiped away with pure angel magic.

I turned and headed out of the emergency room bay doors. The town car sat idling in a parking space, and I crossed to it. The driver opened the back door for me and waved me inside.

"Instead of taking me to the apartment, can you take me to Marist College in Poughkeepsie?" I asked.

"Mrs. Ryan had strict instructions..." he started.

"Take me to Poughkeepsie," I said softly and pushed with my mind.

"As you wish," he said with a smile as he helped me into the vehicle and closed the door behind me.

Two hours later, the driver pulled into the college campus and stopped in the parking lot, his headlights illuminating a small piece of it.

I pulled out a fifty from the cash in my pocket and handed it to him. "Thank you. When you get back, you can let the Ryans know where you dropped me." I stepped out of the car and waited until it pulled out of sight before I headed towards the Home Depot sign I had seen before we pulled into the campus. The grounds of Hudson River State Hospital were beyond the massive construction store, and if it were too close, I couldn't see this being a place that Lucifer would camp out in.

As I crossed the street and took to the narrow sidewalk, the hair on my arms rose and my skin itched. I knew I should find a hotel room and rest for the night, but I wanted to do some reconnaissance on the layout of the state hospital campus before I went barreling in.

The closer I got to the nearest building, the more my chest tightened. I crouched behind an overgrown bush and looked between three structures closest to the Home Depot parking lot. A high-rise building, a smaller building next to the high-rise, and a concrete monstrosity.

According to the research I had done at the hospital, there was much more to this asylum than just these three buildings, but they were the first of the sprawling campus and the closest to civilization.

The wind shifted, and all I could smell was wet, burned wood and Death. I covered my mouth, and again second-guessed my wisdom of being here alone.

Movement out of the corner of my eye pulled my attention towards the concrete building. A rat scurried across a patch of whitened concrete and into a hole in the wall. I suppressed a shiver and looked back at the large building. It was too close to civilization. I closed my eyes and concentrated. I couldn't read any of the buildings here, so I pushed my mind farther, but I couldn't sense anything in the space except an ominous cloud that wouldn't allow me to penetrate it.

I turned and glanced at the box stores behind me and did the same thing. The noise that filled my head made me cover my ears. Not only did thoughts accost me, but the living souls caressed me with warmth. I focused back on the black hole before me. Even in the Farm colony on Staten Island, I felt the ghosts' energy.

The absence of anything pushed me forward, and I darted across the lawn towards the large brick building with EVAK and TOAST spray painted in white, which stood out even in the semi-darkness.

I made it to the door tucked in the middle of the building with my heart pounding, and I leaned against it to catch my breath. Iron chains blocked the door, so I closed my eyes, concentrating on breaking the metal. The rattle and thump on the overgrown path followed. I opened my eyes and tried the doorknob, but it didn't budge. Still holding the knob, I concentrated on unlocking it from the inside. The creaking of the lock turning was loud enough to set my nerves on edge.

I twisted, and the door opened. Dust and decay wafted out with a hiss of air. I coughed and covered my mouth. I paused because I did not want to cross the threshold until the tickle in my nose abated. With a final sneeze, I stepped through the door and closed it behind me. Darkness enveloped me. I let the sparks on my fingers turn to a controlled flame, lighting a small area before me.

I moved slowly and took shallow breaths, but even so, the air left my mouth stale and dry, like it was trying to turn me into a relic like the building itself. I used the walls as a barrier between me and my back, always trying to make sure nothing could come from that direction. The floor creaked under my weight, and each step announced my presence.

I paused and pulled a blade into my free hand before I stepped out of the trashed lobby and into the long, dark hallway that led into the belly of the building.

Nothing stirred. I kept to the side of the hallway, avoiding the middle that occasionally sagged, but even that didn't stop the groaning of the boards under me. Leading with the knife, I shuffled halfway down, peeking in each room to see if it matched Gabriel's description or showed any indication of similarity to what I saw on television.

It was darker than either, but it was nighttime, so no light but my flame penetrated the darkness. When I closed my hand, blackness engulfed me. The kind that made my heart drum in my chest and my saliva dry in my mouth. Dust tickled my nose and I stayed still in the dark, leaning against the wall.

I used my otherworldly senses and spread my essence throughout the building like I had on Staten Island, but I took my time. In my mind's eye, I was actually walking from room to room, starting on the top floor and moving downward until I happened upon my form, standing like a frozen sentry.

Nothing sparked my senses. Not even spirits. The complete absence of anything, even a rodent, made me pause. I opened my eyes and unclenched my fist, letting the fire lick my fingers and light up the hallway.

I hadn't gone down to the basement because the thought gave me a shiver. The stairwell was just a few steps away, across the sagging floor. I hurried across, trying to be light on my feet. The creak that ripped through the hallway claimed my breath. My foot sank, and I leaped the remainder of the way.

The floor where I had catapulted from crumbled away, leaving a small hole that seemed to grow with each lasting vibration. I escaped into the stairwell and nearly teetered off the landing into an abyss below. I grabbed the railing to steady myself. Of course, my fire went out. I stood still in the blackness with my breath coming in ragged pulls.

I tucked the knife away in the sheath and let my fingers spark into a flame. The entire building seemed to shake now. I was only a few hundred feet from the entrance, but when I looked back into the hallway, most of the floor had caved into the darkness below. Either way was going to be difficult.

I had no idea what was below, but at this point, I had ruled out this building, and now with the floor caving into the basement, I doubted Lucifer would put himself in such a precarious position.

Alex's phone buzzed in my pocket, but I didn't have the time to answer it. I had to decide which way I was going to go before this building collapsed on me. I chose the hallway and jumped from edge to edge like Kylee and I had done across the quicksand.

I fell out the front door onto the grass and scrambled to my feet as the rumbling got louder. I ran towards the concrete building to the right side of the monstrous structure before the middle section dipped noticeably, tilting the side wings drastically enough so people would notice at first light. A plume of dust puffed out the door, but I was out of the debris zone by the time it cleared.

I stumbled and fell on the grass, trying to catch my breath. I sat up and stared at the building. That was just too convenient to be a coincidence. I was positive now that Lucifer was somewhere on this campus.

The phone buzzed again, and I pulled it out of my pocket, answering it with a swipe.

"Hello?" I said, still panting.

"F-Faith?"

"Mr. Ryan?"

"Y-yes. Th-they w-want me t-to s-stay overnight f-for observation."

Hearing him struggle to speak broke my heart. It meant the hit on his head was worse than I had thought. "Is Valerie there?"

The phone shuffled.

"Faith, where are you?" she asked, concern flooding her voice.

"I'm fine," I said, ignoring her question. "Your mojo didn't fix him?"

She took a deep breath. "It will, but sometimes when it's this serious, it takes time. The hit to his head triggered his stutter again. But it should be fine by morning. By the way, the cauterization job you did was fantastic. You sure you don't want to go into the medical field?"

I laughed softly. "Yes, I'm sure." I would be a disaster in an operating room.

"T-tell her to w-wait f-for me," CJ said in the background.

"Tell him to get some rest. I'll be careful," I said, not really answering him. I disconnected the call before he could get into my head. I had no intention of waiting. Not when I knew Lucifer was here, and I was pretty sure he knew someone had breached one of the buildings.

If anyone else had gone into that building besides me... I shivered at the thought of them falling through the floor and having the building partially implode on them.

I tucked the phone into my pocket and climbed to my feet. The light from the Home Depot parking lot cast long shadows over the land between me and the concrete building. I was out in the open, so I bolted to the nearest tree and leaned against it as my heart pounded at my stupidity.

Despite the adrenaline still surging in my veins, the aches and pains of the day were rearing their heads. My shoulder throbbed in time with my heartbeat and my legs ached from being in a car for so long. I was glad I was on my feet.

I took a moment to assess the building I was heading for. The geometric pattern of it struck me as odd, but it was concrete, so unless Lucifer had it wired with explosives, it would probably be the safest building here. The door hung on the frame in the entry, and it swayed any time the wind blew, creaking and in need of some oil to stop the grating sound.

I scanned the rest of the area and then zeroed my focus on the door. Before I reached the count of three in my head, I was bolting across the open field. Thankfully, I was wearing black. At least my clothes blended in with the night.

I maneuvered around the door without touching it and squared myself with my back to the open air. I stepped as lightly as I could. The floor was solid and didn't announce my presence as I made my way across the graffiti-decorated entry.

Shadows filled the area, but at least I could see in the semi-darkness thanks to the lighting filtering in from the parking lot across the barren field. The farther in I got, the more the light faded, and dusty decay filtered into my nose, causing me to itch before I sneezed.

Unfortunately, I'd never been able to sneeze quietly, so when three escaped in quick succession, the echo filled the concrete chambers, bouncing against the walls until it returned to me like a mountain yodel.

Whatever element of surprise I had was surely killed.

Still, I moved forward with flames licking my fingers for light. When I stepped beyond the weirdly placed walls and into the main hall, I stopped. That familiar itch centered between my shoulders. I imagined my deadly barrier surrounding me, and I stepped forward, more sure of myself now that I had my protection up.

Something leaped from the dark. I didn't have time to react. It hit me with the force of a car, sending me flying into the hard wall. My barrier hadn't worked, but my fire certainly did. I sent a plume in the direction it came. An inhuman shriek of pain filled the air, and I glimpsed a large entity moving out of my sight. A moment later, the door banged on its hinge.

I had hurt whatever it was pretty badly from the scent of burned flesh hanging on the air, but I didn't know if it was a fatal blow or not.

I counted to ten to get my nerves settled, then continued crossing the open space to the sets of doors on the other side. I made it halfway across when four shadows surrounded me. I grabbed the knives and let the flames engulf them. I hoped the metal wouldn't melt, but a flaming knife was much more intimidating than just a blade. The shadows paused, but then they charged forward.

I spun with my arms wide and let an arc of angel fire loose. The shadows burst into ash hanging on the air like a fog that choked me. I coughed and stumbled through what was left of the dead.

I reached for the door and was tackled. My injured shoulder hit the ground hard. Hard enough to rip a yelp out of me and send one of my knives bouncing over the hard ground. I tried to use the other one, but whatever had tackled me had its full weight crushing down on me. He knocked the knife away easily.

A fist landed a punch on my side, knocking the breath out of me. I tried to roll, but he wouldn't let me.

"We've got you now." His growling voice snarled in my ear.

"That's what you think," I muttered and mentally pushed. Nothing happened. I kicked my foot and miraculously hit the magic spot between the bastard's legs.

He "oofed."

I was able to roll enough to send a blast of fire at him that threw him into the wall, where he crumpled to the ground before exploding to dust.

I struggled to my feet and crossed to where my knives had gone, then sheathed one of them with shaking hands. I obviously needed my hands free in case there was another attack.

"Six down..." I muttered to myself and took a deep breath. It seemed only my fire powers were consistent, and I glanced around at the building again, thankful that it was concrete and not wood.

My side ached where I had been punched. I closed my eyes, mentally searching my immediate surroundings. Nothing came through. I snarled low. Now I was sure Lucifer was on the grounds somewhere, and I wondered if he was the one who was stopping me from using the Ryans' powers and not my own epic failure.

I let flame lick my fingers and took a deep breath before stepping through the darkened doorway. I didn't even make it over the threshold when something grabbed my wrist and swung me around into the wall hard enough to knock my breath from my lungs.

Another hand gripped my free wrist and raised both hands over my head. Weight pressed against me with enough force to nearly crush my ribs.

"You're a feisty one," he growled in my ear.

I wiggled my hands to the right angle and let them ignite with the same fire I used to cauterize CJ's wounds.

The pressure holding me to the wall released with a hiss, and I was tossed farther into the room. A yelp ripped from my mouth when my hip connected with the concrete.

The shuffle of more than two feet catapulted my pulse into overdrive. I clenched my fists, dousing the flame and plunging the room into absolute black. I crouched low and listened as I attempted another force field.

Even with the panic slowly filling my cells, I couldn't muster up the same energy that I had on the island with Kylee. Nothing buzzed in the air to signify success. I pressed my lips together and concentrated.

Is Lucifer in here? Is he watching this slow torture?

Noise came from my right. I shot a plume of flame in that direction, lighting up the entire room and missing my mark by a couple of yards. My stomach plummeted at the six demons surrounding me. Six armed demons with feral grins that nearly let my bladder loose.

I had nowhere to run, either. The only exit was the door I had come in, and there were three demons blocking my escape. I closed my hand again, and spots flared in my vision.

I stood and put my arms out, splaying my fingers and sending jets of fire in both directions, hoping I would hit at least two. My aim was off, and I only succeeded in torching one before the business end of a whip lashed around one of my forearms.

I screamed at the sting. The yank that followed nearly tore my arm from the socket. I fell. But this time, I had a lead on where the whipping demon was. One blast took him out. I rolled away, grabbing the whip and pulling it towards me so no one got the same idea.

The others had moved closer. With only four, I wasn't sure just blasting haphazardly would work, but that was my only option. My hand knocked the knife hilt on my thigh as I turned clockwise.

I bit my lip and pulled one out, listening closely. I launched the blade towards the nearest shuffle and was rewarded with a groan. I opened my palm in the same direction and unsheathed the second knife.

I blasted the demon trying to remove the knife from his thigh and shot the knife at the closest one to him. Unfortunately, that one dodged the blade, but he wasn't able to dodge my flame.

I didn't have time to turn before the last two demons tackled me. The fool who stepped on my wrist to pin it obviously didn't understand physics. My aim was dead on, and he went up like an old dried-out Christmas tree.

The one lying on top of me went to slap something on my wrist. His lips peeled back in a growl that promised all sorts of pain. But he wasn't fast enough to stop my initial blast before metal encased my wrist.

His dust choked me, and I coughed and rolled onto my hands and knees. I waited, mentally counting my attackers in my head. I thought that made a dozen demons, but I was so disoriented in the dark that I couldn't be sure. My hands wouldn't spark and the spit in my mouth dried as I tried to pry the metal off my wrist.

A chain attached to the cuff scraped the ground, and I yanked at it, pulling link after link until I reached the other end holding a similar cuff to the one clamped on my wrist. Relief flooded through me. I wasn't attached to anything.

I needed to get out of here and wait for CJ. I could not do this on my own. Not with whatever this thing was on my wrist. I turned around, searching the dark until I could make out the door. I took a step toward the change in light, and something hard connected with the side of my head. Stars transitioned to blackness so thick I could hardly breathe.

Judgement Day
Chapter 12

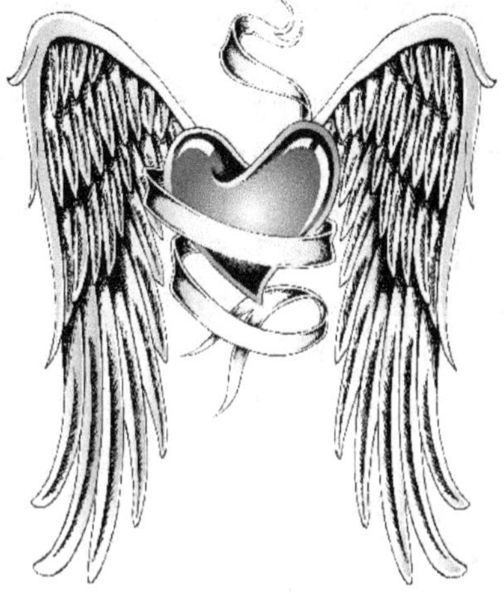

THE FIRST THING I became aware of was that every inch of my body ached. The second was the foulest smell I'd ever encountered. Worse than the subways and worse than anything I ran across in Hell, including the slaughter yard.

I couldn't turn my head away from the stench, and my arms and legs wouldn't work to turn me so I could run.

Blinking, I tried to reconcile what my eyes were seeing through the limp strands of my red hair. I gagged and tried to curl up against the cramping. Bloated bodies lay on the concrete a few feet from where I stood, and a couple of bodies were chained to the wall, each form in various stages of decay.

I attempted to flip my hair out of my face, and that's when my gaze landed on him.

He smiled at me, and my heart melted. Damn my father for using Alex's smile against me. Grace kneeled next to him in shackles, the necklace holding Alex's soul hanging from her neck. She looked every bit as insane as Gabriel had said she was. It wasn't a surprise to me. I couldn't envision spending twenty minutes with Lucifer, never mind close to six months.

She straightened so I could see her fully. The protrusion of her belly made my throat close against a thin stream of vomit.

I looked away, and my eyes caught what held me in place. My wrists were chained, each to an opposite wall, and shackles held my legs in place. At least I was still wearing my boots, which meant he probably hadn't done a full search of the weapons I had at my disposal.

I closed my eyes, searching the shackles with my mind, trying to feel it out like CJ had taught me. When my silent command to release echoed in my mind, nothing happened. I opened my eyes and yanked. Again, nothing.

These were the same type of cuffs that the demon had secured on my wrist. Hot panic pulsed in my temple.

He looked on with a bemused smile, and his hands clasped before him.

I struggled, yanking at both my wrists and my ankles. The panic mounted at my inability to break free. The power coiled inside, but I couldn't release it.

"Sigils." He nodded towards my wrist bonds. "I had them specially forged to keep you from tapping your power. They would work on CJ Ryan as well if he dared show his face."

"You son of a bitch," I breathed. The curse felt dirty in my mouth.

I glanced down at my legs. None of the weapons I'd had when I stepped onto the asylum grounds were still attached.

"Looking for these?" he asked as he stood and dropped the knives I'd had attached around my legs. And then he crossed, reached around me, and pulled out the gun I'd had tucked in the back of my pants.

Just his close proximity and his arms around me sent my heart into overdrive. Both attraction and revulsion brewed in my blood. He undid the clip and tossed it away. Next, he raised the ninja stars that had been on my belt before he shot them into the bodies hanging from the wall.

"Or this?" He held up the potion that had been in my coat pocket.

I glared at him as if he had stripped me of all my hidden gems, and I tried to move my legs.

When he pulled Heaven's blade out from behind him, my heart plummeted.

"I'm guessing this is what you really were hoping we wouldn't find. It was so cleverly hidden inside your boot. The boots that the boy recognized immediately." He inspected the knife in the small space between us. "You do understand I have the memories associated with this body."

I held my breath, staring at the blade, terrified.

He looked beyond the blade, wearing Alex's thoughtful expression.

"Let Alex go," I said with authority. I knew it was foolish, but I had to try.

He smiled, and amusement danced in his eyes. He placed the tip of the knife to my neck. "You never should have been born."

I swallowed, and the chains rattled with the shakes that gripped me.

Instead of slicing my skin and erasing me from existence, he leaned closer. "I am conflicted." He leaned back and met my gaze. "While I would love to run you through with this knife, that would annihilate my grace which lies within you." He turned and placed the blade on the bench and returned to the spot in front of me. "Just in case I get carried away."

The hardness in his eyes belied the softness of his voice. I broke out in gooseflesh, more scared now that he didn't have the knife in his hands. He grabbed my shirt and tore it in half, exposing my skin.

"I find the attraction that this boy feels for you strange."

He was close enough for me to feel the heat radiating from him. He ran his hand down my cheek, but I pulled away from him.

"The boy is having an all-out fit right now. He's worried that I might act on his *feelings*." Lucifer enunciated feelings as if it were a dirty word.

If I could have kicked him, I would have, but all I could do was level a glare that I hoped would give him pause.

He just laughed. "He knows your greatest fear," he whispered and ducked under my bound arm. He pressed against my back and wrapped his arm around my throat, squeezing my neck with the inside of his elbow. "And he knows you are going to die today."

I couldn't claw him away. I couldn't fight. I was completely helpless. My airway constricted with the force of his tightening arm. I yanked at the cuffs holding me in place, and they dug into my skin.

His arm released slowly. "But you won't die of asphyxiation," he whispered in my ear as he reached around my waist and unbuckled my belt from behind.

I snapped my head back, connecting with him. The growl that came from behind was followed by a punch to my kidney. My breath locked in my chest as spiraling pain pulsed through my body.

He went back to pulling my belt loose. He smacked my legs with it, pulling a hiss from my already tight lungs.

He slowly paced in front of me. "You've caused me quite a bit of grief since your mother died. I think perhaps it's only fair to repay the favor." He spun and his fist connected with my nose.

White light flashed, and then heat like someone had put an iron on the middle of my face blasted through my nose. I gagged on the hot liquid sliding down my throat. My face throbbed in time with my heartbeat. I didn't scream, though. I was too shocked to make a noise. I blinked the lights away and spit at him.

The light in the necklace around Grace's neck became chaotic, like Alex's soul was struggling to be freed from his glass prison.

I couldn't wipe the blood from my face. It dripped on the black leather of my jacket.

Lucifer licked his lips as he stared at the blood dripping from my chin. His fist connected with my stomach. "When I am done with you, the screaming fool in my head will finally shut up." He landed bruising punches to my torso and then swiped one of my knives off the ground.

He stared at me with a cruel expression I had never seen on Alex. He twirled the knife and looked at my wrists like he was contemplating cutting my hands off. Instead, he flicked the knife, cutting my chin.

He looked at my pants, and the evil gleam in his eyes chilled me.

He leaned closer and pressed the blade against my stomach, leaving a thin cut. "He's always wanted to taste you." Lucifer dropped the knife, and it clattered on the ground as he swiped a thin strip of blood onto his finger. He slid it into his mouth suggestively and closed his eyes as he sucked it clean. "I'm sure that wasn't what he had in mind." He winked at me and picked up the belt, moving behind me again.

Drawing air was difficult, and he made it more of a challenge when he wrapped the belt around my throat and yanked, nearly crushing my airway.

"Do I kill you now?" he whispered in my ear. "Or do I make you watch?"

I shivered with revulsion and struggled in the chains, pulling one foot up and then the other. The wheeze from my mouth was the only noise I could make.

He snapped his fingers. Grace crawled over the arm of the chair, and she had the audacity to grin at me as she spread her legs in a wide invitation.

He sauntered to Grace with a grin. "Here kitty, kitty," he said in the same seductive tone I'd heard in my dreams.

I screamed breathlessly and struggled in the chains, closing my eyes against what I knew was coming. Lucifer whistled.

A hand grabbed a fistful of my hair and pulled my head back, tightening the belt on my neck. A large hideous demon stared at me. His disfigured face made me blink. It sported the scars of a burn. A burn I probably delivered. His slow smile sent a rush of frigid air over my body.

I didn't think I had left any demons alive, but then again, I had been knocked out by something. My guess was it had been this monstrosity.

"Make sure she watches." He approached Grace from behind as he unbuttoned his pants. "If she doesn't, make sure she feels it."

In that instance, I hated him with every fiber. I didn't care who he was wearing. I was going to rip his heart out with my bare hand.

I kept my gaze on the ceiling. Even when the demon's hand wandered over my torso. He pushed down on a bruise and chuckled when I winced.

"She feels so good," he purred in my ear.

I clenched my teeth and yanked at my legs. The bolt holding my feet loosened. I kept struggling and staring at the ceiling as this creature held my head in place and rubbed his body against my back like we were at an orgy and I was fair game.

"I will burn his soul," Lucifer growled.

My gaze snapped to him. He smiled as he held Grace's hips and rode her hard. He knew that threat would bring my gaze to him, and he knew I wouldn't ever be able to unsee the lewd scene. He closed his eyes, and an expression of ecstasy appeared on his face. The same one I had seen on Alex's face in the panic room when he'd made love to me.

My heart clenched.

"You bastard," I whispered, choking on blood and tears.

He smiled.

I had inspected enough of CJ and Tom's memories to understand what he was doing. If by some blind luck we made it out of here, this moment was meant to make it impossible for me to fall into Alex's arms again.

I knew his tricks.

I knew his twisted mind.

And there was no way this side of Hell I was going to let him win.

He shuddered with a throaty groan and then pulled out, swatting Grace's behind. She obediently sat back down on the floor by his throne, her face pained, like what he had done was no pleasure for her whatsoever.

That small tell gave me a flair of satisfaction.

He zipped himself up and crossed, waving the demon back to wherever he had been stationed. The belt around my throat loosened. He stared at me, and I struggled in the chains, yanking one foot and then the other.

"Want to know a secret?" he whispered and stepped too close. "He thinks she's much better than you were." He pulled back enough to look into my eyes.

His proximity offered me an opportunity, and the sudden flare of fury took control. I slammed my knee upwards, and the bolt in the floor sheered, freeing my feet. My knee connected to his groin.

"Liar," I hissed.

The "oof" that escaped his lips, followed by his slow descent to the floor, gave me a weird sense of satisfaction. I kicked out, aiming for his reddened face.

He rolled out of the way. His glare was as deadly as the fire raging through my blood.

His hands curled into fists again and he slowly stood and stepped close like he was purposely tempting fate.

I tried to knee him again, but he grabbed my knee in his hand and squeezed. Hard. Hard enough to do damage.

Burning pain gripped my leg. I ripped it from his grasp with the small latitude of movement I had. I kicked his shin with a growl.

His jaw tightened. "The boy tells me he will kill me if I so much as touch you again. That would be a neat trick since he's on lockdown," he said through grinding teeth. His fierce anger made me shake, and my tremors shook the chains holding me in place. He stepped close, and I caught the brimstone scent of his breath. "Enough of this game. I want *my* grace back."

I braced myself for the pain, but it didn't help. A cry still ripped out of me when his fingernails dug into my skin. A cry with Alex's true name on it echoed off the walls, shaking the foundation we stood on.

I needed Alex to take control.

I needed him to stop this, or otherwise, I was as dead as I wanted Lucifer.

The light in the orb around Grace's neck flared just before the glass shattered. The brightness shot like a bullet and slammed into Lucifer with the power of a lightning bolt. His skin lit up like a true Nephilim as Alex's soul knocked Lucifer clean out of his body.

Black smoke swirled. My eyes widened at Alex standing in front of me. My Alex. His aura radiated white, and there was a power in it that had never been there before.

Grace roared, struggling against her chains at the turn of events.

Alex's angry blue eyes met mine, and he tore his nails from my skin while the black smoke formed behind him. He dug into his pocket and pulled a key out. The key to the shackles. He unclasped my right hand and moved to the other shackle.

The black smoke coiled to strike.

"Watch out!" I splayed my right hand over Alex's shoulder, aiming my palm towards the oncoming smoke as he worked the lock for my other wrist.

The moment the shackle released, fire shot out. Lucifer's soul dodged it, twirling away. He slammed into Grace with such force, her own soul didn't have a prayer. Lucifer consumed her, and the chains holding her in place shattered.

Before Alex could turn towards the oncoming danger, Lucifer launched, turning into Grace's tiger in midair. He hit Alex hard enough to drive him into the ground a few feet away from me.

Alex bellowed as the tiger's claws ripped into his shoulders.

I lunged for Heaven's blade, swiping it off the bench, and threw myself at them while praying my blind aim was true. The blade ripped through the tiger's flank before it scraped on the concrete floor.

The tiger bellowed and shot a glare at me. I propped myself up on my elbow with the blade gripped tightly in my hand. Lucifer's eyes went to the knife and then widened as the transition turned him from a tiger back into Grace's form.

"You bitch," Lucifer said in a weakened female voice.

"Damn straight," I said.

Alex's face filled with fury, and he shoved Grace's form away from him. When he put his hand out to me, I knew what he wanted. I slid the blade across the ground and Lucifer lunged for it, but Alex was faster, even with his injuries.

He snatched it, and before Lucifer could scramble away, in one violent motion, Alex slammed the knife into Lucifer's chest. Burying it all the way to the hilt before he released. He pushed himself back against the wall.

They say when Heaven and Hell collide, it's as powerful as an atom bomb.

They weren't wrong.

The explosion that took Lucifer and Grace was magnificently bright, but instead of annihilating us and everything in the room, all that hit us was pure wind. It pulled at me until I tumbled back into the wall, hissing with the pain of impact. Alex covered his face with his arms, and his open shirt rippled like he was in the eye of a tornado.

And then it sucked back into a bright spot in the center of the room and blinked out with a pop. The knife dropped from the air with a clang.

I stared at the blade, blinking, waiting to snap out of existence, just like Lucifer had.

And then my focus landed on the blood coating the blade.

If the knife had wiped Lucifer from ever existing at all, the blade would have been clean, if it even had been forged at all. But there it was, in all its bloody glory.

My gaze snapped back to Alex.

My Alex.

My wonderfully sensitive, loving Alex, whose eyes were full of every ounce of emotion he had lost months ago.

Tears blurred my vision as I crawled to him. Sobs echoed on the concrete along with the scraping of the metal ankle chains that were still attached to me.

His shoulders were torn and bloody, but he still had a smile for me. The smile that made my heart clatter in my chest despite all the bruises and cuts traversing my body.

His eyes widened at something behind me. I spun and shot my fire. The jerk who had held my head and fondled me turned to embers in a blink. I lay on my back, staring at the ash floating in the air, before I looked back at Alex.

"You've gotten really good at that," he said, his voice slow like he was just getting used to being back in his own skin.

I lifted my legs and willed the cuffs on my ankles to release. Nothing happened.

I laid my head back down. "It doesn't always work," I said with a heavy sigh and opened my palm, blasting fire through the center chain. It disintegrated, but the chain heated to a point it scalded my ankles. I closed my fist and lay back on the concrete with one more injury to deal with.

I turned, crawling the rest of the way to him, giving into the burning need to make sure he was real. I pressed my lips to his and sighed. His kiss was soft and warm, and the void in the center of my body shrunk to nothing.

Until he gently pushed me away. My heart plummeted. Maybe Lucifer hadn't been lying.

He must have seen the hurt filling my eyes because he cupped my cheek despite the scowl of discomfort. "While I would love to kiss you into eternity, and trust me when I say that is what I want, I do not want to do it here." He glanced around the room and shivered. "And maybe we can get my mom before I bleed out?"

My gaze jumped to his wounds. I hadn't realized just how deep the tiger's claws had ripped. I dug his phone out of my jacket pocket with shaking hands, punched a button, and handed the phone to Alex.

He took the phone and put it to his ear, blinking at the voice on the other end. "Dad?" He closed his eyes, and tears dripped from his lashes. "I kind of need, Mom." His eyes opened, and he looked at the ceiling with his lips pressed together in agony. And it wasn't just physical. He handed the phone to me.

Even from this distance, I felt the mistrust coming over the line. CJ did not believe this was his son. He believed it was another one of Lucifer's tricks, and after the last couple of months, I couldn't blame him.

"Mr. Ryan, I'm sorry. I wasn't thinking when I gave him the phone. This isn't a trick. It is really Alex. Our Alex," I said, and closed my eyes. "And he really needs Valerie."

Quiet permeated the line.

"Are you okay?" he asked, but he still had doubts as wide as the Grand Canyon.

I let out a laugh. "I'm a mess physically, but I'll live. Mentally, I'm the best I've ever been. I almost feel like I could fly." I opened my eyes and stared into Alex's soulful baby blues. "I have all of him back, Mr. Ryan. All. Of. Him," I whispered, and a new set of tears sprang to my eyes.

Alex smiled and his chin trembled as tears leaked from the corners of his eyes. He lifted his palm again and cupped my cheek as his thumb caressed my bottom lip. "You've had all of me since I first saw you," he said in a shaky voice that I didn't think Lucifer could ever mimic.

The change in CJ hit me—hope flared through the phone and the air shimmered next to me. I looked up into Valerie's wide eyes.

"I swear if this is a trick..." CJ said on the phone, his voice shaking with barely contained emotion.

"It isn't a trick, Chris," Valerie said loud enough for her husband to hear. Then she dropped to her knees next to Alex. She covered his face with kisses through sobs of her own. Each kiss bloomed light over his skin that traveled directly to his wounds.

"Enough, Mom. Jesus," he said, pushing her away. His cheeks turned crimson. "I get it. You're glad I'm back. I am too." He wiped his face and glanced at me as his jaw tightened and his breath came in long, slow pulls until the light dancing across his skin faded.

We both knew his mother's magic didn't work on me, so when she reached out and tweaked my nose, I didn't expect the flare of pain.

"Ouch," I said, and my eyes teared up from the sudden relief that followed.

"I just snapped it back in place." She smiled at us and stood. "Hurry home," she said, and then faded.

I disconnected the call as Alex climbed to his feet. He offered me his hand. That crooked smile gracing his lips sent a chill up my back. I had just a moment where I thought maybe Lucifer had tricked me, but when he nodded for me to grab the knife, I knew that was impossible. Lucifer would never trust me with Heaven's blade.

With his arm around my waist and Heaven's blade in my grasp, I slid the knife into the built-in holder on the inside of my boot. I limped with him towards the broken stairway, but I paused before we left the room.

"We can't leave them like that." I lifted my palm towards the grotesque scene. I focused, because this place would go up in flames faster than Naomi's panic room had if I didn't control this. And I was sure we needed a little time to get out of the building.

I needed angel fire to purify the room, and I needed to be careful. I didn't want to annihilate the entire building with us in it. But I needed to get rid of the bodies if Alex ever had a hope of fabricating some logical explanation for the videos Lucifer sent to the news stations.

I scanned the area once more and sucked in a large breath. I met Alex's gaze and smiled. "Here goes nothing."

I opened my hand, and pure white light filled the room, wiping all traces of human occupancy away, along with the makeshift throne and anything that could be traced back to Alex, or Grace, or Bridget, or Tom, or Gabriel or Naomi. When I closed my fist, all that swirled in the air was white dust.

I hoped it was enough.

Alex squeezed my hand and then put his arm back around me as we climbed our way out of the dilapidated asylum and into the clean air of the New York countryside.

Nick was leaning against the brick a few feet away, and when he saw us, he straightened.

"Have you been here the whole time?" The thought that Death was lingering about really set my teeth on edge.

"No. I came when you used the blade." He held his hand out.

"Did you know where he was this whole time?" I couldn't help the escalating anger. If

Death knew where to find Alex and didn't tell us, I was going to slam him right out of existence.

His jaw tightened. "If you do not give me that blade..." He pressed his lips together and closed his eyes at my glare. "Faith," he started and glanced at Alex. "I could not intervene."

"You knew?" I hissed.

"I knew as much as Gabriel and Naomi did." He met my gaze. "I knew enough to get Tom that blade." He pointed to my boot. "Now I need it back."

I crossed my arms even though the movement hurt. I wasn't feeling like obeying. Not after everything that had happened. It was Alex's non-reaction that pulled me out of my obstinance. He just stared at Death, dumfounded like nothing that had been said computed.

Instead of continuing this crazy argument and letting the darkness blooming inside me take over, I pulled the blade out and flung it towards Nick. He jumped back as the blade sliced into the ground between where his feet had been.

"Just take the cursed thing," I snapped.

Anger and the malignancy of Lucifer's grace scraped at my insides. I pushed it down into a box, mentally locking it before it lashed out on its own.

I turned towards the building, remembering CJ's plan to exonerate Alex. It was something to let my aggression out on instead of taking it out on Death.

I raised my hand, pulling forth only fire this time, and shot a blast right into the entry we had climbed out of. I forced it to incinerate the room where we had just escaped from, using my aggravation and anger to power it. The dry tinder of the building caught immediately.

I closed my hand and turned, expecting to see Nick still standing there, but he was gone and so was the knife.

We needed to get out of there, too. I hobbled away as fast as I could, with Alex by my side.

As soon as we were off the grounds and away from the burning building, Alex stopped and pulled me into his strong arms.

His hug hurt and I winced, but I needed his arms as much as I needed the air around me. He loosened his grip and put me on the ground again, leaving very little space between us.

He pushed my hair out of my face and stared down at me. "I never thought I would see you again." He delivered a searing kiss that nearly knocked my knees from under me.

When the kiss broke, I whispered, "I thought I would have to kill you." Tears filled my vision.

"Would you really have done that?" He searched my eyes and then closed his, nodding. "If you'd had a chance while Lucifer was in me, you would have taken it." He broke away from me and started walking again, blocking me from his head. His gait announced aggravation.

"Alex?"

He kept walking.

"Ty?"

He stopped and stared at the ground, kicking the dirt. I approached him, limping. When he turned, his face was washed in tears.

"I would have done the same damn thing," he whispered, and pain filled him. "I was present for all the hideous acts he did. I was there, climbing the walls of my own head, and Grace had the rest of my soul locked in that glass orb. For months, I wanted to smash that thing. I wanted to knock that bastard out of my body and find my way back to you." He swiped his face and looked at his hands. "*My* fist punched through both Naomi's and Gabriel's chests. *My* mouth swallowed their hearts." He shook his head and turned away. "When Bridget didn't bring you with her, he used *my* fists to pummel her to death. The sick bastard reveled in it."

I put my hand on his arm. "Ty."

His eyes closed. He covered my hand. "I'm damaged, Faith. Fucked up beyond belief. I don't have those rose-colored glasses I had when I first met you, either."

"I don't care. I've been to Hell and back. Literally." I laughed at his cocked eyebrow. "We had to jump through a breach to escape an avalanche."

"Really?"

I nodded. "That's what took me so long. What seemed like days down there were months up here."

"I thought you had given up on me." His eyes were serious, and my heart just about tore in two.

I stood on my tiptoes and pressed my lips to his. "Never. I always clung to the idea that I could somehow save you."

"And you did."

I shook my head. "I couldn't do anything in those chains. He had me helpless. Well, as helpless as a mere human is. I still got a solid shot at his balls."

He grimaced, and his hand went to his crotch like he remembered the pain, too.

Heat bloomed in my cheeks. "I think *you* broke that orb. I was chained by some serious mojo and couldn't do a thing. Nothing. At. All."

His mouth popped open.

I laughed under my breath. "You have a little more of your father in you than you think."

"Don't bullshit me right now." He crossed his arms.

"I'm not." I stood taller, wincing, and his gaze dropped to my ripped shirt. He blinked like he hadn't noticed that my entire torso was exposed. My little black lace bra peeked out, along with the bruises dotting my abdomen.

His eyes narrowed and his head tilted. When my shirt slid back, exposing more of my chest, his eyes widened. He stared at the exposed crescent marks of Lucifer's nails. But my shirt kept moving.

I grabbed at the fabric before it slid off my shoulders, covering myself up again.

"Well, shit," he said. A slow smile gained traction on his lips, and a chuckle escaped. "So I could lock the keypad on my father next time?" He wrapped his arm around my waist, and his eyes twinkled with the prospect.

I shifted, uncomfortable with his arm pressed against the bruises, but I didn't want to lose the connection. However, Lucifer's words painted doubt in my mind.

I clasped my shirt together. "Was what he said true?"

His smile faded and his fingers traced the welts on my skin that he had been an unwilling partner in inflicting. He met my gaze and shook his head. "No. There is no comparison to what we had. Fucking Grace made my skin crawl. The memory of making love to you is what kept me holding on. My promise to you kept me sane even with every fucked-up deranged thing Lucifer did."

"Stop swearing," I scolded and licked my lips.

"Sorry," he mumbled and offered me a strained smile.

I stretched on my tiptoes ignoring, the stabs of pain in my body, and kissed him softly. "I'll let *you* take the heat for locking the door next time." I lowered myself back to the ground.

His smile became more natural. "You still want a next time?" He teased by running his fingers down the line of my bra, careful to avoid the painful welts his nails had left.

When I didn't answer right away, his smile faded.

My skin dotted with gooseflesh at the motion of his fingers, momentarily erasing my ability to speak. Whatever connection we had seemed to shoot me into the stratosphere.

Worry flared in his eyes enough to help me find my voice. "Despite the damage Lucifer tried to do to both our psyches, I still want the first, the last, and the always with you."

He cupped my cheek. "I go where you go," he whispered, closing the distance to my lips.

The beep of a car horn made us jump apart. I was acutely aware of our bloodied condition, along with the spark of carnal need in both of us. When the car stopped and the car door opened, a German shepherd jumped out and trotted up to me.

"Are you done with your little venture?" Levi said.

I glanced at Alex and back at Levi. "No." I wanted Alex time.

The dog had the audacity to roll his eyes at me.

Josh stepped out of the driver's seat. "I'm told there are hundreds of minor breaches to close." He leaned on the door. "And no time to waste."

"She needs rest. Like a month-at-a-spa kind of rest," Alex said, looking between the talking dog and our resident pilot.

"We aren't going to leave you two in a hotel room for that long," Josh scoffed. "You're still sixteen."

Alex gave him a sideways glare. "I turn seventeen next month."

"Sixteen, seventeen. Same thing," Josh said with more than a little exasperation.

Alex's lips thinned into an aggravated line. "My dad sent you. Didn't he?"

Josh grinned and nodded. "We are your chaperones for the next however long it takes to do this. He needs to do some damage control before you can go home. Besides, he knows there isn't anything this side of Heaven that would separate the two of you, and this stuff needs to get done. So, here we are." He spread his arms out.

"Mother..."

I gave Alex a look that stopped the swear from continuing. He put his hands on his hips and glanced at the sky. That familiar countdown started in his head, and I stifled a warm laugh.

Sirens wailed in the distance, coming closer, and that made up our minds.

"Fine." He stomped toward the car, and I followed with a smirk still plastered on my lips.

"Damn teen angst," Levi muttered and joined us in the back seat of the car, wiggling himself right between us.

"Really?" I said.

His tongue extended from the side of his mouth as he gave me his weird canine grin. I fell back in the seat and sighed as I looked at Alex over at our diligent little monster chaperone.

His blue eyes sparkled with unshed heat. I reached over the dog and clasped Alex's hand in mine despite Levi's warning growl.

"Oh, go eat some demons," I said under my breath. "I'm holding my boyfriend's hand, and if you try to stop me, I'll blow you out of the car."

Both Josh and Alex snorted laughter at my terse tone as we drove away from the darkness that had overshadowed our lives for far too long.

Judgement Day
Epilogue

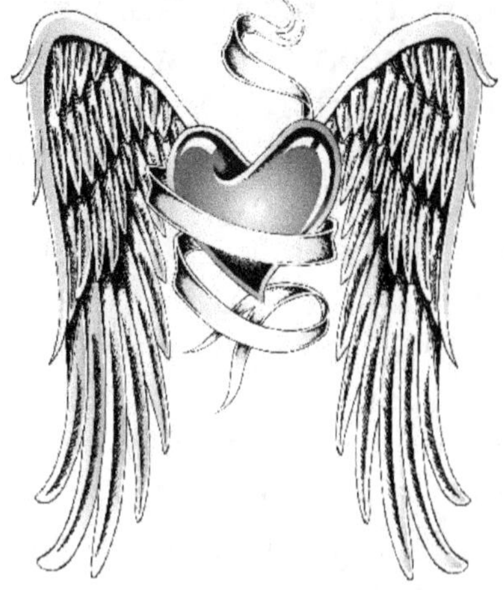

THE JET ENGINE WHINED, and I turned on my side on the bed in the back room. Thankfully, Levi hadn't followed me in tonight, but I was sure he was guarding the door from the other side like he had been for the past two weeks.

Knowing Alex was on the other side of that door left me restless. My fingers caressed the hem of Alex's flannel shirt, trying to get rid of this build-up of nervous energy. This was the same shirt I had worn to bed every night since I found out Lucifer had taken him. For me, because of my little jaunt through Hell, that equated to a period of a little under three weeks. For Alex, here in the real world, it was a few days shy of six months.

The day we beat Lucifer was an adventure for more than one reason. Just having Alex comb his fingers through my hair while I lay on his lap on the couch in the main cabin was as near to heaven as I had been since we had made love in his basement. But that contentment ended the moment he flipped on the television and our faces were splashed all over the airways.

Apparently, Lucifer had turned on the live stream when I woke up in that godforsaken basement, and the world saw what transpired

I'm sure it wasn't what Lucifer had intended, but it helped our ruse of filming a movie. We executed CJ's cleanup plan last week. Alex had been perfect. He delivered the scripting that CJ had put together with conviction and as smoothly as a seasoned actor. He had the same natural stage presence as his father once the camera turned on.

As for me, makeup still couldn't cover the blackness surrounding my eyes, but I was the only one that seemed worse for wear. CJ had an explanation for that, too, and it was one of the reasons we didn't get to finish making the film. Apparently, our execution of the stunt hadn't been as crisp as when we'd practiced, and after we filmed that scene, we left to get my nose looked at. Unfortunately, we left the generator on, and it overheated, which is what they believed started the fire that burned down the building.

CJ made sure that was what made it into the fire marshal's report.

However, with Tom, Naomi, and Gabriel looking as fresh and alive as everyone else, we couldn't have done better with what we had at our disposal. At this point, we could still get in trouble for the fire, but at least we believed we'd addressed the televised deaths.

We just prayed it was enough.

Valerie gave me back Raphael's grace, and the darkness inside me was again balanced. That left me to solely focus on the breaches without worry that Lucifer's grace would somehow taint me.

So, for now, Alex and I relished the limited freedom we had together with our ever-present and insanely diligent chaperones.

Neither Levi nor Josh had let their guard down enough to let us have more than a blink of alone time.

So, when the door cracked open and Alex slid inside the bedroom and quietly locked the door behind him, I sat up and rubbed my eyes to make sure I wasn't dreaming.

He put his finger on his lips, and then he crawled across the bed and pulled me to him. He kissed me with such reverence that I sighed under it. He cupped my cheek and leaned back, staring into my eyes. He glanced at the bright light coming from the bathroom and raised an eyebrow.

"Nightmares," I whispered.

His thumb caressed my bottom lip with a slow stroke. "I get them, too."

I traced the stubble on his jaw. In six months, he had gone from the pristine, clean-shaven boy to a rough-edged young man. His filter had returned, which was refreshing in some cases, like his bad language filter, but I missed the frankness of his near-soulless self.

"You want me to be more direct?"

I had not gotten used to him being able to hear my thoughts. He was growing into his powers, and anytime he stretched his mind to do something, it seemed so easy for him. I still struggled unless I was holding his hand. The only thing I was consistent with was closing the breaches with my fire.

He smiled and cocked an eyebrow, waiting for me to stop lamenting and answer his question.

"Yes. I don't want you to hide your thoughts from me."

He pushed me down onto my pillow. "Do I have to tell you what is on my mind right now?"

I grinned up at him and shook my head. His desire radiated in his eyes and his aura. "No, that I can read pretty clearly."

His smile faded as he stared down at me. "When I'm with you, I think maybe neither of us survived, and this is Heaven."

I palmed his cheek. That same thought had crossed my mind a time or two over these last couple of weeks, but with the sentries we had making sure we didn't have *this* kind of time together, I knew that was just my fears blooming bright. I got lost in Alex's thoughtful gaze and the slow progression of his fingers unbuttoning my shirt.

"They don't need planes in Heaven," I finally said as he pushed the fabric aside and traced the faded bruises traversing my abdomen.

"Do they still hurt?"

Not enough to stop whatever you have in mind.

Dimples appeared in his cheeks, followed by that smile that rivaled Heaven's light. He leaned over and pressed his lips to the first mark, like he was trying to erase the damage that Lucifer had done with *his* fists.

My skin tingled, and a soft light spread over my stomach. The bruise faded away, along with every other blue and purple discoloring of my skin. Even the scabbed crescents over my heart turned to unblemished skin.

Alex grinned. "I guess I've got a little of my mother's mojo, too."

I ran my hand over my abdomen, and then, as an after-thought, bent my knee. All the pain was gone. I lifted my leg, and the burn mark around my ankle had faded, too.

"And it works on me." Awe filled every fiber of my being and I met his loving gaze.

"Well, you do own my heart." He went back to what he had started. Each butterfly kiss sent a chill through me that resulted in gooseflesh, and a burning need ignited my blood.

This was not like the rushed session in his basement.

This was slow, sweet bliss.

Every glance from him was fueled with heat that sparkled in the bright blue of his eyes. Every stroke created another layer of flame between us. Every flick of his tongue brought me to the flash point.

"Ty," I exhaled his proper name like a prayer of thanks to the gods.

His reaction was immediate and carnal but controlled in a way that he hadn't ever been before, and his ministrations made me soar higher than the mountain peaks we were flying over.

When he finally returned to my mouth, he whispered, "I love you, Faith." And then he delivered a kiss that transcended all of Heaven.

The End

Continue with more of the Ryan clan in THE DEATH CHRONICLES II.

ABOUT J.E. TAYLOR

J.E. Taylor is a USA Today bestselling author, a publisher, an editor, a manuscript formatter, a mother, a wife, a business analyst, and a Supernatural fangirl. Not necessarily in that order. She first sat down to seriously write in February of 2007 after her daughter asked:

"Mom, if you could do anything, what would you do?"
From that moment on, she hasn't looked back.

Besides being co-owner of Novel Concept Publishing, Ms. Taylor also moonlights as a Senior Editor of Allegory E-zine, an online venue for Science Fiction, Fantasy and Horror, and co-host of the popular YouTube talk show Spilling Ink.

She lives in New Hampshire with her husband and during the summer months enjoys her weekends on the shore in southern Maine.

Visit her at www.jetaylor75.com to check out her other titles and sign up for her newsletter for early previews of her upcoming books, release announcements, and special opportunities for free swag!